A GIRL LIKE YOU

A GIRL LIKE YOU

NOW & THEN SERIES

KATE RYAN

LAST PAGE PUBLISHING

A Girl Like You

Kate Ryan

Cover by Jacqueline Sweet

Dedication

Mr. Everything,

I have an idea.

You take my back.

I love you.

You love me back.

I see a scorpion inside the house.

You kill it for me.

Acknowledgments

First or firstly, a huge thanks to Adriane and Barbara. Adriane, you're my barometer and enthusiast. Barb, always and forever #nofilter. You both kept me writing and are so, so special to me. Margaritas poolside? Oh hell yes – anytime, anywhere – but I vote for Adriane's house.

Second or secondly, every woman needs a *Village*. I am blessed beyond measure with mine, and thank you doesn't begin to cover the extent of my gratitude. In alphabetical order (because organization is an important life skill): Amy, Angie, Bonnie, Carlee, Carole, Claudia, Danielle, Genie, Hayley, Heather, Heidi, Jen, Jennifer, Karen, Karla, Kristi, Leanne, Michelle, Robyn, Ronda, Rose, and Sheila. Please know how appreciative I am for your hole-poking, feedback, questions, and sharing your own relatable stories with me throughout the creation of this series and our lives.

Third or thirdly, enormous mad love for the amazing sister combo of M & M. You make all things possible *within reason*. You make all things *funny* and *artsy* and *blurby* and *think outside the boxy. "Yes, we know the boots HAVE TO BE RED. Focus, Kate. Focus. We've totally got this."*

Last or lastly, thank you to the Readers of this series. If you grow to care about Amanda even half as much as I do – imperfections, neuroses, and all – I will be thrilled. Please laugh, cry, and cringe throughout the twists and turns during her journey through life. I endeavor to keep you guessing before leaving you satisfied with Amanda's *happily ever Now & Then*.

CONTENTS

ONE

Sunday, July 8, 2012
Age: Thirty-nine

I COULD BOLT FOR THE door, but I won't make it very far. Even if I could squeeze by the solid frame of my husband, the keys to the minivan I never wanted are in his pocket. He won't hand them over or offer me a ride home because I've changed my mind. My current circumstances are both voluntary and my idea; I've chosen to take this proverbial fork in the road, and there is no turning back. Soon he'll leave me here alone to face my shame without drugs or pills or my favorite pillow, to return home and contend with all the responsibilities of house and family along with his career for at least the next twenty-eight days.

Truth be told, he's already been doing this mostly alone for the last three years regardless of my presence in our home. Yes, I play a role—I bring in a significant portion of our income, I handle our finances, pay bills, and make sure money funnels into 401K accounts. I issue directives and make decisions from the confines of our lovely, albeit generic, four bedroom, three bath suburban ranch home some seventy-five miles away in the city of Chandler.

Maybe over the next twenty-eight days he'll come to the conclusion that their lives are ultimately easier without me. He's tall and handsome with the large build of a former football player. He's generous with his affection—which I no longer want, engaging in conversations—which I no longer participate in, and he has a successful career—the details of which make my eyes glaze over.

There are plenty of age-suitable single women out there. Perhaps demure Ella from his office? She was devastated by her husband's affair with the younger woman he met at the gym. Or maybe he'll take an interest in single Stephanie, Nicki's "class mom" two years running. Stephanie divorced a CEO, doesn't work outside the home, and lives off spousal support and venti coconut milk iced coffees.

His options for a real wife and decent mother for our daughter are infinite and ripe with possibilities. Whoever she turns out to be, they—my ex-husband and his new wife—are astute enough to involve a family counselor to aid in the blending of their families. My daughter loves her and tells me stories about their family adventures when I see her every other weekend.

Meanwhile, due to the sum of my child support payment schedule, I can barely afford the rent on my two-bedroom apartment north, not south (shudder), of the Loop 202 freeway. And, of course he has primary custody because I'm a well-documented drug addict thanks to my subpoenaed medical records. The state requires that I piss in a cup once a month to hang on to my pathetic unsupervised visits.

New Wife moves her family into my house with the granite counter tops that I personally selected from Arizona Tile & More. Maybe they'll pick out a new sofa—one that doesn't contain a permanent indent of my hip from the glassy-eyed hours I've logged on its cushions watching reality TV on Bravo when I should have been delivering stimulating feedback presentations to prospective clients or interacting with my family.

New Wife makes him happier than he's been in years; she's a super woman with an ass designed for yoga pants who gives blow jobs in the shower, and she excels at feeding my daughter home-cooked nutritionally-balanced meals every night and keeping my house in a constant tidy state of "company-ready."

I hate her. Damn it—no way, New Wife. He is my husband. It took me thirty years and immeasurable quantities of shattered expectations before he slid that gold band on my finger and promised me forever. He's mine. Nicki is mine. The career I've built and the short-term disability covering this leave of absence—mine. It's all mine, including those granite countertops.

Our great room overlooks the spacious backyard complete with in-ground pool—resurfaced two years ago with sparkling glass tiles and a new water feature. We splurged— because, hey, we deserve it—on a table that doubles as a fire pit and a weather-proofed outdoor sofa with matching chairs that swivel and rock. Just off the outdoor shower on the side of the home, we have a large cabinet that houses clean towels, swim goggles of assorted colors and sizes, foam exercise equipment for the pool, and a variety of pool and spa chemicals.

On the uppermost shelf of this cabinet, tucked behind the Spa pH Up container, was a small glass pipe so beautiful with its swirly blue and purple patterns. As of this morning, it's not there anymore. I threw it away in a white Hefty garbage bag after Jenny drove off with my daughter.

I didn't cry as I filled Nicki's beach bag with towels, sunscreen, goggles, water toys, and a change of clothes. Jenny stood just inside the front door while Nicki clamored around her.

"Auntie Jenny, I have a new nail polish," Nicki shared. "It's pink and it *sparkles*. And wait until you see my cannonball. My splash is *ginormous*."

"We're going to have a great day, Nicki." Jenny smiled.

"Auntie Jenny?" Nicki tugged on her hand. "Mommy is stuck, and the doctors are going to unstick her."

Jenny's eyes filled with unshed tears. She leaned down to stroke Nicki's still not brushed and therefore very tangled dark hair. "Yes, baby. That is a very good thing."

I froze for a moment. Yes, that's what we—my husband and I—told Nicki together yesterday evening. Mommy is going away for a little while because she is really sad. She's stuck in her feelings of sadness. Mommy needs to see a doctor who will help her get unstuck so she can feel happy again. Mommy loves you very much. We can talk to her on the phone while she's away, and you can draw pictures for her.

I didn't cry when I hugged my girl, helping her into the SUV and adjusting her seatbelt while Jenny started the engine to fire up the air conditioning. Jenny closed the SUV door and turned to my husband. "So we'll see you around six? I'll have dinner ready, okay? Nothing fancy—burgers or something. Maybe bring your swim trunks—and bring Miles. He's fun." It was sweet of Jenny to include my husband, child, and our 110-pound yellow lab in their evening plans. I wished I could join them.

"Thank you for everything," he said.

"Of course." She turned and threw her arms around me. "You just concentrate on you. We got this... I'll help with Nicki as much as he needs. Probably more than he needs. But don't worry about anything here. Okay?"

My arms locked around Jenny's trim frame. "I love you."

"I love you, too." With an extra squeeze, she looked back to my husband. "And I love you. Whatever you need... I'm just a text away."

Nicki waved goodbye to us, oblivious to the adult conversation, excited for a day with Auntie Jenny and her daughters, Maisy and Sydney. The SUV moved down the mesquite tree-lined street. It turned right at the stop sign and disappeared from sight around the corner.

After Nicki left with Jenny, my husband followed me around the house with the Hefty. I looked through dresser drawers and the "hers" closet off the master bath suite. In the recesses of my closet, I located a large metal box that used to contain Christmas cookies. Now it contained several pipes—one glass and two metal with copper screens in the bowls, cleaning solution, pipe cleaners, excess screens, and a half dozen or so empty small zip lock baggies with the sticky remnants of pungent green flecks affixed to the plastic.

My dignity already in a damned state, I smelled the inside of each baggie before tossing them into the Hefty. I also located two smaller tin boxes—one housed goldfish crackers and the other *Haribo Goldbären* sent to us last Christmas in a box of goodies from my sister in Germany. Containers of the shameful detritus that is my double life.

"Jesus, Amanda..." Not bothering to hide his disgust, he used my full name scornfully. It sounded so strange coming from his lips that I cringed. My eyes filled with more tears because it was killing me to throw away my constant companion in passive respite that kept me numbed to my very core for the last several years. Still, I didn't think Jesus should be brought into this humiliating moment in my closet, but I didn't share this with him, although he knew that I wanted to.

Not because I was religious, mind you; it was more of a habitual response to the use of the name Jesus outside of church. I couldn't recall the last time I set foot in church. It was not something we did as a family, and, in recent years, I only went with Mom on a major holiday. I am firmly Team Darwin because I have spent copious amounts of time praying to God and it hasn't helped. Perhaps God doesn't answer prayers from people who only selfishly call on Him in moments of need and never in gratitude. Perhaps there is no God.

If I'm honest, which I'm not quite ready to be because denial is my go-to reaction, I haven't attended many school functions or kids' birthday parties, or taken my daughter to see a movie at the theater in years because I can't bear to be separated from the contents of these tin containers. And therein, I suppose, is the crux of a problem I've finally admitted to myself, my husband, and my best friend

Jenny. Although... I hesitate to label my behavior as a problem per se, because I don't mind being dead inside. In fact, I prefer it.

But in rare moments of lucid contemplation, I've allowed myself to consider that my life isn't just about me and my wants and needs. I can admit that my behavior is reckless and selfish because of the fact that my life isn't my own. As a wife, mother, and daughter, my life is more like several critical pieces of a much bigger picture. If my life and job, husband and daughter, and the other people who rely on me were a giant jigsaw puzzle, the puzzle would remain unfinished because I'm too stoned to snap my pieces into place.

For years, I've told the unfinished puzzle to fuck off. The uncertainty of how long I can sustain this lack of participation in the world around me is my motivating reason to change. I could lose my job. I could get pulled over with drugs and children in the minivan. My husband could—and probably should—seek comfort in another woman's arms.

He is exceptionally patient with me. Too patient, some might say, because he watched me drift away and sink into darkness. Yes, there was that one night a few months ago when he lost his temper and called me an addict. I became enraged and responded with pure evil, "And you're a fucking loser who can't let go of the past." That shut him up. I'm a master at turning it around and making things his fault.

I'm certain that he is tired of this sorry version of a woman he didn't expect to find himself married to. In our earlier years, I would crawl onto his lap during the middle of a football game, whip my Colts jersey over my head, and ask him to call the play on my field—you know, penetrate my slot. That tactic always elicited a smile that I once found sexy and ended with our naked, sticky, satisfied bodies tangled together on—or over the back of—the sofa.

But things happen in life. Bad things happen to good people. Do you know that? While I was not exactly impervious to this little fact of life, I'd successfully weathered every setback and disappointment in my semi-charmed life until I no longer could.

* * *

We're ushered into a small office where Joy, an elderly plump woman with a sing-song voice, starts keying information into a computer from the early 2000s. "Have you pre-authorized with the insurance carrier?" she asks.

My husband looks to me for the answer because he has no idea how our insurance works or how the bills get paid without checking with me. "No," I answer. "My psychiatrist knows I'm here, but I didn't call the insurance company. But I did complete all the FMLA paperwork for my company, and I'm approved for leave and short-term disability."

"That's good, Amanda. I'll run this through the insurance, but you should know it's likely going to be rejected. They always want the patient to try intensive outpatient therapy first."

"That wasn't a viable option," my husband responds.

She smiles warmly and replies, "That is the case with most of our patients." We sit in silence as she plugs more information into the computer before sending several pages to the printer. She places them in front of me, and my husband scoots closer in his chair so he can see, too. "This form details the financial obligation for a twenty-eight-day stay. The daily rate doesn't change, so you can use this number to calculate additional costs should you need more time with us. Also, we require a 25% deposit up front. The total balance is due on your final day with us. I need your initials here, here, and here, with a signature and date at the bottom."

The number is staggering—astronomical with no insurance. With wide eyes, I stare at my husband. He nods impassively and directs, "Initial and sign."

I initial and sign and then reach into my purse to find our checkbook. I ask Joy not to cash it for at least forty-eight hours because my husband will need to transfer funds from savings to checking.

"Of course," she replies. Moving on, there are more forms and releases—one for them to bring my bags over to the clinic where they will be searched for contraband during my medical exam.

I briefly think about my *contraband* in the Hefty at home and wonder how my husband will dispose of it. I picture him with his buddies at his favorite outdoor spot in the desert, where we go for target shooting. Anything unwanted is fair game for target practice—glass bottles, rickety furniture, and, our personal favorite, pumpkins after Halloween. I envision him lining up the sight and carefully blowing my glass pipes to smithereens, filling my tins with holes. And I suppose that's a poetic and deserving ending.

"Now, once we finish up the paperwork, I'll give you a few minutes alone to say goodbye. You'll need to leave, sir, when we bring your wife over to the clinic." She hands him a piece of paper. "This is the phone schedule. Family visitation is on Sundays from noon to 2 p.m. You need to call by Thursday of each week to arrange the Sunday visit. That allows us enough time to seek approval from the patient."

"Approval?" he asks for clarification.

"Yes. Patients decide if they are ready for visitors—not the other way around."

My eyes dart to his again. He sighs and says, "Okay, we'll take it as it goes."

"Now, depending on how well Amanda responds to the treatment program," Joy continues addressing my husband, "your Family Week is currently scheduled on these dates." She circles a week on the calendar. "It's important that you clear your schedule. The first two days of family week involve family members working with counselors separately from the patient, although you will have lunch together each day. The final two days can be somewhat... intensive in nature. And the entire process is designed to talk through the emotional impact of addiction with the important people in your life and provide the family with tools and a plan following discharge—boundaries, expectations, aftercare treatment. It is not recommended for children under the age of twelve." She scans the computer. "And I see that your child is younger." Joy continues. "You may also include other close family members impacted by addiction—siblings, parents, close in-laws and the like."

I look to my husband. "My mother?"

"No," he says. "This is between us."

"I'm going to have to tell my mother," I press him. She lives two hours away and thinks I'm in the midst of a nervous breakdown from the stress and depression of losing Dad as we did. She's partially right.

"When you're ready," he tells me. "It doesn't have to be today, during Family Week, or even two months from now."

"She needs to know," I argue. *I'm always right.*

He takes a bold stance, and I'm not used to him putting his foot down. It makes me angry, really. *I make all the decisions. I make the world go around, and I tell* ***you*** *what to do.* "No. Claire is not married to you—I am. Family Week is for us, and I don't want her there. We need the time. Period." I tilt my head, blink rapidly, and then settle into a scowl.

Joy ignores the dynamic and states cheerfully, "The patient will make that decision when the time comes."

"It's decided," my husband growls.

Joy repeats her previous statement with a kind but firm tone. "The patient will make that decision when the time comes." I feel vindicated. *See, big guy, I still call the shots.* "Now," she says, standing, "I'll give you some privacy to say your goodbyes. I need your purse at this time and if you have a cell phone, you might want to leave that with your husband because they're not permitted on campus. You'll receive a pay card for the in-house telephones to make outbound calls during scheduled hours."

"No cell phone?" I echo; somewhat chagrined. *Apparently, I do not call all the shots.*

"Privacy," Joy says. "We protect the anonymity of our patients—some of whom might be more well-known but are no more important than others. You'll be known only by your first name. If there is more than one Amanda, the first initial of the middle or surname will be used. Cell phones distract from your journey and place anonymity and privacy in jeopardy."

"All right." I power down and hand my husband the phone and Joy my purse.

"You can say goodbye here and then join me in the lobby. Take as much time as you need." Joy leaves us alone.

"I need your passcode," my husband says.

"For?"

"Your phone—in case I need to get into it."

"Why would you need to get into it?"

"Jesus," he growls.

"Not part of the conversation," I counter with equal malice.

"What's on the phone that you don't want me to see? Texts to your dealer? Sharing naked pictures with your boyfriend?"

My phone only has a passcode because it's a security requirement in order to access work email and company apps—nothing nefarious, but, yes, there's probably a string of texts between me and my dealer, so he's got me there. Now that the phone is powered down, it's too late to delete those. Oh shit, my Facebook account and all those private messages... Will he read those? If he does, how will he react?

"Now, big guy," I try to soothe, "we both know I'd have to leave the house in order to have a boyfriend." His smile is sad. "I guess there's nothing on my phone—just Facebook and email. Please don't go through my stuff. But you'll need to use the Chase Bank app to pay a few bills and transfer funds if you don't want to go into the branch. So," I locate a pen and sticky note, "here's the passcode. If you enter it incorrectly more than five times, the phone will self-destruct. No joke—my company will wipe it clean for fear of hackers. Here's the login and password for Chase. If you have any questions about the bills or whatever, you can ask when I call."

"Will you call tonight?"

I look at the schedule. "I don't think so. I'll try for tomorrow evening, okay?"

"Okay."

"My mom..." I continue.

"Enough about your mom."

"No, this isn't about Family Week. It's about the house search." My mother is selling my childhood home to find a place near us in Chandler in one of the dozens of active adult communities that line Riggs Road. The house in Pine Ridge is a huge responsibility, and the maintenance was Dad's job. Plus the five hour round trip every weekend to visit Dad is wearing on her. I haven't been there in months, anyway. The house contains thousands of happy memories, and I expect Dad to walk through the door at any moment and our lives to be as they were *before*.

Hating for her to be alone after she visited Dad, I'd invite her to spend the night at our house. It was always a sorry, miserable time where we drank too much wine, I snuck out to the garage to get high, she barely noticed the granddaughter who used to light up her world, and my husband had to remind her every other minute to keep her voice down so Nicki didn't overhear her incensed rants about the indignities of it all. Still, even if Nicki couldn't hear it, she felt it—the permeating wretchedness of our new reality. She reads it on all our faces while she struggles to make some sense of it all in her innocent mind.

He was an amazing grandfather—fun, doting, enchanted by his little granddaughter who reminded him of when he was a new father, giving the same love, albeit liberally and without doling out consequences to her. He'd take her out for ice cream or to the park and lie on the floor and endure countless games of Candyland. He snuggled while reading to her, and in my favorite moments, I'd watch her on his lap, safe and content inside his strong arms while he'd read *The Paperbag Princess*. He'd tell her that she was way too smart and beautiful for a schmuck like Ronald. I'd laugh, and he'd catch me watching them. He'd smile and say, "It feels like I stepped back in time." I'd melt at the words, proud that I could give that to him.

"I'll stay on it," my husband assures me. "I'll go to as many viewings as I can and get involved in the negotiations."

"Thank you." I'm uncharacteristically grateful and so rarely acknowledge what he does for me and my family.

"She's my family, too. I made Michael a promise, and I'll take care of her."

Over a year ago, Dad turned to my husband and said, "You're the patriarch now. Please watch over my girls." My husband stood up a little taller, and my dad's slouched posture put them almost eye-to-eye.

I knew he wanted desperately to hug Dad, but since he couldn't, he choked back his tears and used his firm, deep man voice to reassure him. "I will, sir. I promise that I will take care of them—all of them."

* * *

We stand and my husband wraps his arms around me. He holds me so tight I can barely breathe. "I'm afraid that when this is all over, you won't want to come back to me," he whispers.

"I'm afraid that you won't want me to come back," I admit. "Nicki... you... Things will be happier for you now that I'm gone."

"Happy? It'll be chaos. Jenny's going to have to teach me how to braid hair."

"Ponytails are easier—stick with those, but make sure you use the wide tooth comb and the spray on those tangles. Start from the ends of her hair, not from the scalp." What else won't he know how to do without me? He's going to blow up Jenny's phone over the next month.

I break down and start to cry. "I'm sorry. I'm so, so sorry for everything. I don't know how this happened to me—to us." I don't understand why I couldn't stop this time around.

"Every low point became a new normal," he responds with a sniffle. Damn, he's crying. "I miss my wife. I need you."

"I've been gone for such a long time. I don't even know who I am anymore. I feel dead inside."

"You'll find yourself again. That's why you came here, right?"

"What if I don't like what I find?" I start to sob.

"I remember who I married. I liked her a lot." With a final squeeze he lets me go and places gentle kisses on my snotty face before looking me in the eyes. “I know you’re in there, and I’m so fucking proud of you right now. You need to be here. And I need to get back to Nicki. We’ll talk tomorrow?”

“Okay.” I reach for him again—another hug, another kiss coated in my phlegm—our phlegm.

“I love you.” And with those words and a tender assessment of my face, he offers a miniscule smile before walking away, leaving me to face the consequences of my poor decisions.

TWO

Joy walks with me on well-manicured brick pathways over to the clinic. The property is gorgeous with natural desert landscaping, huge saguaros with bird nests burrowed into the flesh, and every plant imaginable that thrives in this climate. We pass a padlocked pool, tennis courts, a raised seating area with several round tables, a gym, and countless outbuildings. I'm exhausted to my bones. My mouth is dry. I would kill for a joint, but eventually I'll settle for a cigarette.

My last drag was last night, somewhere around midnight. After I finished packing my bags and Nicki was in bed, I smoked myself into a stupor on the back patio. Concentrating on the clouds of smoke, I watched them twist and turn in the porch light before they disappeared into the sky.

My husband sat in a swivel chair off to the side. He watched and said nothing. I told him, and he'd agreed, that I would have this last night to indulge out in the open—no sneaking around —and he would not interfere.

I smoked and smoked and smoked until my lungs and throat burned and my head and body felt encased in a layer of concrete. Alternating between several heavy drags from my pretty glass pipe, I smoked a full cigarette in between. When I could smoke no more, I went inside. I drank a glass of water at the kitchen sink and walked to our bedroom suite. I used the toilet, washed my hands, brushed my teeth, took off my shorts and bra but left my tank top on. In the medicine cabinet I reached for the bottle of pills next to my antidepressant medication which had been on the same shelf, in the same place for—I'm not sure—the last twenty-four months or so. They didn't help, so I stopped taking them. The other pills, those were very helpful—so helpful that I had two different doctors prescribing them for me.

Shaking four pills into my hand, I swallowed them down before climbing onto my side of our king bed. As my husband got settled on his side, I kept my back to him, my body curled on my side, away from him. He crossed the invisible line on the mattress and spooned around, holding me inside his solid frame while several minutes ticked by.

Eventually, I released a sigh as tears rolled silently down my face and onto my pillow. He sighed in return. He let me go to turn off the lamp on his side of the bed. I could hear the rustle of him settling back into his space, and I looked forward to slipping into my sleep coma. I drifted off but was pulled back by the sound of his voice in the dark room. "You smell terrible," he said. I'm sure I did, but I could not have cared any less.

* * *

In the clinic, I'm asked to take a seat on a pleather couch. A young girl in scrubs brings me a sandwich with fruit and bottled water on a tray. She tells me that a nurse will come get me shortly. I'm not hungry, so I push the tray away on the coffee table and stare out the windows. A blond woman, maybe ten or fifteen years my senior, walks by. Our eyes meet through the glass; she offers me a huge smile and friendly wave. I wave back half-heartedly, no smile, because what the fuck do I have to be happy about right now?

Eventually, I'm escorted into a small examination room where I'm measured and weighed, and my body is inspected for marks, bruises, or other imperfections, which are noted by the nurse in my chart. There are many imperfections, but not from drug use. Just the usual imperfections of an overweight, inactive mother—cellulite and stretch marks on my breasts and stomach. I wonder if she's writing those down or just looking for needle marks. I don't have needle marks.

She runs though questions about my medical history—current medications, any diseases, pregnancies, prior surgeries, etc. She asks about my alcohol and drug use—which substances, my frequency of use, and the last time used. I answer honestly. She takes a few vials of blood. She hands me a cup for a urine sample and explains that they'll do an 11-panel drug screen. They have to rule out pregnancy before any medications can be prescribed or administered later today.

Attempting a feeble joke as I head off to the restroom, I wave the plastic cup in the air and say, "You know I'm going to fail this, right?" She offers me a wry smile.

The nurse might have asked me for the last date of my nonexistent period, but she didn't ask me how long it's been since I last had intercourse. Two years? Two and half years? I can't recall. When was it—the month, the year? Was it enjoyable? Did we laugh, or did I just go through the motions? I don't know. I have no memories of the last time, yet so many of our first time and hundreds of other times. In the beginning, I couldn't keep my hands off of him; he felt and tasted so delicious, all I wanted was to be consumed by him.

Sunday Night

I'm in a hospital-type room inside the detox area of the clinic. There are two beds and a bathroom, but I'm alone. Every so often I hear crying, yelling, and the sounds of someone throwing up across the hallway. Occasionally, a patient representative named Carmen knocks on my door to bring me dinner or offer me water, but she's probably making sure that I am still alive.

I'm reading a book called *SPIN* by Catherine McKenzie. It's about a young woman in treatment, and, really, I might be dead inside but I enjoy the irony. Silent tears fall, and I try not to climb the walls because I have absolutely nothing to turn off my brain. For the first time in years, I'm experiencing emotions without marijuana, and I hate it.

Off the end of the detox center there's a tiny smoking patio with two plastic chairs and a coffee tin for an ashtray, shaded by bougainvillea and Palo Verde trees. I go outside almost once an hour and smoke two cigarettes at a time.

I am invited to attend "Community" at 9 p.m., but I decline. It sounds like something where I'll have to meet people. Around 9:30 p.m., from the smoking patio, I spot a small group of young men on the walking path. One of them meets my eyes and peels off from the group approaching the fenced in area. He looks left then right and hops over the railing, plopping down into the seat next to mine.

"Can I have one of those?" he asks.

"Sure. Help yourself."

He does and lights up. "Name and malfunction?"

"Amanda."

"Jacob." He reminds me of a guy I used to sleep with my senior year of college—*God, what was his name...* young with thick dark hair, brown eyes, and a heavy fringe of lashes. He's adorable. "Malfunction? What are you in for?" he asks. When I don't answer right away, he provides a list of options. "Alcohol, drugs, both, mental disorders—gambling, maybe? There's a chick here for gambling. They still make her piss test—like, what's she going to do, piss out a poker chip?"

"Drugs," I answer.

"Yeah? Molly, benzos, meth, blow, speedballs, crank, poppers?"

"I don't know what most of those things are."

He laughs. "That's funny. Then why are you here? Hey, how old are you?"

"Thirty-nine."

"Wow, you're like my mom's age. Holy shit. Not many MILFs here—mostly kids my age and old people. You'll probably hang out with the old people."

"Jacob, are you trying to make me feel naïve and ancient?" He's so unconcerned with his candor that I answer, "I'm here because of marijuana."

"That's not a drug," he says.

"Yes, it is."

"Uh... no, it's not. That shit grows in the wild—it's medicinal. You do anything else?"

"I take too much Klonopin. Does that make me more interesting to you?"

His face lights up, because apparently it does. "You pop benzos?"

"What's a benzo?"

He laughs. "Benzodiazepines. Did they cut you off? Detoxing off that shit will suck."

My head is spinning. I hear what he's saying, but I have no idea what most of it means. "I don't think so. I'm supposed to pick up meds... right about now, I think, and they know I'm taking it."

"If you're staying in the clinic, they'll bring them to you. You'll probably move into a cabin tomorrow. Unless you're too sick. Are you sick?"

"I'm not like throwing up or anything. Is that what you mean?"

"Yeah, that's what I mean. I threw up for four days when I got here."

"How long have you been here, Jacob?"

"About twenty-three days. Mandy, right?"

"Amanda," I correct.

"Right. Amanda, is this your first time in a place like this? You seem like a normal lady."

"Ha—yes, first time. I'm not so sure about the normal lady thing." I laugh.

"It's not so bad. The food is really good, once you get out of Detox, the beds are super comfortable."

"Is this your first time in rehab?"

"Hell, no. This is number four, five maybe... Probably my last one, according to my dad."

"How old are you?"

"Nineteen." *Good god, he is a boy. Just a boy who's been in rehab four or five times—so many times that he can't remember?*

"Why are you here, Jacob?"

"I'm fucked up," he responds on a laugh.

I hear a female voice call out from the doorway, "Jacob, no fraternization outside of the common areas. You know the rules."

He jumps up and hops back over the fence. "Sorry, Carmen." He holds his hands up in mock surrender. "Just trying to be neighborly. She's, like, my mom's age, so no harm, no foul. And no ticket, please."

"Go home, Jacob," Carmen points her finger toward the men's cabins.

"Thanks for the smoke, Amanda." He heads back down the path.

I look up at Carmen. "I'm sorry. I didn't mean to break any rules."

"You'll get a list of them tomorrow, Amanda. You're fine. But we keep men and women separated except for common areas."

"Oh." And because I'm clueless I ask, "Why?"

"I'm not a therapist, just patient advocate, but it's common for a patient in treatment to substitute one form of compulsive behavior for another that feeds the reward center in the brain. Sex is the most accessible form of compulsive behavior in a treatment center."

I can't fathom wanting to have sex with my own husband, much less some boy/man in rehab, but I'll take her word for it.

"You'll get a list of common areas and a complete tour tomorrow. Come on in when you're finished. I'll take your blood pressure and bring meds to you in your room tonight. Would you like some sleep tea with honey?"

I would like a big fat joint. "Tea would be nice. Thank you."

I sit on the patio and have one more cigarette. The desert is alive with sounds—crickets, frogs, rustling leaves. I can't for the life of me remember that kid's name from college so many years ago, the one Jacob reminds me of, and it's driving me crazy. I mull this over and over and over in my foggy brain until the name finally comes... *Noah. His name was Noah. He wasn't complicated.* Feeling more settled now that I've recalled that name from my ancient history, I head back inside the clinic.

Monday – Day Two

I slept like shit. I'm exhausted when my door swings open and a man with silver hair enters my room holding a breakfast tray with—*God bless him*—coffee. "Hi, Amanda. I'm Rex," he greets me with a smile. "How are you this morning?"

"Happy to see that coffee."

He laughs and sets the tray down by the bed. I reach for the coffee. There's milk but no sugar. Beggars can't be choosers. "Everyone is always happier to see me when I bring coffee." He sits down on the other bed across from me. "I'm a patient advocate. Rex, as I said."

"It's nice to meet you, Rex."

"This morning, you'll eat, I'll bring your meds, you can shower, and then you'll have a physical with Dr. Weiss and an appointment with Dr. Martinez, our psychiatrist and the acting medical director. If she recommends it, we'll do a formal orientation, tour, and get you moved into a cabin so you can start your schedule—get into the routine."

"Are you sure I can't just hang out here? Maybe watch some soap operas?" I tease, surprised that I have any sense of humor, but Rex looks like a nice man. I can see it in his eyes—he's fatherly and cares about people.

He smiles. "There's no television here, at least not for patients."

"Darn it," I faux grumble and snap my fingers.

* * *

Dr. Weiss, a physician, is older than time with a dry wit. He confirms that I did indeed fail my drug test. My THC levels are impressive and not in a good way. He reviews my intake chart from yesterday and performs a fairly routine physical exam. I then answer many of the questions that I was asked yesterday by the intake nurse. I have the impression he's looking for consistency in my responses, and I'm certain I deliver because he's checking boxes as opposed to taking notes. He provides me with a scary pamphlet of information which describes the effects of chronic marijuana use on the brain, lungs, and body in painstaking detail. *And Jacob thinks pot isn't a drug? He's so wrong.*

Seventy pounds overweight—although thirty of those pounds I come by naturally—I'm at risk for type 2 diabetes, my cholesterol is too high, and my self-esteem is lower than ever after this conversation. However, Dr. Weiss informs me that I'll work with a nutritionist while I'm here; the menu is gourmet and healthy, and I'll have plenty of opportunity for exercise during my stay. It's possible that I will lose a decent amount of weight over the next twenty-seven days, and I'm hopeful. I've betrayed and abused my body, and now it's working against me.

Dr. Martinez is nothing like my psychiatrist back home. Dr. Anderson's known me since I was twenty-one years old. She cares about me, and her demeanor is warm and comforting. She asks questions so nicely. Dr. Martinez's questions are direct, pointed, and I start to feel mortified. This woman dances around nothing—everything is a direct hit to my center. She assesses me; she's reading my expressions and body language as much as she's listening to the words I offer in response.

Within five minutes flat, I'm reduced to a blubbering idiot. She doesn't pass me a tissue. I have to get up and get it myself. After filling her in on the last few years, she asks me to tell her when I first started using drugs. Digging deep in the recesses of my mind, I try to piece it together, but my brain is not entirely forthcoming with the finer details. I also mention Dr. Anderson and her diagnosis several years after I started using alcohol and drugs—the depression and social anxiety, and her theory that these mental disorders led to my use in the first place.

Dr. Martinez nods and adds, "I would also diagnose you with PTSD."

"Post-traumatic stress disorder? Don't you need to experience severe trauma to have PTSD? Like seeing people die in combat, or getting beaten or raped, or worse?"

"While uncommon in nature, the trauma you've experienced and your related symptoms—nightmares, intrusive thoughts, anger, isolation, guilt and sadness—and the need to use chemicals to push these feelings beneath the surface, are signs of PTSD. Research shows an association between PTSD and functional changes in the amygdala, the part of the brain involved in the formation of emotional memories, especially fear-related memories. Over time, trauma or even chronic stress can decrease the number of neuronal connections in the brain. Just because you weren't active in combat or you weren't violated or abused in a more conventional manner, doesn't mean your reaction to the trauma is any less significant. You need to acknowledge and address this while you're under our care, and I'll make sure it's included in your treatment plan."

"So I'm a substance abuser with depression, social anxiety, and PTSD?" I ask, because save for the PTSD reach, none of this news is new to me.

"As we work with you and get to know you better, that diagnosis may change. For example, you may well try out the term *addict* as opposed to *abuser*. But that's why you're here—for the treatment of inter-related, co-occurring disorders."

Finally, she wants to know if coming here is my decision. "I don't want to do this," I reply. "But I have to. I have too much to lose." When she shares that it's unlikely my insurance will cover the cost, I say, "If I didn't separate myself from the drugs, from my problems at home, I wouldn't stop. I couldn't stop on my own. So I'm staying, no matter what."

"You're better off than many people who come through these

gates—forced into treatment by legal situations, family members, friends or employers. When you want to quit before the program is over—and you will want to quit—don't lose sight of why you came here."

And with that, our first session is over.

Walking back into the clinic's detox area, Rex is waiting for me with lunch, a thick binder, and a clipboard. As we sit in a back room while I eat, he takes me through an extensive list of rules and restrictions. I sign off on a few more forms agreeing to the rules and associated consequences of breaking them.

Once assigned to a cabin, Rex helps me wheel my thoroughly searched baggage from the clinic to the cabin. There's another occupied bed, so I select from one of the remaining two. I choose the far back corner, closest to the window air conditioning unit. I'll be allowed to unpack later, but, first—or is it firstly?— Rex takes me on a tour of the campus.

As we walk some of the thirty-acre property in the foothills overlooking the city of Tucson, it strikes me that I'm in a very familiar section of the same city where my problems escalated and spun out of control for the first time—a place where I experienced beautiful and horrible times. It's apropos that I'm back where it began.

Rex ends the tour in front of an office door—one of dozens in this long, low, U-shaped building. "This is where you'll have Group weekdays after lunch from 1 p.m. to 3:30 p.m. Your therapist's name is Jeff. He's waiting inside. No need to knock."

Inside the room I meet several people. Jeff is about my height, maybe a few years older, slightly balding and chunky around the midsection. His smile is brilliant, and his green eyes are warm and welcoming.

Mostly we just talk about ourselves. Lara and Amber arrived a day before me, and we'll have two other patients join over the next few days. Lara is fifty-two years old. She's from Menlo Park, California, and dressed head to toe in coordinating Lululemon gear. Her platinum blond hair is cut in a shoulder-skimming bob, and her makeup is understated and well done. She looks relaxed, happy to be here, like she's spending time at a spa. She welcomes me with a hug. Her twenty-year-old son is in another treatment center for marijuana dependency and alcoholism. Lara says that she enjoys her Chardonnay a bit too much, so she's here to set an example for her son and two other children. If he's going to be sober, she will do it with him.

The other person in the room is a young girl named Amber and just her name alone makes me smile. She's the same age as Jacob from last night, in between her freshman and sophomore years of college. Her parents made her come because she got kicked out of the dorms after getting caught drinking twice, and the third time she got caught—which was when she got kicked out—she had alcohol and weed. She's facing criminal charges but insists she doesn't have any issues with control because it's all under control. *Sure it is, Amber. When I was about your age, I used to think that, too.* Her smooth skin is dotted with miscellaneous piercings on her pretty face—eyebrow, nose, lip—and too many to count up one of her ears. Amber's smile is endearing, slightly crooked, but her shorts are way too short and her shirt dips way too low, displaying the top of her skimpy lace bra.

"One of the first things you'll do," Jeff explains after our chatter dies down, "is a Timeline exercise. In the hallway of the Lodge, you'll find a huge roll of paper. Off the hallway, look for the Timeline Room. It's full of crayons, markers, paint—whatever supplies you might need. But first, you tear off a section of paper." He smiles. "Amanda, you might need more paper than Amber, and that's perfectly all right. You and Lara have more life experiences. What you're going to do visually, any way you want, is break out your life into decades and sub-section the decades into years. Think about significant memories, people—family, friends, teachers, love interests—and events in your life. They can be positive, negative, or completely run-of-the-mill stuff that stands out to you. Go back as far as you can in your life, and try to dig deep. Throw yourself into it. All of these experiences and memories make you the person that you are today."

Ugh. I could barely remember Noah's name last night. How am I going to pull this off?

"There's more." Jeff explains further. "When you're finished with the timeline of your life, you're going to visually represent your timeline of use over the timeline of your life."

"Use?" I'm so clueless.

"Substances—alcohol, drugs, risky behavior. But try to put it in a visual that's measureable and overlays the events in your life."

"Like plumes of smoke?" I offer.

Jeff laughs. "I've seen a few plumes of smoke in my day. Sometimes the clouds are small or hang long and low. Other times they take over a person's life. The important thing is that you're honest with yourself—as honest and open as you can possibly be. Which can be hard for people in treatment. Some of you might be masters at covering your tracks, but there's nothing to fear here, no reason to hide. Can we all agree on that?"

Lara looks ready to jump out of her seat and get going. Amber curls her legs up in her chair and wraps her arms around them. I can no longer see her cleavage, but now I have a view of her crotch. *Jeez, does she know she's giving us all a show?* Probably not.

I look away from Amber's crotch and check out the ceiling. *Dig deep. Be honest. Nothing to fear.* Fuck, I'd kill for a joint, but I'll settle for a cigarette before I get started on dissecting my life.

THREE

TIMELINE

Decade One: July 1972-June 1982

AGE THREE. WE LIVED IN San Francisco—city noises, preschool—Miss Iris loved me. She said I was smart like my big sister. Daddy went to work. Mommy took care of me. We had a pool. Our dog was named Zilber. She liked to snuggle. I cried because I didn't know how to read and Brianna did. That wasn't fair.

Age Four. We moved to Pine Ridge, Arizona. We lived in a tiny house with gold shag carpeting. We had to wear shoes inside because there were pins that poked through the carpet. We had a cat named Pepper. Brianna and I found a horned toad in the front yard. We wanted to keep it, but Dad made us set him free. I cried.

Age Five – First Grade. I skipped kindergarten—testing straight into first grade—where I met Jenny on the swing sets on the first day of school. The tarantula I brought in for Show & Tell climbed out of the shoe box. We screamed. Mrs. Farnsworth scooped it up with her bare hands and put it back in the box. I had to wear the *Tattle Tail* in class because I got in trouble for being a tattletale. My grandfather died. He liked me. My grandmother didn't like me, but she liked Brianna because she could sit still and knit. Brianna and my mother yelled at each other all the time.

Age Six – Second grade. My mom made me cut my hair like Dorothy Hamill. Jenny had long hair and Mom would braid it and tell her that she was pretty. Strangers called me "young man." I cried.

Age Seven – Third grade. I went to birthday parties and slumber parties. Ronald Reagan liked elephants. Scrawny Tanner Rawlings was new to Pine Ridge Elementary. He chased me around the playground and put grasshoppers down my shirt. Grease was the way we were feeling. Brianna hated it here. I liked it. I had a lot of friends and Jenny was my favorite. My family moved into our new house. It took a long time to have it built. Daddy coached Pop Warner football. I couldn't play even though those stupid little boys could. Daddy gave me a job on the sidelines.

Age Eight – Fourth grade. The school nurse embarrassed me. She told everyone how much I weighed. *Eight-five pounds! My, what a* ***big girl!*** Everyone heard her. Jenny only weighed fifty-two pounds.

Mom told me about sex. It was a spiritual experience for married people. I shouldn't do it until I had a husband, but here's how it worked... I spent time with Daddy on the sidelines during Pop Warner practices and games. I had an important job—keeping stats.

Age Nine – Fifth grade. My first bra was a B-cup. Jerry snapped the back of it, and Tanner still put grasshoppers down my shirt. Jenny kissed a boy. Gross. Mom was my English teacher. I got in trouble a lot. Everyone started calling me *Amanda Grace* because that's how my mom would yell at me in class. You're so tall. Such a *big* girl. Embarrassing.

Decade Two: July 1982-June 1991

Age Ten – Sixth grade. Matt Neilson moved to Pine Ridge. He was taller than me and so, so cute. I loved him, but he loved Jenny. I sang a solo at the spring concert—*Let There Be Peace on Earth*. Daddy showed up at the last minute. He watched me from the entryway of the gym. Brianna hated me. She was so mean, but I knew way more about football than she did. Daddy asked my advice on play strategies with his Pop Warner team.

Age Eleven – Seventh grade. We moved to the junior high school. I had to ride the bus. Brianna went to Germany for a whole year. Matt Neilson danced with me. Then he spent the rest of the time with Jenny. I loved softball. I played first base, and my swing was solid. I hit a lot of home runs. I had braces on my teeth. Ugh.

They hurt. I started my period. My Dad congratulated me at dinner. I started crying and ran out of the room.

Age Twelve – Eighth grade. I got mad at Jenny. Matt Neilson loved her. I still loved him. We didn't talk for a long time. Trina was my new best friend. The school nurse made a group of girls come to her office. She told us that we weighed too much. It was humiliating. I wore a size 10. I was the tallest girl in school. Brianna was home from Germany. She yelled at Mom and Dad all the time, and they yelled back. She still hated me.

Age Thirteen – Ninth grade. Jenny was my best friend again. We didn't have many classes together. I didn't play sports anymore. I worked with the football team. Tanner became my other best friend. He played football and sat next to me on long bus trips. He was still scrawny. Brianna went to college in Massachusetts. Our house was peaceful. Dad and I talked about football all the time. Coach Wendall taught me a lot, too. I loved football and liked the funny, sweaty, foul-mouthed boys. They treated me like a little sister—only nicer than Brianna ever did. Two girls I knew got pregnant. Dr. Cartwright told me I should come to him for birth control before I decided to have sex with a boy. He wouldn't tell my parents. Yuck.

Age Fourteen – Tenth Grade. Mike Haines tried to touch my boobs on the bus coming back from an away game. He didn't try to kiss me—just went right after my D-cups. I went back to my seat in the front of the bus. Tanner got mad at me for leaving my seat.

I was smart and took all honors classes. So did Tanner. Jenny had sex with Ricky Herbert. She was fifteen years old. I couldn't imagine doing that. I still loved football, but when Coach Wendall moved to Colorado after football season I cried.

The summer between sophomore and junior year. Tanner and Jenny got driver's licenses and cars. Jenny's was a restored MG convertible. Tanner's was a beat up Chevy pickup. He started coming over to my house almost every day to talk to Dad and eat Mom's cookies and dinner. We went camping overnight at the lake every chance we had. My skin was tan and covered in freckles. Jenny had sex with Robert in the back of his pickup truck at the lake one night. I slept in Tanner's truck. We laughed at the noises but didn't do a thing together. He was too skinny for me. I turned fifteen years old in July. I was younger than all of my friends, and it started to feel weird when they had more freedom than me. I got my braces off. Tanner went through a growth spurt. Overnight, he was almost as tall as me now. Almost but not quite.

Age Fifteen – Junior Year. I fell in love.

***

Fall Semester 1987

It is the first day back to school after summer break in Pine Ridge, Arizona—our small, lazy, two stoplight town just a few hours north of Phoenix nestled in the shadows of mountains. It sits at the 6,000 foot elevation—high enough for freezing fall nights and snow in the winter, with hot arid summers prone to massive monsoon storms in July and August. People move here to escape the relentless heat and sprawling pavement and crime in Phoenix. It's one of those towns you might pass through on your way to somewhere else and think, "*Hey, those mountains are gorgeous, there sure are a lot of pine trees, that café on Main Street looks like it's been here since the time of the settlers.*"

Certain family trees date back that far—families rich in history and tales of "*when I was your age...*" Most of those families aren't tolerant of outsiders. While my family didn't settle this town, we've been around long enough that we're accepted, and my roots continue to grow into the dark rocky soil.

Despite being born in San Francisco, life in Pine Ridge is all I know. Mom was my fifth grade English teacher at the only elementary school in Pine Ridge, and Dad owns a real estate company—residential, not commercial. He belongs to Rotary, chairs a few committees for the Town Council, and provides a very comfortable life for our family.

Our custom-built brick home blends into a hilltop where it offers sweeping views of the town parks and fishing ponds and the mountains. Long and low to the ground, our house has dark wood floors, twenty-foot high wood-beamed ceilings, and a massive stone fireplace in the open concept main living area. The front door opens into a sun room that's full of plants and comfortable places to sit. Plentiful windows in the front and back frame the views like pictures. The back deck is expansive—a place to grill out, host company, watch the sun sink behind the hills in an awesome display of changing colors streaking the sky, and enjoy the beauty surrounding us.

My folks, as far as parents go, are relatively open-minded. Our relationship is based in trust. The consequences of screwing up are crystal clear, so I have few restrictions or rules. I couldn't get away with anything anyway in a town this small, so there's no point in rebelling, drinking, doing drugs, having sex (as if that were an option), or otherwise misbehaving. I have goals, plans for beyond Pine Ridge. My parents will pay for the college of my choosing and encourage me to get good grades and make wise choices. I want for nothing, and especially now that Brianna is away at college there's very little family drama.

I have my own dramas going on inside my head—insecurities, anxieties, struggles with maintaining a 4.0 GPA, and fears of going to Germany for a year between high school and college. I have day-dreams about the boy who will give me my first kiss and worry that no guy will see me as more than a friend. I don't think I'm ugly—just more of a fixture. Dependable Amanda Harrington who's been around these people forever. Tall and overly curvy, the burly jocks on the football team seem to prefer petite physiques to my solid frame.

Beside my father, I feel 'little'. A former defensive lineman during his Boston College days, he's an imposing six foot five and tips the scales somewhere between his target range of 260 and 270. With massive hands and feet, a deep booming voice, and a confidence that I don't possess, he passed along many of his genes to me.

Like Dad's, my eyes are brown and hidden behind tortoise shell glasses to correct my terrible near-sightedness. I have contacts but only wear them on special occasions. My hair, also brown with copper sun streaks, has spiky bangs and spirals wildly over my shoulders in an untamable, decidedly regrettable perm. After the Dorothy Hamill situation, I insist on keeping my hair long and throw a fit at any suggestion to 'take off a few inches.'

I've always had plenty of friends and run around in a comfortable clique of like-minded kids—a mix of guys and girls all sharing the goal of getting out of the confines of our small town someday but content to be where we are in the meantime.

The swing sets are a metaphor for my friendship with Jenny because she's been pushing me my whole life. Any time I've been in trouble, Jenny was right by my side—or rather, leading the way. She's a hell raiser who exudes energy and good times, and, if I didn't have evidence to the contrary, a girlish innocence. She's also tall at five foot seven but with delicate features and a slim build. She runs track. She loves boys and boys love her—especially her current boyfriend, a senior named Robert.

At the moment, I'm pressed for time and in a hurry to find my newly assigned locker, because they gave me a lower, which is totally unjust for someone five eleven. Miss Patty in Administration saw it my way and gave me a new assignment. I round the corner of the row of junior lockers and stop in my tracks.

There is a boy—a new boy—and he is a beautiful boy. *Oh my god.* He stands in profile fiddling around in his locker, and he stops my heart. He's taller than me by several inches (rare), and his broad shoulders fill out a well-worn tee, olive green cargo pants, high tops with laces undone—not the usual wardrobe for guys at my high school. His shaggy dark blond hair falls over his forehead. It's almost like the first time I laid eyes on Matt Neilson in the sixth grade—you know, the same Matt who fell hard for my best friend—only it's one thousand times more flustering.

Moving to my locker just feet away from his, my heart is pounding out of my chest. Slick with sweat, my hand slips off the lock causing me to fumble and recheck the combination. I watch him from the corner of my eye as he throws a stack of books haphazardly in the locker. I turn my head and wince because proper organization is an important life skill. He sighs and mutters *Jesus* before slamming his locker shut, leaning against it with shoulders slumping in teenage defeat.

He looks up and catches me staring at him. *Awesome. I'm so smooth.* My skin flushes, but I offer him a small smile. His eyes are blue like the sky on a perfectly cloudless sunny day in Pine Ridge, but they seem cautious as they meet mine. He doesn't return the smile, but he maintains eye contact while crossing his arms over his chest. I grow uneasy under his gaze.

I'm about to speak when I'm unceremoniously shoved from behind right into his personal space. We don't make physical contact but I'm acutely aware that the three feet separating us has now become mere inches.

"Panda!" Tanner shouts, using his body to push me around like an uncoordinated puppy reunited with his favorite human friend. It's a good thing I find puppies adorable. My dad often jokes that Tanner is growing into his paws, and when he finally does, he'd better keep them off of his daughter. It never fails to make Tanner blush, though he's never laid an inappropriate paw on me.

Despite my having seen him just the day before, Tanner moves into my space to give me a bear hug. That's his way with me. He eyes the beautiful new boy with open curiosity while placing one hand lightly on top of my sky-high bangs, moving his hand up and down as if they're spring loaded. "Nice volume, Amanda-panda." He offers his trademark grin and teases, "If it weren't for all that hair, I'd be taller than you."

I return his hug and grin before placing my hand on his chest and push him away a few inches. "No way—I still rule." I gesture to the beautiful boy. "And thanks for freaking out the new guy. I'm sure he wants to make new friends and influence people while getting knocked on his ass by a girl."

"You're a girl?" Tanner winks as I give him the look. "Hey, dude." Tanner reaches around me and extends his hand. "Tanner Rawlings. Apologize that Amanda-panda here is so clumsy."

The beautiful boy hesitates before his posture changes. He stands up tall and clasps Tanner's hand in a firm dude shake. "Braden McLaughlin. New guy."

"Welcome. You related to Coach McLaughlin?" Tanner refers to the new history teacher and varsity football coach whom I'm excited to meet later today.

"My father," Braden replies.

His father, my future father-in-law, is the new football coach?

"Going out for the team?" Tanner asks.

"Yeah. I'll see you on the field."

"Cool. Nice to meet you." Tanner notices the crumpled campus map in Braden's hand. "Put that shit away, dude. Campus is microscopic. We'll show you around, right Panda? What's your first class?"

We have it together, which means we'll likely have most of our classes together. As the five minute warning bell rings out, my locker is still unorganized. I'll have to save it for a later time. After stacking the rest of my books inside, we walk Braden to Honors English.

Turns out, Braden already has one friend at Pine Ridge High School—Becky Haines, little sister of attempted boob groper, Mike Haines. Becky is conventionally pretty, super competitive about her grades, and determined to go Yale after graduating top of our class. I've known Becky for years—we run in the same circles—but now I kind of hate her because it's blatantly clear that Braden adores her.

When we walk into the classroom, his face lights up in recognition. It's the first time I see his smile, and it's directed at freaking Becky who jumps from her seat and gives him a hug that lasts way too long. As she starts introducing him to everyone, I learn that he's her *good friend Braden*, he just moved here from Phoenix, they've *known each other since the cradle*, and their fathers are best friends going way back to their college days at Arizona State. *Isn't that great*?

I was right. Since Braden's an honors student like Tanner and me, we have five out of seven classes together—except he takes Spanish while I take German, and guys and girls are separated by gender for Health/PE Class. I have all day to stare at Braden. *How awesome*. My GPA is going to nosedive.

FOUR

AFTER SCHOOL, I GO TO the training room. It's a windowless square space just off the locker rooms. This is my room. These guys would take advantage of any display of weakness, so I demand respect. When the athletes walk through the door, they don't give me any shit. The ones that don't know better quickly learn that I'll add extra rows of tape to the top of the wrap job making it more painful to remove, or I'll 'lose count' of how many minutes they've been soaking a limb in an ice bath.

Before this first practice, I tape ankles, wrists, and fingers of the athletes who are known to me. I inform the underclassmen that I need direction from the Frosh or JV coaches before I can attend to them. It's a lot of fun, but it's not for the faint of heart. Boys smell, swear, and say really disgusting things, but I take it for what it is, and in return they are exactly who they are in front of me—no pretense.

I've become one of them. I'm really interested in having a career in sports medicine one day.

I finish up and head onto the field. It's nothing fancy. Our campus is small, just 350 kids from Pine Ridge and few of the small surrounding towns. We have to travel long and far to play other schools in our division. When I'm not tending to the athletes, I study the playbook, keep stats, and respond to orders from the coaches.

As the guys are warming up under barking orders from the JV Coach, I meet Coach McLaughlin for the first time. "Who do we have here?" he booms. He's a boisterous man-version of his son. His eyes are the same shape and shade of blue, but his don't make me swoon.

I introduce myself and explain my role with the football program for the last two years. He says that he's grateful to have the extra set of hands to hand out icepacks after a tough hit. I correct him. "I don't just hand out icepacks, Coach. I was raised on football. My dad was a linebacker at Boston College, he coached Pop Warner for years in this town, and I grew up on the sidelines with him. Coach Wendall made me learn everything you'd expect from the players—plays, signals, strategies—so I can help you from the sidelines. I want the same opportunity to learn from you."

"Okay, honey."

I shake my head and correct him, "It's not *honey*, Coach. It's Harrington."

He bursts into laughter. "I hear you, *Harrington*. You do your usual thing this afternoon, and I'll give you time after practice to make sure we're on the same page this season."

* * *

True to his word, Coach and I sat on the bleachers after practice. He walked up, took a seat next to me, and said, "Hit me, Harrington." That made me smile as we talked through our game plan. Over the next few weeks, I became familiar with his coaching style. I memorized the playbook, hand signals, and call words. I earn Coach's respect, and he earns mine.

During practice scrimmages and heading into our first games of the season, the players know they can look at me to reconfirm a signal from the sidelines. Everything we signal is with the hands. Both hands signal the front. The left hand—line movement. The right arm and hand designate the blitz. Palm open facing down: Neilson. Fist closed at waist: Haines. Palm open at shoulder height: Rawlings. Both arms are used to designate a defensive back blitz. Hands facing in and pointed up at chest: Hound. Arms stacked and palms in at stomach: Fox. Hands facing out and fingers like claws at chest: Cat. The coverage is signaled using the fingers on the right hand. Calls and signals follow the same order every time. *Easy.*

We don't have a fancy stadium, but we have a decent travel coach with comfortable seats, huge storage compartments underneath for the gear, and a tiny bathroom in the back which I try to avoid at all costs for understandable reasons. It's white with green script—Pine Ridge Bobcats—and a huge picture of our mascot.

Coach McLaughlin also fears for my innocence; I think—just as Coach Wendall had. During those long dark nights rolling over Arizona highways, I have to sit up front, but Tanner is right by my side, as he has been for the last two years.

Tanner and I talk about anything—everything—on these long bus trips. His home life is rough, which is why he gravitates to my family. His folks scrape by with various blue collar jobs, and his dad definitely does not belong to the Rotary Club. Tanner's dad drinks too much beer, and he has an explosive temper. His older brother and two sisters are pretty much losers, and I've never been invited into his house—which is not really a house; it's a rundown trailer in a mobile home park.

Tanner puts in odd hours with an old mechanic off of Main Street to make money to support his truck, football, and social life, so I suppose he scrapes by, too. Unlike his father, Tanner has concrete plans for his future. For all his easy laughter and kidding around, he knows exactly what he wants in two years. He's going to earn a scholarship to the University of Arizona, go pre-med, and eventually become a doctor—pediatrics or family practice. He wants a big family with a hot wife, six kids, and a nice house that most definitely is not an old trailer. Until then Tanner keeps his eyes on the future. He studies hard and keeps his head in the game on the field—so much so that I don't think he's noticed the way girls look at him now, especially the underclassmen who never knew scrawny Tanner.

We're so close, with similar coloring and such an easy way with one another, we could be mistaken for siblings. Often it feels like we are because if I'm out with Jenny or another friend, I'll come home and see Tanner's truck parked in front of the house. He's inside with Dad—watching sports or huddled together over his homework. Way before I was born, Dad's first career was as a high school science teacher. He loves helping with our homework.

Ever since their Pop Warner days, Dad's kept an eye on Tanner and his home situation. Dad's experienced Mr. Rawlings' drunken temper and outbursts from the bleachers many times. Dad is not a fan, and since Tanner got his license several months ago, Dad slips him cash for gas money. Tanner quit protesting after Dad insisted that he's doing him a favor being my chauffer—especially since our bus rolls into town in the middle of the night every other Friday night. Sure he is, but I know that Dad just wants to help Tanner out any way he can.

As for the other guys on the bus, they're super friendly, sometimes smelly, and free with physical affection for me that includes sweaty armpit hugs, playful punches, and the occasional pinch on my ass. I'm surrounded by green and white jerseys and firmly established in the friend zone. Whenever I share this reality with Tanner, he says, "You're in the friend zone 'cuz Coach and me keep you there, and that's where you're staying." Then he laughs in my face and offers, "But you ever wanna make out, just let me know." *Whatever.*

Of course there's more to my life than football. There's school—the academics and the friendships. There's Coach's son. Braden is swept along into my core circle of friends, and I'm obsessed, fascinated, consumed by thoughts of him. He's a part of my everyday life, my extracurricular activities, and the subject matter for all of my daydreams. Our interactions fill the pages of my diary—innocuous encounters documented and preserved to revisit and build on my fantasies. His responses to my jokes are psychoanalyzed along with every word he says to me and every look or gesture, no matter how mundane.

I can't explain why I'm so crazy—crazy about Braden, that is. Yeah, he's good-looking, but it's more than that—intelligence delivered with either a dry wit or an offensive but funny comment.

Braden's also really sweet—at least to me—and maybe kind of awkward, too. Even though I fit in here, I still feel like I stand out—but not in a good way. Braden seems uneasy in his new surroundings, and although we quickly embraced him as one of our own for obvious reasons—sports and academics—I think he's holding back huge pieces of himself. For all his foul-mouthed jock banter, he's guarded and introspective. The layers of his mind would be fascinating to peel back and examine.

Irrationally possessive and jealous, I document his interactions with other girls. As the cutest new guy our town has seen in, well, forever, he gets a ton of female attention during his first few months at Pine Ridge. From the friend zone, I watch other girls try and fail with him. He isn't mean or rude—just detached from the Pine Ridge scene, except for his group of new friends, and, of course, Becky Haines.

When he stares at her with a wistful look on his face, I hate her for it. A typical guy would've been all over the variety, but he doesn't bite, *thank God*. But I bite—I bite my tongue, grind my teeth, and spend way too much time wondering how I can make him notice me as more than a friend. Braden is mine. He just doesn't know it yet, and I have no idea how to make it happen.

We study together in groups—his place, my place, someone else's place. Braden's a study all by himself—a study of contradictions. With a foul mouth and a brooding disposition, one minute he's a guy's guy, shoving Tanner into a locker or dropping the "F" bomb four times in one sentence as a noun, adjective, verb, and adverb. In the next moment, he's eloquently translating Shakespeare's flowery prose into plain old English for the class.

On weekends, we do more of the same—changing out studying for game or movie nights—living our self-absorbed teenage lives in a pack.

Braden calls me every once in a while for quick stuff, like:

Did you catch what Mrs. Robertson said in biology about the regulation of eukaryote genes? How do you spell eukaryote, and when am I ever going to use this again in my life?

Mom wants to know if you and Tanner will pick up a few bags of ice on your way over tonight.

Are we studying at your house tonight? And can your dad help explain this inheritance patterns chart so I don't have to ask Tanner—again? So I blow at biology—his Spanish is shit.

I make up excuses to place similar types of calls to him, but it's total bullshit. I'm a good student. My notes are detailed and I always have my act together. I don't need his help, but he doesn't need to know that, right?

A self-proclaimed expert on gauging his moods, finding the right combination of words to earn myself a grin or a shake of his head, hopelessly fixated to the point where our exchanges determine my own mood—I've lost it. After doodling *Braden & Amanda* and *Amanda McLaughlin* all over the pages of my diary (surrounded by hearts) for weeks on end, I confess this to Jenny. She has some ideas on how to move things along.

As luck would have it, Braden and Robert, Jenny's boyfriend, are neighbors. They hang out, spend time together, and Jenny knows Braden perhaps better than I think I do. She offers to find out what he thinks about me. I'm scared, but since I have no moves of my own, I allow it. Jenny reports back that she talked to Braden about me: *Isn't she nice? What do you think of her? Maybe you should ask her out.* He offered very little in return. *Yeah, she's nice. Amanda is really smart and she's funny. I don't know—I don't really date.*

I still have nothing to go on.

October 1987

On this particular Saturday evening a few weeks before Halloween, about a dozen or so kids are gathered at the McLaughlins for game night. Pictionary is a favored activity, and Braden's house has become our preferred hang out. It's sprawling, perched on a hilltop across town from mine. He basically has his own wing off the kitchen—a huge family room with space for everyone, a half bath for guests, and his bedroom/bath suite are off the entertainment area.

The sliding door off the back deck leads directly into the family room. That means we can come and go—and we do—without disturbing his parents. They even landscaped a lighted foot path from the driveway, around the side of the home for easier navigation in the dark. As with my folks, there are few rules placed upon us in their home. We are welcome anytime, but drinking or drugs will earn you a prompt ejection from the circle of trust—and a call to your parents.

We partner up for Pictionary, and Braden picks me with a nod in my direction. Although it's far more strategic to partner with someone who shares history and inside jokes, I'm ecstatic to be acknowledged. We're all loud and playfully argumentative—smack talk routinely fills the room. Jenny and Robert are cozied up, Tanner partners with Trina, and we rotate turns.

About an hour into the evening, Becky enters through the slider, followed by a blast of cold air and Kyle Greenway. Kyle is a quick witted sophomore—tall, dark, cute and smart. He runs track and is expected to beat his own state record this year in the 800M. It's not unusual for a guy to date an underclassman, but when a girl does it he has to be someone worthy of an exception to social taboo. Kyle is most definitely worthy.

Greetings are exchanged. Kyle helps remove Becky's coat before shrugging off his green and white letter jacket and placing them on the pile of other outerwear in the back corner of the room. When he sits beside her, their hands join. This is the high school equivalent of a public announcement of their relationship. From the looks of these two, Braden stands no chance with Becky. *Thank God. I'm so relieved.*

Braden must reach the same conclusion, but he's not relieved. Without a word or a backward glance, he stands up and walks outside. Becky watches his retreat and leans to whisper in Kyle's ear. He looks concerned and strokes her cheek with his thumb before laying a quick kiss on her pouty lips.

"Hey, Becky, I'm his partner. We're up next. You guys take our turn, okay?" I ask, standing up. Her snarky smile serves as confirmation.

It's freaking cold outside, considering the family room is so full of hot air. I'm wearing a thin red sweater over jeans and my favorite cowboy boots—red leather with pointed toes, tan embroidered details. My jacket is buried somewhere in the massive pile inside. I can see my breath in the crisp air. Braden's back is to me, but I'm positive he's brooding because that's what he does.

"Braden," I call out, letting him know I'm there. "You, um, left me without a partner. Pictionary without a partner isn't much of a game. It's just some girl standing around drawing really bad artwork with an audience, and that is kind of... sad."

My jesting earns me a snort of laughter. A prize. He doesn't turn around but stretches his arms toward the sky, brilliantly decorated with a million stars. He gestures to the heavens. "Too many city lights in Phoenix to see this shit. I mean, look at all these fucking stars. I had no idea there were so many fucking stars up there. What else don't I know?"

"Is that a rhetorical question, or should we make a list?"

Another chuckle. Another prize. "Rhetorical. Your list will only prove I'm a bigger dipshit than I care to admit." He releases his signature broody sigh.

Silent and chilled to the bone, I remain on the other side of the deck. My teeth start to chatter, and I consider going back inside when Braden asks, "Are you cold? I can hear your teeth chattering all the way over here."

"Freezing."

"Do you prefer Amanda or Panda?"

I wrap my arms around myself, as if that can ward off the near freezing temperatures. "Tanner owns the nickname Panda. I mean, he's the only one who calls me that."

"Does he? What else does he own?" He turns toward me. Surprisingly, his expression is playful as opposed to morose. I shrug because I'm not sure what he means. He crooks his index finger at me. "Come here. I'll keep you warm."

Keep me warm how, exactly? I'm afraid to move, mostly because

I feel a heart attack coming on at the mere suggestion of getting near him. "Unless you want to go back inside?" he amends. "Or unless Tanner might try to kick my ass if I touch you."

I take a few steps in his direction. *What's with all the Tanner references?*

"Hang on." He crosses to a deck box near the door and lifts the lid to retrieve a blanket. He adjusts the back of a lounger so it's lying almost flat and takes a seat. His legs are spread wide resting on either side, and he pats the space between his legs with one hand and holds the blanket off to the side with the other. Again, he pats the space between his legs. "Have a seat. Right here."

I tentatively sit on the far end of the lounger.

"No, no, no," he chides, sitting up to wrap his arms around my waist. "Slide back. Lie back against me."

"I'll crush you."

"Maybe my heart, but not the rest of me. I take hits on the field, remember?" He pulls me back against him. "Good girl," he soothes and spreads the blanket over us before guiding me back against his front to "relax" on the lounger. Tucking the blanket under my chin, he runs his hands up and down my covered arms. I shiver but not from the cold.

"Still cold?" he asks.

"Maybe my heart." I'm rewarded with a third chuckle—*my favorite sound, like, ever*. I adjust my body against his, concerned he's uncomfortable. I shift and squirm.

"Hey, hey..." his voice conveys unease.

"What? Am I squishing you?" I try to sit up.

He holds me in place with his hands. "No, no, but you're rubbing against my, you know—you're rubbing on my, um... my dick." Mortified, I shoot straight up. "No—" His arms lock tight around me. "Come back here, silly. I'm freezing without your body heat." He tugs me back down. "Now take a minute to get situated and then stay put."

I find a comfortable position and hope it's comfortable for him, too. I have a million thoughts running through my head, mostly *what the hell is happening here?* Instead, I again voice my five foot eleven girl with curves concern. "I don't want to crush you."

"Amanda, stop it. You're not heavy. You're warm and cozy, and," he draws in a deep breath through his nose, "you smell like a girl—sugar cookies—which I happen to love." *Butter-freaking-flies. Just kill me now and I'll die happy.* "Tell me something about you and Tanner."

"What do you want to know?"

"Well, you're always together. But you're not *together*?"

"No, not together-together but, yes, usually always together..." My voice trails off lamely.

"Why not together-together?" His fingers attempt to comb a path through my tangled hair, but he's thwarted by my spirals. He settles for running his fingers on top of my hair rather than through it. If I was a cat, I'd be purring right now.

"It's not like that."

"So you and Tanner never..."

"No. Never. And eww..." I elbow him gently in the thigh—at least I hope it was his thigh. "I was seven when we first met. He was totally scrawny——like a head shorter than me most our lives. Until recently." *Okay, maybe I've looked at him once or twice lately and noticed he's becoming more man than boy. His efforts in the gym are paying off, and I should probably gracefully concede that he now has me by at least half an inch.* These thoughts disturb me, so I share, "He put grasshoppers down my shirt for years. Live grasshoppers, although sometimes he'd tear off the legs first... and throw those in my hair."

This confession produces prolonged laughter—not a Braden snort or a chuckle but full-blown from the belly laughter. As he cracks up, he tightens his hold on me.

"And so," I conclude, "he's more like the brother I never wanted."

"That might change."

"I don't see that happening," I explain. "I suppose things *could* change. Anything is possible. But there's a big difference between possible and probable, you know?"

"Yeah. Still, you're tight."

"Totally tight," I confirm. "And he's that way with my family—my dad especially. Anything else would be beyond weird, and it's both possible and probable that Dad would never forgive him, and he means a lot to Tanner—and vice versa—so..."

"Your parents seem cool," he shares. "I mean, I've only talked to them a few times, but your dad was really helpful with our biology homework. And your mom—she makes killer cookies."

I smile. "Yeah. My parents are great. No complaints."

"Really? *No* complaints?"

"Well, who doesn't have complaints about their parents, but it's nothing serious. I'm lucky, and complaining about things that aren't important seems silly."

"Biggest complaint?"

I consider the question before responding. "They have really high expectations."

"How so?"

"I have an older sister—"

"—me, too. What's her story?"

"Brianna is a junior at Amherst. You know, Amherst College, as opposed to U Mass Amherst—which, if you make the mistake, she'll correct you right away, so don't worry."

He laughs. "Ah... one of *those*."

"Totally one of *those*, but I feel more like an only child because she's not around much. So my parents have a lot of time to, um, focus on me."

"I imagine that can be both good and bad. I get that with Fiona out of the house."

"Exactly," I say, pleased that we're discovering more common ground.

"So define high expectations for me."

"Nothing crazy. Just more about my grades and behavior—no drinking, drugging, teenage pregnancy."

"Is that a possibility? The last one sounds the most interesting."

"Ha—it's highly improbable, unless you believe in Immaculate Conception, which I do not, by the way."

He snickers. "Me either, but don't tell Father Francis—or my mom."

"Your secret is safe with me."

"Excellent." He pushes for more information. "Good grades, no drinking, drugging, or babies out of wedlock. What else?"

"I'm going to Germany after graduation—as an exchange student. Did you know that?"

"No, but it explains why you're not in my Spanish class. Germany? What's that about?"

"Brianna was a junior in high school when she spent a year overseas. She's actually going back for spring semester of college in a few months. And because she did it, it seemed like something I should do, too. Plus there's my age and everything."

"Your age?"

"I just turned fifteen in July."

"Damn. You're really young for a junior. Skip a grade?"

"Kindergarten, I guess."

Braden comments, "The things you learn about cute girls on a freezing fall night."

He thinks I'm cute? "I'm not that interesting. It's just you're asking a lot of questions."

"I'm trying to get to know you better, Amanda. Am I prying too much?"

"No, no—not at all. I'm kind of an open book, just not one that grabs a reader and sucks them in." I laugh.

"I don't know... I'm a little sucked in right now. I mean," he tickles my rib cage, "I'm not falling asleep or anything. I like getting to know you. Most of our conversations are about school and ace bandages. Not very deep, right?"

"Maybe I'm not a very deep person."

"Yeah... I've listened to you take up a counterargument in class. You have some pretty deep thoughts going on in that head of yours—even if you are like half my age."

"That's funny, Braden. It's just a few years."

"It's like a year and half. I'll be seventeen in February."

"I'll be sure to get you a nice present."

"You can bake me some sugar cookies. I'd like that. Or you can just come over and let me smell your hair. I'm easy to please. I won't be around for your birthday, though. We spend every summer in Michigan." I want to ask questions about him, but he continues. "What does your age have to do with Germany? And, why do I have the feeling you don't want to go?"

I sigh. "I don't. But when I graduate, I'll only be sixteen years old. Dad won't put me on a college campus until I'm, um, legal age, so I have this gap year to fill. I don't want to work at Walmart, so... I guess, I kind of made this decision going into high school, and my parents are holding me to it. I guess I might as well go."

"Why *wouldn't* you want to do that?"

This chat is about to take a turn for the *deeper* as I admit, "I'm scared. Beyond scared. What's worse than scared—terrified, petrified?"

"Why?"

"Change. The unknown. Starting over. Being different. You name it; I'm probably scared about it."

"You won't have any problems making friends. People here think the world of you. My dad does, for sure. The team, too."

"That's because I belong here."

"You can belong anywhere."

"Except Arizona State, so your dad should stop trying to talk me into the sports medicine program there."

"Mortal enemies. He still loves my sister, though—I think. She goes to U of A."

"What about you?" I ask. "What's your plan after high school?"

"Depending on grades and stuff, I'm considering Iowa—creative writing, writers' workshops, English Lit major possibly. They have strong programs."

"I had no idea you were into writing."

"It's not something I really talk about."

"What do you write?"

"Fiction, science fiction, mostly. I don't know if it's any good; guess I'll find out one day. But it's a good escape for me and some of the sick shit in my head."

I muse, using his words, "The things you learn about cute boys on a freezing fall night."

"I'm not an open book, but I don't mind sharing certain things with you as long as you don't spread shit around. You don't spread shit around, do you?"

"Generally, no."

"You think I'm cute?"

"Very much so," I say and quickly cover my confession with a question. "Can I read any of your great works?"

"No. I'm not ready to share that part of my head with the world. You understand?"

"I do. I have quite the collection of things I'd never show the world on the pages of my journal."

"So you're also a writer?"

"Not really. Just a documenter of experiences and, you know, my hopes, fears, and dreams."

"I bet it makes for great reading."

I cringe and grow warm at the thought of exposing my fantasy word to Braden. "You'll never know," I state.

We fall into a companionable silence listening to the muffled laughter coming from inside the house. I have no idea how long we've been outside talking. But, with a slight shift of my body and his, I am comfortable and cocooned, our bodies keeping each other warm.

"Amanda?" He breaks the silence.

"Yeah?"

"I honestly thought that you and Tanner were a thing."

"We just covered this. Just friends. End of story."

"He's more than a friend. He's like your own personal cock blocker."

"I, uh... I... I..." I stutter. "I don't like the word 'cock.'"

He belts out a laugh. "Just saying—that's all. It would appear that Tanner's got you locked down."

"I'm free to do as I please," I affirm. "You don't date either, and not because you lack options."

He sighs. "No, I don't date. Fear of teenage pregnancy and all..."

Turnabout is fair play, and I can't help myself. "You've known Becky your entire life— longer than me and Tanner even—and you've never...?" He stiffens beneath me and not in a good way. He also doesn't respond. A fair amount of uncomfortable silence follows, so I offer, "I'm sorry. I didn't mean to upset you."

"You didn't." He says nothing more while I lose track of time. While holding me loosely with one arm and stroking my hair with his free hand, his breathing deepens. I think he smells my hair again, which is just fine with me. Eventually his body relaxes and he speaks. "I think at our age... this is all temporary, a point in time, and relationships can get too heavy—too complicated. I watch dudes tie themselves up in knots over a girl who doesn't give a shit, or the other way—he's got her where he wants her and doesn't give a fuck after he gets a fuck. I'm not sure Becky and I can come out of this situation as friends, and I feel pretty fucked up about it."

"You had a... a *situation*?"

"We've had a *situation* for a few years. We made some plans, and those plans didn't work out, which created a new *situation*."

"Did you get, um, serious with Becky?" *Please don't throw up.*

"I did. She didn't—said, 'I don't have time for a boyfriend with school and obligations.'" He mimics Becky and, while not very kind, it's a fairly decent impression. "I know that she has all these goals for her future and stuff, so I believed her and we went back to close friends. But now... she has time for Kyle, and Kyle is playing Pictionary in my fucking house with the girl who didn't have time for me."

I feel bad for him. "I'm sorry. I didn't know. That must hurt," I say quietly.

"You didn't know? Aren't you and Becky friends?"

"More like friendly acquaintances. I've known her a long time and we've always been part of the same circles, but it's not like we talk on the phone every night and have sleepovers."

"Like you and Jenny?"

"Yeah. We tie up our share of phone lines and, well, we have plenty of sleepovers." I smile.

"I bet you guys look all cute in your jammies having pillow fights and all," he teases. His tone switches to serious when he says, "But it's good to know Becky's not spreading our business around. I'm kind of a private person, you know?"

"Privacy and Pine Ridge aren't exactly synonymous, Braden. More like exactly the opposite."

"Another reason to keep things to myself," he mutters. "I like Jenny, though. She's cool but she's..." he searches for the right word, "typical. She's not my thing. She's not like you."

My pulse quickens. *What does that mean? Is that a good thing or a bad thing? If you think she's typical and different than me and you're not into Jenny, does that mean you could be into me? I love touching you. You smell like Polo—the green bottle, not the blue—am I right? And I love you.* I ask for clarification. "If I'm not typical, what am I?"

"Smart. Kind of intense... I don't know any girl as into football as you are. And cute—definitely cute." *Just let me stay in this moment forever.* And it is such a great moment, but then I receive the ultimate prize of the night. "Hey, do you want to come over tomorrow night? Have some pizza, watch a movie or something? I'll come pick you up, take you home, and all that." *Yeah, this moment kicks the other moment's ass.*

I mentally tick off a list of friends' parents still married that met in high school. I can name at least six couples without thinking too hard. *It's totally possible. Not too young for it to last forever. You'll take me to prom in a few months, maybe get a hotel room—but who needs a hotel room when you have your own wing in this big house? You'll have to get to know my parents. My dad is cool with Tanner, but that's probably only because Tanner isn't having sex with his daughter. We're going to have sex—someday... Jenny and I will be able to talk about life on a whole new level. You're perfect for me. We're perfect for each other. Are you going to kiss me tonight? I love you, Braden.*

Instead, I say, "Yes."

"Cool. I'll call you tomorrow. We can figure out a time."

Oh my god, I have a date with Braden. I think. This is a date, right?

The distant sounds from inside suddenly ring out full force. Tanner's voice calls into the darkness much too loudly for our actual proximity. "Panda? You out here?" *Buzzkill, Tanner.*

"I'm right here." I struggle to sit up and instantly regret the loss of Braden's body heat. I peek over the top of the chair. "Here."

"What are you doing out here? It's fucking freezing, and I looked all over the house for you." He walks around the chair, appears surprised to see me with Braden but recovers quickly. "It's almost curfew. Do you want to call it in?"

I have a midnight curfew, but it's loose. If I want to stay out later I have to call home by midnight with my name, rank, and serial number. "Do you want me to call it in?"

"Naw. Save it for another night. I'm tired—ready to roll."

I'm disappointed to leave Braden but flying high on the potential of time alone with him tomorrow. "Okay, let me grab my jacket and purse."

"In my hands, duh. You blind?" Tanner replies. "I don't just hold any chick's purse."

"Ah, yes—" I scramble to my feet, and he holds my jacket open so I can slide my arms in. "It's a nice look." I pinch his cheek while liberating my purse. Braden doesn't get up. He tucks the blanket around his solo form and offers Tanner a mock salute.

"Let's roll, Panda." Tanner turns to head for the stairs.

"Uh... Thanks for keeping me warm," I stutter. My earlier visions of prom, giving him my V-card, and living happily ever after dissolve into the cold night air.

"Thanks for being warm. I'll call you tomorrow."

FIVE

October 11, 1987
First "Date"

I'M IN MY ROOM WITH my diary, listening to my parents clanking dishes around in the kitchen, discussing whether or not it's too cold to put the chicken on the outside grill tonight. My dad insists that it's only too cold when he has to shovel a path of snow in order to get to the grill. Since there is no snow, it's not too cold. It's going on late afternoon and Braden hasn't called.

Climbing my Bon Jovi, Lost Boys poster-covered walls, I'm obsessing so hard that I think everyone in town can hear my thoughts—like they're posted on that light-up sign outside the KFC, updated weekly.

Braden asked Amanda for help with pre-calc problem #4.

Braden told Amanda a secret.

Amanda loves Braden.

Braden is not going to call.

Amanda needs professional help.

Dr. Cartwright, call Amanda and get her help.

I might be obsessed, I muse, but at least I still have my sense of humor—no matter that it's self-deprecating.

The phone rings, startling me. Did Dr. Cartwright read the latest update as he drove by KFC? Clearly he did, and he's calling as soon as possible to schedule my appointment.

Mom enters my room, cordless in hand. "Honey, Braden—for you."

My face turns four shades of red as she hands me the phone. Her eyes zone in on mine. Five shades, six shades... Quite certain I'm approaching purple, I ask her to close my door on her way out.

"Hi, Braden," I say into the handset.

"Hi yourself." *Jeez, swoon.* "What are you doing?"

I look at the unfinished sentence in my diary and share, "Not much. You?"

"Do you still want to hang out tonight?"

"I do." *I love you.*

"Can I come get you in, like, half an hour? We'll hit Blockbuster and Pizza Stop. I know it's a school night, but I'll have you home by, what... ten?"

You can have me all night. "Yeah... hold on a sec, all right? I need to check with my parents."

"Sure."

Leaving the phone—and Braden—on my bed, I go ask my parents. Dad is massaging the chicken with his special dry rub. "Ten is late for a school night," he objects.

"Yes, but I don't go to sleep until eleven, so it's not really that late," I reason.

He looks to Mom. She asks, "Who else is going to be there?"

"Coach and Braden's mom. It's just pizza and a movie. He'll drive me both ways, and I'll be home by ten." My eyes beg Dad's, *pretty please.*

Dad's ruling on the field is in my favor. "All right. But tell Braden to come inside when he picks you up."

"Yay! Thanks!" I bounce back to my bedroom and pick up Braden. Dialing back the exuberance, I tell him, "My parents said yes, but you have to come inside and talk to my dad before we can leave."

"I wasn't going to honk for you from the driveway. My mom raised me better than that." He laughs before posing a relevant question. "Is your dad in a good mood today?"

"I think so. He probably just wants to intimidate you a little bit."

"Great. I'm really looking forward to that. See you in a few, Amanda."

Flying into action, I get dressed in my comfy black leggings and a super soft pink sweater that has a flattering V-neck and comes to mid-thigh. My red boots complete the outfit. After fixing my hair, I pop in my contacts and I'm finishing with light makeup when the doorbell rings.

I put my personal stuff back into drawers and under the sink because bathroom clutter triggers Mom's OCD. Shoving a few items into my small purse, I grab my winter jacket off the back of my desk chair.

I'm greeted by the sight of beautiful Braden in my living room, hands in pockets, rocking back and forth lightly on his feet and nodding at whatever my dad is saying. He's wearing his signature cargo pants, and a tattered Banana Republic tee peeks out beneath his dark blue Banana Republic sweatshirt.

"Hey. I'm ready," I declare cheerfully.

Braden turns his killer blue eyes to me and smiles. *You're picking me up for our first date. You're going to look incredible in your prom tux and rocking our first born in the crook of your arm.* What? *Shut up, voice in my head.*

"Mr. Harrington? Anything else, sir?"

"No. Have her home by ten, and don't do anything stupid." Dad's tone is cold, flat, and seriously serious. Although he's met Braden and his parents many times before, Braden is still an outsider with a black sports car driving away with his fifteen-year-old daughter in the passenger seat for the first time.

I roll up on my toes to kiss Dad's cheek and call out to my mother who's up in the loft, "See you, Mom. Love you."

"I'll bring her back by ten, in one piece, sir," he assures my dad over his shoulder as we walk to the front door.

In return, Dad slaps him on the back a little too hard and says, "You don't deliver on that promise, we got real problems."

I snicker and roll my eyes, but Dad's not playing—he's glaring at Braden's back.

As we step outside and navigate the steps of the front porch, Braden places one hand on the small of my back. He opens and closes the car door for me. Sliding into the driver's seat, he turns and says, "Amanda, your dad scares the crap out of me. Does he treat Tanner like that?"

"Uh, no," I laugh. "You must be special."

* * *

The selecting of the movie at Blockbuster turns into a bit of a debate, so we walk out with two movies. Braden's mood is carefree as we make small talk and drink fountain sodas waiting on our pizza—which was also a debate because I love just pineapple on my pizza, which Braden finds disgusting, so we had to order a half-and-half. Our conversation flows from movie titles to favorite music to our stuck up sisters.

"Pink is a good color on you," Braden compliments. "You look all innocent and sweet."

Swoon. "That's because I am innocent and sweet."

He studies me. "You look different today. It's not the pink... it's something else?"

It's my love for you written all over my face. "No glasses." I provide a clue.

He snaps his fingers. "That's it. I can see your eyes really well." He leans in closer. "They're not just brown. Around your pupils you have flecks of... green—hazel, maybe. I've never noticed that before."

"Maybe because you haven't really looked before—at my eyes..." I feel my blush blotching and spreading.

"I guess you have other things I'd rather look at," he teases. *Oh my god.* "Such as, you have these," he taps his finger lightly over my nose and cheeks, "adorable little freckles."

I sit back out of his reach because my skin is on fire now. I blurt, "I have freckles all over my body." My blush deepens. *Why did I say that?*

"Maybe I'll get to see them sometime."

"Oh, you will." *Shut up, Amanda.*

His eyes widen in astonishment. *Now I've made him blush.* "And where," he takes a sip of soda, "exactly are these freckles?"

"Pretty much everywhere. If you go to the lake with us this spring, you'll see they're all over my shoulders and arms, and, um, chest... but you can kind of see some of those right now because of my sweater..." I trail off because I just directed his attention to my cleavage. *I suck at flirting.*

"Innocent?" He arches an eyebrow.

"Yes," I insist. "*And* sweet..."

I will wear contact lenses from here on out.

* * *

If Coach is surprised to just see me walk into his family room, he doesn't show it. "Harrington, who's taking the Territorial Cup this year?" he booms.

Dating back as far as 1899, Arizona and Arizona State started battling on the football field for bragging rights and the Territorial Cup. In 1964, it became an official annual grudge match held after Thanksgiving, and it gets vicious out there between these arch rivals—often called the Duel in the Desert. The only thing both teams can agree on is that they hate each other. They fight it out on the field until the bitter end.

"That can't even be a serious question because, *duh*, Coach—Arizona is taking it. We have the last five years in a row," I wisecrack.

"You're not even ranked," he fires back.

"Like that matters. It all comes down to who wants it more, Coach."

"I don't like this side of you, Harrington." He winks and gets up from his seat on the sofa. "All right, I'll leave you kids to it."

Braden turns to me. "Why are you such an Arizona fan, anyway? Didn't your parents go to Boston College?"

"Yes, but my mom got her Masters' Degree from Arizona. My parents always rooted for Arizona. Besides, everyone knows it's the superior school—academically and in NCAA sports. Except baseball—I'll concede that ASU owns baseball, although that could change."

"I don't know if I should break out some old game tapes or pop in one of these movies."

I pretend to think about it before chanting, "Movie, movie, movie."

"You're going to make me watch your movie, aren't you, Mandy?"

"It's one of my favorites," I smile at him.

"Jesus," he mutters. "Those eyes..."

"Braden, is He part of this conversation?"

He laughs. "I might need Him to get through this movie."

"Here's the thing about John Hughes..."

"Oh, please, enlighten me more about the cliché genre."

Yes, this was part of our debate in Blockbuster. Braden is not a fan but I totally am.

"Actually, clichés are exactly the point. John Hughes brings to the screen the emotional roller coaster of life through the experiences of upper middle class high school students—sure mostly those from Chicago's North Shore but no less applicable to other parts of the country, except for all the weather and scenery and stuff. But it's this painfully honest, although some might argue semi-satirical, depiction of cliques and hierarchies and how they both define and confine us. And in the end, when we're lucky, we get to see his heroes and heroines come out on top and have a better sense of self."

He looks up at me from the VCR. "Did you just make that shit up on the fly, or have you given this a lot of thought?"

"I've given it a lot of thought."

"Of course you have." He shakes his head with a smile and finishes setting up the movie. There is that awkward—at least for me—moment after he kills most of the lights and decides where to sit. I'm curled up in the far corner of the couch against the armrest with my legs, sans boots, tucked underneath me. Pulling up the ottoman, he sits in the middle next to me, but not right next to me, stretching his legs out in front of him. His arm rests on top of the sofa, behind me but not touching me.

I try to focus on the movie, which I've seen at least a half dozen times by now, but all I'm concentrating on is the warmth radiating from his body, his breathing pattern, and his propensity to fidget. No matter how still the rest of him is, there's always at least one part of his body in motion—fingers drumming, knee bouncing, foot tapping. I use my hand and apply pressure to his knee. "You're jiggling my view."

"Sorry—nervous energy. And I don't like this movie," he admits.

We're not even that far into *Sixteen Candles*—after Jake Ryan finds the note Samantha Baker dropped in study hall and starts making inquiries but before Samantha is forced to bring Long Duck Dong with her to the high school dance.

I narrow my eyes. "How dare you? *Sixteen Candles*—fantasy ending, despite the whole panty incident—that's coming up. What girl wouldn't live to capture the heart of Jake Ryan? And *The Breakfast*

Club—we know all of those people 'in the simplest of terms, in the most convenient definitions: a brain, an athlete, a basket case, a princess, and a criminal,'" I quote the film's ending. "Yes, they are those things, and so much more." I should probably stop talking, but I'm on a roll and keep going. "And Watts in *Some Kind of Wonderful*—she's really a better person than Amanda, and Keith finally follows his heart instead of his hormones. But poor Duckie Dale. He doesn't get a happy ending. Wait, no—Duckie's actually from *Pretty in Pink*, but still—poor Duckie, because Andie winds up kissing Blane, who's kind of a jerk for most of the movie but he's very redeemable in the end..."

"Pick one character from *The Breakfast Club*. Which one are you, Mandy?"

"Oh, I love this game. Press pause." He does as I ponder my options. "It's impossible to pick just one. I'm a princess and a brain. And also a bit of a basket case." *And what's with Mandy? No one calls me Mandy.*

"Clearly," he laughs. "I'm almost afraid to ask, but since I'm sure you've given this a lot of thought, which John Hughes character do you most identify with and why?"

"I'm Samantha Baker-esque. Realistic. Resigned to my place in the natural order. I don't expect the unexpected, and, if the unexpected ever happened to me, I'd want to be totally surprised. Like when she runs out of the church with her sister's veil only to find she's gone. Then the traffic clears, and Jake Ryan is waiting for her in front of his red Porsche. I mean, she never saw that coming."

"You just gave away the ending."

"Don't worry, that's not the actual ending. There's more."

"So you're a girl who wants to be taken by surprise?"

"Yes. *No.*" I shake my head. "I guess I like these movies so much because everything turns out the way that it should in the end. John Hughes is genius. I rest my case."

"Have you considered law school?" he asks.

"No. Why?"

Instead of responding to my question, he asks, "Are you sure it's not a red Trans Am?"

I challenge, "Do you dare doubt my knowledge of all things Jake Ryan?"

"That would probably be a big mistake on my part. If you say it's a Porsche, it's a Porsche."

"Oh, it's a Porsche, all right."

"Hey, since we're on pause, do you want something else to drink?"

I ask for another Diet Pepsi, and he heads into the kitchen. While he's gone, I stand to stretch and wander the room, looking at family photos from years gone by. I lean down to check out their large fish tank which houses schools of colorful little fish. They frantically swim back and forth but get nowhere.

"All right." He returns, drinks in hand. "Let's get this over with."

"You have Free Will, you know. You don't have to watch this."

"You've already ruined the ending, but since you like it so much..." He plops into the corner seat—my seat. He stretches his arm out and nods at the crook. "Come here. If I have to watch the rest of this shit, I'm going to do it holding you."

Smiling but nervous, I resume my previous position, only this time instead of leaning into the arm of the sofa, I lean into him. We could be watching any movie in the world, and I wouldn't care because I can't think about anything but Braden; I'm overwhelmed by the sensations of his warmth and scent. He *has* to wear Polo—the green, not the blue.

I settle in closer and rest the side of my face on his shoulder while he cracks jokes at the appropriate times and skates his fingers down my hair, shoulder, and arm. I'm not relaxed—*oh, hell no.* I feel like a ticking time bomb. I want to know what he's thinking about right this second because I don't want to watch this movie; I want to climb onto his lap.

Iconic. Epic. Totally romantic. Jake and Samantha sit cross-legged on the glass table, a beautiful cake adorned with sixteen candles—*duh*—between them. They're drawn slowly—oh so slowly—toward one another until he places a cinema-worthy first kiss on her virgin lips. I can't help myself. I'm so happy for her that I release a wistful sigh.

"You're all gushy and crap," Braden snickers. "Over that?"

"I love it. I wish I knew what came next—after the kiss. Like, not in a perverted way, but what happens to Jake and Samantha? Do they date? Does he fall in love with her? What happens when he leaves for college next fall?"

"They break up. Long distance relationships at that age never last."

"That's just great, Braden." Rolling my eyes, I explain, "Samantha finally gets what she wants, but we only get to see that moment of initial gratification. Now you're telling me she gets dumped. But maybe not... Maybe Jake Ryan stays local for college and they live happily ever after. Or maybe he's a total asshole who pressures her into unprotected sex because Caroline puts out so he expects it from Samantha. And then he knocks her up, drives off in his *Porsche,* and she's stuck living with her parents changing dirty diapers between shifts at Walmart. Ugh... But I don't think he does—because Jake Ryan listens to his heart, not his hormones."

"Oh, he so wants to get in her cotton panties. He's just doing the pre-work, breaking her in with romance. A teenage guy will always follow his hormones. You should probably know that for future reference with the defensive line."

I pout then ask, "What if a teenage guy can follow his hormones and heartstrings? You know, to have a physical and emotional relationship?"

"Best of both worlds, I'd imagine." His response is immediate—and promising.

Because I was too afraid to move for fear of terminating the delicious hair petting and arm rubbing activities, Braden and I haven't changed positions in forty-five minutes. Now I feel off-balance, weird, nervous... I'm waiting, wondering what's going to happen next.

"I don't want Jake Ryan to be an asshole. And my neck hurts." I sit up and stretch with an exaggerated groan while reaching for the painful kink.

The corners of Braden's eyes crinkle when he smiles at me—clearly amused by my final declaration. Without a word, he stands and stretches as well before extending his hand to me. I take it and he pulls me to my feet. Face to face, my hand still in his, he says, "Good news is, Mandy, since Jake and Samantha aren't real, their story can end however you want it to."

"What's with the *Mandy* thing? No one calls me that."

"Do you like it or hate it?"

"I haven't decided yet."

He grins at me. "I like it. It suits you."

I'm melting. "Then I like it, too." I smile back, my hand still in his.

He uses the back of his other hand to stroke my face from temple to chin. Tremors roll through my body. If I lean forward ever so slightly—with significantly less distance to close than Jake and Samantha—our lips will meet. At the thought, a rush of heat follows the tremors causing me to shiver. My breasts tingle, my stomach feels heavy, and I have the urge to rub my thighs together.

He moves his hands to my torso and turns my body around so my back is to his front. Placing his hands on my neck and gently massaging, he asks, "Where does it hurt? Here?" *Soft moan.* "Here?" *Ahhh....* "Here?" He digs his fingers into my flesh. *Whimper.* His hands move from my neck down my back, kneading. "Here?"

"Ahhh.... Feels so good," I sigh my appreciation.

"Good. Enjoy it." Stretching my neck slowly from side to side, his hands and fingers deliver pressure to different muscles on my neck and back. This goes on for a fair amount of time before he asks, "Does your neck feel better?"

"Yum..." *Yum? Yeah, I said that.* "But please don't stop," I request.

His hands move up over my shoulders, descending until his fingers knead along my collarbone. This motion continues on a slow downward slide—*so slow*—until his palms skim over my breasts, down my rib cage to my stomach, to the band of my leggings, over my clothing, heading south—sliding across my lower belly and coming to rest on my hips over my pink sweater. “This sweater is really soft,” he whispers in my ear.

SIX

Is it possible for my heart to burst out of my chest and land on the floor? Can you hear my heart pounding, Braden? His front is now firmly against my back with no space between us. *What is this?* I feel his hot breath on my neck as his hands gently knead my hips. Heart—hammering. Knees—rubber. Brain function—unreliable.

I blurt out, "Did you just feel me up, Braden McLaughlin?"

"Technically," he whispers in my ear, "I just felt you down." His hands travel further south to mid-thigh and the bottom of my pink sweater. Slipping them underneath the fabric, they travel the same path only in reverse, from my hips to my lower belly to the waistband of my leggings. His skin meets mine, and his hands are chilly. *Goosebumps, like everywhere.*

"This..." He pauses, skating his fingers up and down my rib cage. *Why are you stopping there? Wait—am I supposed to stop you there? I'm not going to stop you.* I can hear his breathing intensify; maybe he's unsure about which play to call now that his hands are under my shirt. After a small delay of game, his hands slide up until they reach the smooth satin material of my bra. Gently, he places a hand over each breast, cupping me tentatively. "This is feeling you up," he concludes with his lips on my neck behind my ear.

Well played, Braden. My nipples pebble with his words and touch. No one has touched me like this before and it feels... *oh my god...* His hands lightly massage my breasts while his lips touch different spots on my neck—hot breath, soft lips, the wet tip of his tongue—thumbs circling in slow discord over each nipple, brushing one and then the other.

Shouldn't an innocent and sweet girl throw a flag on this play? Probably, but instead I fail to swallow a soft moan. I've never felt my body *feel* so much. Aware of every inch of my flesh, while at the same time it's like watching this happen to someone else. *What is this? What does this mean? This spinning, whirling, hazy, bliss... is it for real?*

With confidence that must come from my failure to throw the flag, his pressure increases—more daring, firm, and very deliberate. His breathing becomes louder, uneven. "Mandy?" he whispers. His thumbs stop moving.

"Braden..." I breathe back his name.

He devourers my neck in earnest, kissing and nipping at my tender skin with his mouth, tongue and teeth. His hands resume their exploration, tweaking and pinching my nipples over the thin barrier of material, experimenting with the correlation of his actions to my reactions. I groan and push back into him to get closer—completely out of control, high on adrenalin.

With one final brush of his thumbs over my nipples, he withdraws his hands and grabs me with force, jerking my body on unsteady knees around and into his. His arms pull me closer, my arms curl around his neck, we tilt our heads, and our lips meet for the first time. This isn't in any playbook I've studied. It's instinct—and it is better than any daydream I've ever had.

Our heads tilt and trade sides to explore different angles and nuances of our mouths, our tongues, our lips—biting, teasing, sucking... *Oh my god.* He tastes like Dr. Pepper, sweet and sticky. His hands are everywhere at the same time—pulling hair, squeezing breasts, grabbing my ass. I may not be a very good flirt, but I'm a natural at this kissing thing, or maybe it's just natural to do it with Braden.

Our mouths separate when my sweater is pulled over my head and tossed aside. Despite his mouth making contact with the swell of my breasts—when the cool air hits my bare skin I snap back to reality. I place my hands firmly on his chest and step back, instantly regretting the loss of contact.

Trying to catch my breath, random thoughts rapid-fire inside my head. *My sweater is on the floor. Why is my sweater on the floor? How far will this go? What time is it? Do you love me, Braden? Too much. Too fast. Too soon. Can't think. Sweater on floor. Do you love me? Do you?*

"Braden, we have to stop," I blurt. "We can't... I can't... I..." I don't know what to say. What I know is that Amanda Harrington's parents would be disappointed if they could see her—me—right now, half naked in Coach's family room with my sweater crumpled on Mrs. McLaughlin's plush carpeting.

"Right." He shakes his head as if trying to clear his own thoughts and assesses my face. His hands immediately go to his head where he pulls on his hair near the scalp. He turns his back on me and walks away. *Walks away!* In the kitchen I hear the sound of the refrigerator door, rustling—the sharp snap of a can of soda opening.

Dread... fear... anxiety—all those awful feelings swirl around in my gut. *He walked away.* Tears fill my eyes and spill down my cheeks. *Why are you crying? Stop crying. Put on your sweater before he comes back. Will he come back?* I dress quickly, wipe the tears away, and sit on the couch before my legs give out.

Finally, he returns from the kitchen, chugging a can of Dr. Pepper. When he reaches me, he holds out the can. "Want some? Or I can get you your own?"

"No, thank you."

He polishes off the can in consecutive gulps, suppresses a burp, and asks, "Should I take you home?" He's not looking at me. *Why won't you look at me?*

"Braden, what just happened?"

He gives me nothing—no eye contact, no explanation. *Wow, silence* is *actually deafening.*

"Braden, say something," I whisper, trying to meet his eyes. *He won't look at me.* He doesn't say a word. My chest muscles seize, and I swallow whatever shred of pride I have left. I stand and place one hand on his arm. "Please. Say something to me."

He jumps as if startled by my touch. Again, still *not looking* at me, he *finally* mutters, "I'm sorry, Mandy." This is followed by, "It's a little after 9:30. I should get you home."

* * *

For the next few weeks we have a new routine... one that's called avoidance with stiff politeness when forced to interact. Braden barely looks at me, and our friends feel the chill and start to ask questions. I'm fairly certain that Braden, like me, gives them nothing to go on. What could I have said? He felt me down, he felt me up, he apologized, he drove me home in dead silence, and now he won't look at me.

We were friends. I thought he wanted to date me. I thought he cared about me. He touched my freaking boobs. And now we are two people existing in the same social circles, who can't make eye with each other. What a crappy *situation. Update KFC: Situations **suck**.*

Several Weeks Later – November 1987

Tanner drives us down the washboard dirt road; his Chevy pickup rattles in in protest with each pothole. We pass Robert's house, then he slows down to make the hard right turn up the McLaughlin's harrowing driveway. "Amanda-panda?" His voice is uncharacteristically tentative. "You gonna tell me what's up with you and McLaughlin? And don't tell me nothing. That'll just piss me off."

"Nothing," I reply.

"Sick of you avoiding my questions," he retorts. "I'm not stupid. Share. Now."

Instead of words, the familiar tears that come often and without warning these days sting my eyes and roll down my face. With his eyes on the long winding driveway cut into the hillside, Tanner doesn't notice until a pitiful sob escapes my throat.

"Amanda, what the fuck?" *What the fuck, indeed, Amanda?* Ashamed not to be in the privacy of my own room as I break down, I can't hold it back. Tanner stops his truck in the middle of the driveway, puts it in park, and pulls the emergency brake. I unbuckle my seat belt and slide across the bench where I promptly dive under his outstretched arm and bury my face in his chest.

He holds me while I cry—sob actually—into his flannel shirt. "You can tell me anything. I won't judge you."

"I don't know where to start."

"The beginning is usually a good place."

"Right... the beginning... Braden and I have a *situation*." *My use of the word is quite clever, right?*

"Define *situation*."

"We, um, kind of..."

"Define *situation* before I have to use my imagination and lose my mind," he orders.

"We messed around, and it didn't end well."

"What?" he barks and slams his left fist on the dashboard. "Did he hurt you?"

"No!" I insist, needing him to understand, but he's too busy flipping out.

"You're bawling all over my favorite flannel because he *didn't* hurt you?" Grabbing me by the chin forces me to look up at him. *"Answer me."*

"You're freaking me out," I tell him.

"You're freaking *me* out. Why aren't you answering me?"

My face crumbles, but I have a little fight in me. "Because you're yelling at me, Tanner! Quit yelling at me. I'm crying and you're yelling. You shouldn't *yell* at a girl who is *crying*!"

He releases a very lengthy sigh and speaks to the roof of the truck. "Please, God, gimme patience not to yell at Panda while she pulls her head out of her ass and gives me a fucking explanation."

"I don't think you're supposed to talk to God like that," I inform him. He glares—*glares* —at me. "Please," I swallow, "calm down, Tanner. I'm just having trouble putting this into words, but I'm sure it's nothing as bad as what you're thinking. As in, not a big deal—except to me."

His face softens immediately. "I'm sorry, babe. I am." His voice is warm and kind. "I care about you. Tired of watching you hurt without being able to help."

I take a deep breath and nestle my face back into his chest. "We just kissed and hands might have roamed—but not very far. I threw a flag on the play, he stopped—immediately. And then things got awful. So the *situation* is beyond awkward, you know? He won't even look at me, much less talk to me. Why? Is he upset that I threw the flag? Is he sorry that he touched me in the first place? Maybe he's repulsed by my breath or my boobs? I don't know. Why won't he talk to me?"

"Okay, we're getting somewhere now. You fooled around—fucking shocked, by the way—and now neither of you knows what the other is thinking about it. Got that right?"

"Yes."

"Just to clarify so I don't kick his ass when I see him here in a minute, nothing happened you didn't want?"

"That's correct."

"He didn't hurt you?"

"Just my heart, but don't worry. It's pretty much cold and dead by now, so hopefully it'll stop aching soon."

"And he got to touch your boobs?"

"Tanner!"

"*Lucky fucker.* Listen, Panda." He squeezes me tight with his right arm. "You just need to get in his face and start a conversation. That's all. Look, shit happens—just not usually to you. I talk to Dude all the time—not about you as of late, but he asked if I was bringing you tonight. He specifically asked, which means he wants to see you."

"You think?"

"I do. Otherwise, he'd be all, 'Dude, don't bring Amanda over.' Right?"

"I guess."

"I speak dude. Trust me, I'm right."

Tanner makes me feel like laughing, so I do—whimpers mixed with laughter while he holds me tight and assures me that everything is going to be okay.

"Your flannel..." I say meekly. "It's covered in my, um, snot."

"Don't give a crap about the flannel," he responds with kindness. "You and your cold, dead heart are another story." It feels so good to laugh with my friend that my cold dead heart has renewed signs of life and optimism. Tanner makes it seem so simple, and maybe it is.

Headlights from behind flood the cab, and a horn beeps. We're blocking the driveway, but I'm not finished clinging to Tanner. He waves his hand to signal the driver behind us. Without letting me go, he releases the parking brake with his left hand, crosses his left hand over his body to put the truck in drive. The tires spin on the gravel before they catch, and we continue up the hill. He parks with his left hand and kills the engine.

He speaks into my hair. "Love you, Amanda. I'd kill for you. Not sure I'd die for you, but I'd definitely kill for you."

I grin up at him. "Love you, too, Tanner."

"Now have some fun tonight, and you guys talk this shit out and quit making things strange for the rest of us."

"Hey!" I swat at him.

The playfulness dies when he asks, "You have feelings for him?"

"I do."

"Explain."

"You're pushy."

"I wanna know where your head is."

I admit, "It's my heart, Tanner. I love him." He says nothing, so I feel it necessary to elaborate. "I don't think it's a crush. I think I'm beyond crushing, and I might be crazy."

"Does he know that?"

"God, no. I don't think so. I mean, I haven't *told* him."

"Girl like you, Panda, you wait for him to show his cards first. He should say it first, work for it if he wants you."

"A girl like me?"

"One without experience. One with a good heart but who overthinks everything way too much—and has boobs that are so far from repulsive, it's not even funny."

"That's, like, the sweetest thing you've ever said to me, Tanner."

"It's true, especially the part about your boobs. I love your boobs. I'll show you how much right now if you'll let me."

"Shut it." I laugh and clamp my hand over his mouth.

His voice, although muffled, is clear. "Is that a no to touching your boobs?"

* * *

"I'll take her home," Braden's declaration is a command. Not a question. Not a statement.

I look up, stunned. For the first time in weeks his blue eyes meet my brown and our gazes don't waver. Game night with our friends was like the last several weeks at school. Braden and I shared the same space but didn't interact. Everyone scattered for the night while Tanner took his sweet time talking to Trina out on the back porch. She's waiting outside for him to drive her home, and, even though I have Braden on the brain, I'm dying to ask Tanner why he's taking Trina home.

"Okay with you?" Tanner asks me.

"Yes."

"Call your dad. I'm not taking blame when you miss curfew."

"I will. Thanks, Tanner."

He gives me a hug and pretends to whisper in my ear while staring Braden down over my shoulder. "It's deer season. This doesn't go your way, I'll make him disappear." I grin and squeeze him back.

Braden interjects, "There's no need for rifles, John Wayne."

Tanner snickers in appreciation of that retort before firing off a final glare in Braden's direction. "Known her a lot longer, dude. Just saying, I have to pick sides, teammate or not, I'm picking hers."

Braden walks him to the slider door where hushed *dude words* are exchanged before Tanner disappears into the inky night. Braden locks the slider behind him and turns to face me. "I don't want anyone showing up. Mom and Dad are in bed. I'm going to kill the lights and try to unfuck this *situation*." Lights off, save for the glow of the tropical fish tank, Braden leads in with, "Mandy, I feel like... we... you... I'm just... Fuck. Can we sit over here," he gestures to the leather sofa, "and I'll try not to make this worse?"

He waits for me to choose my spot, but instead of sitting next to me, he pulls up the ottoman and sits across from me. Once settled, he cradles his head in his hands. When he finally looks up at me, instead of speaking he drags the ottoman a few inches closer so our knees touch. He remains silent before pushing my legs together and sliding in closer still, my legs nestled inside of his.

"Do you have something to say, Braden?" I prompt. *Because I love you.* "Because if I'm going to miss curfew, I have to let my dad know where I am."

He looks relieved that I have the ability to speak and knows the drill with my folks. "Yeah... make the call." I hop up and buy myself more time with a story about an unfinished movie and a ride home from Braden. Not a *total* lie, which makes it a half truth, right? I make my way back to the sofa, but instead of climbing back over him to sit between his legs, I sit off to one side, still close enough for the outside of my leg to rest against his.

"Look, I'm... I don't know how this is going to come out, but if you could maybe listen and not put words in my mouth while I try to do this..."

I figuratively zip my lips and toss the key over my shoulder. His lips turn up in a smile that reaches his eyes. He can't help himself because clearly I'm a laugh a minute. He shakes his head and reaches for my hand. I allow it because I have to. *I love him.*

"I was thinking about what you said about, um, *stupid* John Hughes movies... And I thought... I thought maybe it could be like that with us—except not the part you made up after the movie with the coerced sex and dirty diapers. I've been so hung up on Becky—for years—and I wanted to know how it would feel to go there with you. I haven't been like that with anyone other than Becky. You haven't either, right?"

"I don't know where you've *been* with Becky, so I can't really answer that question."

"I'm still a virgin, Mandy. Aren't you?"

"Well, that's pretty direct."

"I'm not embarrassed," he declares. "You shouldn't be either."

"I'm not... I'm not embarrassed or experienced *at all*... except for what happened with you. Well, I'm kind of embarrassed, but not about being inexperienced."

He nods as if I make sense, which I'm not sure I do. "What happened between us seemed to escalate so damn fast. When you said stop, I felt like a total asshole. I took your shirt off."

I rub at my forehead with the palm of my hand. "It wasn't so bad."

He shakes his head. "'It wasn't so bad?' The shit you say sometimes..."

"I say a lot of things, Braden. More than I should when I'm nervous or feel strongly about something, but I say a lot of, um, things.

All the time. And a lot of those things don't make any sense. But some of them do."

And for the second time this evening, a boy in my presence looks to ceiling and asks God for strength before he continues speaking to me. "You have these freckles and big eyes that say things to me."

"Did my eyes tell you to take my sweater off?" I ask.

"That's what I mean about the shit you say... I can't tell if you're okay with it or pissed off about it. You haven't said anything to me in weeks."

"Um... what?" I snap at him and jerk my hand from his. *This is bullshit.* "I haven't *said anything* to ***you*** in weeks? Because you haven't *looked* at me in weeks. How is it even possible not to *look* at someone who's around you for *hours* every day? Really, I mean, you have to actually make a conscious decision not to look at someone who is *in your face every minute of every day.*" I take a deep breath and admit, "And now I am pissed off. Not about the shirt thing—about what happened after what happened...happened. This *situation* pisses me off."

"I'm sorry."

"Yeah. You said that already—after you took my sweater off, remember?" I flop back into the sofa cushions and cross my arms over my chest. I also cross my legs so we are no longer touching in any way, shape, or form. *Does air have a pulse? Does it pulsate? Because I think I feel it pumping, or maybe it's just my heart.*

"I don't know what I'm doing with you," he admits. "I want to make things right—normal—between us."

Okay, maybe I can uncross my arms because my posture is quite defensive, and it seems to me that we're both equal levels of utterly clueless. I soften my tone. "I like you, Braden, and I'm really sad because that first kiss between us—it was my first kiss *ever*. And it was my first groping, by the way, and so I thought... I thought you had feelings for me, too, but then you shut down on me."

"I thought you were pissed at me."

"No," I counter. "I tried to get you to talk to me after, but you wouldn't. I wasn't angry. I was just kind of... in shock, maybe. Definitely confused."

"So here's the other thing. Including not handling any of this well, I still have feelings for Becky." *Ouch. Did he have to come out and say it like that—no sugar cookie coating*? "If she changed her mind about our *situation*, I'd be with her. I'm not in a place to make any promises to another girl." *Double freaking ouch.* "It felt too good with you. I wasn't thinking about stopping. That isn't right—at least not with a girl like you."

"*A girl like me*?" I air quote because Tanner used those exact words earlier in the evening.

"You are the kind of girl who should be respected—by me, by any guy, by the whole defensive line."

"Hey," I snap. "The defensive line respects me."

"They do, along with the offensive, because you're kind of intense in the training room and on the field. But you know what I mean, Mandy. You deserve respect, and I hope that if— when—you get into something serious with a guy, it's not with some guy who has feelings for another girl." *Shit. Shit. Shit.*

"So you don't have feelings me?" *God, how sad for me.*

"Please don't twist what I said. If I didn't care about you, I wouldn't want to make things right again. I wouldn't want to be friends."

"So you have feelings for me?"

He hesitates and delivers a broody sigh. "Yeah, but I don't know if I'm that guy for you. Not right now..." He trails off and looks away while my heart threatens to break. He looks back at my face and says, "The thought of taking things too far and not being able to be that guy for you... Wouldn't that be a dick move on my part?"

SEVEN

I'M SILENT BECAUSE I DON'T understand the question. I do understand that my skin is crawling and my stomach is sour. I sit and think a few moments before asking, "There are no guarantees going into any sort of relationship, right? That's why people get together and break up all the time, right?"

"No guarantees—just decisions and consequences. Becky and me, we're not in a good place. As in, we may never be friends after all our years of friendship because I'm having a hard time dealing with how things went down. And I don't want you all weird around me and have shit end up all '*Fatal Attraction*', and then we can't even be friends because you hate me."

"Except you don't have any bunnies. Or pets at all, really. Not even a cat, right? Because I've never seen a litter box and cats can't live outside here because of javelina and coyotes. You have those, um, fish over there, and if I wanted to boil something to make a point, those fish are way too small. And they're pretty..." His composure slips—again—and he laughs. "But, personally, I don't think boiling a bunny over Becky is worth the sacrifice. She's not even that nice of a person, Braden."

He raises an eyebrow. "No?"

"Have you ever gotten a higher grade than her on an assignment?" He grins and shakes his head. "Well, I have, and, trust me, she's not nice. Like scoring better on a test will keep her out of Yale. If you have feelings for me, and I have them for you, then why can't we find out what happens next?"

"I can't make you any real promises."

"But you also stated that you have feelings for me—beyond friendship. Did you not just say that?"

"Definitely law school," he mumbles. "Yes."

"So what's the problem?"

"Where's the line, Mandy? If I'm not ready for a real relationship but I want to rip that sweater off your body and kiss you stupid? What does that do to you in the end?"

"You want to kiss me stupid?"

"And rip your sweater off. Fuck," he clips. "We're getting nowhere, and now I have a hard-on."

"I think we should discuss our options, Braden. You're making assumptions. In fact, you and Tanner make assumptions—*everyone* makes assumptions—about *the kind of girl* I am." I throw in the air quotes again. "I'm really tired of being a girl like me, because a girl like me never seems to get what she wants. Except *respect*. I get a lot of *respect*, apparently."

"If you don't want *respect*, what do you want?"

"It doesn't matter what kind of girl you think I am—or should be, or may or may not turn out to be—because we... we decide to explore what we feel. I'm not asking you for a promise or a money back guarantee when I... When I just..." *When I just want you to love me*. "When I want to spend time with you."

"I want that, too. I just don't want to hurt you."

"Isn't that my choice to make? We should come up with a list of options and think through them logically and come to a decision."

"Options?"

"Yeah... like Option A: Pretend that night never happened and go back to how it was before. Option B: Maybe date or spend time together and see what happens..."

"I'm a guy." He smiles, "I know what will happen with Option B. You're going to wind up underneath me."

That takes my breath away. "Good to know... We could have Option B with some physical limitations, you know, ground rules about what we do and don't do together, and we can re-evaluate at a later time if necessary. And Option C... Option C... Jeez, I can't come up with any other options. So we're either just friends—that's the line—or we give it a go and see if it turns into more. Or you come up with other alternatives."

"Option A is the simple answer." *No. No. No.* "I'm not ready for a label, you know, girlfriend/boyfriend and all that crap. So if Option B is on the table, you have to promise me that this is our business—yours and mine. You understand? Private."

"I've heard this before." I harken back to the night on his back patio.

He jokes on a wicked grin. "Option C might be something like we throw down, get naked, and screw until we're experts."

"Um, I'm not ready for an Option C in my life, which I'm sure is not surprising given my fear of unplanned pregnancies and dirty diapers and having to work at Walmart."

"It was worth a shot. I'm teasing—mostly."

"Okay, so recapping our viable list of options... Wait... Can you get me a piece paper and a pen?"

"This isn't AP Biology. You don't have to take notes or make a flow chart."

"Good notes help me organize my thoughts and aid in memory recall and good decision-making. Jeez, Braden, everyone knows that. Get me the paper and pen." He does, although begrudgingly. By the light of the fish tank, I spend several minutes notating and then studying my work.

"Care to share?" I believe he's more amused than exasperated. I mean, we have five classes together, participate in the same study groups, and I call plays on the field. He has to know how my mind works by now.

"Sure, but I haven't made up my mind. Just so we're clear. Don't expect a response yet."

"Option A: It never happened. With good faith, we re-establish our friendship as it was before that night. Which might not be possible—for me, at least. I mean, you did just spend the last several weeks ignoring me, and I'm not over it yet."

"Option B: Date and/or spend time together and see what develops. This option will not be discussed with any third parties without consent from both parties—you and me, and it will most likely include physical relations because you're a guy with hormones, but it may or may not result in a relationship or love or whatever you want to call it. I should also add—"

"Mandy, come on," he interjects.

"This is important." I silence him with a glare and clear my throat. "I should also add that Option B puts the future of our friendship in the most jeopardy. The variables are not defined, there is no control group, and we have no hypothesis. Or differing hypotheses, at this point in time. And we would need to discuss the ground rules, of course. And then there's Option C, which is not viable and therefore did not make the list. Is there anything you would like to add or remove? Maybe it would help you to read it yourself?" I try to hand it over but he declines with a shake of his head. *Whatever*. "I know which option I want."

"Option C?"

"Not a viable option, Braden."

His smile melts me from the inside out when he reaches for my hand and asks, "We're going to see how this plays out?"

"Yes."

"I get to kiss you stupid whenever I want?"

"Yes, but before we do anything really stupid, we need ground rules," I state.

"You don't have those already jotted down on your little list there?"

"Not yet, but I will," I say, tapping my pen on the paper.

"'Course you will," he smirks.

"These ground rules are ours—not just mine, Braden. Okay?

Amendments can be negotiated at any time after we come to an agreement."

"I say we take things one day at a time, keep it private, and try like hell not to make things weird—weirder—between us," he suggests.

I write 'Ground Rules,' with an underline and a colon, and write out the words before speaking them out loud. "Okay, take it slow, private, honesty. All agreeable to you?" He nods with a smirk. "I need to hear you say the words. This is a binding agreement."

"I suggested them in the first place; those are all agreeable ground rules."

I review our meager list of bullet points and share, "There should be more to 'take it slow.' As in specifically no sex—intercourse or, um, otherwise—which, as you recall, is the gist of Option C, which is not viable. We should probably have a ground rule that certain clothes don't get ripped off in the heat of the moment—like underwear. I think a lot of bad things can happen without underwear, so that should stay on at all times. Do you agree?"

"I can't believe I'm having this conversation."

"Say the words."

"I agree that I will not rip off your underwear without asking first." He rolls his eyes. I write it down. When I'm finished writing he says, "I can't believe I'm going to add to your little list, but the whole 'no means no' thing should be included—for your benefit, not mine, because I probably won't ever say no." He chuckles. "You don't like what's happening, you say stop, I stop. Or you don't like what's happening; you tell me what I can do to make it better for you."

Oh, I love that. "I agree. These can be subsets under respect and honesty, yeah?" I sub-bullet 'no means no' and 'trust.'

He smiles when I show it to him. "I'll say the words, Mandy. I'll do my best to be honest with you and with myself, and I'll do my best to be respectful of your feelings and that other girl shit. Are we finished here?"

"Do you think we should both sign this or something?"

"Fuck no," he clips and rips the list from my hand. It goes into the pocket of his cargo pants.

"Hey, I need that in case we need to reference or amend."

"I would ask if you're fucking serious, but I already know the answer to that one." He fishes it out and hands it over. I get up to tuck it away in my purse. He stands up to stretch, arms to the ceiling, neck popping.

As I round the couch, he hooks me by the waist and says, "Let's go to my room."

* * *

Braden fiddles with the CD player and the sounds of INXS fill the room. He adjusts the lighting, closes the door, and depresses the lock. He gestures to his double bed where I take a seat on the edge. He kneels down on the floor in front of me, pushes my legs apart and crawls between them, his arms wrap around my outer thighs, and he looks me directly in the eyes.

He reaches up to cup my face in his hands and angles my head down just so before closing the gap and touching his lips to mine—tentative, gentle, sweet. We press together softly for a few moments before suggesting that we 'get comfortable.' We settle on the bed, on our sides, facing each other, foreheads touching, legs tangled together, arms... well, we figure that out quickly. Like the first time, it's instinct. Pure and simple. We kiss and kiss and kiss, experimenting with different angles, nibbles, bites, tongues in and out of each other's mouths. Before one kiss ends, another begins. There are soft moans and groans as we explore these sensations.

Our bodies align perfectly—five foot eleven pairs with six feet three inches of muscular high school football player—everything is within reach. Where he's hard and defined, I'm soft and yielding. As this state of play could easily take on a life of its own, the ground rules put me at ease, leaving me free to roam his upper body over his clothes. Wanting to taste his skin, I tip my head to the side and place my lips, the tip of my tongue on his neck. I administer dozens of kisses, tiny bites —salty and delicious.

"You're killing me, Mandy," he groans several minutes into my exploration.

"What? How? Did I do something wrong?"

"That's fucking hilarious—no, no, you're an angel. You," he grabs my face so he can kiss me again and again, "you are so perfect. You're so warm. I want... I want to see you, touch you. Can I?" he's tugging at my shirt.

"Unfair," I protest the play.

"How so?"

"I'm the one who wound up half naked last time."

"I'll make it fair," he says and pops up on his knees to pull off his sweatshirt and drop it to the floor.

I believe that he believes that no means no—after all, he set the ground rule. But apparently he also believes that in the absence of a direct no, he can do what he wants. He swings his body over me and sits over my thighs, pinning my legs together with his weight resting mostly on his knees. "Your turn. I need to see you, Mandy."

With his leverage and in my surprised state, he's able to wedge his arms underneath the back of my shirt and use his momentum to pull it up and eventually over my head. Now this is awkward only because my arms are trapped inside and he requires my assistance. *Wait—no, never mind.* Shirt in one hand, he uses the other to restrain my entangled wrists together, and with a sharp tug, my arms are free.

He's slightly out of breath and looks a bit crazed perched above me. Eyes travel from my face to my neck to my breasts and back again—like my body is a map and he's considering which route to take. As he kisses me from mouth to neck to collarbone and everywhere in between while rubbing his hands all over my breasts, he gives his verbal approval of Option B. It comes out like, "I fucking love Option B. You're fucking amazing." I'm certainly no expert, but I believe that's articulate speech for a teenage guy who has a girl pinned to the bed.

Even though the lighting is dim, my eyes are well-adjusted and I can see every expression on his face and in his beautiful eyes. And he can see everything, including the front clasp on my simple satin bra. He kisses a trail between my breasts, licks the mounds of flesh that spill over the top while he palms and squeezes me from underneath. Hands move to the front clasp before he looks me in the eyes. "This is coming off."

"No. I'm scared." I have to consider my limits because my heart, my very soul, feels exposed to him for the taking and the crushing.

"Can you just lie with me—maybe talk for a while?"

He rolls to his side next to me. "Yeah, of course. Whatever you want." He reaches for a throw blanket and wraps it over us; his arms circle me tight, my face buried in his neck. "Please don't be scared. I want you to feel safe with me, Mandy. Are you all right?"

"Yes. Totally. And I want to do more, but we don't have to do everything in one night, right? Because I really like the kissing, and the, um... touching, but I'm not... ready."

He strokes my hair. "It's all good. I like the kissing, too. I especially like the kissing combined with the touching. I just get so excited, and your tits are... and... ugh, I don't think my dick has ever been this hard."

"What? Eww... No..." Yet I'm flattered? *Yes, you're flattered.* I've spent enough time around burly jock guys to know that they use crude names for girls' body parts, and they talk about the size of their junk and the stuff that comes out of their junk. And while Braden is so much more than a burly jock guy, he's still partially a burly jock guy, so I shouldn't expect poetry.

I say, "I'm a fan of Option B, too." He laughs, and I nibble at his neck again. "Do you wear Polo—the green, not the blue?"

"Are you an aftershave expert?"

"Just, you know, I spend a lot of time on busses with football players after postgame showers."

"Good nose, Mandy." He touches his lips to the tip of my nose, and I tip my head up so our mouths can meet. While we kiss, I take the opportunity to explore his bare skin. My hands skim and dance across his chest, noting the dips and plains of his muscular frame and the fine layer of hair sprinkled across his chest. He is so beautiful. He kisses me softly on the lips, forehead, and nose while my touch becomes more confident. Inhaling from my scalp, he whispers, "You smell so fucking good." His hand moves to cup my breast; my nipple erect against the thin layer of satin. His tongue tangles with mine, while his thumb rubs over my nipple. And then he groans reaching for the clasp in the middle, "I want to—"

"It stays on," I decree.

"All right, Mandy. I won't even try, okay?"

"Thank you," I whisper.

I'm not sure how much time passes—enough for INXS to play all the way through—and I might have, all right, I totally did, silently cry a little bit during *Never Tear Us Apart*. If he noticed, he didn't call me on it. And with a click and whir, Bon Jovi is slippery when wet. He lets it rock and gives love a bad name before we're living on a prayer. Through each track, we continue to kiss and touch, moan and sigh, and he talks a lot about Jesus while we press together. Sometime during *Never Say Goodbye*, I realize that I have to say goodbye.

The digital clock on his nightstand tells me that I've blown through my extended curfew. I pray my father is fast asleep and unaware, which he probably is since the McLaughins phone hasn't rung. Feeling completely disheveled, there is no other condition I'd rather be in, nor anywhere else on this earth I'd rather be.

* * *

"Stop here—around the corner," I order before he can drive his car up our loud, crunchy gravel driveway. His headlights will shine directly into my parents' bedroom window if he pulls all the way up.

After parking as instructed, he kills the lights but not the engine. We haven't spoken much on the fifteen-minute drive from his house to mine. My brain is creating the sentences that will soon fill the pages of my diary. I'm emotionally drained while my body still tingles.

He puts the Celica in park and pulls up the emergency brake between us. "About Option B, Mandy... We'll talk on Monday, right?

"Unless you decide to ignore me."

"I won't."

"I want to believe you."

"You'll see," he assures me. "It doesn't have to be weird. Only if we let it."

I release a sigh worthy of Broody Braden as I reach for the door handle. There's no need to fish out keys, because the side door will be unlocked for me. "Right. Only if we let it."

"You're too quiet," he states. "Are you okay?"

"I'm just tired." *I'm thinking. I hate thinking. Stupid thinking.* "You wore me out."

He chuckles. "Then we must've done something right."

Needing to get inside the house before my dad hears the car engine idling, I want a goodnight kiss but he's not initiating it. Facing forward, hand gripping the gear shift, this should be his play to call, but—as we sit in silence—I grow more self-conscious with each passing second. "Thanks for the ride, Braden." I open the car door, step out, and lean back in. "Good night," I whisper.

"'Night, Mandy."

I close the car door as quietly as possible. While tiptoeing up the driveway, I hear him pull away. Half expecting to find Dad waiting for me when I sneak in the side door, I'm relieved there's no incident.

In the bathroom, I study my face in the mirror. My lips are bright red and chapped, cheeks flushed, and I have minor abrasions here and there from the scruff of Braden's skin. I also have a few marks on my neck and one above my collar bone. *Hickeys? Great—don't let Dad see those or Braden is a dead man.*

After washing my face and brushing my teeth, I finally relieve my bladder. As I wipe, I notice the slick, clear discharge between my legs. There's a lot of it. My panties are soaked, and I'm not sure why that is. I change my underwear, put on my favorite sleep shirt, and crawl into bed.

I want to tell my diary everything, but I'm spent. *Dear Diary, I love him now more than ever. Please pass along the update to the crew at KFC.*

EIGHT

Second Semester, Junior Year 1988

We have our football Awards Banquet after the New Year, and Coach presents me with my very own Pine Ridge Bobcat football jersey. The guys whoop and holler when I hold it up, beaming. It's green with "HARRINGTON" silkscreened across the back in white lettering. My honorary number is 89 for my graduation year.

"This is so awesome, Coach. I love it!" I give him a hug.

"I'll never smack you on the ass, but you're part of my team, Harrington. I expect you to wear this with pride next season."

I am, and I will. But I wouldn't mind one bit if your son smacked me on the ass...

I wish I could tell you that Braden changes his tune and makes a public declaration of his feelings. That doesn't happen. We share schoolwork and laughter with our mutual friends. We hang out in our pack or sometimes we go out somewhere without them, but I live for our stolen moments together in the dim light of his bedroom where we share conversations and thoughts about life along with lots of kisses and bare skin.

As Option B plays itself out, I don't ask him to verbalize his feelings—or lack thereof—for me. On some level, I know he cares. I see it in his smiles, in the sly looks and smirks. I hear it in his laughter when I prattle on and become too analytical or passionate about study notes and flow charts. I feel it during our fevered kisses and in his enthusiastic hands.

Maybe because Braden makes no promises except to respect me and he tells me no lies, and because he doesn't date or initiate an Option B with another girl, we're able to maintain our friendship as we become more intimate behind his locked bedroom door. When I'm honest with myself, I own up to and frequently wallow in the sad feelings in my heart as we part ways following our Option B-related activities. After he drops me off at the bottom of my driveway or when he doesn't call me the rest of the weekend, I don't like that. This time with him is *everything* to me, but it is not enough.

He doesn't even take me to prom. Apparently Braden has a phobia of school dances and monkey suits and crepe streamers and balloons. When I tell him that I'm going with Tanner, Braden says that he hopes we have a good time. We do, even though Trina spends half the night staring at Tanner.

Tanner is ultimately my one transgression regarding Option B. I confide in him because he asked me what happened on the night that he left me at Braden's house on the hill. So I tell him the truth, with as few details as possible, about the options we came up with and the one that I selected. Tanner thinks the options are 'so fucking stupid' and worries that I'll get hurt, but he doesn't interfere. He listens when I want to talk, holds me when I need to cry, and cares for me as any good friend would.

Age Sixteen
Summer between Junior & Senior Year – 1988

At the end of junior year, Braden leaves to spend the summer with his family at their cabin on Lake Michigan. I'm not expecting to hear from him because there's no phone at the lake house, but Becky calls me after she, Mike, and her parents return from spending a week there with the McLaughlins. I don't know why she feels the need to fill me on her vacation. We're not phone friends. But her news is reassuring—she's still wild about Kyle and doesn't mention any parties or girls hanging around Braden this summer.

On July 22, I turn sixteen, and we have a small party at my house that turns into a lake party with my friends. As the sun goes down over the lake, someone blasts *Amanda* by Boston over a boom box. Instead of the happy birthday song, I receive a serenade of *Amanda*—as I often do from the guys on the travel bus. Yeah, it's funny, but, jeez, after two years it's also old news.

A few days later, I get my driver's license and the keys to a brand new Chevy C1500 with an extended cab, side step, and a short bed. She's bright red with silver trim, and when my parents lead me out to the driveway, she has a huge silver bow across the hood. I jump for joy because I wasn't expecting a car. Brianna never got one. Following crushing hugs of gratitude, I calm down and christen her Cherry.

Even though I no longer need to bum rides, Tanner's truck is a fixture at my house. He takes most meals with us when he's not at the shop. Mom, not Tanner, tells me that Dad's encouraging him to apply to the best colleges in the country and offers to pay the application fees. My father allows him to drive us around in my new truck since his is less reliable. Just as we did last summer, we spend as much time at the lake as possible. And while I'm having a happy-go-lucky summer vacation, I miss Braden. I miss him every minute of every day.

* * *

Braden comes by unannounced a few days before senior year kicks off. We're eating dinner when he knocks at the door. I see him through the glass, jump from my seat, and run outside. "Hey, Mandy," he greets. His familiar blue eyes sparkle, and the skin around the corners of them crinkle. His hair is super blond and his skin so incredibly tan that it makes his eyes all the more blue.

I can't help myself. I throw my arms around his neck and squeeze tight. Then I grab his hand and drag him off the front porch, away from the prying eyes inside. "I missed you," I confess. "So, so much." I step into his space, wrap myself around him, and give him a kiss to back up the talk. He's game and participates fully. I'm reassured that it's not—we're not—over. *I am so in love with you, beautiful boy.*

"Me, too, you," he says. "So much that we just got home an hour ago, and I was hoping you'd be here. Tanner inside?" He nods toward his truck.

"Yeah, with my parents. We're having dinner. Do you want to come in?"

"Sure. I can stay for a little bit. But," he gestures to Cherry, "whose truck is that?"

"It's this girl's—this girl right here." I point at myself and grin. "A lot happened while you were gone. I have an official driver's license and my Cherry."

"You had your cherry when I left."

I smack him. "Cherry is my truck, smartass."

"She's cool, Mandy, and I hope you don't lose her anytime soon. I mean, I at least want a ride first." *What?* "So," his smile is brilliant, "what's for dinner?"

Senior Year – 1988-1989

Senior year is insanely jam-packed with activities. More AP classes, special projects, study groups, football, college applications, socializing with friends, and creating memories. Really, it's exactly like junior year, except I head into it with Braden entrenched in my life.

Tanner now has four inches on me, and he holds it over my head (pun intended) every chance he gets. He's filling out courtesy of Mom's hearty meals and all the time he spends in the gym. Were it not for the fact that he's still Tanner Rawlings with his incessant teasing and propositioning and laughing in my face every chance he gets, I might find him hot. Other girls do—especially poor Trina, who's asked him out on several dates. They've gone to movies a few times and shown up for social events together, but Tanner insists—at least to me—that he doesn't have the same feelings for her. I feel bad for her because she's been wanting more for over a year now, but there's a part of me that's relieved. Even though I don't have those feelings for Tanner, he's sort of mine. I'm almost comforted to see him keep his focus on the field and his grades. This is a huge year for him, and nothing will stop him.

Jenny and Robert can't sustain a long-distance relationship now that he's at CU-Boulder, so she selectively picks and chooses—primarily from the defensive line—new guys to date/bang. We make an effort to spend time together, but we're drifting apart with our different academic tracks and life goals. She favors beer and bonfires in the woods to Pictionary and movie nights. Eventually she settles on a linebacker named *Matt Neilson*, but I don't care. Middle school was years ago, and he waited a mighty long time to have her.

And, of course, there's football and smelly athletes, taping limbs, keeping stats, and learning some new plays and hand signals. Our team is fairly decent this year—not good enough to win a state championship, but we have way more wins than losses. On the travel bus I have my usual seat—up front and next to Tanner, and the team still loves to play and sing *Amanda* for me.

Even though Braden's in my life in a completely different way now, there is no big show for other people. He doesn't ask or refer to me as his girlfriend, and he treats me pretty much the same in front of the team. I guess that's okay—I wouldn't want the guys to give me a hard time.

One cold day in November, Braden jogs off the practice field and puts his letter jacket around my shoulders. I want to be buried in it, but I wear different player's letter jackets all the time when it's cold. Since he didn't ask me to keep it or tell me that it meant anything more, when I go over to his house later that night I return it. He doesn't give it back to me, so...

Braden definitely has his hopes set on the creative writing program at Iowa. The rest of his picks are also out of state, except for the obligatory ASU application, and his schools don't coincide with mine. We talked about where we were applying, but not in any context of trying to stay together. Of course, I consider putting in an application to Iowa but don't. I hate cold weather, I'm not particularly fond of corn, and isn't it pathetic to follow Braden when we aren't serious or committed or committed to being serious? He seems fairly accepting of our eventual goodbye.

My intention is to major in Biology with a Sports Medicine emphasis, and I've applied to The University of Arizona and Northern Arizona, with Stanford, Berkley, and Duke as long shots. I'm not sure why I picked Duke. I'm a PAC 10 girl. And nagging me, never far from my thoughts, is the fact that no matter where I decide to go, I have to defer admission for a year because I'm still leaving for Germany next July.

Oh, and Becky gets into Yale—early admission. Merry Christmas to her.

Christmas Break, Senior Year 1988

Brianna is home for Christmas—which is weird. Brianna hasn't come home since her sophomore year of college, opting to stay closer to campus and spend holidays with our uncle and cousins who live thirty minutes from campus. For a while, she would spend time off from school with a boyfriend named Isaac who hails from an obnoxiously rich family in New York City.

We don't often share details with each other. We're not close like many sisters are, possibly because we're very different in temperament and interests. Brianna spent her years in Pine Ridge in a perpetual state of loathing—self-loathing, peer loathing, mother loathing. She had a few friends along the way, but it was never easy for her. While I slid right into things as a first grader, she came to Pine Ridge as a gawky red-headed ten-year-old with thick glasses and bony knees—maybe a little too intelligent for her own good. Adding insult to injury was the fact that Mom was a new teacher at Pine Ridge Elementary, and a strict one at that. Most kids shudder of at the memory of facing Mom's wrath in class.

Little kids can be mean to each other, and then they turn into vicious teenagers. Her final year in Pine Ridge was pure hell. She went overseas her junior year and returned—after a taste of freedom and a life without being teased—to the same asshole people who had started a rumor about her while she was gone. Brianna didn't go overseas—oh, no. She was sent away to a private school because my parents didn't want the whole town knowing she was pregnant. It was utter bullshit, but it cut her deep and severed any ties she might have wanted to have with this town. She showed them though. She graduated near the top of her class and left town for the Ivy Leagues.

Maybe she harbors resentment for my good fortune and her lack thereof. Maybe that's why we aren't close. It's hard to say. I have a lot of memories of snide comments, loud arguments between her and Mom, and her steely determination to escape this place and never look back. Still, she is my sister and I love her. It's just a totally different dynamic when she's in the house.

Brianna just spent her spring semester of college at a university in East Germany—you know, on the other side of the Wall. Following that, she segued into her senior year without coming home. Although Dad has been out to visit her several times, Mom has not. They communicate by phone almost every Sunday evening at 6 p.m. Mountain Time. Our calls on the speaker phone with the whole family last about fifteen minutes. Sometimes, I'll take the handset and walk off to my room so Brianna and I can have a private, sisterly conversation. More often, we don't.

With Brianna home, my mom is on edge and speaks slowly, as if she's vetting out the consequences of each word before it passes her lips. Dad is Dad. He and Brianna are golden—always have been—while I'm close to both Mom and Dad.

It's a few days before Christmas, and we just finished dinner. Tanner and Brianna got into a heated debate about the actual need for a Women's Studies program. Poor dude. You'd think he would've learned by now. Arguing with Brianna is futile, and Tanner's knowledge of the subject matter was akin to him bringing a dull switch blade onto a battlefield with rocket launchers. After taking his plate to the kitchen, Tanner hugs Mom and me, nods at Dad, grimaces at Brianna, and quickly escapes with his tail between his legs.

"Kiddo," Brianna says, "come help me with the dishes. I don't know where anything goes. And I wouldn't want to put something in the wrong place, *God forbid*."

My mom purses her lips together in a very tight line before she starts clearing the table. It is law in our home that everyone brings their own plate into the kitchen and helps put away the condiments. Mom and Dad alternate nights with me finishing off the remaining cleanup. It's actually kind of nice. I get to spend quality time with them individually after a family meal. It's a chance to delve deeper into our dinner table discussion or change topics completely. This is our routine, and Brianna hasn't been part of the rotation in a very long time.

Once the table is clear, Brianna gives my mom—it being her turn—the night off. She rinses while I load the smaller items into the dishwasher since I can duplicate Mom's mad skills in this area. "Tanner, huh?" she asks. "That boy's been following you around for years now."

"Tanner? No, we're just friends. Things aren't good at home—like, at all. He's here a lot, so I don't even know if his mom buys groceries for him anymore."

"Oh. Okay. That's a nice truck you have. Must make all your little jaunts to pep rallies and parties around town easier."

I give her the side stink eye, "Jealous much?"

She waves a dismissive hand. "I've no need for a car, what with public transportation and Uncle Daniel so close by. It's not practical for my life, but it's nice that you have one. You'll need it in Tucson. Right? You still plan on going in-state?"

"If you think it's so nice that I have my little truck, why does it sound like you hate me for it?"

She laughs. "I don't hate you. You're my baby sister."

I sigh and look directly at her, "Maybe we can just cut through the crap, yeah? Big sister to baby sister, Ivy League genius to kiddo. Because this is my last Christmas at home, and the way you treat Mom is... It sucks. I have a lot on my mind, and I don't know anything that's on your mind, so maybe we can make better use of this rare time together. What do you say?" I arch my brows and extend my right hand, "Truce?"

While I'd classify her smile as more of a smirk, she takes my hand and gives it a firm shake. "When did you grow up?"

"Yesterday. So," I resume my loading activities, "tell me about your life. Senior year, Women's Studies and History major, what's next after graduation?"

"I'm going back to Germany."

"Really?" I'm actually excited that we'll be in the same country next year.

She nods. "I'm looking for a job and have a room lined up in an apartment. It's a really crappy room in a really crappy apartment," she confesses. "But I've got to start somewhere."

"Back to Neubrandenburg?" I refer to the East German city. "Is that allowed?"

"For a year, and then I'll either have to attend graduate school or move to West Germany or get married," she shrugs. "I'll see what happens."

"Wait—I thought all Women's Studies majors were lesbians," I jest.

"Who said anything about marrying a man?" she jokes back. "But there is a man."

"Yeah? A German man not named Isaac Goldstein, I hope."

"He's nothing like Isaac. We were only together a few months, but it was intense and we're not finished."

"Wow, this is really big news, Bree. I'm going to miss you—even though you're never around anyway. And I hope things work out for you—the job, the man, the whole thing."

"Thanks, kiddo. I'm driving your truck while I'm here, you know."

"My truck is your truck. But you have to call her Cherry."

“Cherry?” she snorts. “Very classy.”

NINE

CHRISTMAS VACATION PROCEEDS WITHOUT MAJOR incident. It's tense, but not as much. Brianna and I fashion a new bond. We talk long and often. She's still condescending because she's still Brianna, but we're able to open up to each other. She promises to visit me in Germany—no matter where I'm sent—and I'm comforted.

We're curled up on my bed when I ask her to make more of an effort around Mom, and she tells me some of her reasons behind the anger. Most of it boils down to control struggles and Brianna seeing life one way while Mom sees it another. "Oh God, the fucked up way she gave me the sex talk in fourth grade. It was all very clinical, and then she launches into this bullshit about two souls joining as one—"

"—in the sanctity of marriage," I finish for her and we laugh. While factually accurate in how babies are made, Mom led us both astray during the sex talk, or rather, she led us down her path—which is definitely not the road most taken and not what my friends are doing.

"Right? I mean what kind of bullshit is that? And did she tell you that you should wait for marriage for it be all 'spiritual', but if you fall in love and decide to have sex before marriage you should be smart about it, and you can come to her to get on the pill?" I nod. "Because that's bullshit, too. In case you don't already know. Do you? Do you already know?"

This time I shake my head. Brianna says, "We'll get to that later. When I was home that summer after freshman year, she made me an annual appointment with Dr. Cartwright. I asked him to put me on the pill, he did, and she lost her shit when I told her about Isaac. *Lost her mind.* It turned into this whole lecture about STDs, pregnancy—because the pill isn't 100% effective, and if I have to have an abortion, it might make me sterile—the STDs and/or the abortion—so I'll never have children when I want them. On and on and on she went. She still hasn't stopped judging me, telling me what to do. Trying to make me feel so freaking guilty when I just want to live my own life. God. I can't wait... *cannot wait* to tell her where I'm moving after graduation. Keep your mouth shut. I'm saving that for the day before I leave the country."

"I can't say that I blame you... It explains a lot about you and Mom, and your, um, attitude. But maybe she isn't trying to tell you what to do. Maybe she's trying to understand you. You're kind of a mystery to us." I shrug. "My relationship with her is different, though."

"That's only because you haven't done anything *wrong*—yet. But I'm warning you, if you decide to sleep with someone, don't tell her, and don't get the pill from Dr. Cartwright. Go to Planned Parenthood in the Valley somewhere, and if you need to talk with someone, I promise you that person is not Mom. You can talk to me about anything, understand? I'm not here, but pick up the phone and call. I won't judge."

"There is a guy... but we're not there—yet. Or maybe we won't get there at all. I don't know."

"How long has this been going on?"

"Since last year—just messing around and stuff. We're not having sex so..." I'm uncomfortable telling her this and it must show on my face, which I can feel burning.

"Amanda, big sister to kiddo, I'm going to tell you what I wish someone had told me. And maybe you've heard it from your friends—that Jenny, no doubt—but I want you to hear it from me. It's like my big sister duty."

I nod. "You have my undivided attention."

She takes a deep breath and her green eyes—damn her recessive genes with that dark auburn hair and green eyes—display genuine friendliness and openness. "The first thing that you should know is that sex is amazing with the right guy. I think it's better when you're in a good relationship—definitely with someone you trust and he respects you, and blah, blah, blah, but I've screwed a few friends and that was fun, too. Sex can be for love, for sport, physical release, fun, for whatever. It's not just about love."

"And also, and this is important, if you—when you—decide to do it, you have nothing to feel ashamed about. It's natural, it feels good, and it's a biological necessity to, you know, repopulate the Earth. Don't ever let Mom or anyone else make you feel bad about what you decide to do with your body. Ever. It's yours. That being said, don't be stupid. We know enough teenage moms in this town. Don't become one of them. Condoms always, preferably condoms with the pill, and don't skip the condom because you're on the pill. Some guys are dogs, and unless you're 100% sure he's clean and you're exclusive, he might give you way more than an orgasm."

"And last—because this is starting to sound like a lecture not advice—I'll repeat that you can always, always, always come to me. Until the day I die. Or you die. You'll probably die first because I've experienced the way you drive."

Something else Brianna and I have in common besides sharing an uptight, sexually repressed mother —we Harrington girls can't leave a tender moment alone.

New Year 1989

The McLaughlins host a New Year's Eve party for everyone, kids and parents alike. The entire family is game to attend, although we're taking two vehicles because my parents will probably bow out before midnight. I haven't seen Braden since school let out. His sister Fiona is home from Arizona. I've only met her once before, and she's a bit snarky and carries an air of superiority. She and Brianna will either become fast friends or try to out-snob one another. Brianna rides shotgun with me in Cherry.

"I'm excited to meet your guy."

Rolling my eyes, I beg, "Please, be cool." She now knows all the intricacies of our clandestine pseudo-relationship. "Don't make a big deal out of meeting him, or he'll know that you know and..."

"Relax, kiddo. The more I think about it, this strategy of yours is brilliant."

"Um... What?"

"When I was your age, I had to be home by midnight. Period. End of story. Never mind that I'd lived a year in a foreign country and did just fine without Mom's thumb on my head. But you... Somehow you've managed to get all this freedom that I never had. Totally jealous, by the way."

"At least you have way more baby pictures. By the time I came around, babies were old news."

She laughs. "No, I was just cuter. Mom is way more trusting with her second little darling. Your extracurricular activities with Braden are completely under the radar. They have no idea that you and this Braden are macking in his room every weekend, right?"

"It's not every weekend."

She shrugs. "Whatever. My point is that they have no clue that you and Braden are involved, so you have a free pass to do whatever you want practically under their noses. Brilliant. If Mom had any idea, she'd fit you with a chastity belt, and I can guarantee Dad would grill him often, without mercy. While it's not the whole high school fantasy relationship, it's still a sweet deal."

The house is packed with people of all ages. Braden greets me with a grin and a hug. Brianna beams. I might slap her. I make introductions, he makes introductions, and we spend a lot of time mingling—just not with each other. It's fine, though. With the diverse combination of party-goers, there are plenty of people to spend time with.

Brianna and Fiona become fast friends. They chat each other

up, perhaps discussing the importance of applying qualitative and quantitative research data in theoretical inquiries. I'm able to catch up with Tanner, who keeps a wary eye on Brianna lest he be forced to engage in word-to-word combat. It's festive and fun and a great place to ring in the New Year.

As expected, my parents head out before the clock strikes twelve. The tape delayed *Dick Clark's New Year's Rockin' Eve* in New York City blares from every television in the house. As the countdown approaches a few minutes before midnight, I search the room for Braden. By the time I locate him, he's already making his way over to me. "Hey." He bumps my arm with his. "Are you having fun?"

"Yeah. It's a great party. So nice of your parents to host half the population of Pine Ridge."

"Sorry I haven't been able to spend more time with you."

"No worries. Your hosting duties come first."

"Doesn't apply to my sister, apparently." He nods in the direction of Brianna and Fiona. "Fucking-A, look at those two. They're thick as thieves. Should we be worried?"

"They are way too cool to concern themselves with the likes of us."

"Good. Because," he speaks directly in my ear, his hot breath—and hot words—giving me goosebumps, "there's a girl I have to kiss at midnight."

"Oh? Anyone I know?"

"I'm certain you're well acquainted."

"And you have to kiss *this* girl, why exactly?"

"Tradition. All the way back to the Romans." I arch my brows in skepticism. "Hey, I didn't create the tradition—obviously, since this one goes way, way, way back. I'm enthusiastic about certain traditions."

"A traditional enthusiast?"

"Not all traditions. But this one in particular—I'm a big fan. Come here." He grabs my hand and tugs. We slip into his bedroom steps away from party-goers. He does a cursory walk through to make sure his bathroom is also unoccupied before closing the door and pressing my back against it with his body. He sprinkles soft kisses on my face and neck. "Practice for the big moment," he teases as we hear the thirty-second countdown begin on the other side of the door. By the time the New Year rings in, we're already well into our private celebration of the big moment, which includes lots of tongue and substantial amounts of groping. "Happy New Year, Mandy," he says, nuzzling my neck.

"Mmm... Happy New Year, Braden." *I love you.*

Spring Semester – Senior Year 1989

I don't want to go, but no amount of begging, pleading, pouting, shouting, or name-calling results in a pardon from my impending journey across the globe. My dad settles the matter with decided logic. "You will be a sixteen-year-old kid with a high school diploma in her hand—barely seventeen—by the time you leave this house. No barely seventeen-year-old should live on a college campus with grown men who have one thing on their minds. Hell no. You're going as planned." *Stupid plans.*

The Rotary Club, my father a past president, approved my

application last spring. Before graduation, I'll find out the name of the town and receive a bio on my host family. I'm not sure what else to expect other than I'll attend Gymnasium (German high school for smart kids) and, of course, learn German because I've only had three years in high school, which is a total joke. I can say things like: my name is, I'm from, may I please have, and where is the bathroom? It's not enough to build a conversation on, much less a new life.

We have heard back from all the universities. The University of Arizona, Northern Arizona, Berkley, and, to my surprise and delight, Stanford—freaking *Stanford*—are happy to have me. Duke can kiss my ass. After much deliberation and longing for something about my future that feels somewhat familiar and concrete, I opt for Arizona.

Maybe it's stupid to turn down Stanford for a school that doesn't carry the same clout. I'm forced to think long and hard about that because Dad asks me that question repeatedly. Okay, he actually *yells it at me* during some heated *discussions* about my future. He even gets Brianna involved, who calls to tell/yell at me that I'm insane, but ultimately it's my play to call. I'll save my parents shit-tons of money so they can retire sooner. With that decision behind me, I have something to look forward to after my year of banishment from this country and all the horrible things that will happen to me over there.

Senior Prom Night, April 1989

This year Braden takes a preemptive approach on the subject of prom. He informs me that he's not going, but I should 'feel free.'

"I want you to take me," I tell him. "It's important to me." And, really, it is. We don't have much time left together, and I want that stupid prom photo and those memories with him. Besides, my dress is really beautiful. I've never seen him dressed up or even shared a dance with him.

He sighs. "It's not my scene, Mandy. I just don't get into that stuff. Hell, we haven't been to a school dance together, and you haven't ever made a big deal out of it. Maybe we can do something else together that night?"

I grump, "Like make out in your room instead of getting dressed up on the one night a year where a girl's supposed to get all dressed up?"

He grins. "You can get all dressed up before we make out. That's cool with me."

I give him the stink eye. "You don't get it. It's our *senior prom*."

"Have Rawlings take you again," he suggests.

"Fine. I'm sure Tanner will be happy to take me to prom—*again*—because he's not lame."

* * *

Even though I know he's scraping together every bit of spare change for college, Tanner agrees to take me. Of course he does. Tanner isn't lame, and he hardly ever says no to me. Ironically, he borrows a tux from Braden. To eliminate the financial burden, my parents spring for the tickets and dinner, and Dad offers to let Tanner drive us in his BMW E32-7 series that still has that new car smell.

The gym is all decked out, reminiscent of last year, with a new theme of "Forever Young." We take pictures, and Tanner compliments me for the fifteenth time on my dress. It's floor length with a slit up one leg to the knee, V-neck and V-back, and the shoulder straps are thick enough to hide my bra straps. Made of shimmery satin covered by a matching layer of red lace; red like my cowboy boots—which I'm totally wearing because this is Pine Ridge, and they are the best cowboy boots ever. My hair is pinned up with untamable tendrils spilling down, and I'm wearing more makeup than I've ever caked on in my entire life.

When we dance, he holds me a little too close, and his hands occasionally wander. "What are you doing?" I ask as we sway to Patrick Swayze's *She's Like the Wind*. "You are *handsy* tonight."

"Enjoying myself," he replies. "See how you have to reach way, way, way up to wrap your arms around my neck?"

"See how your hands are reaching way, way, way down to grab my ass? Stop it."

"Wish I could, but you feel like a real girl tonight." He rubs my ass with great exaggeration, and I swat his hands away. He laughs in my face. "I'm feeling a lot of things for you right now. If I don't get this under control, you're gonna feel how much I'm feeling."

"Stop it, Tanner." My tone is still light. We're still joking around—I think. He cuts the nonsense and places his hands a respectable distance above my ass and continues swaying me around.

Then, out of the blue, he says into my ear, "Why stop?"

"Because this is not what we do."

His brown eyes are still gleaming with good humor when he says, "It could be what we do. I mean, why not us, Amanda?"

"Because you put grasshoppers down my shirt—"

"—years ago."

"And you're my best guy friend."

"Key word being *guy*."

"I'm in love with Braden."

"Who is not here with you again this year. Why is that? Why have I taken his girl to back-to-back proms?"

"I'm not his girl."

"That's right. You aren't his girl, Amanda, or he'd be here right now trying to cop a feel instead of me."

"That's mean."

"I'm not trying to be mean. I'm being honest."

"He's your friend, too, Tanner. There's a girl code, so I'm assuming guys have a code as well."

"I don't owe him a thing. He sent you off with me—again—with his blessing. Hell, he even provided the formal attire knowing I'd wear it holding you." My eyes start to burn; I can feel the liquid building up. I stop moving and stare up at him.

His chocolate eyes fill with open sincerity. I've looked into his eyes at least a million times over the course of my life; they are more familiar to me than my own. "Don't cry, Panda Bear. There's no need for tears. I'm just asking you to think about it. He handed you over to me tonight. I've always been there for you. Always. What do you have to lose by giving this a shot?"

"Your friendship." My response is instant.

"That's never gonna happen. You and me have too much history. We kiss and it sucks—which it won't—we laugh it off and go on. It doesn't suck, we do it again."

More shocking than his words is the unexpected wave of anticipation that rolls through me. "Braden deserves better from you as his friend and me as his... his..."

"As his Option B? As his, 'not his girl?' And seeing how you're not his girl, you don't owe him anything. He's a dead end anyway, Panda. You leave town, that's it."

Spot on, direct, and very sad, I consider that while Tanner may be my dearest friend and most trusted ally in the history of dearest friends and trusted allies, I'm also saying goodbye to him in July. "You're also a dead end."

"I'm not. I'll see you in Tucson when you get back. We still feel the same way, we pick this back up. Have our whole lives ahead of us after next year. Yeah, it's a different place and a different time, but we'll both be there. While Braden's in Iowa learning how to put his dreams on paper, we might be living our own dream."

"*We*? What is this *we* stuff? There is no *we*—no *us*."

"There is a *we* and an *us*," he retorts. "Has been for most of our lives." This is also true, but not in the way he's suggesting. We have a bond that defies the laws of nature—a girl and a boy who are intimately close without actually being intimate. Without question, *we* are part of each other.

Damn it, if I'm not considering his words in a new light. "This is wrong, isn't it?"

"Doesn't feel wrong." He pulls me closer and runs his hands up and down my back with a firm touch, this time dropping back below my waist. "We decide what's right or wrong. If it's right, you might find yourself really happy with me one day."

I can't think of a single time that Tanner hasn't been there for me when I've needed him, along with all the times he's been there without me having to ask. He knows how to make me laugh, he's held me when I've cried, and he's told me often that he loves me—sure, in the context of friendship, but love comes in many forms, and it's not a solid shape. It changes. It grows, it goes away, it gets deeper. "I don't know what to say..."

His broad smile and warm eyes melt my heart. "You don't have to say anything if you'd just shut up and let me kiss you..."

"Everyone will see." *Wait—I'm considering this? Yes, I'm considering this.*

"Don't give a crap. It's prom; everyone's kissing their date. Got nothing to hide. I'm always proud to be with you."

Damn it, that tugs right on my heartstrings. Maybe Tanner is the best of both worlds—hormones and heartstrings? He's making perfect sense. '*Have our whole lives ahead of us after next year. Different place, different time but we'll both be there. Braden's a dead end.*'

He touches his hand to my chin and tilts my face up—you know, because he's so much taller than me now. His eyes... those deep chocolate pools that consistently show me comfort and care. '*We kiss and it sucks— which it won't—we laugh it off and go on. It doesn't suck, we do it again.*'

When Tanner kisses me, he's not sweet or tentative—he is confident and doesn't hold back. He pulls back for a split second to lick his lips, tilts his head, and comes right back for more. When I part my lips, his tongue immediately sweeps into my mouth and finds mine—*whoosh*—adrenaline and heat rush through me. It so far from sucks that we don't stop. We do it over and over and over again with one of his hands locked behind my head and the other fastened to my ass.

There's no need to grip me so firmly because my body molds to his. I can't get close enough, and I can feel what he's feeling as he crushes against me. Keith Whitley's *When You Say Nothing At All* becomes more fuel for our little fire. Tanner guides me in a subtle two-step because country music on a dance floor necessitates a proper two-step regardless of what any other parts of your body might be doing. On and on, we dance and kiss, and I am entirely lost in him—or maybe I've been found.

One Friend by Dan Seals—*God, are we building our own soundtrack*? Tanner relinquishes my lips to say softly in my ear, "If I had only one friend left, I'd want it to be you." The words move me so much —so, so much—that I pull his face down to mine and reach for more of his lips, his taste, his touch.

Jesus, Tanner. And is Jesus part of this moment? Is this a religious experience? Probably not since I want to climb him right now.

"Holy shit, get a room," Jenny hisses in my ear. I'm rudely brought back to reality. And to both of us, as we part our locked lips, she says, "What the hell is this, *lovebirds*?"

"I'm not sure," I stutter at the same time Tanner tells her to get lost. She glares at him then stalks away. He takes my hand, stops at our table to scoop up my wrap and purse and the keys to Dad's car without letting me go, and he pulls me behind him out the creaky gym doors.

We spend a fair amount of time in the high school parking lot fogging up the windows. We don't talk at all. We just make out like our diplomas depend on it. That is, until I remember that we're in the school parking lot and probably close to drawing attention from a chaperone, which would be so embarrassing because I'm still Amanda Harrington, after all.

I throw the flag. "Tanner, we have to stop. We're going to cause a scene."

"A little late for that." He laughs—*laughs again*—right in my face. He looks so pleased with himself. "But yeah..." He gives me a little distance, maybe collecting his thoughts and wondering how long it's going to take for his hard-on to go away. "You're right. This isn't the place for what I want to do to you."

There's no need for clarification about what he wants from me, and the thought makes me quiver but he needs to know my line. "Tanner, I... We aren't going to have sex tonight."

"We're taking the car back. You're changing out of that dress, I'm getting out of this getup, and we're taking Cherry down to the lake." Without another word from me, he starts the car and we're out of there.

My parents don't bat an eye when we walk into the house just a few hours after leaving. "Hi, kids," Mom calls out. "Home so soon?" We walk into the living room where my parents are watching TV. "How was it?"

"Sweet ride, Michael. Thank you for trusting me with it," he says, tossing the keys to him. "When I'm a doctor, I'll let you drive my sweet ride around for a change of pace."

"Can't wait, son," Dad replies.

"Claire." He smiles at Mom, "Prom was nice—you know, gym decked out and all. Good music. And Amanda looks beautiful tonight. Well, she's always beautiful, isn't she? But tonight —damn—extra beautiful." He winks—*winks*—at my dad with that one, and my dad apparently thinks that's *just fine* because he smiles and nods and is *so totally clueless* right now. Tanner announces, "We decided, since we've been there done that, we're gonna change clothes, maybe grab a quick bite." He charms Mom with another wink and rubs his belly. "And then take Cherry down to the lake for the night."

"Okay," Mom says.

Okay? *Okay? Are you people blind? No, they trust you.* I share a mental high five with Brianna.

"Gotta grab a bag from my truck. Be right back."

While he's outside, my mom follows me to my room to help me unzip my dress. She hangs it back up and perches on my bed while I move around my room changing into shorts, a t-shirt, and my flip flops. "But you kids had fun?"

"Yeah, Mom. We always do."

"Well, that's just great. Shame you didn't stay longer, but I imagine prom is a different experience when your brother takes you."

"I guess. I have no comparison, right?" I laugh, praying that I sound like myself.

"Well, it's nice that Tanner is your... Oh, what's the expression from that Tom Cruise movie? Wingman. Sidekick. Cohort. Do I have that right?"

"Yeah, Mom," I snicker. "You're the bomb."

"I'd like to think so. Tanner's hungry, so I'll pack up a few things for you kids to take to the lake. Are you going to have a big crowd there?"

"I'm not sure who's going, but, you know, the lake is a popular place for after-parties." *Not a lie.*

"Well, it's a special night, so we'll see you when we see you." She gets up to go the kitchen. I change quickly. I want to wash my makeup off and grab a scrunchie, but Tanner's using the bathroom to change so I join my mom to help with food prep.

Tanner walks into the room a few minutes later in gym shorts and a tee. "I love you, Claire—the mother I always wanted," he wisecracks as he assesses the small mountain of food. "Lemme grab a cooler." He returns sixty seconds later from the garage, cooler in hand. "I'll pack up Cherry." And he goes back to the garage again.

He's 100% comfortable in my world. My parents adore him, and he moves around our house like he owns the place. I know he's in the garage grabbing camping gear and firewood. He doesn't have to ask where anything is because he's done it so many times before. Mom doesn't have to ask what he wants on his sandwich or if she should include a bag of marshmallows in our haul—she knows.

We're ready to take off some thirty minutes later. "What time should I expect you home?" Dad asks me.

Tanner answers, "Oh, we'll be here in time for breakfast. Pancakes, Claire? That'd be awesome."

TEN

The Next Day

LATE AFTERNOON ON THIS BLUE-SKIED Sunday, I've long since washed the campfire scent off my skin and out of my hair, had some lunch, and taken a cat nap. I'm hunkered down in my room with *Dear Diary* trying to figure out how the hell to explain myself. The phone rings and I groan. Jenny's called two times, and I've managed to be in the shower or sleeping. I could make a break for it, lock myself in the bathroom again, but I decide it's time to face her. Maybe she can help me sort through this quandary I'm in. If I don't take her call, she'll just show up at some point.

Mom knocks lightly before opening the door holding the handset. "Honey, Braden for you." She drops a bomb without warning. To be fair, she doesn't know it's a bomb—to her it's just a phone call.

I wait for her to close the door behind her and, honestly, I use this time to say a little prayer. "Hi, Braden."

"Mandy."

Silence. *Tick tock, tick tock, tick tock.*

"Um, you called?" I ask.

"Yeah," he sighs—never a good sign—and this one is long and ominous.

More silence. Copious amounts of silence.

"Becky stopped by earlier," he says. His voice is flat, deep, and controlled.

"Oh?"

"She had a lot of news to share about last night."

"Such as?" My heart is *pounding*.

"She's Prom Queen. Bummed Kyle wasn't eligible for King."

"Yeah, that's too bad... But Prom Queen is great. Good for her. I'm sure she was thrilled. Too bad she's already in at Yale. She could add that to her list of accomplishments." It's weak, but it's all I have.

"It sounds like news to you that Becky is Prom Queen." *Shit. It is news to me.* "Weren't you there last night *with Rawlings*?"

"Yeah," I answer with extreme caution. "I was there, but we, um, left early and I haven't really talked to anyone today."

"You talked to Rawlings today." With his flat tone I can't tell if this is a statement or question.

"I have."

More silence. Another freaking sigh. "You know, Pine Ridge is such a small town. Everyone knows everything. They like to get in other people's business, tell stories *out of school*. Do you know what I mean, Mandy?"

"I do. That's been my experience pretty much all my life."

"Do you have anything to tell me about last night? Any *situations* that I might find *interesting*?"

I gulp. I'm shaking. I need time. I need Jenny. "I do, but, um, not over the phone, all right?"

His slight chuckle is laden with darkness. "I'll give you that, Mandy. But we're not going to have this conversation weeks from now. You come here after dinner—tonight. Seven-thirty." He hangs up on me.

Dear Diary, when did the boys in my life get so bossy? Oh, and while we're at, please update KFC: Amanda is a dumbass.

* * *

Braden's parents are watching TV on the other side of the house when I arrive. I'm sitting cross-legged on his bed, fidgeting and perspiring just a little bit. He's sitting up against the headboard, arms crossed over his chest, legs in front of him and crossed at the ankle. Save for 'hi,' we haven't said more than two words to each other.

"The floor is all yours, Mandy."

"I'm sure you can appreciate that this is an uncomfortable *situation*," I start. He shakes his head and looks at me in... *Is that disgust or disappointment or anger*? "So before I say anything, I would like to know what you've heard." He glares and gives me nothing. "Because, you know, it's like that game Telephone where you sit in a circle with a bunch of people. One person makes up a story and tells the next person and each person passes it along, and so on, until the last person in the circle tells the story out loud and it's," I laugh lamely, "not even close to what the first person said."

"I'm familiar with the game, so you can stop explaining how it's played."

I'm not stalling, not really. I need a frame of reference so I know where to start. Because stupid Jenny didn't answer her phone, and it's not like I could call Tanner for advice. "What did Becky tell you?"

"I want to hear it from you. What happened last night?" He's studying me like a textbook. His blue eyes are narrowed, cool, appraising. The scrutiny is too much; I look down to pick at imaginary lint on my jeans, except I'm wearing shorts so that's not helpful.

"Would you say that you're more pissed off at me or, um, hurt by me?" I ask.

"I haven't decided yet. I'm waiting on you to tell me what the fuck went on last night."

"Surely you must be feeling one way more than the other?"

"Amanda," he grinds out my full name, which sounds foreign coming from his lips. "Enough."

"You aren't making this easy on me, Braden," I snap back. "I told you that this is really... uncomfortable."

"Right. And this is totally comfortable for me, too," he retorts. "Did you sleep with him?"

I meet his eyes, which are still narrowed, but mine are wide with shock, "No, of course not. I'm actually offended that you would even ask me a question like that." I read a sense of relief on his face. "That would be a total cliché—as opposed to tradition—and if it were, say, a tradition, it wouldn't be one I'm enthusiastic about. Like, um, kissing to ring in the New Year. That's a good tradition..."

"It is." No smirk, no chortle. Nothing but frosty.

I switch tactics to garner more information. "I don't know what I owe you right now, Braden. I'm your friend."

"You are more than my fucking *friend*, Mandy, so cut the *innocent and sweet* bullshit act."

I hold up both hands, palms facing out in surrender. "It's not an act. No promises, remember? You didn't make any. I didn't make any. So I don't think you should be *swearing* at me and acting like I wronged you. Because, *technically*—"

"You're going to try to get me on a *technicality*? Jesus. Fuck—totally a future lawyer. I'd hate to see you miss your calling in life. I'm not *acting* like you wronged me; I know that you wronged me because I feel it like a fucking gut punch."

This is developing news, and I need to think it over before responding. "We've been exploring Option B with ground rules for..." I do a quick mental calculation, "approximately eighteen months. We... I... we... no, wait you—over the last eighteen months, not one time have *you* attempted to clarify or redefine our relationship beyond the terms of our original *agreement*." And, yes, I use air quotes.

He glares at me.

"Braden, give me something to go on here, because, as previously stated, we aren't exclusive."

"I didn't think I had to renegotiate our *agreement*." He also throws up air quotes because he's mocking me. "You're the only girl in my life. And I was under the impression that I was the only guy in yours."

"You are." I catch my mistake before he can jump all over it. "You were. And there's Becky..."

"Fuck Becky. Becky's been nothing but a friend since we got

involved. I don't kiss Becky, I don't lie down with Becky on my bed and take her fucking clothes off. Haven't spent the last eighteen months doing anything with Becky or anyone else because *I'm with you.*"

I rub my hand over my mouth and tug on my lips while I absorb the force of his words. Apparently, I misunderstood our *situation* because he's so angry and looking at me like he wants to boil my bunny right now.

"You still haven't answered my question. I'm going to ask you one more time so the question is fresh in your mind and crystal fucking clear. What happened last night with you and Rawlings?"

"Again with the swearing at me. You really want to know?"

"Fuck, yes, or I wouldn't have asked you five fucking times already." His voice rises in volume and force, and each word is sharply punctuated.

"I'm not really comfortable sharing, um, details. Like—no play by play."

"Spit it out or this conversation is done. I'm *fucking* done repeating myself." He's angry, no doubt, but he looks defeated, too. I don't think he wants to be done, and I know I don't want things to end this way—so ugly and sad.

"Tanner and me... We kissed in front of half the school last night. And then we did it some more, not in front of half the school, because it didn't suck."

"Because it didn't suck?"

"No." I shake my head. "It didn't suck, and I'm... ugh. This is so *confusing*. It just happened."

"What? You just stumbled and landed on his fucking mouth?"

"No... It was sort of like a... like a test drive. I never got to test drive Cherry, did you know that? My dad just picked her out and bought her home. He didn't ask me what kind of car I wanted. And I'm not ungrateful—like, at all—because who wouldn't want a car on their sixteenth birthday? That's awesome. But maybe I would've preferred a Ford or a bigger truck. No, not a Ford," I amend. "We're a Chevy family, and big trucks are really expensive, so he actually made a good choice for me after all. But the point is—"

"Is there a point to this?" he clips.

"Yes. The point is, I never got to test drive the truck. Tanner's been my friend my whole life, but I've never taken him out on the road—so to speak. So I did. And it should've felt awkward or weird, but it didn't. It didn't suck. And, wow, that was probably the worst analogy of my entire life."

"Not your best work." His voice is barely above a whisper. "Is there more?"

"More?"

"You let him near the end zone? Maybe no touchdown, but did he score a field goal?"

"No." I hang my head. "He did not. And, I should point out that it would not have happened if *you'd* taken me to prom." I look back up at him, "Why didn't you want to take me? Two years, Braden. *Two years* you sent me off to prom with him." My voice is weepy and pathetic.

"I would've rather just hung out here with you last night, but I didn't want you to miss out on any high school experiences because it's not my thing. And it seems that you didn't. Miss out. On anything."

"It seems that we're both pointing a finger at the other. We could do this all night, except I have to be home by ten—firm curfew, non-negotiable. It's a school night."

"I thought it was safe to leave you with Rawlings." He uncrosses his arms to run his fingers through his hair, to pull it at the scalp the way he likes me to do it when we... "*Fuck*. I'm so stupid – Becky was right. Where did you leave things with him?"

"Unresolved?" I shake my head in disbelief. "I look forward to another awkward conversation in my near future." I want to ask what Becky was right about, but I hold back.

"Perfect," he mutters. "What a fucking mess."

"I'll fix it—with both of you. I promise." I laugh dryly, "Hey, look at that. I just made you a promise."

He doesn't find it funny. "How are you going to fix this? I'm out of here in six weeks. By the time I come back from Michigan to get ready for Iowa, you're long gone. I'm not going to be in some fucked up *situation* for the next few weeks. If you want Rawlings, you should go for it. Just let me know what you decide."

"Braden, when I'm close to you... It is everything to me."

"And Rawlings? Is being *close* to him everything to you too?"

"It's not the same thing."

"You can't have it both ways. You choose him, I'm out."

"Do you want me to choose you? Because it would help me to know that you still want me. Do you?"

"It's been eighteen months, and I haven't touched another girl."

"Would you please answer the question more directly?"

"Jesus, Mandy, without question, I *want* you to choose me. I care about you so much. You have to know that. Right?" When I shake my head his face falls. "I don't think a declaration of everlasting love is, um, smart when we're so close to going our separate ways. When we leave Pine Ridge and do what we need to do, I want to see you again—however that comes about. Fuck, maybe you and Tanner will introduce me to your kids one day." He grimaces. "I can't tell the future, but I know that wherever you are, whatever you're doing, I want nothing but the best for you. I swear to God, Mandy, that's the truth."

Update KFC: Amanda Made a Huge Mistake

Monday after Prom

Becky corners me before I can set one foot out of my truck in the school parking lot on Monday morning. "I can't believe you did that to Braden," she hisses at me. "He knows. I told him."

"Yeah, thanks for that." I look up at her.

"I can't believe you, Amanda. Playing two guys at once. Playing Braden like that. How could you?"

"I didn't play anyone." *Did I*?

"How could you do that to him?"

"Becky, this doesn't involve you—at all, so I would appreciate you stepping back and staying out of my business."

"He's my friend. He is my business."

"Okay, he is your business, but I'm not. Back off." I have six inches and at least sixty-five pounds on her—she'll move. I grab my backpack from the passenger seat and climb out of the cab. She holds her ground. I look down on her and say, "Get the hell out of my way, or I'll shove your Prom Queen tiara up your ass."

That does it. She moves.

* * *

Next up, Tanner. He finds me walking up the concrete path to the student center where all the admin offices and student lockers are located. "'Morning, Panda." He breaks out a smile for me.

"Hey."

"Your parents miss me last night?"

"Yeah." I smile back. "We have a ton of leftovers, though. Um, thanks for giving me some recovery time last night... I was really tired, and, um, Braden—fair warning and all—Becky couldn't wait to tell him what she saw us doing on prom night."

He shrugs. "Figured someone would. You think he's going to get in my face?"

"I really wouldn't know. That doesn't seem like his thing. I talked to him last night and he made it really clear that I did some damage. I don't want to lose him. I can't lose my best friend either. We need to talk."

"Sure." He's affable, open, the same old Tanner. "And by best friend, I assume you mean me." I nod; he grins. "Cool. After dinner tonight. You good with that, or does this need to happen sooner?"

"I'm good with that." Because, really, I'm not sure what I'm going to say to Tanner, and I need time to figure it out.

He slings an arm over my shoulder and we walk the rest of the way to the student center together, where we round the corner to my locker and find Braden. When Tanner doesn't drop his arm, I slide out from under it and move to my locker. Trying to pull off casual nonchalance, I address Braden with a quick smile and, "Good morning," but he's not looking at me. He and Tanner are playing chicken with their eyes. I open the locker, drop off the things I need for later and grab my books for first period. I shut the door. They're still staring each other down. *Whatever. Where the hell is Jenny when I need her?*

I don't see Jenny until lunchtime. I approach from the side while she's talking to Matt. "Hey, Matt." I grab Jenny's arm. "I hope you don't have lunch plans because I need you. Right now."

"KFC?" she offers.

"Anywhere but there."

Over breakfast for lunch at Denny's, I lay it all out for her—the whole shebang, no detail spared. We talk so long that lunch turns into fifth period and we need more time. There is a first time for everything, including ditching class. I'll deal with that later. Over the course of our conversation, she mostly listens when she isn't blurting out, "Holy shit I can't believe I don't know any of this." I do feel guilty about that, how far apart we've grown. Even though I haven't bared my soul to her in quite some time, it's easy to do. Jenny and I are who we've always been—two girls who met on the swing sets in the first grade and have been there for each other ever since. With all my secrets spilled, Jenny asks an important question. "Tanner or Braden?"

"Ugh..." I groan. "Why didn't Braden clarify things sooner, or, you know, ever?"

"Why didn't you ask?"

"I was afraid of what he would say."

"You are such a dork, Amanda."

"*Duh.*"

"Tanner or Braden?" she asks again.

"That's the problem because I don't know."

"You do know, Amanda. The beauty is that you don't have to think beyond the next few weeks. Do you want to keep getting busy with Braden or Tanner?" I start to open my mouth, but she stops me with her hand in the air. "And before you start weighing all your freaking pros and cons, neither of them will be in your life for at least a year after high school. Who do you want to make out with? Answer me—now."

"Braden."

"There you have it."

Update KFC: Amanda Still Loves Braden.

ELEVEN

I STOP BY DAD'S OFFICE on my way home from Denny's. His car is in the parking lot, and after exchanging pleasantries with the receptionist, I find him in his office combing through a contract. "Hey, Dad."

He looks to the clock. "Brown Eyes, what a surprise. What brings you by?"

"I just want you to know that I skipped my afternoon classes today. This is forewarning that the school will probably call, and I'm going to need a note. And, most of time, you're cooler to deal with than Mom."

"You skipped school? Are you sick?"

"No." As always, truth is the best option, "It's just I got caught up at lunch with Jenny. We had a lot of things to talk about and time got away from me, and then I figured screw it—I'm a rebel with a cause.

U of A isn't likely to revoke my acceptance, and so I just went with it."

"Senioritis?"

I snicker. "Something like that."

"It happens. I'll give you a 'get out of jail free' card and call the school before the office shuts down for the day."

"Thank you, Daddy."

"It's a one-time pass, kiddo. Got it? No more ditching class."

"Totally. My first time will be the last. I'm sorry." I toy with the familiar business card holder on his desk—a Christmas gift from his staff many years ago. It reads: "Michael Harrington" and scrolled underneath are the words "Broker at Large." Punny. Funny. The bookshelves behind his desk are full of serious-looking real estate books and cluttered with plaques and awards. Family pictures over the years are sprinkled liberally throughout. A family photo from the Dorothy Hamill haircut days, pictures of me, Brianna, and Mom in various combinations of togetherness.

Studying one of my favorites photos of me as a preschooler sitting on a piece of yellow playground equipment at Casa de Adobe in San Francisco, my head rests sideways on my arms while I look straight into the camera. My eyes are big but sad, and my lips make a full-on pout. I'm wearing a white jacket with red roses and red corduroy pants. You can make out the letters "anda" embroidered on the back pocket. I have no memories of that day, but I look pensive and contemplative—even at such a young age. Why do I look so sad? I'm a little kid. What on earth is there to be sad about? Or am I just lost inside my own head? I'm always lost inside my own head.

When I look back to my father, he's busy trying to read my face. I can't remember the last time he's looked me over so methodically. "I think there's more to it than a case of the giggles between girls. Some people tell me that I provide sound advice," he offers.

"That is a fact, Daddy. I guess it's just, like, a really weird time. Everything is winding down and we're all going our separate ways—running out of time. And I wish..." I take a deep breath. "I don't want to go to Germany. The thought of going makes me..." I trail off as tears well and spill out.

"We're back to this again?" He passes me a box of tissues. I flop down in a chair across the desk from him and wipe my eyes.

"It all comes back to this because it's totally against my will."

He treats me to a slight eye roll. Then his eyes, which are basically my eyes too, stare directly into mine. "Here's my sound advice." I sigh and treat him to a slight eye roll of my own before crossing my arms and legs. "We're sending you to Germany, not prison camp. You wanted to do this. We had a deal. Learn the language, make new friends, travel Europe on my dime, and try to find one person in this world who thinks it's not the opportunity of a young person's lifetime. Come back when you're eighteen and go to college—again, on my dime. Dry it up, kid. This is a done deal."

* * *

After dinner with my parents, Tanner and I sit on the back deck with the beautiful views of the park and mountains off in the distance. He asked me to say whatever I needed to say, and I tried. I think I've done a good job of explaining what's going on inside of my head and what's in my heart. I'm winding down and conclude, "And so while it definitely didn't suck—at all—my heart is still... I'm not ready to let him go."

He laughs and elbows me in the side. "It so did not suck."

"Do you think that's bizarre? Because I kind of do."

"I think it's awesome, Panda."

"Even though it's not going to happen again?"

"Just because it's not gonna happen now, doesn't mean it's not happening again."

"Tanner..." I'm off kilter because I thought I'd made myself pretty clear.

"Panda..." He mimics my tone. "Been thinking about taking a shot for a while—seemed like the right time. Turns out it was, and it turned out good, right? No regrets, yeah? Not gonna push for more, because what's the point? We can revisit this in a year—or not. Either way, we have each other."

"So we're cool?"

"We're cool. McLaughlin and me, probably not so much, but whatever. I'll try to smooth it over with Dude so we finish out the year with good times, good memories."

"Thanks for making this so easy."

"It is easy. You spend way too much time overthinking things." He smiles and shrugs. "It's a personality flaw. Well, some might call it that. I think it's kinda cute." I wrinkle my nose at him. "Hey, we explored something. There's chemistry, and now we know it." He stands and fishes his keys from his pocket. He leans down and pecks my cheek. As he walks back inside to say goodbye to my folks and take off for the night, over his shoulder he comments, "It's always easy with us."

* * *

True to his word, Tanner doesn't waste time attempting to smooth things over with Braden. While they aren't back to best buddies, I don't need a knife to cut through the hostility. Tanner and I fall back into our normal routine. Even though I can't call what I share with Braden normal, we spend a lot of time together during our final weeks of school. Of course, there is gossip and more dagger eyes from Becky, but so what? Becky has her own problems—like unraveling her heart from Kyle's before she heads off to Yale.

While the spring weather is way too warm to wear Braden's letter jacket, we've changed publicly. He reaches for my hand in the hallways, nuzzles my neck up against our lockers, and keeps a hand at the small of my back or our legs pressed together under the lab table in AP Chemistry.

Tanner is around as well—for dinner, of course—but we don't spend as much time together. He's giving me space and no guilt about the amount of time I spend with Braden, who calls me more often at night and confirms plans in advance for the upcoming weekends, effectively shutting down the peripheral group gatherings in favor of time alone together.

My dad busts us in a clinch on the front porch and blinks the porch light on and off until we pull apart. Dad is not amused. We go out together all over Pine Ridge and we watch a lot of movies on the leather sofa in his family room, curled up and playing with each other's hands. Coach and his mom don't blink twice when they walk in on us. Sometimes one or the other or both join us to ask about my family or talk about plans after graduation. Sometimes they just smile and walk the other way.

In the darkness of his bedroom, behind the locked door, we listen to music while we kiss, moan, and grind together on his bed. We always stop a few yards short of the end zone, usually winded and completely wrecked. I'm drenched between my legs from excitement and the friction of his hand or knee rubbing against me. These sensations leave me overly sensitized and more than a little frustrated, but I don't try to amend those ground rules and neither does he. He's already confessed to finishing himself off the minute I'm gone which is, I guess, a viable option to alleviate his frustrations. Although, he recently started wearing contact lenses so maybe there's some truth to that whole 'it'll make you go blind' thing.

Going into May, there's studying for final exams and papers to finish. My Rotary packet arrives in the mail with the name and location of my new host family. It includes information about the area and a family bio with a group photo. They are tall, slim, and blond, except for the father who is quite bald, about the same height as his wife, and has a rounded beer belly and a friendly smile. Siegfried (Siggy) and Inge Schmidt of Bielefeld, Germany, population 225,000 and Germany's nineteenth largest city. There are two host siblings—Lars, nineteen, going into his final year of Gymnasium, and little Hannah, age six. They love to vacation in the south of France, tour the countryside by bicycle, visit art galleries, and they have a cat named Biscuit. I share the contents of the packet with my German teacher, parents and friends, and Brianna, and everyone is so excited for me—excluding yours truly.

Introducing the Graduating Class of 1989

One hot Saturday afternoon in late May, we sit through Becky's trite valedictorian speech in the packed auditorium, our names are called one-by-one, tassels are turned, caps are tossed in the air, and high school is officially over.

It's been a busy time for my family. My folks did a turnaround trip to Massachusetts for Brianna's graduation last weekend and helped move stuff from her dorm into Uncle Daniel's basement. While they were gone, Braden slept over both nights—all night, with us pressed together in my tiny full-sized bed. We played house, shut out the outside world, and it was magnificent.

Brianna flew back with them to attend my graduation, and we're having an open house-style party at our house tomorrow afternoon/evening to celebrate both major milestones. She plans to break the news sometime over the next few days that she's moving to East Germany in August. Right now, my parents are under the impression she's going to work through the summer in the admissions office at her college (which is true) and then move to Boston to start an internship (which is partially true). Her internship in Boston is actually a job in East Germany. I want nothing to do with the aftermath of Brianna's confession, but she's asked me to be there when it happens and have her back if Mom tries to kill her. I don't think it will come to that. Dad will support her decision, and Mom will have to fall in line. I mean, she's an adult, and this is her life, right?

I'm excited for our graduation party today. We—my crowd—are going to meet at the lake once we've had a chance to go home, change clothes, and load up our trucks with coolers full of food, firewood, air mattresses, and blankets.

Before we're allowed to scatter, my mom takes a series of pictures with Jenny and me in our caps and gowns, holding up our shiny new diplomas. We've taken a picture together at the end of every school year, so I hope these turn out along with the rest when we get the actual photos back from Walgreens.

Mom beckons to Tanner and Braden and takes several shots of the four of us. Tanner stands between Jenny and me, and I'm between Tanner and Braden. I'm looking forward to selecting the perfect photo to display in my new bedroom while I miss them all terribly.

Jenny decides to attend a party down the lake first with Matt and his beer guzzling crowd. She promises to stop by our campsite at some point during the evening. It's a clear, warm day at the lake that turns into a mild evening. We float on rafts, swim, listen to the Eagles and Aerosmith, talk smack, and have a great time.

As the evening turns to night, a few kids go home, some continue to splash around in the warm lake, while others pair up and start to bed down in the back of their trucks. We're parked as usual in a half-circle with tailgates facing the fire and overlooking the lake.

Tanner catches me coming out of the water. Ever the gentleman, he stares at then compliments my boobs and hands me a beach towel. "What would you say if I told you that I'm spending the night with Jenny?"

"Huh?"

"Yeah, that's not much of an answer, Panda."

"Um, you kind of caught me off guard. I didn't realize she was here."

"Yeah. She's buzzed, possibly drunk. Not sure yet. And pissed off at Matt—don't know why yet. Anyway, I left her with an empty cooler in case she barfs. I took her keys away, so looks like I'm her keeper for the night. Thought you should know."

"Why does she have to do this shit? She drove down here wasted? It's so stupid."

He taps a closed fist lightly on my chin. "Guessing this reaction right here is why Jenny doesn't want to see you right now. Makes you feel better, she didn't get on the main road—just the access lane."

"Yeah, that makes me feel so much better." My voice drips sarcasm. "Shit. I should check on her."

He shrugs. "You can if you want, but you'll get sucked into her drama, and you probably have better things to do tonight. Braden leaves this week, right?"

"Four days."

"No worries. She'll be fine. You can chew her ass out another time. She's not going anywhere until she's sober. Scouts honor."

"Silly, Tanner, you were never a Boy Scout," I remind him.

"Least I never got kicked out of the Scouts."

"Hey." I smack him playfully, "That was totally Jenny's fault."

"Always is. Story of your lives." He chuckles. "Might not have been a Scout, but I'll take care of Jenny tonight—promise."

I hug him. "You're so good to us."

He latches on and drops his hand to my ass and squeezes. "You're my girls. Anytime I can be good for you, just ask. You can return the towel later." With another ass squeeze and a quick peck on my mouth, he heads back to his truck and my wasted Jenny.

* * *

I'm damp from the water and the night is setting in, bringing a slight chill to the air. I scan the shore for Braden and find him sitting by the campfire looking right at me. As I approach, he smiles then slides his eyes back to the dancing flames. I sit next to him on the sandy beach and knock his knee with mine. "Penny for your thoughts—or maybe a dime because, you know, inflation and all..."

He chuckles and Broody Braden sighs, "I'm tired... exhausted actually. I kind of want to go home and feel sorry for myself. But I'd rather feel sorry for myself with you."

"Why do you feel sorry for yourself?"

"I have a million things running through my head right now, and none of them have a happy outcome—except for being alone with you. Let's get out of here."

In addition to the other things I haven't done with Braden, like scoring a field goal—never mind a touchdown and not even a 2-point safety—we haven't slept together under the stars in the back of a pickup truck. I shake my head softly, communicating my disapproval. "I love camping out under the stars. Please stay and do that with me. It's like a Pine Ridge rite of passage. It might actually be state law."

His eyebrow quirks. "Everyone has to sleep under the stars with you?"

"Not necessarily *with* me." I smack his arm. "Just everyone should sleep under the stars—with me, not with me. It's something I love to do, and I want to do it with you."

He gives me a soft, drawn out kiss in front of God and anyone else who might be watching. "If it's something you want to do, I won't let you miss out." Chills run through my body as he continues to share, "I'm sad because it's almost the end of my time with you." With those words, my eyes fill and tears trickle down my face. "Hey." He kisses me again and uses his thumb to brush away the droplets. "I didn't mean to make you cry."

"Oh well, I cry at pretty much anything these days—especially those Folgers coffee commercials where the son surprises his mom for Christmas. Oh, and that one for AT&T where that college girl calls home because she misses her dad, and he picks up and she's all '*Daddy*?' Gets me every time right in the heartstrings."

"You know what gets me in the heartstrings?"

"What?"

"Seeing another guy put his hands on you."

"Tanner? Just now? That was nothing."

"That guy is going to try to put his hands all over you again the second I leave town. Just another one of those thoughts running through my head on a loop. And now that I've seen, I can't unsee it."

"He didn't mean anything by—"

"Oh, he totally does," he interrupts.

I capture his lips with mine. I let them linger gently before I lean in and nip his bottom lip, trapping it and sucking it into my mouth. When I pull back, I have his attention. I share, "Jenny's drunk in the back of his truck right now. I don't know how drunk or what's going on because he's taking care of her so I can be with you." I place a few more kisses on his mouth, "Let's go get cozy."

"I'd love to."

TWELVE

WE END UP DRIVING CHERRY further down the shore, away from the noise and laughter of others. I'm still in my damp two-piece with a beach towel wrapped around me. Before climbing into the bed of my truck, he changes into dry shorts on one side of Cherry. On the other side, I take liberties with one of his well-worn Banana Republic t-shirts. I slide it over my head and remove my bathing suit underneath. It smells like *Essence of Braden*. I'm so caught up in the scent that I decide he's all I want to wear.

I open the extended cab to pull out my boom box and hand pick a few CDs. I place them on the wheel well inside the truck bed. He helps me "make" the bed from the opposite side, arranging the bedding. An unzipped sleeping bag covers the air mattress wedged in the back. I pull out a soft blanket for warmth. It's horrifically gold, probably a leftover of my parents' 1970s bedroom linen collection, but it's clean and it's cozy. I toss him a pillow for his side and he says, "I've never done this before."

"Done what?"

"Co-ed camping."

"Too bad you spend all your summers in Michigan. Don't fret, little camper. You're with an experienced coed camper. I'll show you the ways..."

"Jesus, Mandy, don't say that again."

"Is He part of this conversation?" Braden chucks the pillow back across the truck bed. I'm unprepared, so it bounces unceremoniously off my face. "Hey!"

He laughs at me. "I don't want to hear another word about your *experiences*—unless they are with me."

Update KFC: Braden is Hot When Jealous.

* * *

We climb into the truck bed and settle into each other. Our lips meet. Our hands wander. In less than five seconds he notices, "You forgot something." His hand runs over the bare skin of my ass.

"I'm not a forgetful person."

"No, you're not. You are, in fact, very detail oriented." I laugh at him. "You're bold tonight. Cheeky." He emphasizes his pun with a light smack on my bare bottom. "*Butt*... we have ground rules, Mandy."

"Um... It's part of the coed camping experience. I mean, our coed camping experience. Are you uncomfortable? Because I can—"

"Uncomfortable that you're not wearing any underwear, Mandy?"

"Yes."

"Ha—only my dick." I catch his drift because I can feel it against my stomach.

"Just because I'm not wearing any panties doesn't mean you have to touch me below the waist."

"Oh yeah it does." His hand is freely and firmly massaging my ass, which feels amazing. "You broke the rules; you're going to have to face the consequences."

"We should revise the ground rules," I suggest.

"What do you have in mind?"

"Right now, I'm thinking about how much I'd like to face your consequences." We laugh, but I add in all seriousness, "No sex."

"No sex," he agrees.

I know what I want. Over his boxers, I've gotten Braden off before, and I want to know how that feels. "How about some music and we'll see what happens?" I suggest.

"What do you have over there?"

"I have a plethora of options, but there's really only one song I want to hear right now, so I'm just going to put it on replay until you, you know, get sick of it and break my boom box."

He chuckles and promises, "I would never break your boom box. Hit me, Harrington."

I fiddle around to queue up the right track on the right CD, but before I hit play, I turn back to him. "I need to tell you a few things."

His eyes quiz mine, "What's on your mind?"

"First of all, you should probably know that when I play this song, I'm going to cry—a lot. Like more than during the Folger's Coffee commercial." He smiles sweetly. "And secondly, I'm totally keeping this t-shirt. It smells like you. And also kind of like a campfire, but I'm willing to overlook that. I love the way you smell. I love how after we're together I can smell you on my skin. Like I'm covered in you."

He groans and pulls me closer. "I love the smell of you on me, too. I'll leave you with another one, too—one that doesn't smell like a camp fire."

Without hesitation I tell him, "I want the light blue one—the one with the lion, not the rhino. It matches your eyes."

"Yours." He's agreeable and anxious to move this along because he starts kissing my neck and around my ear which makes me insane.

"Wait, wait—I'm not done talking yet. Time out on the field."

"I can kiss and listen at the same time," he grumbles into my skin.

"I can't be kissed by you and think straight because of my *stupid hormones*," I tell him, and he laughs.

In four days, he will leave town, and by the time he comes back to Pine Ridge to pack up his things for Iowa, I will be 5,457 miles away. I know because I looked it up and calculated the distance. In four days, I will have only my memories and two of his t-shirts, and he will have my heart. It's not exactly a fair exchange.

"I'm going to miss you so much. I wish that our relationship had been more like these last few weeks because I'm proud to be with you."

He props himself up and half covers me with his body, holding me and stroking my face. "I really thought that you knew how I felt about you. I screwed up because, apparently, I'm no Jake Ryan with big gestures, but I want you to take this to heart. You mean so fucking much to me, and I'm going to miss you like crazy."

"Ugh, I hate this. I don't want to say goodbye to you. It hurts so, so much."

"It's like that saying... what is it? This isn't goodbye. Not forever. It's *until we meet again*. And I will see you again. I know it's not this, but that's the point at our age. We have to go and do what comes next. I'll make it a point to come to Pine Ridge next summer so we can catch up, or maybe you'll want to come to Michigan. I'd love to show you the lake and lay you down in a rowboat... But, listen—let's not leave here holding ourselves back from what comes next, okay? Whatever we do while we're apart—no guilt, no regrets. Just go and have a great experience. Please."

I take some time to digest his words. I want him to know that I love him, but question if that matters at this point. He alludes to some sort of future while making no concrete promises, and that is so very Braden. "Everything you just said, I take it to heart."

"That's exactly where my feelings for you belong—inside your heart." Maybe this moment feels really heavy for him, too, because he prompts, "Music?"

"Reminder—the song is on replay until you break my boom box."

"I won't break your boom box."

I reach up to push play and settle back under his warmth and weight. With an ironic laugh during the musical intro, his voice softly joins Bob Seger's in *We've Got Tonight*. It says it all. My eyes fill with tears but, surprisingly, they don't spill over. In the quiet seconds before the CD repeats the track, Braden says, "John Hughes would be so proud of you."

I agree. We've spent so much time together with music playing in the background. So many songs that I imagine whenever I hear them in my future, I'll be brought back to very specific moments in time with my beautiful boy. But this song—this is ours. An anthem for our relationship with the uncertainty of any future.

That night—which turns out to be our final night alone together—we take things farther than we ever have. When he pulls my t-shirt over my head, I'm bare to him in the moonlight. His eyes slowly scan my body. He's seen most all of me before, but this is different. I feel insecurities bubble to the surface of my thoughts. I'm not thin. My breasts are heavy, my body is thick but strong, everything is too round—belly, butt, arms, thighs.

Ever the mind reader, he chooses that moment to tell me, "You are so beautiful, Mandy." He kisses and touches me tenderly from temple to navel while he occasionally whispers fragmented thoughts of sweet and dirty words. I allow Jesus to be part of this moment because I feel like we're engaging in a form of worship.

When he slides off his shorts, we're completely naked together for the first time. I touch him—all of him. I've never held him in my bare hand before, and his skin feels like silk over a steel rod. I don't know if it's big or small in comparison to other boys. I only know that I want to make him feel good. I'm nervous, but he talks me through it in such a gentle voice.

When I have a rhythm with him in my hand, we begin to kiss in earnest. Our mouths stay locked, and his tongue drives into my mouth in rhythm with his thrusts into my hand. Right before he comes, he warns me before his body seizes then relaxes in quick successions. He grunts and groans, and he also involves Jesus in the moment along with numerous expletives as he spurts liquid—thick, hot, and sticky—into my hand and onto my belly.

I continue to touch him until he begs, "No... no more. Too sensitive." I release him. He assesses the state of my skin covered in him, and says, "Let me clean you up."

"No," I reach for his arms with both hands as he starts to move away. "Stay here with me." He watches me while I rub him into my skin, like lotion. His eyes are glazed over, mouth agape.

When I'm finished, he shakes his head and says, "Jesus, Mandy. That is so hot. I'm all over you. Fuck." I must have called the right play. "I want to make you feel so good."

He uses his hand, his fingers, between my legs. His touch is light at first, but he starts to explore with great curiosity. "God, you're so wet... so warm," he whispers as he moves his fingers over me. "Tell me what feels good."

"I've never... I don't really know. Maybe just..." I adjust his hand and place his finger where it burns the most. "Ah... keep doing that... right there on that spot," I gasp. Eventually the pressure of his fingers on and in the most private part of my body creates a slow burning sensation.

There's no blinding flash of colors or temporary loss of consciousness like I've read about in some of the books I swiped off my mom's bookshelf, but something happens. The slow burn turns into a soft pulsing that grows stronger until I moan and beg repeatedly, *"Please, don't stop, Braden."* The sensations roll through me and eventually subside. I bury myself in his arms.

We drift off to sleep. Sometime during the night—maybe minutes or possibly hours later—he wakes me with his hands and his kisses and we begin again. Me first and, *oh my god*, I could do this for the rest of my life. He's on top of me resting his weight on his arm, and when he pulls his hand away from my center I can feel him, his silky hardness poised between my legs. I open them wider and tilt my hips up. Just a nudge, a push from him, and we'd be together.

Fuck the ground rules. My first time should be with the boy I love. We don't have any birth control. We can't. But wait. An unplanned pregnancy would put a kibosh on this Germany fiasco. Don't be stupid. You've seen "For Keeps," and it did not end well for Darcy and Stan. My hips rock slowly into his. I can't help myself. I can feel him right there, and my body gravitates to his of its own accord.

As I fight warring emotions, he throws the flag on the play—because, you know, he can read my mind. "Not like this, Mandy." He's right and thankfully our voice of reason. I roll him to my side and satisfy him with my hand before we curl back together, sticky and content, and fall asleep again under the stars.

Until We Meet Again

Braden comes over on Wednesday afternoon in early June, four days after our night at the lake. The McLaughlins will head down to Phoenix soon and fly up to Michigan in the morning. He's already thanked my parents for all of their hospitality—the food and help with homework, and for raising the girl who helped him survive his time in Pine Ridge.

Brianna is attentive because she's fully informed about everything, including our night under the stars. She said that she has a lot of respect for him, for throwing the flag and taking care of me. And so she's uncharacteristically friendly and charming, chatting him up about the lake house, Iowa, and his plans for his first year of college. She smiles and wishes him well, and tells him that she hopes they meet again.

We're in my driveway sitting on Cherry's tailgate. It's time for our "until we meet again" moment. I'm wearing Ray Bans and his Banana Republic tee from graduation night (which I'm keeping until it disintegrates) with well-worn cut-offs and flip flops. My hair is in a messy updo, and my toenails are bright sparkly pink. His light blue lion tee is draped across my lap. I asked him to wear it a few times before he gave it to me. I swing my legs as we sit side by side, shoulder to shoulder in the bright sun. I'm determined not to cry.

"I have your address." He pats his pocket. "I'll write first because I don't have one to give you yet."

"You better write. If only to dispel the Bielefeld conspiracy theory." In my Rotary packet, I read and shared this odd little conspiracy theory about the German city with Braden. The theory goes that if you don't know anyone from Bielefeld, you've never been to Bielefeld, or you don't know anyone who has ever been to Bielefeld, Bielefeld cannot exist.

"When you write back to me, I will be able to disprove the conspiracy theory, although I'm more a fan of proving them. That seems more interesting, right? But for your sake, I hope this place exists. And that won't be the only reason I write to you. Are you feeling any better about going?"

"No. So I might run away from home. Or maybe I'll get a job at Walmart and hang out in Pine Ridge until Dad lets me take Cherry down to Tucson."

"You might not have your cherry when you go to Tucson."

"I will. My parents will drive her occasionally while I'm gone—use her for hauling stuff or whatever. And then I get to take her to college."

"Um... I wasn't talking about your truck. I was talking about..."

"Ugh. Okay, stop," I groan. "I must be off my game because that went right over my head. See? I'm perfect for stocking shelves at Walmart." I need to know so I ask him, "Was it hard to turn me down the other night?"

"That's not what happened."

"It is what happened."

"It is not. Please don't see it that way. It wasn't going to happen—you know, not a viable option. It would've been a mistake. Something we can't unfuck, for lack of a better word." He sighs, "But yeah, it was really hard, er... difficult, to stop myself. I was thinking about the whole 'just the tip' thing... And then health class, and, then babies." He shudders. "And I promised to respect you, right? Have I done that? Did I take good care of you?"

"Yes."

He smiles. "I'm glad. I figure, *a girl like you*, you shouldn't look back on your first time and think about how it was in the back of a truck with some guy."

"You'll never be *some guy* to me."

"I will be *some guy* when you fall in love with the guy who takes your cherry."

I can't imagine that ever being the case. And I should've given more thought to naming my truck Cherry. "So... you'll write?"

"I will." He nods.

"And you'll miss me?"

"So, so much."

He makes me laugh. I love it when he endearingly mocks my little quirks. "Okay. If I decide to get that job at Walmart while you're gone, I'll leave a message on your parents' machine."

"Don't do that. I'm serious. Go. Have adventures. Take lots of pictures. Maybe get drunk. I'd pay to see you drunk. Let loose. Write and tell me about it. Although, if you decide to let loose with Tanner before you leave, I don't want to know."

"That's not going to happen."

He shrugs. "No promises. Just... If it does, I don't want to know."

"Okay, but I don't know if I'm capable of that. You know, the drinking, letting loose—the whole anti-Amanda thing." "Sure you are. Any moron can lift a glass to her mouth." He elbows me in the side. "Even you. Have some fun. Enjoy yourself. Damn," he slides off Cherry's tailgate, "I have to get back before Mom has a shit fit. Oh, and I have something else for you." After fishing around in the pocket of his cargo shorts, he produces a cassette tape. "Mix tape. It's for the airplane and whenever you get homesick." "I'm already homesick."

He cracks a smile. "I didn't list the songs, so you'll be surprised. But they all remind me of you, most likely for the rest of my life. Like, burned into my subconscious. And some other stuff that I like or figured you would enjoy. No country—that's too redneck for me.

And no cheating. You have to wait until you're somewhere over the pond, got it?"

"Got it." I set the tape aside, next to me on Cherry's tailgate. "Thank you. I wish I'd thought of doing something like that for you."

"You've already given me a lot to remember you by, and it's all up here." He points to his head and smirks at me. "And I'm going to remember you often—with great fondness and in very explicit detail." He moves his body between my legs, which I open to accommodate him. After he tugs the Ray Bans off my face, I squint in the bright sun. Since I'm seated, he has to lean way down to take my mouth. And he does take my mouth in a fierce, profound kiss.

When he breaks it off, I feel branded for life, but I want more of *everything*.

Looking me directly in the eyes, he runs his hands down my face and lays them to rest them on my shoulders. I study him—amazing bone structure, full lips, strong jawline, and, jeez, those beautiful blue eyes.

"My sweet Mandy, don't put *all* the juicy stuff in your letters so we have something to talk about next summer." He tweaks my nose and mutters, "Those freckles are adorable. I'm going to miss them—and you." His expression sobers as he says. "Until we meet again."

I wrap my arms around his waist and bury my face in his chest. I ask him, "What other options are available to me?" When he laughs, I feel his body vibrate against mine. I wrap my legs around him for maximum contact. I hold my beautiful boy tight on that bright June afternoon in Pine Ridge. I hold him tight until he lets me go.

Age Seventeen—Over the Pond

July 1989

It isn't easy. I'm talking about my Dad getting me on that international flight out of LAX. He flew with me from Phoenix to LA and helped me navigate to the international terminal. We went through security, where we're now waiting for my flight from LAX to Heathrow to board. I'll change planes in London and land in Hannover, Germany, where I'm supposed to meet a representative from Rotary who will deliver me to my host family about an hour away.

I'm bargaining, "It's not too late, Dad. We can fly back to Phoenix, and I'll be all 'just kidding, Mom.' She cried when I left, so she'll be happy I'm home. And what kind of father puts his barely seventeen-year-old on an airplane to Europe to do God only knows what in a city that might not exist? You shouldn't have so much trust in me. I've done things you don't know about. Devious things. Terrible things. You'd be ashamed of me, really..." I trail off. His expression is dubious.

"You rob a bank?"

"No."

"Kill someone and bury them in the woods?"

"No."

"Are you pregnant?"

"Does that question belong in this felonious line of interrogation?"

"Answer the question."

"Why? Wait... Oh my god, Brianna was actually pregnant when

you sent her away?" I feign astonishment. "Crazy how history repeats itself."

Dad is struggling between ire and mirth. I enjoy watching him grapple—can't wait to see which way this goes. Maybe we'll have a huge argument and he won't want to part ways with his baby girl in anger. I'll miss my flight. We can be home in time for dinner. "Amanda, you are getting on that plane. Period." *Damn—ire.*

Of course, when the time comes to walk down the jetway, I make a scene—a huge scene. I wrap myself around Dad, cry, "I don't want to go. Please, no." And then the big guns because—so what if people are staring—I'm desperate here. "*Daddy, please don't make me go. Please don't make me go...*"

But I'm no match for Daddy. He pries me off, turns me toward the jetway, and shoves the small of my back. "I love you, Brown Eyes. Start walking."

* * *

Twenty hours later, the black Mercedes winds through rolling hills on narrow roads. We pass incredible scenery with storybook houses—the likes of which I've never seen in person—at alarming speeds. I worry about death. Like, will I be killed instantly when this Mercedes collides with a tree, or will I have time for my life to flash before my eyes before I bleed out?

I cried in my seat most of the way to London. Worse yet, I had to sit near the smoking section, so I'm pretty sure I have lung cancer now. Somewhere over the pond between LA and London, I pulled out my yellow Walkman and Braden's mix tape. That's pretty much when the bulk of the crying happened.

***

With no sleep and nerves of mush, the car pulls into a circular drive in front of picturesque farmhouse—if farmhouses can also be mansions. It's white with bright blue shutters and a double glass front door trimmed out in bright yellow. Flowers bloom in obscene riots of color, and they frame several rolling lawns covered in the lushest grass I've ever seen. No, Amanda is definitely not in the high elevation desert anymore. The air is sticky with—what's the word I'm looking for? Ah, yes, humidity.

Siggy and Inge are my host parents. Somewhere around the age of my parents, they are both about my height. Siggy is round and bald with a bushy salt and pepper beard. Inge is slim with platinum blond hair styled in a sleek bob and bright blue eyes. They greet me at the door and start babbling in German. I'm patted and hugged, my bags are whisked into the house, and I'm swept inside. I'm trying to remember German for "I don't understand," but the exhaustion is kicking my ass.

I'm taken through the house and right back outside again to the back garden. Sitting at a picnic table next to an enormous rectangle pool are my new brother and sister. They're tall and lanky with defined armed muscles, blond hair, blue eyes, and sun-kissed skin. They ask me questions—about what I have no idea. I smile weakly and nod, and then Inge brings me a small bottle of sparkling water and says something. *"Verstehst du?"*

And suddenly it clicks—the German words for 'I don't understand.' I bust out with, *"Ich verstehe nicht."* And then, *"Ich habe nicht verstanden,"* because I'm uncertain of the proper verb conjugation for present or past tense.

Inge replies, "All right, then we will speak English at first, yes?"

"Yes, please."

She chatters in German to the family—I catch every fourth word—but I have no clue what sentences she's actually forming. Then the heavens smile down on me and they all start speaking English, even little Hannah. Inge shares, "When Lars was quite young, around Hannah's age, we lived in Ohio on Siggy's sabbatical. Two years. Our cat, Biscuit, is an American like you. Now, please tell me how much German you have learned so we know where to begin."

I explain that I've only had three years of high school German and that I have never applied it in the real world. "So, you know, I have a lot to learn," I conclude. Then I add, "And I'm very sleepy. And sad." And with that, I start to cry. *Oh, scheisse (shit).*

Inge, with Hannah trailing behind, shows me compassion and takes me inside. I'm given a tour of the home, so traditional and different from my own. I meet my fellow American, Biscuit, who is so old he must be on the last of his nine lives, and eventually I'm shown to an adorable bedroom on the second floor with slanted ceilings and a charming window seat overlooking the pool and gardens. It has a wardrobe instead of a built in closet and a miniature attached three-quarter bath, but at least I don't have to share.

Inge suggests that a nap might improve my spirits but warns it's far better for me to wait until night so my body clock can begin to adjust. With a smile and a promise of *abendessen*—dinner—soon, she leaves me to my unpacking and organizing, which is an important life skill. One of the first things I do is fish out the framed photo from my carry-on bag. I place Braden, Tanner, Jenny, and me on my dresser.

When school begins, there is much discussion about what to do with me at my new high school. Since I'm already a graduate and I don't need actual grades or credits for a diploma back home, I'm given a few options and find one more preferable than the others. I'm placed with Lars in the 13th grade which is the equivalent of "senior year" in the States, but it's way more intense. The first two-thirds of the year are spent reviewing and becoming experts in the materials learned over the past several years. In the spring, the students break for about six weeks to prepare for a series of written and verbal final exams before receiving their diploma.

I'm allowed to participate—or not—in class. No homework, no exams, and in the spring I can travel. Sounds easy, right? It should have been, except I learn something new about myself and I don't like it all. I'm shy. I'm scared of these new faces and this foreign guttural language that I barely understand, much less speak or write. With the exception of my host family, I have a fear of talking to anyone in German or English, so I don't talk much at all.

It's not like anyone is mean to me. It's more that I simply exist, and it wouldn't matter to anyone if I was there or not. I'm lonely without my friends, but I don't know how to make new ones. I've never had to do that, and the thought of putting myself out there and being rejected... I can't do it.

I'm disappointed in myself, but I don't know how to flip the switch to *on*. And so I retreat into myself. I spend my days feeling self-conscious. Afternoons and evenings, I fill my journal with depressed thoughts. I'm not just shy—I'm pathologically shy.

Inge soon institutes a German-only mandate in the house, so I'm forced to speak German with the family, and they are good sports about it. It's really the only place where I shed a layer of self-consciousness because my host parents are lovely. My 'little sister' Hannah is adorable. We watch cartoons together, which actually helps me learn German.

Sometimes I screw up the language so badly that Hannah laughs until milk comes out of her nose, and Siggy and Inge can't choke back their amusement. Lars, I think, isn't sure what to make of me. He's not unfriendly at all, but I don't get warm vibes either. He has his own life, and his own circle of friends—sort of like my clique in Pine Ridge—and a beautiful girlfriend named Sonja.

At school, I continue on in radio silence, except in the English class where the instructor teaches 'real English'—the British kind. He likes to point out my accent and mispronunciation of words to the class—words, mind you, that are my freaking native tongue. Herr Merckel has a hard-on for trying to make me sound and/or look stupid. In return, I mumble snide comments under my breath, such as:

Herr Merckel: *You Americans speak English as if your mouths are full of hamburgers.*

Me (speaking as if my mouth is full of hamburgers): *You sound like you have a meter stick shoved up your ass.*

Herr Merckel: *Excuse me, Amanda. Would you repeat that? I could not understand you because you are mumbling.*

Me: *Oh, it was nothing important...*

There is a boy who catches my eye. He's in several of my classes but isn't friends with Lars. He knows that I exist because I've seen him smirk at my sarcastic exchanges with Herr Merckel. Curt seems like the broody type—hence my initial attraction, I suppose. I may have a "type" because he's tall with broad shoulders. His dark blond hair falls over his eyes, and, even though he's never assessed me with his eyes, I know that they are blue and pensive.

Curt doesn't say a lot—to anyone, but when he does speak out in class, he's articulate. At least I think so, because he appears to search for very deliberate words and other students smile or laugh out loud. From what I can understand, I'd say that if he does possess a sense of humor, his is bone dry and riddled with intellect. Curt reminds me of Braden. Of course, I'm drawn to him.

In September, I take a Rotary-sponsored four-day/three-night trip to Berlin with about thirty other exchange students, most of whom are American. Staring at *The Wall* is a sight I'll never forget. Imagine building a *wall* around an entire city and shooting people for trying to get from one side to the other. I mean, we don't even protect the Mexican-American border like that, but these East Germans have it down. We should take notes. I marvel that Brianna is somewhere on the other side. I can't wait to see her. She's coming for Christmas, but Marcus is iffy—they're doubtful she'll get permission to travel to West Germany.

My first night in Berlin wasn't that great because I'm still me—still shy—just not pathologically, because at least I can communicate with these strangers in English. I don't talk a lot, but I listen and I discover that I'm fairly alone in my feelings of isolation. The vast majority of these exchange students are having so much fun in Germany. They're making friends and enjoying their freedom. *Why can't I do the same? What is wrong with me?* They tell stories of beer, festivals, discos, and encounters with uncircumcised penises. I'm not sure what that is. I'll have to ask or do some research.

On the second night, a small group of us leave the youth hostel and head to a 'disco.' I follow the lead of my fellow exchange students; I belly up to the bar, order, and receive my first 'legal' beer. It tastes like shit, but after two more followed by a few shots provided by some US Army men, I can't feel my face much less taste the beer.

It doesn't take long before I'm shit-faced drunk for the first time in my life. I loosen up. I crack jokes and I laugh. Everything is funny—even me. As we dance, one of the soldiers takes a liking to me but probably has no idea I'm under the age of eighteen. It doesn't matter though. I wind up letting him take me into a dark corner to kiss and feel me up.

Honestly, I don't feel much of anything with Army Guy, but I go through the motions because it's been so long since a guy has touched me like this. With no spark to speak of, the experience leaves me longing for Braden. Even Tanner would do nicely right now. When Army Guy tries to convince me to leave with him, I decline and stumble back to find my Rotary group.

We return to the dingy hostel before the doors are locked for the night. I wake up in the morning hours and spend the next few hours on my knees barfing my guts out into a toilet. Veronica from Colorado checks in on me. She brings me a scrunchie to hold my hair back and encourages me to take sips of water so I don't get the dry heaves. I still get the dry heaves. I spend day and night three in the hostel, too hungover for life itself. I vow to never drink like that again.

Day four, I rebound. Good thing, because we tour on the bus before we're dropped off to catch trains, busses, or get picked up by our host families. Siggy picks me up at the train station in Bielefeld. He's such a nice man, and he lets me get away with more English when Inge's not around.

Back at home, I tell Familie Schmidt about the trip and my low tolerance for alcohol. They're all quite amused, except for Hannah, who hasn't experienced alcohol-induced dry heaves. The family talks about relatives that live in East Germany, and I try to hang with them—asking questions when I don't understand, which is, of course, quite often. I think Siggy is trying to explain some sort of political situation going on in Germany right now. I'm ashamed to admit that I don't understand the talking heads on the evening news, and I can't read *Die Zeitung*, and I'm a little lost.

Heading into October, still feeling lonely and sorry for myself, I continue to retreat inside my head and my room. I read and re-read letters from home. I've received two letters from Jenny, postcards from Brianna, a care package from Mom—and we talk every other week, letters from a few other friends, but nothing from Braden.

I stare at the graduation photo of the four of us on my dresser—Branden, Tanner, Jenny and me—and I wonder what they are doing. That, of course, leads to crying, which leads to not wanting to leave my room because everyone will know that I'm in my room crying. It's a vicious cycle. I want my life back, except that life doesn't exist anymore. Everyone has moved on.

I get permission from Inge, calculate the time difference, and place a call to Coach. Thankfully, he answers. I put on my very best *everything is just wonderful* voice, and I tell him about my trip to Berlin, my new school, and my host family before I ask for Braden's address at Iowa. He forks it over and makes me promise to visit him before I go to that terrible school in Tucson next year.

Over the next few weeks, I mail out a few postcards to Braden. They are innocuous in content, but I use my best *everything is just wonderful* handwriting and sign them with (until we meet again) *UWMA, Mandy.*

In Jenny's first letter, I learn that she and Tanner are—*what the fuck?*—roommates. They share an apartment and bills and meals. At least, that's how she describes their relationship initially. Why she moved to Tucson when she had no plans to do so is not, however, described to me. Last I'd heard, she was moving to the Phoenix area to share an apartment with some girls from Pine Ridge, find a job, and take classes at a community college. By the second letter, I grow more suspicious because I'm missing major details. I call her out by sending a postcard with a beautiful picture of the Bielefeld Art Gallery. Other than their name and address, the only words I write are: *Dear Jenny and Tanner—**what the fuck???***

That seems to do the trick because in the third letter from Jenny she confesses her love for Tanner. *What the fuck???* This letter is accompanied by three additional pages tucked inside a separate, sealed envelope from Tanner. Now they share everything, apparently. Not just postage. I feel duped. Something serious happened in his truck bed on graduation night—something so serious that they kept it between them. Jenny, with her long legs and lack of moral compass, and Tanner, with his hot body and smart mouth, well, they're together-together, and I feel really damn stupid. I've shared a lot of things with Jenny over the years, but Tanner was never one of them—always way more my friend than hers.

My hands shake as I open his letter. I feel anger, rage, and, if I'm being honest, a certain degree of despair. Tanner is mine. *Tanner used to be mine.* Tanner loves me. *Tanner loves Jenny. What. The. Fuck???*

October 18, 1989

Dear Panda,

I can almost see that what the fuck look on your face. I can hear the words coming out of your mouth. I told you I'd take care of Jenny, right? We really wanted to tell you before you left, but it didn't feel right. You were in such a crap mood about going to Germany we didn't want to make it worse.

OK, I also didn't want to see that what the fuck look on your face. Call me a chicken shit. I know you want to. I said some intense things to you. I meant them when I said them, but you picked Braden and Jenny picked me.

She's insane. You know that. She's full of wild ideas and plans and those things are cool sometimes but distracting. I have 18 credits and a part-time job on campus. My job sucks ass by the way. Sucks. ASS. I have to keep my GPA way up, or I lose the free tuition. I can't afford that hit. I can barely afford to live as it is. I have to concentrate. The classes are fucking HUGE. I'm talking lecture halls with 300 students and some T.A. at the front of class droning on and on and on until I start to drool. I'm doing all the prerequisite stuff—bullshit repeat of high school crap. Be prepared that some of your AP classes might not transfer or you will have to fight for the transfer—convince them it meets the next level of requirements, not just the pre-requirement of the actual requirement. Understand? Don't worry, I'll explain it to you.

She's taking six credits at Pima Community and works at Bennigan's full-time. I'm not sure how we wound up living together. Well, I know because I was there when I agreed to it. But it was her idea so we wouldn't have to do the long distance thing and save money on a place, since she planned on paying a certain amount in Phoenix.

I will hate you forever if you tell her any of this. I mean it. I won't forgive you. Got it? I hope so because I don't want to hate you. I don't know what the fuck I'm doing with her. The sex is hot. She's hot.

I stop reading because I have to vomit. I feel the bile rising up in the back of my throat and it bubbles to the... *Fuck*. I drop the letter on my bed, and I run for the bathroom, throw up the lid, and fall to my knees while I wretch and cry and spew my guts into the toilet bowl. I'm barfing into this stupid German toilet bowl while Tanner is having 'hot sex' with Jenny. Hey, *Jesus*, do you want to be part of this conversation, too, because my heart is... Wait—is my heart breaking? Is that what this is?

I lift up my head, close the lid, and flush from my seat on the bathroom floor. I open the lid again and rest my head back on the seat in case there's anything left to purge. I'm sweating and sobbing and trying—trying so hard—to find a piece of logic to cling to. I close my eyes and dig as deep as I can for wisdom. I wait and wait and wait. Nope, no wisdom, but no more vomit. I walk back into my room and eye that stupid fucking letter. I snatch it up in my hands, but I can't bring myself to finish it.

THIRTEEN

Letter in hand, I leave my room. The house is dark and quiet. Thank goodness, because my face is streaked with tears and possibly vomit, and I might scare someone. I go downstairs and flip on the light in the kitchen. I search for some cold *flat* water. These fucking Germans don't put anything in the refrigerator. Why even *own* a fridge if you're not going to *use* it properly—like **cold** water or **cold** Diet Pepsi or freaking anything that should be served ***cold***. I can't find any flat water—just the gross kind with bubbles—so I sit at the table, rest my head in my hands, and cry.

"Amanda?" Lars' voice startles me. I jump in my seat and whirl around to face him. He speaks to me in quiet, slow German. "You are sad."

Responding in German, I admit, "Yes. I'm very sad."

His smile is tentative. "Why are you crying?"

I wave the pieces of paper in my hand. "This stupid letter from home."

"Do you want to talk about it?"

Do I want to talk about it? How? All the words and feelings are jumbled in my brain. It's too difficult. I switch to English. "If we can speak English."

He switches to English and laughs. "I won't tell *Mutti* if you won't."

"I don't think I know enough bad words in German for this conversation."

He barks out a laugh, and his blue eyes twinkle. "I will have to teach you some bad words."

"And I will use them."

He sits at the table with me and I ask, "What does an American girl have to do around here to get a glass of cold, *flat* water?"

"Outside in the garage." I love how he says garage. It comes out like garrrrr-raaaaage. Hard to explain. I guess you have to be here.

"I think I need something stronger."

"Whiskey?" he suggests. I nod. I've never had whiskey, but Dad enjoys a tumbler of it every night after work. Maybe I will, too. He gets up and fixes us both a drink. "Does the American girl want hers over ice?"

"Yes, she does," this American girl confirms with a smile.

He chuckles because, well, I'm always asking for ice, so his question isn't even necessary. My craving for cold beverages loaded with ice is known far and wide in the Schmidt family. He adds ice to my glass—stupid little tiny cubes that have to be cracked out of one pitifully small tray in the microscopic-sized freezer compartment—but whatever, I have ice and whiskey, and possibly a friend when I really need one, and that's all that matters. Holding the drinks, he suggests we sit in the TV room because it's more comfortable. I agree. "I will bring the drinks," he says. "You get the bottle."

"Done." We get settled in the other room on the couch, and he's right, it's dimly lit in here and way more comfy on the couch. I sip my drink, which initially burns going down, but that feeling fades quickly. I pour out my stupid feelings as he refills my glass before I hit empty. Lars is an excellent listener. He looks at me attentively and asks qualifying questions while I share the back story of Tanner, Jenny, Braden, and me.

It's kind of a long story, but he doesn't seem to mind, and it feels cathartic to talk about the people I love. I cry again when I talk about the letter and where I left off. I conclude with, "And I don't know why I feel this way. They have every right to be together. Maybe it's because he's always felt like mine, and I've been so lonely without my friends. I miss him like crazy—*crazy*—and sometimes when I'm feeling the most lonely feelings of loneliness, I think about what it'll be like to go home and see him—and Jenny. But I don't want to see them together. Oh, God..." I trail off, so grateful for the packet of tissues he passed me ten minutes ago. I'm an absolute wreck.

He nods and asks, "What else is in the letter?"

"I haven't finished it because... because... I threw up... upchucked." I act out the motion in case my words are unclear.

He laughs and gives me a few German words for barfing, *"Spucken, sich übergeben, oder kotzen.* You should finish it."

"The drink?"

"No, American girl, the letter."

"Wait. I have to use the bathroom. I'll be right back." When I stand I notice that the room spins just a teensy bit. Am I drunk? Maybe tipsy? What's the difference between drunk and tipsy? Jenny would say it's the difference between screwing ugly and fugly. *Fuck Jenny.* I have to brace myself and make sure my legs are steady before I leave the room and stumble through the still not quite familiar enough to be walking around in the dark, especially after drinking whiskey, house. When I come back to the TV room, Lars is right where I left him. He turns on a side table lamp, presumably so I can see. Lars is nice.

"Do you want to read it to me or to yourself?"

"Do you really want to hear this?"

"The life of an American girl is interesting. So if you read it to me, I will not be bothered." I take it from the top and come to the part where I left off. I chug some more whiskey because, why not? We have an entire bottle and it makes me warm inside. I read on, out loud to Lars:

> *But that's all it is. Hot sex and fighting. She can pick a fight about anything. I say the sky is blue and she's going off on me. The fights usually end in hot sex, but it's a fucked up way to live. I thought I'd be in a dorm and ease into this shit. But I didn't, and I wish I could've talked to you because you would've talked me out of this. Right? Please tell me that you wouldn't have done something stupid like supported us.*
>
> *I don't know how this will end. Badly. It has to end eventually, but I'm tied to her right now. Financially. Emotionally.*

Physically. I wonder if this is what it feels like to get addicted to drugs. I hate her. I love her. I want her to fuck off. I want to fuck her.

"Oh, God." I pause and look up at Lars. "This is really bad, isn't it?"

"It seems that your friend—Tanner?" I confirm with a nod. "Tanner does not like her very much."

"He never has, Lars. That's why this doesn't make any sense to me."

"He is confused. *Durchgeknallt* because of a pretty girl."

"Yeah. Jenny is a good person, but not for my Tanner."

"Your Tanner?" he asks. "Braden is your boyfriend or...?"

"No. Braden is not technically my boyfriend. His university is so far away from mine. I can't be with Braden, but I could be with Tanner. God, I *could* have had Tanner, and now I can't. That's why I'm so upset." Suddenly I see a glimmer of logic in my thought process. *Whiskey brings clarity to a* situation—*who knew?* "You must think I'm *durchgeknallt*—a little bit crazy?"

He smirks and gives me a one-shouldered shrug. "I have a sister and a mother and a girlfriend, so I already know that all women are a little bit *durchgeknallt*."

This makes me laugh, and I take another drink and continue reading:

But more than anything, I want to be a doctor. I have to be a doctor. I have a plan. Must focus on the plan. Must stick to the plan. This relationship with Jenny is not part of the plan. God, I would give anything to talk to you right now.

I miss you so much.

I need to get away, so I'm going to spend Thanksgiving with your parents...

"He's going to spend Thanksgiving with my family?"

"The Indians and the turkey?"

"Yeah... yeah..."

He chuckles. "I made a turkey with my hand when we lived in Ohio."

"Oh, Lars, how very American of you," I chide, but he looks pleased with himself. I take another sip of my whiskey. This is actually a really nice moment between us. Lars is always a cool customer with me—polite but extremely reserved—and I haven't known what to make of him or get a read on how he feels about having me crash his academic and family life. I'm seeing glimpses of his real personality and depth of compassion, and, as always when I find something here that brings me comfort and peace—a tiny sense of stability—I'm grateful. He's wading through my shit with me, and I really, really, really need a friend away from friends.

I need to talk to Michael. He'll help me get my head on straight. And Claire's cooking... Damn, I miss dinner at your house. Jenny can't cook for shit. I don't have time for that shit so we eat a lot of Bennigan's. Did Claire tell you that she sends me care packages? They come every few weeks. An inspirational letter, a few dozen cookies, and money. The letters are sweet. I'm saving them to show you. The cookies are gone. And the money. It's embarrassing to get a handout from your folks, but the money helps more than they know. Well, they do know, because Michael made me tell him how little of it I have. I can't wait to see them. I'm going to sleep in your bed, Panda. Wink. Wink.

"He calls you Panda? Like the animal?"

"Yes. What's panda in German?"

"Panda." He smiles. "See, German is not so difficult."

"Ha! It's his nickname for me—Amanda-panda. And sometimes just Panda or Panda Bear. But," I raise my finger and point at him, "don't you get any ideas there, Lars. You may not share this with anyone or start calling me Panda."

"Most people believe pandas are docile because their looks are..." He searches for a word in English.

"Deceiving?" I offer. "Deceptive."

"I think so—tricky—*trügerisch* is the German word."

"See, English is not so difficult." I polish off my glass and Lars moves in for a refill. "No, thank you. I think I've had enough. I don't drink very often."

"Yes, we do not want the American girl to upchuck again. Vomit, barf, throw up. *Sich übergeben,*" he supplies the German word. *"Aufs Neue,"* he teases, throwing in the German phrase for doing it all over again.

I laugh and laugh. I laugh from my belly and my heart. This is the best conversation I've had in a very long time. Lars joins me in my laughter. As it dies down, we stare at each other with shit-eating grins on our faces. He asks, "How does your letter end?"

I look back down and read the rest to him.

I'm sorry that I didn't tell you any of this in person. We owed you that. I hope you aren't upset or still making your what the fuck face. But I'd give anything to see your face right now. I miss our bear hugs. I miss shooting the breeze and the shit. I miss killing time with you. I miss everything about you. I'm sorry that I didn't give you the chance to tell us what a horrible idea this was. You would've slapped some sense into me. At the very least, you would've made a PROS and CONS list so I could see that sex, while I won't argue the fact it's a pretty stellar PRO... You would've helped me with the CONS.

I keep pretty current with your news—at least the news you tell your parents. We're going to call you over Thanksgiving, Michael said the 'usual time.' I'm excited to hear your voice.

We cool, Panda? Write me soon, please. I'm going to worry about your feelings and shit until you share them with me. I might talk to you before I get a letter back, but I need to know we're still cool. I need your advice. I need you.

I will take care of Jenny. I promise not to kill her before you get home.

Out, Tanner

As I finish, it doesn't feel as bad as it did before. I'm here with my new buddy Lars, and I'm no longer crying. I might ü*bergeben michs aufs neue* later, but all is not lost. My head and eyes feel heavy, my belly warm, my limbs and mouth loose. I need sleep.

Lars asks, "How do you feel now?"

I respond in German, "Better. Thank you, my German brother."

He smiles and also responds in German, "You are welcome, Amanda. We had a good conversation."

I smile back. "We did. I hope we have more. But I am tired. I'm going to bed."

"Good." He stands, as do I, although I think he's decidedly steadier on his feet than I am. "I will hide the evidence." He gestures to the glasses and bottle of whiskey on the table. "Good night. Sleep well."

"You, too," I respond *auf deutsch*. Once back in my room, I get ready for bed—face, teeth, etc. And as I lie in bed about to drift off, I feel the weight of the alcohol pull me into the mattress. The bed spins a bit, or maybe that's just my head. I push the dark thoughts away and fall into a deep sleep until I wake early in the morning to *übergeben michs aufs neue*.

***

I guess the best thing to come out of that night is that Lars and I are friends. Just friends—there's no weirdo sexual attraction going on here, but we share more conversations and laughter and whiskey in the TV room during the late evenings. He likes to study in there, and I'll join him with a book or my journal. Sometimes we don't talk. Other times we cover a variety of topics, and I learn that he's at the stage in his life where I was just a few months ago. After the Gymnasium, he'll move on to a university, and it's likely that he and Sonja will end up in separate cities. I have higher hopes for them because Germany isn't that big and there are buses and trains aplenty.

He invites me to join him and his friends out on occasion. I'm still pathologically shy, so I mostly sit around, drink at least three beers to kill the taste, and I people watch instead of interacting with the people, but at least I'm not in my room all the time.

My parents and Tanner call after the Territorial Cup on

Thanksgiving weekend. We won—again—28 to 10. Bear Down, Arizona! I have them all on speakerphone, and we chat until my parents turn the phone over to Tanner.

"Are you pissed at me?" he asks.

"I'm worried about you."

"Your dad just chewed my ass out, but I asked him to give it to me straight, so it's all good. I'm gonna ride this year out, and it's over. I'll spend more time at the library."

"How are classes going?"

"Not too bad right now."

"And Jenny?"

"Yeah, when I say it's over at the end of the year, she's what I mean. We're breaking up—if we make it that long—and I'm gonna move on campus. I'll pick out a coed dorm for us. We can apply for the same place. You like that idea?"

"Wait, you're going to keep living with Jenny for another semester when you already want to break up? *What the fuck*, Tanner?"

"There it is," he says, laughing. "Been waiting to hear that from you. We're locked into a lease, can't pay the rent without her, so... I'm kinda stuck until then. Fuck, this was stupid."

"Yes, I am pissed at you—both of you. One of you should have told me what was going on before I left. Instead, I get this fucked up letter, and God, Tanner, it really hurt my feelings that you guys were together behind my back for half the summer."

"I know. I'm sorry, Panda. Like I said, you weren't in a good place, and I didn't wanna upset you. How's your place now? I don't hear from you. Are you doing okay?"

I hate it here. I want to go home. "I'm doing fine, Tanner. I miss everyone, but it's all right. My family is really great, and my German is getting a lot better. Listen though; I know these calls are really expensive, so we'll have a major catch up session when I get home. And I promise to write more often."

"Good. I'll probably stay in Tucson for the summer, though. I wanna take some classes. You cool with me picking out our dorm? Your parents can submit paperwork in a few months, so I'll tell them which hall to choose."

"Tanner," I chide, "haven't you learned your lesson about asking a girl to move in with you?"

"Ha! Fucking hilarious. For the record, she asked me. But, really, I want to have you close so we can do shit together, cool? It'll be fun."

"That sounds great, Tanner. It really does. I'm so glad you guys called. I love you all."

"We love you, too, babe. Bear Down."

"Bear Down, Tanner."

I hang up the phone and smile. I mean, on one hand, I do feel bad that they're both in this *situation*, but I'm relieved to know that I'll have Tanner to help me adjust to life at college. I just have to survive the next seven months in Germany.

Braden's first letter arrives inside a package in late November. *Finally!* What took him so long? I jump for joy to the amusement of my family and race up to my room. I can hear his voice as I read the words.

November 14, 1989

Dear Mandy,

I have to know about the Bielefeld conspiracy theory. Do I actually know someone who's been to Bielefeld? You have to prove it—postcards don't count. Send me a picture of you in front of a landmark holding a newspaper with the current date. Like a hostage.

Speaking of postcards, thank you for writing to me. I did write to you first. I promise I did. My first letter came back, and I got worried about the conspiracy theory. Turns out, I screwed up the address, and by the time I got the right one from your mom (she says hi), all the stuff in my first letter was old and it was lame when I read it back, so I'm glad you didn't see it. You would judge me for being a loser and use it as blackmail when I become a famous author. I'm sorry it took so long to get a letter to you so I'm making up for it by sending an early Christmas present.

I'm still figuring out which way is up but doing better. This place is huge. My classes are huge, and I couldn't get registered for much of anything that has to do with my major. So it's like prerequisite crap. Everyone says that it's easier to get more specialized classes as a sophomore. I'll let you know. It's fucking cold here. Cold and flat. I miss mountains. I guess I took them for granted. What else is new?

Please tell me that you're having fun. Sometimes I look at the clock and wonder what you're doing right now. And then I have to figure out what time it is where you are, and I think that if you're not drunk then you should be sleeping. If you're not having fun, please lie to me because I want to picture you happy. I also picture you in bed. I said I would use my memories for creative purposes. Great, now you're probably saying "gross, Braden," and wrinkling your little nose with all those cute freckles.

Anyway, I don't know if Arizona will be anything for you next year like Iowa is for me right now. There are so many people around all the time. It's hardly ever quiet and my roommate is a douchebag. I've met some cool people, and I'm busy. I met this girl Jessica. She's from...

FOURTEEN

Who the ***fuck*** *is Jessica?* I can't do this again. I can't face another guy in my life moving on without me. My heart contracts and stays like that—like he just stabbed his hand through my skin, grabbed my heart, and he's squeezing it with his big burly football player hand. *Stupid hand. Stupid heart. Stupid me.* Who the fuck is Jessica—besides a Braden-stealing whore? Why would I think he's not hooking up with someone?

> *...some shithole town in Nowhere, Iowa that's way smaller than Pine Ridge. Maybe 25 kids in her graduating class. I'll be shocked as shit if she makes it through first semester without getting carted off in a straitjacket. Can you imagine coming from such a small town right into a huge university environment? There should be something in between for people like that.*

Anyway, I did a little research. Your city looks like a mix between old and new. Lots of greenspace and walking trails and stuff. I see castles next to modern art museums. Have you seen much? Gone out of town or the country yet? And then there's this event called The Fall of the Berlin Wall. I'm not sure if you heard about it or seen any of it, but it's all over the news here. "OPEN THE DAMN GATE." Have you seen the gate yet?

What is German high school like? Cracks me up that you're still in high school. What are your new friends like? Are you fluent now? And I have to know about the beer and letting loose. I want to ask about your cherry, but that seems intrusive. Although I just indirectly asked about your cherry, so you owe me an answer.

I'm not so good at writing letters, which is kind of ironic considering my major. But since I'm stuck in freshman English, I should get a pass on that. I'm spending Thanksgiving in Iowa but will be home for three weeks over Christmas. It will be weird not to see you, but me and Tanner are going to catch up. I might stay with him and Jenny for a couple of days and kick around Tucson with Fiona. Tanner and Jenny? Did not see that one coming. Maybe I'll call the house and try to get a current number for you. My parents can pay for the call. If you're able, you can call me, too. My dorm number is 319-555-2216. I'll be there from December 19–January 15. Shit, that's like a whole month in Pine Ridge without you. Good thing I have my memories.

Now you know I'm thinking about you—alone and in bed. I hope you're happy, Mandy. If you're not, please try to be.

Love,

Braden

Jessica—poor Jessica—is some girl from a small shithole town in Iowa. And I'm insane. And I still love him. With hope for a phone call from him in a few weeks, I unwrap the present wrapped in Des Moines Register Sunday cartoons. Inside is the brightest gold sweatshirt I've ever seen. It's Arizona State gold, which is so not my color, but it boldly displays the words "Iowa Hawkeyes" in black lettering with a large logo of the mascot. As I shake it out, a piece of paper falls onto the bed. It's folded into a rectangle and "Mandy" is scrawled across the outside in Braden's rather terrible handwriting.

I promise I'm not cheap, but I decided to send you my first Iowa sweatshirt. I wore it a few times and didn't wash it because you said that you like the smell of me on you. When you wear it—alone at night—please think of me. Then think of me thinking of you. –B

I'm not proud. I pull it to my face and inhale. I inhale *Essence of Braden* and relive a hundred beautiful memories. Of course, I cry. I miss him so, so much. I strip off my shirt and slip on his oversized, smells-like-my-beautiful-boy sweatshirt. I never want to take it off.

Christmas 1989

Two days before Christmas, I'm anxiously riding shotgun with Siggy as we drive to the train station to pick up Brianna and Marcus. We converse in German. His is perfect; mine is still sad but it's coming along.

"You are excited?" He smiles.

"Yes! Will you drive faster?"

"The train arrives when it arrives. My speed is irrelevant."

"Thank you for hosting my sister and her boyfriend."

"More people, more merriment."

More indeed. I can't recall ever wanting to see Brianna more in my entire life. I'm going to wrap myself around her and make her love me back. As she steps off the train, I do just that. I launch myself at her and throw my arms around her, effectively blocking the exit for other passengers, but I don't care. My sister is here! My sister, my sister, *my sister*!

"Kiddo," she grumbles after releasing me while I'm still attached to her. "Let's get out of the way."

"Fine," I acquiesce most ungraciously. She has a duffle bag over her shoulder, and as we make our way to Siggy, a blond man relieves her of her bag. We set everything down on the pavement and introductions are made. Marcus is very tall, at least six foot five; he's lean with long legs that go on forever in his Levis. I wonder how hard it is to find jeans in his length with his narrow waist and hips. Marcus simply towers over our matching five foot eleven frames—one of the few things Brianna and I have in common, really. His face is open. He's looking from Brianna to me, and smiling as if he's discovered the cure for cancer. He offers me a hug. I accept because I'm starving for affection and because he seems really, really nice. Maybe too nice for my sister.

Brianna 'ohs' and 'ahs' as Siggy pulls up in front of the house. "So charming," she says in German. "Beautiful."

Inside is a flurry of activity. The entire family is home and rolls out the red carpet for my sister and Marcus. Drinks are offered and poured, coffee cake appears, and Inge whisks us into the main living area where we sit around and engage in light 'let's get to know you' conversations. Of course, Marcus is a huge focus of interest. He's a real live East German and, aside from vacationing in Poland, this is his first trip to the West. Talk turns to the fall of the Wall and the political climate, especially in and around Berlin, and, of course, the potential for total reunification of the country.

I'm sure most of the finer details of the conversations fly right over my head. We all speak German—that's the law, er, rule at Familie Schmidt's house. Who cares? I don't. Brianna is here for four entire days, and while the fall of the Wall is a big freaking deal, nothing is more major than having my sister with me this Christmas. It's so important that I crowd her on the sofa. I sit too close. Hell, I'd sit in her lap if she'd allow it. I touch her arm and leg and grin at her often. Maybe she'll let me hold her hand? Doubtful, but I try it. It lasts about five seconds before she softly squeezes our hands then guides them back to my leg and shakes me off. *Whatever.*

Eventually, Inge provides a tour of the home and snow-covered grounds, and I show Brianna and Marcus to their guest room down the hall from mine. Marcus can't stop looking up and around and commenting on the sheer size of the home. Brianna shares their living arrangements. After two months in a crappy apartment with friends, she moved into an even crappier apartment with Marcus. They don't even have their own bathroom. It's a shared hallway bath for several apartments. I can't imagine Brianna living in near squalor conditions, but the gleam in her eyes tells me that she's so high on love she would probably live in a tent with Marcus and be happy. While they unpack, I sit in the rocking chair until Marcus excuses himself so we can have time together. He kisses Brianna and gives me another hug saying, "It is so good to finally meet you, Amanda."

As soon as the door shuts, I turn to Brianna and state the obvious, "I love him for you."

"Me, too, kiddo. I've never been happier." She tells me—in English—more about their lives in Neubrandenburg. Her new job, his childhood friends who are now hers, how quickly she felt at home, and more about the rapid pace of their relationship. Head over heels, no doubts at all. But she has one more tidbit to share. "Kiddo, you're going to be an aunt."

"What?" There's no point in trying to hide my shock—no chance.

"I'm having a baby. I'm fifteen weeks along. Obviously, I haven't told the parents. Just you. We're telling Marcus' family and friends on New Year's Eve. Eventually," she narrows her eyes on me, "when I'm ready, I'll tell Mom and Dad."

She is way too calm for an unwed, pregnant young woman starting her adult life in a foreign country. At least, I think so, and I have a million questions which she answers in a composed voice with a relaxed expression on her face, in her eyes. She is not scared. She's thrilled and so is Marcus. They've no immediate plans to marry and, as far as I can tell, not a care in the world. Marcus is five years her senior, so he's "ready" for a family and excited for their future.

"Was this planned?" I have to ask.

She turns a little pink—not a full on blush—and admits, "No. He definitely gave me way more than an orgasm."

I shake my head in mock reprimand and mimic Mom, "How sad that you wound up as just another statistic." That sends us off into bouts of laughter, which, again, feels amazing.

While her news is nothing short of *huge*, Brianna shifts the conversation to me. We've talked on the phone, she's read my sorry-ass letters, and she's worried about how I'm adjusting—or not—to my life in Bielefeld. She offers empathy and words of encouragement, but I still wind up in tears. "I've never had to make a friend in my entire life, Bree. These kids don't give a shit that I'm here. And I'm shy. I'm really fucking shy, and I had no idea. I mean, who knew? I'm afraid to speak, I don't smile, and I hardly ever laugh. I spend a lot of time in my room telling my journal how much I'd rather be anywhere than here. I'm just biding my time and praying it'll be over soon."

"You shouldn't do that," she says.

"I can't help it. Ugh. I'm a loser." I fall back on her bed. "I want my life back."

"This is your life, kiddo."

"I don't want it. I just want a plane ticket home."

"Your family seems very nice."

"They are."

"The little one, Hannah, she's sweet, yes? You finally get to boss someone around." She grins. "And Lars—quiet but typical German. Do you get along with him?"

"I do. We're fine around the house. We've had some good talks, and he takes pity on me every once in a while and invites me out with his friends."

She stifles a grin, but I can see it in her green eyes, "You have to make an effort, kiddo. Not everything is going to be handed over to you on a silver platter with a red bow on top."

"You are still jealous about Cherry," I accuse. "And the bow was silver, not red."

She lets the grin fly before she gives it to me straight. "I didn't get a car when I turned sixteen, Amanda. I didn't have the friendships in Pine Ridge that you did. I didn't fit in—at all. So I can relate to how you feel right now. I can. When I went to Amherst, I still didn't completely fit in, but I found people who made me feel good about myself. I found my place, but I had to *make* that happen. It wasn't easy," she shrugs, "but it was worth it. If you stay in your room and cry about it, you're going to miss out on so much. They—these kids—are going to miss out on you."

"Why are you being so nice? Pregnancy hormones?"

"Hardly. I'm the big sister, and it's my job to help you along in life, even if I have to kick your ass to get you moving. And I will. I will kick your ass."

"There she is," I mumble. "There's my bitch sister."

My bitch sister takes matters into her own hands and initiates a direct and slightly uncomfortable, at least for me, conversation with Inge. She shares my shit while I sit back and share next to nothing, and then they set about making plans to fix my sorry life. And, really, thank God, because after we had a wonderful family Christmas, my crappy life took a turn for the better. Her name is Monika.

On Christmas Day, Brianna and I had a great phone call with our parents who were thrilled that their daughters are together and actually enjoying each other's company. On the day after Christmas, the Schmidt phone rings, and I receive the best present ever—a thirty-minute conversation with Braden. He sounds wonderfully, perfectly, utterly, exactly like Braden. I sit through the discussion with goosebumps, a very warm heart, and moisture between my legs.

He keeps it light—we talk about Iowa, what it's like being back in Pine Ridge, and he asks so many questions about Bielefeld and school and my life. I keep it light, too, in that I don't tell him just how terribly depressed I am and that whiskey makes everything better unless I overdo it. We talk and laugh with familiar ease and comfort, and, God help me, *I still love this boy*. Toward the end of the call, he turns the topic to Tanner and Jenny and his upcoming visit to Tucson while he's back in Arizona.

"Does it bother you that I'm going to see them?" he asks.

"No. I'm just surprised you would want to see Tanner."

"I figure, why not? But mostly, I'd rather visit with Jenny... Did you..." He's clearly hesitating. "Did you and Tanner hook up after I left?"

"I thought you didn't want to know."

He's quiet and assumes—incorrectly—in his response, "So you did." He sighs into the phone, and I can feel the weight of it from 5,457 miles away.

"I did not hook up with Tanner," I say softly, honestly. "There was not even a hook up attempt on his part because he was already otherwise engaged in hooking up with Jenny."

"How do you feel about that?"

"Honestly?"

"Unless you can make up a good lie," he says. I giggle recalling another time he said that to me. I love our inside jokes.

"I didn't take it well."

"Why did you get so upset?"

"My good buddy Tanner and my best friend Jenny..." I don't bother to hide the disdain in my tone. I sigh and believe he can feel the weight of mine from 5,457 miles away, too. "They hit me from the blindside. That's all. I might have had a little whiskey to see things more clearly."

"So you're drinking legally now?"

"Some. Whiskey and some beer, which, ugh, beer is so gross, but if you have enough of it you don't notice the taste."

Finding this more amusing than troubling, he laughs and says, "You're letting loose."

"Any moron can lift a glass to her mouth, Braden—even me."

More laughter, and then, "I miss you."

"I miss you, too."

"Write more often, okay? Please. Letters."

"I will." But I probably won't since there's nothing good or interesting or positive to fill a letter with. And I can't fill a letter with what I really want to say—that I love him and want to desperately to be with him. But I'll write more peppy little postcards that don't say much at all. Hopefully the postcards will remind him of my existence so he won't fall in love with an Iowa farm girl. "Tell Tanner and Jenny hi for me. I'm all right. I'm still here. I miss you guys, and I'm so happy you called me today—more than you'll ever know, Braden. It is so, so good to hear your voice." And I feel the tears boil back to the surface.

"I love it when you *double so* me, Mandy."

Braden, I love you so much. So, so much. "Okay, well, give my best to Coach and Mrs. McLaughlin. Oh, and I love the sweatshirt. Thank you! I wear it all the time even though gold isn't my color."

He laughs at me. "I'm so, so glad. You take care of yourself."

"'Bye, Braden."

"Until we meet again, Mandy," he replies sweetly and disconnects the call.

I spend the next hour or more sprawled on my bed in tears until Brianna locates me. She lies down next to me and rubs my back. "Shouldn't I be the one rubbing you—like your feet or something?" I joke but my voice is flat.

"How's Braden?" she asks.

"Perfect for me, except he lives in Iowa and I'm stuck here," I respond dully.

"Let's go, kiddo. Time to suck it up and clean up. Inge has dinner almost ready, and she just sent out a search party—yours truly—for you."

As with most things in my life right now, I don't want to, but I do it anyway.

FIFTEEN

I EFFECTIVELY ATTACH MYSELF TO Brianna at the train station. Of course, I do. She's my only touchstone to home, and she and Marcus (and my niece or nephew) are getting on that stupid train and leaving me here to fend for myself. But at least we have a plan, and Inge, the queen of efficiency and rule-making, will see to it that the plan is carried out. She untangles my arms from around her neck, tells me to keep my chin up, *kiddo*, and discusses a possible meetup in Berlin so we can experience what remains of the Wall while it's still there and before she's too pregnant. I don't think there's any such thing as a little bit pregnant, but I keep that thought to myself. I give Marcus a hug and they're off. I'm on my own once again.

Except I'm not completely on my own. Inge has a plan, and she wastes no time kicking ass and calling in reinforcements. Before we head back to school, she invites a girl from my school over for *kaffee and küchen*. Her name is Monika, and while she's in several of my classes, she doesn't appear to be close with Lars or his friends, so we've had very limited interaction. She's petite, with a pretty face and angular features. Her light brown hair with blond highlights sweeps below her shoulders, and her fringe of bangs accentuates deep, thoughtful brown eyes. And she speaks English perfectly. Hell yes, she almost sounds like one of my people with just a hint of accent. Inge narrows her eyes when Monika speaks to me in my beloved and highly preferred language. Inge, in German, of course, orders, "*Auf deutsch*."

At this point, Monika politely suggests that Inge allow us some privacy for some exchange student girl talk. I'm curious. I don't know much about this Monika. I'm delighted to learn that she's a friendly, open book. She leads in her almost perfect English, "Amanda, I'm so glad Frau Schmidt contacted me. And I'm sorry that she had to. I should have been a better hostess." I offer her a quizzical looks and she continues. "I was an exchange student last year in Tampa, Florida."

"Oh?"

"I had so much fun, I hated coming back."

"Your English is amazing. You almost sound American."

"Really? Thanks! I totally threw myself into it." She's delighted by my observation. "All of it. And I've heard that you're not—not throwing yourself into this experience."

"No. I'm not," I admit.

"Like I said, I should have had been there for you, and I'm sorry. This is a tough year for me academically. And emotionally—there's a guy in the states I can't wait to see again, but I have to get this shit done before I can do that. The *Abitur* is a time sucker and total buzzkill, and I've been struggling to find some balance. But I'm here now." She smiles.

"I wish I could explain how awesome it feels to hear words like *shit* and *time sucker* and *total buzzkill.* Not just a buzzkill—a *total* buzzkill."

"Totally," she instantly quips, and I fall in love with her just a little bit. "Amanda," she smiles, "I want to offer you my friendship."

I want to pump my fist in the air and scream, *hell, yes*—maybe do a happy end zone, I just scored a touchdown, type of dance, but instead I return her smile and honestly state, "I'd really like that."

"Good. Now that we're officially girlfriends, tell me what's going on with you."

I'm sure it will come as no surprise that as I open up to Monika tears leak and sniffling ensues. "I'm so homesick. I've never been away from my parents or my friends before. I've never had to make friends before. Hardly anyone talks to me, and if they do, I don't know what the fuck they're saying to me. And then I probably seem stupid because even if I do know what they're saying, I don't know the right words *auf deutsch* to string together a coherent response. And I'm shy. I didn't even know I was shy until I came here. I hate meeting new people. I hate being the new girl. I hate being so tall and so big." I puff out my cheeks and use my hands to illustrate my girth. "I hate being away from my people. I hate being here, and I want to go home."

She nods throughout with such a kind expression. "We're going to change that right now."

January 1990

It sounded too good to be true, but it wasn't. When school resumes, Monika takes me by the hand and drags me into her world. I have an awakening. I have people. They aren't necessarily my people yet, but they are around me and, prepped by Monika I presume, they are outgoing and inclusive and so very nice. They 'hang out' and I'm always invited. They meet up at a local pub, and I'm there. They speak to me in English and German. When I completely screw up a word or a thought, they laugh with me, not at me, and give me the right words in German.

Monika encourages me to just go for it with the language. "If you fuck it up, who gives a shit, Amanda? You're here to learn, right? You won't learn unless you get in there and get messy. We don't judge." She shrugs. "We help."

And then there's Curt, who is part of Monika's crowd. Now that I'm in his orbit, I have an opportunity to exchange a few words with him. He interacts with me occasionally, and we speak in a mixture of German and English. His accent is delicious and so is his dimple—which I rarely get to see because, you know, the guy doesn't crack many smiles. When he does, they are captivating but never directed at me.

Curt is unavailable because he's with a girl named Kiersten. I've watched them make out in the corners of dark pubs. I've heard them argue. They are loud, and they do this in front of everyone, and I've watched him retreat to an empty seat and hold his head in his hands after she's stormed out of the room, bar, party—the wherever or whatever. It happens a lot—both the making out and the arguing.

Kiersten did not get Monika's memo about being nice to the exchange student, or she doesn't care, because she doesn't talk to me. That's all right with me because I have an eye on her boy, and becoming friendly with her would make my surveillance more ridiculous than it already is.

Friday – late February 1990

About four weeks after I enter his social circle, he unexpectedly invites me for coffee after school. It's a polite invitation, and he explains that he'd like some help with an English paper—will I read it, check his grammar and spelling? Of course I will. We leave campus together in the drizzling rain and walk to a nearby coffee shop. I order coffee with Baileys. He takes his black—like his heart.

We work on his assignment, and while the overall theme is fine, it's more his butchering of the written words that astounds me. Not just the spelling—that's bad, too—but it's the actual choice of words. They aren't authentic. I don't know anyone who would actually use them in a sentence much less in a writing assignment.

Finally, I look up and ask, in English, with what I hope is a neutral expression, "Where did you find all these big words?"

"Why?"

"It's just that I don't know anyone who would actually use half of these words." He stares at me, and I think I catch a little glimmer of play in his eyes. Or maybe it's a glimmer of not being broody for a second. He cocks his head to the side, says nothing, and continues to look at me. "I would never actually use these words. I don't even know what most of them mean. I can infer the meaning based on the topic of your paper and the supporting details, but if you and I were just sitting around having a conversation, it would never occur to me to choose these words."

"Which words?" he asks.

"Specifically?"

"Genau." He provides the German word for exactly.

"Can I, um, write on your paper? I can circle them?" He affirms with a nod, so I dig out a pen from my book bag. I start re-reading and making circles. I look up and he's watching me like a hawk. "I wish this pen was red. Or another color..."

"The better to see my mistakes?"

I laugh. "It's just when I edit, I like to use a different color."

"Next time I will present you with a red pen."

Next time? That doesn't sound half bad—*next time*. I attempt humor. "I prefer one with a felt tip, not regular ink like a ball point pen." It works. I earn a smug grin as one side of his mouth quirks up, and thank God it's the side with the dimple, and his eyes—they come to life. We sit several beats in silence and evaluate each other before I continue with my circling rampage.

He places his huge man hand directly over the paper and I'm forced to look back up. "Do you find so many of my words offensive?" he asks.

I crinkle my nose at him and try to convey how bad I feel with my eyes. "I do," I answer. "I totally do." I gesture to his hand, "Have

I gone too far?"

"No, Amanda." My name falls from his lips for the first time, and it sounds like poetry. All of the A's are soft as opposed the hard A in the middle. Suddenly my heart is racing and my palms are sweaty and—wait—I've almost felt this way before, albeit some 5,457 miles away. "You have not gone too far. Perhaps we can do this another time."

"You don't want to finish this? It won't take much longer and then we can discuss why I think other words might be more suitable in certain contexts."

"Another time." He slides his paper toward him, slips it back in the folder and into his book bag. Since he's packing up, I put my pen away and finish off my coffee, assuming it's time to go. When he stands, I stand, too. "Would you like another coffee?" I'm surprised by his question.

"Um, sure?"

"Irish?"

"Yes, please."

We talk—in English—and, even so, I follow maybe three quarters of the conversation. It might be the language barrier or that Curt says things in a lofty manner—similar to his writing style. He strikes me as incredibly intelligent, slightly arrogant, possibly charming, and definitely dry. He's into philosophy, heavy reading, Goethe, Nietzsche, and a bunch of stuff I never studied in school and know nothing about. He's definitely university bound after his *Abitur*. He wants to move to Berlin, study philosophy, and God knows what else because it's over my head, but I don't want him to know that.

He's hard to read, hard to follow, but he's insanely handsome. I walk away from our talk feeling off balance, but that might be due to the four Irish coffees.

Saturday Night

And the following night, as it always seem to happen at night, things change. A small group of us are at a disco. We're dancing and drinking. Monika is in her element—queen of the good times. This activity is rarely something I did in Pine Ridge—the dancing, I mean—with this sense of abandonment. And, of course I never danced with an endless supply of alcohol in my bloodstream, but I don't correlate the reckless abandonment with the alcohol. Maybe I'm just too drunk to notice. If this is learning to let loose, I'm a quick study with Monika for an instructor.

Curt arrives sans Kiersten and proceeds to knock back several shots before joining us under the blinking lights and thumping music. He surprises me from behind, grabbing onto my hips and grinding into my backside. I'm drunk and I go with it. His hands wander and the pressure of his grip on me grows firmer. He wants something from me and it's not help with his English paper. I spin around and he crushes us front-to-front. The dirty dancing intensifies. He bends down and kisses my neck. Our bodies gyrate in beat to the music, and his next play includes a few bites on my neck.

Then he takes my mouth—hard. It's the most crushing, thieving, selfish kiss I've ever experienced. It's angry, and he takes what he wants before pulling me off the dancefloor by my arm. He pushes me into a dark corner where he takes more and I give it back to him.

We exchange hard kisses and heavy-handed touching. He's rough with me and I like it. He takes me by surprise by wedging his knee between my legs. His hand moves up under my short skirt, right into my panties; his finger flicks over me before he drives it inside. *What the fuck???* I gasp and I should throw the flag, but at this point in my life, I'm basically starving for physical affection. I'm about to die from starvation and he has nourishment.

This guy is not playing. He knows exactly how to touch a woman, and he does just that until I find myself moaning my orgasm into his ear. He doesn't stop touching me until I collapse against the wall behind me.

It's then that I look up at him and into his eyes. They are dark and he's wearing a smirk. My mouth is agape. *I just came against the wall in a crowded disco.* The pounding music and dizzying lights play on as my orgasm fades away. He leans down, bites my ear and says in English, "I want to fuck you."

I shake my head and say, "No. Are you crazy?"

"Are you a prude?" he growls in my ear.

The music is deafening; I need to make sure he understands me loud and clear. I roll to my toes and nibble on his ear so I have his attention. "No. I'm a virgin."

Oh, he understands me all right—no translation required. He steps back and flicks his blue eyes over my face. They narrow before the smirk returns and he replies, "I'll take care of that."

That's his parting shot. He walks away from me with my panties and brain in a twist.

Sunday Afternoon

"Monika, I mean, what the fuck was that?"

She's laughing, but it's not funny. Fuck, she reminds me of Jenny. If she keeps laughing, I'm going to have to join her soon. Friends don't let friends laugh alone. We're in my bedroom, sprawled across the mattress and, of course, I just spilled the orgasm against the wall story. "Holy shit. That guy is intense, Amanda."

"Um... yeah, a little warning would've been nice," I grumble, but she's still laughing and I'm breaking out into a smile.

"How would I know? He's been with Kiersten for years, and she's a bitch. She doesn't exactly share stories about Curt."

"He wants my cherry. What the hell am I supposed to do?"

"Give it to him—if you want to. But let me make sure it's over with Kiersten. I mean, he's not known for cheating, but I don't want you involved in some sort of *situation*." Her choice of words doesn't escape my attention. "That wasn't your first orgasm was it?"

"Um... no, but it was my first one like *that*. Braden handled me with care."

She looks up at the graduation picture on my dresser. "Which one is Braden?"

It pains me to lift my hungover head from the mattress, but I do. I crawl to the photo and hand it to her. "My best friends. Jenny—you remind me so much of her. That's Tanner—"

"Hottie," she comments.

"And that's Braden."

"Also hot. God, he looks a lot like Curt."

"Right? That's probably why I've been drooling over the dude since I first saw him."

Her eyes light up. "You have? You didn't say anything to me!"

"Well, he's taken—or was taken. I just... there's something about him."

"Yeah, he looks like your boyfriend!" She laughs.

"Braden's at college in Iowa, of all freaking places, doing God knows what, and I'm going to the University of Arizona next year," I point to Tanner, "with that guy who is currently fucking," I point to Jenny, "my best friend."

"Have you ever been with the other guy—Tanner?" I blush, nod, and she breaks into peals of laughter.

"But I'm a virgin, Monika, so it's not like I've *been* with Tanner."

"You're returning to a soap opera." And she finds this hilarious.

"Stop it. Ugh." But it feels good to laugh—really laugh, so I do.

Monday Morning

At school the following Monday, I walk to my first class with Lars. Curt approaches and nods at Lars before taking my hand and pulling me to him. I'm crushed to the side of his body when he wraps a firm arm around my shoulder. I place my arm around the back of his waist lest my bones break. Outside of the classroom he stops walking and pulls me to his front. He hasn't said hi or how was the rest of your weekend or jack shit. Monika is jubilant when she sees us together, his arm around me, my body pressed to his front, his lips on mine. In German she interrupts this embrace with a, "*Na?* Hi there, people. What's going on?"

Curt responds, “I’m saying good morning to Amanda.”

“I see that.” She grins at us. “Nice.” She walks into class.

“Coffee after school,” he says to me in German. I don’t think this is an invitation because it sounds like an order.

I don’t know, Monika. Is this nice? Is it?

SIXTEEN

Over Irish coffee after school there's zero discussion of options or ground rules or boundaries. He doesn't apologize or analyze what happened on Saturday night, and we don't talk about our feelings. He lays out a tentative schedule, and he has a lot of ideas. We will see one another after school two days a week for coffee. Since I don't really have to study, I can help him with English or read books/write letters while he studies. If my host parents agree, I will take the bus to his house after school on Friday and stay the night. He'll talk to them later this week.

Beyond confused, I sit there while he continues drafting the playbook for our—*what the hell is this?*—relationship. When we don't have other plans, we'll come back into Bielefeld together and see our friends on Saturday. Sundays are reserved for his family and church. I learn that he lives in Steinhagen—a small village on the outskirts of the metro area. His father died when he was young and his mother never remarried. His brother is much older and out of the house. Also, his mom works overnight shifts at a hospital and she is either neurotic or highly nervous. I'm not sure and don't ask for clarification. Because, apparently, on the seventh day, I get to rest.

"Question," I say in German. "I have a question."

"Yes."

In English I ask, "Didn't you and Kiersten just end a relationship, like last week?"

"*Like*, yes." It seems *like* Curt enjoys making fun of my "Americanness."

"Isn't this kind of fast?"

"I don't understand."

Nor do I. "It's just that usually when a couple breaks up, one or the other, or more often both people, need time to get over it. You know, work through their feelings of sadness or loss."

"I don't need time. We had a lot of problems. It's done with."

"Are you sure?" I question.

He narrows his eyes, the smug grin falls back into place, and he responds in German "Amanda, I am sure. Done. Finished. Over."

"I didn't realize there were so many German words for done."

"Yes, and none of them are big words." Yes, this man is a dry one.

Thursday

Curt comes home with me after school and has a talk with Inge. And—*what the fuck?*—Friday nights in Steinhagen are *just fine* with

Inge. After he leaves to catch the bus, Inge has a talk with me about birth control. I don't have the German words to say much, which doesn't seem to matter because she's so matter of fact about making sure we use condoms, and if I'm not on the *antibabypille* she will make an appointment for me to see a doctor.

For seventeen years, I've overthought every single decision. Pros and cons, options and ground rules, choices, opinions, alternatives. I used to revel in the decision-making process. My dad would say to me, "Every decision you face is a fork in the road. Once you've chosen your path, you might leave a piece of yourself behind as a reminder that you were there, but you can never go back."

Now it seems like everyone around me is making decisions for me, or at least giving me Free Will to make some pretty stupid ones. I'm Curt's girlfriend, my host mom wants to put me on the pill, and tomorrow after school I'm going to Steinhagen to spend the night at his house while his mother works the overnight shift. Forget Deutschland—this place should be called Oppositeland. What's up is down, what's down is up; if I fork right does that mean I should've actually forked left?

March 1990

Seriously, that's how this plays out over the next four weeks. Curt and I meet up for coffee after school at least two days a week. I write letters and postcards and a whole bunch of sentences that begin with *what the fuck* in my journal. Sometimes I help him with his English studies. I pack a bag Friday morning, and we go to his village after school on the bus. Inge either picks me up on Saturdays or I take the bus back later in the day, and we hit a party or a club with our friends on Saturday night. On Sundays, I rest up and gab with Monika. During this time, Inge takes me to a doctor, and I walk out with a prescription for the *antibabypille*. Meanwhile, Curt and I have not done the deed, but we're doing everything except the deed so I guess it's only a matter of time.

Chronologically, he's only two and a half years older than me, but he's light years ahead of me with sexual experience. I'm unsure how I *feel* about Curt. Yeah, it's nice to have friends and activities, and orgasms are great, but I don't *feel* like this relationship with Curt is love. That's how it's supposed to be, right? I want it to be.

Curt is smug and arrogant, but he's also witty and so good looking. When he removes the pretense and relaxes around me, we have fun together. I don't trust him, though. Often I feel like an accessory in his life—as if I'm there to serve a specific purpose—and, really, a girl should always listen to her gut when it comes to stuff like this. She's usually spot on, and in moments of reflection she will—and should—kick herself in the ass for ignoring that inner voice.

He's brought me to orgasm many times with his hands and his, *oh my god*, mouth. I was shocked at first. It seemed like such a dirty thing to me, but he loves it and wanted me to do the same for him. (He has an uncircumcised penis, so I can check that research off my list.) *Awkward*. I didn't even know where to start, but he told me what to do and eventually I came to learn how to do it just the right way for him. *Is giving head an important life skill?* Jenny would be so proud. I should write to her, but I don't want these private details shared with Tanner, so I rely on Monika for advice.

Curt has no hang ups about nudity—his or mine. He'll do anything in the bright light of day, and he likes to keep a light on at night when we're messing around. He won't let me hide. He's visual, he explains, and seeing me, watching me, is a huge part of what turns him on. Eventually with direct evidence proving his arousal, I accept that but never get over my discomfort.

Germans are nothing if not efficient. The road from Point A to Point B is not a meandering journey. Unless you specifically make plans to meander during your journey, it's just the road from Point A to Point B. It's weird, but it's also a kind of refreshing. With Curt there are very few decisions to make. Yes, I decide how I want my coffee, what I'll have on my pizza, if I want to go dancing or drink at the pub or both, would I like another drink, am I hungry. I don't have to decide if he likes me or wants to be with me. He's decided I am his girl even though I'm temporary. I have an expiration date of Tuesday, June 5, 1990—it's printed right on my plane ticket home.

April 6, 1990

The seniors were released from daily school activities to prepare on their own or in groups for final examinations. Curt and I hop on a train and head for Berlin for a weekend with Brianna and Marcus. I'm so excited because *freaking Brianna*. I can't wait to see what's changed in and around the city of Berlin since I was there last September.

It starts off well enough. We meet at the train station; Brianna is *huge*. Since we have similar body size and shape, I wonder if this is what I'll look like one day. Everyone is in a good mood as we locate our B&B, drop off our bags, and head into the city. I'm chattering Brianna's ear off and keep asking to touch her belly, but she doesn't seem to mind. Marcus and Curt are having deep political discussions. I'm not quite sure what they're talking about—the intricacies are too complicated for me to follow *auf deutsch*.

We make our way to the Brandenburg Gate. The Wall is *gone*. I can see from West into the East as plain as day. Marcus *beams* and runs back and forth across the nonexistent border. He spins in circles with his arms in the air—and he kisses my sister madly. There are vendors everywhere selling souvenirs, particularly magnets and pieces of the Wall. But as we walk further, we find sections of the Wall still intact although in various states of ruin. Marcus, Curt, and I try to pry a section free, but our bare hands are no match for concrete and rebar. Marcus borrows a crowbar; we work until we're sweaty, but we've managed to liberate several large pieces.

Brianna's been snapping photos as we worked. Now she hands the camera to an American from Texas and asks him to take some pictures of our group. We throw our arms around each other and grin, posing in front of the crumbling wall looking mighty happy and proud. Yeah, we have to haul the pieces back to the B&B, but it's totally worth the effort. I have a *huge* chunk of history to bring home and share with my parents and friends.

That evening after dinner out, Marcus and Brianna decline our request to go dancing. Of course they do. Brianna is tired from a long day on her feet. We separate for the night, and Curt and I take off for Alexanderplatz in search of nightlife. It's Berlin—it's not hard to find. As we drink and dance, I think about my first trip to the city, the Army Guy, and the barfing. It feels like one hundred years ago.

I'm not that girl anymore. I have a life here. I have friends, I know the differences between a circumcised and uncircumcised penis, and I've even had one in my mouth many times. Of course, I have Curt. He's so handsome, and as we kiss and grind together on the dancefloor, he leans down and says, "Tonight is our night, Amanda. Let's get out of here."

Back in our room at the B&B, he shuts the door, grabs my shoulders and pins me to the wall. Driving into the kiss, he controls the pace and tempo, which is frenzied, rabid. I'm buzzed—possibly drunk—and turned on, and when he starts to peel my clothes off, I return the favor. Once naked, his hands and mouth seek out his favorite parts of my body until he walks me backward to the bed.

After I come for him, he digs through his bag for a condom. Another important life skill—he teaches me how to roll it on. On my back with him between my legs, suddenly I'm terrified. This is it.

I delay the game and put a hand between us to hold his body away. "Is it going to hurt?" I whisper in German.

He instructs, "Relax, Amanda." The German word for relax doesn't sound very relaxing, especially when it's not whispered with sweet persuasion.

I try to relax. I do. I take a deep breath and spread my legs a little wider even though I consider throwing the flag as he positions himself at the line of scrimmage. I have a request, and I whisper it to him in English, "Please be gentle with me."

As if the soft whisper of those words communicated much more, he pulls back from the goal line and relaxes over me, and his lips become more forgiving; his kisses are softer, and his tongue lingers and explores instead of thrusts. His fingers tease and twist softly between my legs. I correlate these strokes and caresses with feelings that I know—feelings of someone who cares for me and are pleasurable and real. I relax so much and soon feel the slow burn again; I pulse around his fingers, moan and needlessly beg him not to stop. He never stops until my body quiets. He withdraws his hand and brings that finger—the finger—to my lips. He traces my lips with the finger, slides in between them, and I can taste myself on him. When he pulls his finger out of my mouth, he leans down and kisses me passionately. *"Braves mädchen,"* he says.

I search my splintered mind for the English translation. Brave girl? Good girl? *More like—who the fuck is this girl?*

He enters me slowly up until the point of no return. Against my internal wall—the barrier between innocence and impurity—he hesitates. He knows what he's doing, but I have not one fucking clue because when he looks at me and nods, I return one in kind even though this does not feel right. As he thrusts his tongue into my mouth, he breaks through my last line of defense and into the end zone. The shock and pain causes me to cry out. I can't relax, and not only do I wish it hadn't happened, I just want it to be over.

After, I lie in his arms and don't speak—save for the inner voice rattling around in my mind. When I go to clean myself up in the hall bathroom, I'm bleeding and seek comfort back in Curt's arms. Stroking my hair while I cry, he offers calm assurances of *"alles gute."* But *alles* was not *gute* because I'm so overwhelmed by what I just did with him. I profess words of love that I don't believe, but I want to. I gave him my virginity. Aren't I supposed to be in love with this guy? So I say it with the impossible to get lost in translation form of, *"Ich liebe dich."*

He replies in German, *"Und ich hab dich lieb."* It's not the same thing—it's the English equivalent of "and I hold you dear."

Whoa—*wie bitte*? Even though we're speaking the same language, we said two very different things. I didn't mean what I said, but I wanted to—so, so much. Curt, being older and wiser, said what he meant.

***

The next day, we spend more time with Brianna and Marcus bumming around Berlin. Perhaps someone in Pine Ridge updated KFC: *Amanda Lost Her Virginity*, but other than Curt and me, no one else knows. I don't even tell Brianna because words keep rattling around in my brain—*lost, taken, lonely, popped, torn*. I do not feel—*happy, adored, cherished, loved*. It's far from an ideal *situation*, but it's done. I can never take it back.

On the dancefloor at a disco later that night, we have our first argument. Drunk and dancing, Curt leaves me to get refills. I still hate beer, but I can no longer taste it since I've had four by now. Within minutes, I'm joined by an American. Army guys are instantly recognizable. Too loud for conversation, we exchange a brief smile. He comes close, closer, and eventually way too close when he puts his hands on my hips and tries to pull me into him. I resist, he insists, and, of course, this is when Curt returns to the dancefloor.

Since his hands are full of beer, he steps between me and Army Guy, glares in my face, and orders me to follow him. When he gets me in the corner, he yells at me—right in my ear over the music. He swears liberally, calls me terrible things while my face crumples, and I start to cry. He slams his beer down his throat, chases it with mine, and he walks out of the club without looking back.

On the streets of Berlin, it's more of the same as we walk back to the B&B, and he's so irate that he won't let me talk. Vile words are delivered with exceptional cruelty, and I know his words are awful because Lars has taught me some creative uses of German vocabulary. Less than twenty-four hours ago, I was a virgin. Now I'm a *bitch*, a *whore*, a *fat whore*—and that one cuts the deepest. Knowing I'm shy about my body and sensitive about my size, Curt keeps going right for the jugular, and he isn't finished yet.

Finally I stop walking. I stop in the middle of the sidewalk and he goes on a good fifty yards before he realizes I'm not with him. He turns and stalks back to me. If I thought he was pissed before... He might rip my face off, so I find my voice. In English, I yell, "*STOP IT. ENOUGH. I DIDN'T DO ANYTHING WRONG. GET THE FUCK OUT OF MY FACE, YOU ASSHOLE.*" And now it's me who storms away, but with those long legs, he catches up in five paces.

Grabbing me above the elbow with such force that I'm certain it will leave a mark, I find myself up against a brick wall. His blue eyes are ice, like he loathes me. He bites out in German, "You are *mine*. No one touches you but *me*. *Do you understand me*?"

My arm hurts. My heart hurts. My vagina hurts.

"I understand," I say quietly with tears spilling down my face. "I was trying to get him off of me when you walked up. Please, Curt. Stop yelling at me." And, *oh my god*, now I understand why Kiersten was always in such a crappy mood—her boyfriend had multiple personalities and I gave *him* my virginity. Jesus. I am so fucking stupid.

After a short stare down, Curt releases my arm and takes my hand in his like we're some happy fucking couple out for an evening stroll as we walk back to the B&B in silence. I'm still burning inside from what he said to me, but once we're back our room, all of his anger is gone.

His fingers are soft as they run through my hair. "You're so beautiful," he whispers in German. "My beautiful girl." With sweet words and gentle kisses, he coaxes me—the *fat whore*—from my clothing and onto my back. Even with all these thoughts rattling around my clouded brain, I don't resist—I only regret. After he's finished with me, I take a quick shower and brush my teeth, returning to our room dressed in flannel boxers and Braden's IOWA sweatshirt.

He smirks at me and says in German, "You've come a long way in two days. We're going to have a lot of fun together before you go home."

After climbing into bed, I reply in English, "I have a terrible headache. I need sleep."

He leans over and his kind personality kisses me goodnight. My *mind completely fucked* personality, turns my back to him and, when he slides in behind me to cuddle, his touch is unwelcome. The ache in my heart and between my legs is raw, but instead of telling him to fuck off, my tears fall silently onto my pillow and, eventually, I sleep.

* * *

Over the next four to six weeks, I continue partying, drinking, and having sex and arguing with Curt. So quick to anger and saying such awful things to me, when I'm pushed too far and try to walk away, he changes the play and tells me in a soft voice that I make him crazy because he cares so much about me. Our arguments are never as vicious as that first one, but that's because I go out of my way to avoid conflict. Oh, and the sex stops hurting—physically anyway.

Taking side trips to other countries—sometimes alone, sometimes with Inge and/or Siggy or Monika—I visit Paris, Luxembourg, Amsterdam, and Neubrandenburg to visit Brianna, who is ready to pop. I send Braden and Tanner/Jenny postcards from these cities and describe my adventures in bubbly cursive. Meanwhile, I tell Brianna about those two very different nights in Berlin and some of the things that he says to me. She advises me to break things off, but what's the point? I've served the majority of my sentence in Germany—just a few more weeks to go.

SEVENTEEN

May 26, 1990

My expiration date is drawing near. It's late in the month of May, and that's not the only thing that is late. I haven't had a menstrual cycle since I started the *antibabypille*. I've taken it without fail and Curt always wears a condom, so there's no chance, right? I call Brianna, who says that I need to tell Curt ASAP and we should buy a pregnancy test from the *Apotheke*.

I do, and as we wait for the results together at his house in Steinhagen, he's beyond angry. His exams start next week, but this is one test he's dying to fail. I'm a *stupid child* and he can't believe I would try to *ruin his life* like this. If there is a baby, there will be no baby. I'll have to *take care of that* as soon as I get home. If I don't, he wants nothing to do with either of us. In retrospect, I should've passed on the phone call to Curt and done this on my own, but I thought... well, I thought he'd bring me comfort instead of holding me culpable for this *situation*.

Thank God we fail the test with flying colors.

Now that I'm filled with relief, I am finished with Curt. I hate him. After I slip away to call Inge, I wait until she pulls into the driveway before telling him that I don't want to see him again. For added measure, I call him a few choice American English words that start with the letter "F" before fleeing to the safety of Inge's car.

In less than two weeks, I'll be back where I belong. Sure, if I could go back in time and take another fork in the road, I absolutely would. But when you choose the wrong path, there is no going back.

June 6, 1990

I step off the plane at Sky Harbor, make my way down the jetway, and race into Dad's open arms. Then I hug Mom so hard that I almost take her to the ground. We collect my baggage, load it into the BMW, and head north. On the drive up, I chatter on and on in my native language, responding to various questions from Mom or Dad.

As we crest the last mountain just before Pine Ridge, I take in the sight of the beautiful blue skies and the mountains in the distance. My body is thrumming with sensations of relief and joy and regret. I took a lot of forks in the road over the last year, and I'm back in Pine Ridge, but there is no going back to the way it was before. Cherry is waiting for me in the driveway. In a few months, I'll take her down to Tucson. It turns out that Braden was right after all—I won't be taking my cherry with me.

Age Eighteen—Until We Meet Again

August 1990

When I pull into Braden's driveway, he's waiting for me on the front porch. By the time I cut the engine and open Cherry's door, he's right there. He has a huge smile on his beautiful face and throws his arms open to welcome me. Jumping from the cab, I launch myself at him.

We hold on tight before he whispers in my ear, "I want to take a look at you." He steps back, performing a head to toe inspection. My hair is much longer, halfway down my back; it's still curly but with a simple fringe of bangs. I've lost about ten pounds from all the biking and walking; maybe he'll notice. Other than that, decked out in his light blue Banana Republic lion tee, white shorts, and flip flops, I look generally the same from the outside even though I don't feel that way on the inside.

"I like your taste in t-shirts."

"What, this old thing?" I grin.

He captures a strand of my hair in his hands, running it through his thumb and index finger. "Nice. I like the hair." He moves to my eyes. "I really like the hair." Across my nose he traces his finger and says, "Those freckles... still freaking adorable. Just as I remember them."

He continues his full body scan, comically raising his eyebrows as his eyes skim, then linger, on my breasts. When his eyes hit my waist, he places a hand there and says, "You've dropped some weight." He doesn't say whether he thinks that is good or bad. As his eyes travel over my hips, his hand continues its journey over the outside of my thigh, moving all the way down over my kneecap, whereupon he squats down on his heels to stroke my—um, shin. *What?*

He grins up at me. "I'm just checking for leg hair." With one final look at the tips of my toes, he comments, "Still pink."

As he stands up, I pretend to be offended. "I went to Germany, Braden. I didn't become a hairy beast."

We stare a beat before he folds me into his arms again for another full contact hug and asks, "What do you want to do today?"

"Honestly?"

"Now, Mandy," he says, breaking our hug and leading me up the front walkway while our clasped hands swing between us. "I much prefer honesty, but, if you're going to lie, make it creative." I dissolve into a fit of laughter at his old joke. We're still laughing as we walk through the front door, into the cool air conditioning, and make our way through the more formal area of the McLaughlin's home. I think I've walked through the front door twice, maybe three times before. "You want a drink?" he offers.

"Please. Water—flat with a shit-ton of ice," I snicker but he doesn't know why. As he fixes my drink I explain the water *situation* and how I *suffered*; reduced to *begging* for extra ice. "And their fridge was just this tiny thing," I describe. "And Inge—my host mom—went grocery shopping almost every day. Ugh, and the milk—it had these thick chunks of skin across the top. So gross. Like I had to strain it before I could drink it, and it was never cold enough..."

"Poor baby." He offers a fake smile of sympathy, along with my glass of water with a shit-ton of huge ice American-sized ice cubes inside. Ah, heaven. He fishes out a can of Dr. Pepper from the fridge and we walk back to the family room.

"It's kind of strange without your parents at home. I'll see Coach before I leave for college, right?" I ask.

"Yeah, Dad's looking forward to seeing you. He was disappointed you couldn't come to Michigan, but totally understands that you didn't want to travel after doing so much of it. They'll be back in about two weeks."

"Thanks for coming here, Braden. Really, it means a lot to me that you'd give up part of your summer vacation to—"

"Time with you is a vacation." He gestures to the sofa and we settle in next to each other, close but not too close. "Vacations are a pleasure."

"Braden?"

"Mandy?"

"I'm going to cry now." And I do, but it's not ugly. Just a few tears roll down my face as I explain, "These are actually tears of joy. I'm happy to see you. So, so happy."

"I love it when you *double so* me. Always more meaningful than a single *so*," he replies, wiping away the tears with his thumb.

"This is true," I almost whisper my response. It feels absolutely, incredibly amazing to be with him, to study his face and be by his side. He looks more mature with broader shoulders—perhaps he grew an inch, and his hair is shorter than I've ever seen it. His skin holds a healthy tan from the summer at the lake, and as good as it feels to look at him, it's a little unnerving to stare into a pair of blue eyes that are so warm.

"Your postcards started to taper off, but then you rallied there at the end."

"I'm sorry. I got wrapped up in things, but I tried to send you ones when I went somewhere interesting. Oh, and I have something for you, but I left it in Cherry. Later?"

"You didn't have to get me anything," he says.

"I wanted to."

"I'm glad you did."

"But you don't even know what I got you yet."

"I'm just glad that you were thinking enough about me in whatever moment you were in to bring me something."

"Were you always this sweet?" I ask.

"Were you always this adorable?" he responds without missing a beat.

"Jesus," I mutter. And then I hold up my hand. "No, He is not part of this conversation." Braden laughs because this exchange, apparently, will never get old. "You were always this sweet."

He grins. "You didn't answer me earlier. What do you want to do today?"

"This. Just this. I want to sit here and look at you and talk to you about whatever... or nothing. I don't care." I put my glass down on the coffee table and curl into his side while his arms wrap around my shoulders. "I just want to be with you."

And we talk about whatever flies into our brains, and sometimes we fall into silence. I ask about Iowa and college life and classes and people. He shares stories, pieces of his life without me. Some are amusing, others not so much because Jessica is part of them. Braden's closest friend at Iowa is a guy named David Pratt who's in love with a girl named Cecilia who is best friends with Jessica. It nags at me, but I don't probe for more and he doesn't offer.

The silences are good too, because they give me time to process what he just said—time to think about what to say next. The more we talk, the more I feel like the girl I used to be. We cover light topics with our familiar style of banter and innuendo. We liberally insert inside jokes. Often one of us shares something that feels like an inside joke, but it's not because we weren't together when it happened. We have to back up and explain why it's so funny. Like the flat water with a shit-ton of ice cubes.

"So I hesitate to bring this up," he starts, "but I assume you've seen Rawlings and/or Jenny by now."

I nod. "No and yes. I've talked to Tanner on the phone, but I haven't seen him. And I've seen Jenny. I spent a few nights with her after I got back to town."

"You spent the night at Jenny's but didn't see him?"

"Um, yeah... they broke up—she moved out."

"Oh? I haven't kept up."

"I hadn't either until I got home. It was not good—both the relationship and the breaking up."

"Spill it."

"Oh yeah, because it's way more fun to talk about other people's problems." *Truth.* "So... Jenny is living in Phoenix with some girls from Pine Ridge, Heather and Janie, if you remember them."

"Not Tucson?"

I shake my head. "Definitely not Tucson. Oh, Braden, it was bad." With wide eyes and a serious tone, I explain, "They fought—a lot."

"Yeah, I saw some of that."

"You didn't tell me." I'm somewhat indignant.

"I'm not a fucking girl, Mandy. I don't gossip."

"Okay, *Mr. Spill It.*" I roll my eyes. "Anyway, it's not like I can or should take a side. I love them both—just don't love them together. So now Jenny's in the Valley, working, taking classes at one of the community colleges. She's on the slow track—no idea what she wants to do with her life, which is fine. She'll figure it out."

"She will. She's a good person, good head on her shoulders."

"Yeah, just not around Tanner, who is spending the summer in Tucson, taking classes and waiting out the lease on that apartment. He's moving into the dorms this year where he should've been in the first place. He's under so much stress—hung onto his scholarship by the skin of his teeth. *Skin of his teeth*," I repeat. "What does that even mean? I mean, I know it means 'just barely,' but where did that expression come from? Do you know?"

He smiles with a shake of his head. "I don't know, Mandy, but I'm willing to learn, and when I do, I'll share my newfound knowledge with you."

That elicits a giggle from me. "My dad gave him a *come to Jesus* talk while I was gone, and Jesus was totally part of the conversation. My dad ripped into him pretty good, but Tanner came to him for advice. Dad just hated to see him lose his way." I don't share that my parents are helping him out financially, or that Tanner's parents used his social security number to start a line of credit that they can't repay and now he doesn't speak to them anymore. Instead I share, "We're going to live in the same dorm. Different floors but same building."

"Should I be happy for you two? Are you going to share bars of soap in the coed bathroom?"

I must have hit an old nerve. "Yes, you should be happy for

me—and him. Obviously, the kid makes very poor decisions about women when I'm not around to tell him what to do." I change the subject with, "Do they have coed bathrooms in the dorms?" I wrinkle my nose. "Because I can't imagine doing some of the things I need to do in there if boys are around."

He chuckles. "I can't speak for Arizona, but there are a few residence halls at Iowa with them. I didn't," he finishes quickly, "live in one of those. Our bathrooms were separate."

"Did you see Becky this summer?"

"I did." He seems surprised that I would even ask. "They spent a week at the lake house."

"What did Yale do to her, or vice-versa?"

"Yale didn't chew her up and spit her out, but Becky is a bit humbler now. She has to work really hard to keep up, and she's not used being anywhere but the top of the curve so it was a rocky adjustment. She knows what it takes now, and she's determined. I don't worry about her."

"Becky and Kyle?" I ask but can predict their likely outcome.

"Officially done over Christmas break. Becky doesn't have time for that shit. Not that Kyle is shit—just bad timing and soon to be opposite coasts. He's going to Stanford."

"What? No way!" And I think about yet another fork in my road. Maybe Dad was right.

"Yup. I'm sure you can compare notes with him at some point next year and see if you made a huge mistake."

"You mean, yet another huge mistake," I mumble.

"Excuse me?"

"Nothing. Never mind. You never said, but do you think I'm insane for picking Arizona over Stanford?"

"I imagine not many kids who get accepted to a school like Stanford and actually have the means to afford it would turn it down. You made yourself a little list and weighed the decision carefully. Right?"

"Right. Duke can kiss my ass."

"Still hurts, eh?"

I demonstrate the Hurt Scale with my fingers. "Yeah, just a little bit."

"If Duke had sent you a thick packet, you'd be going?"

"Oh, hell, no. I just want to be wanted. Feels better to turn down than be turned down."

"Right? Fuck Duke."

"Fuck Duke," I echo.

"Are you hungry?"

I demonstrate the Hunger Scale with my fingers. It's far greater than the Duke Hurt Scale. He chuckles and tweaks my nose. "You call it."

"Pizza Stop. I want a Diet Pepsi with a shit-ton of ice and free refills."

After dinner I ask if he wants to say hi to my parents. He declines but promises to come by my house soon. "I want to take you home—my home, Mandy, and spend time with you." I'm game. That's all I want.

Now we're on the back porch, side by side in separate chairs, watching the sun set and the array of colors and shadows that are impossible to describe but incredible to experience. It's easy, natural, getting back to us—or a new version of us. While he's touched me and hugged me and he's holding my hand right now, he hasn't made a move to kiss me or take things in a romantic direction. I sit here watching the sky wondering if it's in our future or part of our past.

"What's on your mind?" he asks.

"It's creepy how you do that."

"What?"

"Ask me what's on my mind when I'm deep in thought about something."

"It's not creepy. You're almost always deep in thought about something. It's a question that's certain to produce a response that might make me laugh—or make me wish I hadn't asked. Yeah, the latter of which is most often the case." I release his hand so mine is free to backhand him on the shoulder. And then I grab it again because I crave a physical connection with him. "Dad always says if you ask a woman what she's thinking you're asking for trouble."

"And yet..."

"I can't help myself. I like being inside your head sometimes."

"Messed up place to waste your time."

"You're not a waste of my time. You're more like a preferred pastime."

And so I blurt, "Are you still attracted to me?"

His laughter is nervous. I watch him swallow and take a few moments to think before answering, "Yes. Of course."

"Are you going to do anything about that attraction?" I notice that the most obvious change with our interactions is how we're communicating with eye contact and in complete sentences instead of looking away to stutter and stammer through discomfort. I decide that however he answers my question, I'll be all right, but I don't want to dance around the *situation* because our time together also has an expiration date. I don't want to waste it wondering. Perhaps I brought back a wee bit of *Wisdom* from my time across the pond.

"I, uh... Um... I..." he starts and *oh no, that's a stammer*. But he recovers quickly and maintains eye contact. "I want to, Mandy—so, so much." He winks with his mockery of my abundant use of *double so's*. "It would be easy to lay you down on my bed and pick up right where we left off in the back of your truck, and, fuck," he clips, "now I have a fucking hard-on." I dissolve into laughter while he shakes his head at me.

He squeezes my hand to get my attention, and his face and voice adopt a serious tone. "It would be easy but not smart, I think, until we know a little bit more about each other."

"What do I need to know?"

"I'm just going to say *it*, and then we're going to talk about it."

The part of me that thought she'd gained a little wisdom runs for the hills as my heart sinks into my stomach. I nod in affirmation because I have to hear him out. "You can tell me anything. I might not like it—in fact I'm pretty sure I'm not going to like it—but I'll deal with it."

It stings to witness the internal debate he's having with himself. "Hey," I squeeze his hand and gave it a little shake. "Look at me, Braden. Like you said before you left for Michigan, it's just us, catching up one year later—however that comes about. Whatever you're about to say to me, say it. I'll still be your friend."

He takes a deep breath, and I lose his eyes as they turn to look up at the sky. Words that I can never unhear spill from his mouth into the mountain air. "There was a girl..." And I *know* I don't want to hear the rest, but I have to. I close my eyes and physically brace for the impact. "We weren't in a serious relationship or anything. She had more experience than me. We ran in the same circles, so I figured... Why *not* her."

It cuts deep, but I fight to keep my face neutral. I tell any tears, along with Duke, to fuck off. I die a little inside, honestly, but even as this revelation rips through my soul like Curt ripped through my hymen, I tell myself that Braden had every right to do what he did. No promises.

"Okay." I hope what came out next would be with a calm and steady voice. I dig deep to find it before speaking. "It's not like you killed anyone." To lighten the mood and because my voice actually sounds strong and steady, I add, "You got laid. You didn't kill anyone, right?"

"I did not kill anyone." He turns his gaze on me.

"And you're not currently in a committed relationship?"

"If I was, we'd have had a different kind of conversation today. Please believe me."

"Of course, I believe you."

"Tell me what you're thinking," he requests while intensely studying my face.

I take a deep breath and ask *Wisdom* to join me for a moment. "I am not jumping for joy over here," I pause. "But what right do I have to be angry? Don't answer. It hurts—a lot. I won't lie. But you are perfectly free to live your life as you see fit, right?"

He releases a sigh into the evening air and strokes my hand with his thumb. "This *situation* with us is tricky sometimes. I don't want to hurt you, but felt that I owed you that information before anything physical happened between us."

The words sink in and my mind conjures up images of this nameless, faceless girl. *Does she look like me? Maybe she's nothing like me. Maybe she's petite and blond, and he can spin her around in bed like a toy. Can she make him laugh from his belly? Does she inhale his scent when he holds her? Did he stare into her eyes and study her reaction watching her orgasm for the first time? Does he have a special nickname for her? Does he love her—even just a little bit?*

I can't ask because the answers will consume me. "I do not want to know any details—ever. If I ask for details at a later time, please refer me back to my aforementioned statement and don't tell me anything—no names, no specifics, nothing. *Ever.* Do you understand?"

He nods. "I do." He attempts a joke by asking, "Is this binding?"

"Wait." I can't help myself. "*Jessica*???"

He winces ever so slightly. *It is Jessica! Her name is Jessica, and I want to hunt her down on her pig—or whatever—farm and kill her with a pitchfork. Maybe I'll start with my bare hands and cowboy boots with the pointed toes, kick and beat the shit out of her before I finish off that—*

Braden interrupts my internal rant. "I'd like to refer you back to your aforementioned statement."

—bitch whore who had him first with the pitchfork. I hate you, Jessica. I hate you.

I release his hand because our palms are now sticky with nervous sweat, and I need both of them to support my chin while I fight back tears and the nasty words. I want to scream into the night and light into Braden with a string of obscenities. *I want to hurt you for not waiting for me, Braden.*

Wisdom is still with me, because instead of lashing out I sit quietly and stare into the night. The sun is slipping behind the mountain, almost gone; the colorful beams of its former glory linger sadly.

I didn't wait for him either. I threw it away with Curt.

"Mandy," he breaks into my thoughts.

"The pig farmer's daughter," I snarl before I can stop myself. *Wait—where did Wisdom go?*

"Her parents aren't pig farmers."

With a whip of my neck to face him, I hiss, "No details from you. *She* is whoever I imagine her to be—fat, ugly, stupid, and wallowing in pig shit, and don't you even bother correcting me because I need to believe that she's disgusting and means nothing to you. Let me have that—*please*."

"You're angry."

"My feelings aren't that straightforward. There's no single word that sums up how I feel right now, but... I'm trying, really trying." *I need to retreat and process. I need to make a list—lists are helpful.*

"What about you? Did you meet someone special in Germany?"

I'm still raw. "I don't want to have this conversation with you."

"Oh? This sharing thing is a one-way street then?" I look away and rest my chin back in my hands. I'm quiet and he mutters, "I guess it is..."

We sit in silence. The sky turns dark and the stars come out. I take deep breaths of fresh mountain air and allow a few tears to trickle down my face as I think about what I want to share, what I should share, with Braden. I'm full of regrets, and I hurt so, so much inside right now. *Fucking Curt. Fucking Jessica. Oh my god, he fucked the pig farmer's daughter.* These thoughts churn around and around in my scrambled head.

* * *

"Do your parents have any whiskey?" I look at him for the first time in about thirty minutes.

"What?"

"Whiskey. I'd like some whiskey on the rocks."

His eyes narrow in confusion, he sighs, and eventually stands, "I'll go check."

"Just bring me a glass with ice and the bottle, please."

After he returns with bottle service, I pour myself a healthy volume and toss it back. I refill and toss that back, too. The third time around I sip slowly. When I meet his eyes, which isn't difficult to do because he's staring at me, I offer him an unapologetic smile and take another sip.

"This is weird."

"I agree." I take another sip. "But which part? The whole sharing of information thing or me drinking your dad's whiskey on your back porch?"

"Yes." His laughter is soft. "All of it." I take a few more sips before he says, "But you haven't shared yet. My imagination is taking me to some dark places, and I wish you'd—"

"I made a big mistake, Braden." I tell him about Curt, and I stutter, stammer, and search for the right words. I refill my glass. Oh, and, of course, I cry.

When I finish, Braden's eyes are dark with worry but his overall expression is gentle. "I'm sorry," he says quietly.

"I wish I could take it back. I didn't know how to handle someone like that. Every instinct told me not to but I just... I did it anyway, and then because it was done, and I was so damn alone, I just... He was so mean to me. No one has ever said things like that to me before, and I stayed with a guy like him because I was lonely. What does that say about *the kind of girl I am* now?" I look down at my drink which is now empty and the ice cubes have melted away.

As I refill my glass again Braden says, "I think you should lay off the whiskey, Mandy. That's your fifth glass, isn't it?"

"Is it?" *I'm not sure*. But I feel warm inside, and I feel comforted by that warmth in my belly, the fuzziness in my head. "Last one, I promise."

"I'm not the whiskey police."

"Well, thank God for that because I'd be in the jail on Main Street by now. Did I say too much? Because I said a lot, and I don't want to know any of this stuff about you and the pig farmer's daughter."

"If I hadn't asked, would you have kept this inside and, what—let whatever was going to happen between us happen?"

"Are *you* angry?"

"Yes, but not with you. I'm concerned. Worried—about you. Disappointed for you." He reaches to the back of his neck and gives it a squeeze.

"Yes." He asks *what* with his eyes. "Yes, I would have kept this inside my head and let whatever was going to happen between us happen. Because I've had the best day with you—well, up until about forty-five minutes ago. I felt like me again, and I haven't been this happy to be with anyone else in over a year, not even Jenny, but except maybe for Brianna, but in a totally different kind of way. You feel like... you feel like home."

"So do you, Mandy. I want to enjoy the time we have together before school starts, but I don't want to be another guy who hurts you. I can't be that guy."

"Do you think I'm damaged goods?"

"Fuck no," he clips. "I think some asshole took advantage of a young, lonely, drunk girl, and then I think that same asshole abused you with words and tried to tie your precious head in knots. And I hate that for you. I hate it so fucking much, and I don't know how to help you except to say that you deserved so much better than that."

There's the anger and it's rightfully directed at Curt.

With clarity that only comes from too much whiskey I share, "I know how you can help me."

"How?"

"Take me to your bed and hold me like you used to. I need you to hold me."

He doesn't hesitate. He stands and extends his hand. I take it and leave my glass on the table outside with the whiskey bottle. In his room, I strip down to my underwear. He follows my lead and does the same, and we crawl under the covers. Our bodies know what to do—they conjoin. Skin touches skin, legs entangle, and his arms wrap around me. I breathe in all that is him—not just *Essence of Braden*, but his kindness, warmth, and strength. *I love him.*

EIGHTEEN

In the morning, way too early, the house phones rings. I lose the warmth of Braden's body when he gets up to answer with a muffled, "Hello?" Pause. "Yes, Mrs. Harrington, she's here." Pause. "Just a moment, please."

"Uh.... Fuck," I mutter into the pillow as he nudges me with the handset. "Hi, Mom."

"Is this what we do now? We spend the night at a boy's house?"

I don't like her tone—at all, so I answer in kind, "I don't know what *we* do, Mom, but *I* spent the night at Braden's house." I sit up in bed and adjust the sheet around my upper body. I look up at Braden because he's hot in his boxers and semi-hard, but his eyes display concern.

"We have rules in this house, and your father—"

"*My father* did not mention a curfew or that he expected a call to extend a nonexistent curfew, so there is no curfew, but I apologize if you were worried. I should have called, but I fell asleep."

"*I apologize if you were worried*," she echoes. "This is just lovely, Amanda. I have an illegitimate grandson with one daughter and another gallivanting all over Pine Ridge with intentions to give me another one."

"First of all, Jonathan," my nephew, who I swear has a halo over his head, "is the real deal. I've seen pictures and everything, heard him screaming over the phone, so he's pretty legit." I hear her sharp intake of breath and continue. "Second of all, there was no *gallivanting*, did you say?" I know exactly what she said; this rhetorical question was added for dramatic effect. "No *gallivanting* all over Pine Ridge, unless you count dinner at Pizza Stop, which I do not. Going to Pizza Stop is not *gallivanting*." I wink at Braden. He shakes his head in disbelief.

"Third—or is it thirdly—like firstly, secondly, thirdly... Never mind." Braden stifles his laughter. "Third—or thirdly, I can assure you that Braden did not knock me up last night. Right, Braden?" I address the question directly to him. His eyes are huge and he might be turning a little green. "No chance we created life, right? Or did you do something weird to me when I was sleeping?" I don't expect an answer as it was also rhetorical. "No? Yeah, no, Mom, there was absolutely no knocking up of your other daughter last night—or this morning, so you're in the clear."

"You still live under my roof and the same rules apply."

What a predictable *Mom* thing to say. "Thanks for the reminder about still living under your roof. Now I know where to find my clean clothes and flip flop collection." Braden's concern might be for my safety, or perhaps he's picturing the size of my father and worrying about himself. "As for the same rules, I don't know what you mean. I never had many of those."

"Amanda, you need to come home right now," she commands.

"Yeah..." I laugh at her like a little snot. "No. I'm going back to bed. I'll be home later for a change of clothes."

She pulls out the big guns with the use of my full name, "Amanda Grace Harrington—"

"Did you just Amanda Grace me, Mother. Really? It's too early to be Amanda Graced. I haven't had any coffee yet."

"Come home right now." Her tone is elevated yet firm, and I've heard that tone hundreds of times before, albeit usually reserved for Brianna. She's struggling for control. Poor Mom. I mean, why struggle for control over a daughter she sent 5,457 miles away a little over a year ago?

"Technically, and I enjoy the opportunity to make use of a solid technicality, I'm an adult of legal age and *consent*. I realize that I live under your roof and you pay my bills, but that does not give you the right to control my life. You sent me off into the world—you know, down a fork in the road—and there's no coming back." I will myself to soften my tone, "I'm sorry that I worried you. I'll be home later today."

She releases a long sigh, I hear sniffling. Great, I made Mom cry—a result often only pulled off by Brianna. "You can take this up with your father. I-I-I don't know what to do with you," she says before hanging up on me.

I put the handset down beside me and sigh. "Will you make me some coffee, please? A heavy splash of milk and two sugars. But if your parents have any Baileys, just skip the milk and sugar, and make me a half and half."

He continues to stare at me with those worried eyes. "Grace? How come I don't know that? Harrington comma Amanda G.," he mutters. "Of course, it's Grace. How many decent names start with G?"

I smile. "Not many. Bon Jovi has a *thing* for *Gina*, but that's not a pretty name, and it definitely doesn't go with Amanda. Coffee, please?"

"Yeah... Are you all right?"

"Fine," I assure with a half-shrug. I drop the sheet and climb naked except for my panties from his bed in the light of a new day. I don't make an effort to cover myself. He doesn't make an effort to avert his eyes. I head toward his bathroom. "When you're finished making coffee, you can come meet me in the shower if you want."

The startled expression on his face makes me laugh.

* * *

I locate a new toothbrush and fresh towels in the linen closet. I start the shower and brush my teeth while the water warms up. I plop the toothbrush in the holder next to his, strip off my underwear, and take refuge under the hot stream of water.

"I have your coffee," he eventually calls from the other side of the shower curtain.

"I have your soap," I reply. "Are you going to let me use it on you?"

He peeks inside the shower curtain catching me shaving my legs with his Bic razor. "You're going to dull the blade."

"I'm a *naked* woman in your shower. Would you rather bitch about a dull razor blade or come join me?"

"Oh, I'm definitely joining you."

I take the lead and wash his body with a bar of Irish Spring and my hands. *Has the pig farmer's daughter ever cleaned his body in a shower?* I push that thought aside and focus on his mouth—the taste of coffee, the familiar tenderness of sharing kisses with Braden.

He was a perfect gentleman last night in bed. He held me, stroked my hair and skin, kissed my face softly without taking it further, and whispered sweet things into my ear until I fell asleep. I slept soundly until the phone rang.

Our *situation* in the shower starts to get very hot. Under the water, our mouths are one, and over slick soapy skin, our hands wander. Mine eventually wander to his dick because it's so hard, it must be killing him. I take his circumcised length in my hands and I bring him *almost* to the point of no return with my soapy hand before I pull back. He opens his eyes, mouth agape, and asks me *what the fuck* without uttering a word.

I remove the showerhead and rinse the soap from his body while I kiss him with everything I feel. Then I sit on the edge of the tub, and I take him in my mouth. Braden is perfect —hard and smooth, just the right size and shape. I want to taste him.

He was already on the brink, and I quickly bring him over the edge, ignoring his warning that he's going to come. I intensify the motions and when he comes in my mouth, I swallow. I hold him in my mouth for a few seconds and lightly tease him with my tongue, but I know better than to give further stimulation. With Curt, this act felt like a performance, but for Braden it is an act of reverence—a gift from me to him.

When I let him go and look up at him, I offer him an unapologetic smile.

"Jesus, Mandy." He grips my hand and helps me to my feet where I'm wrapped in his wet warm arms and given a beautiful kiss.

"I hope Jesus wasn't watching," I chide as his hands wander south. I cause a fumble on the field and grab his wrist lightly to redirect his attention. I have other things on my mind. "Coffee?" I ask.

"On the bathroom counter," he responds in a shaky voice.

"Thank you."

"No, Mandy. Thank *you*."

***

He finds me on the front porch. It faces east and is currently the sunny and warm side of the house. I'm on my second cup of Irish coffee. He left the Bailey's next to the coffee maker. My face is warm from the sun, and my insides are warm from Irish whiskey on an empty stomach. I'm wearing the same thing as yesterday, but I have sunglasses on and I helped myself to fresh t-shirt. This one is heather gray and not Banana Republic. It reads "IOWA" across the front in plain black block lettering. While it's clean, I think, it smells faintly of laundry detergent and Polo.

He ruffles my almost dry hair and sits in the chair next to mine, holding a can of Dr. Pepper. He also shakes his head while he looks at me, squinting into the sun.

"Why are you shaking your head so much around me?" I ask. *And there, he does it again. Why does he do that?*

"I'm trying to... Fuck, Mandy, that was... Jesus..." He trails off and *shakes* his head *again*.

"Good for you? The best shower blowjob in your entire life?" I offer suggestions.

Again with the head shaking, but his smile is from ear to ear. "That was good for me. And it was the best and only blowjob of my entire life—in or out of a shower."

"At least I get to be the *first* at something with you." My tone is light and I'm grinning, but either he takes it the wrong way or he's still worried about me.

"You didn't have to do that. I mean, we don't have to, um..."

"I want to. Don't you?"

"Um... I'm a guy. Hell, yeah, I want to, but I don't want you to feel like because you've done certain things, that you have to do them with me. Do you understand? Because I told you last night, I don't want to hurt you."

"Braden, your body, *god*, the taste of you—you are delicious. You're amazing."

His face flames. "Jesus, Mandy..."

"What? Don't you want me, or do you find the thought of sexual relations with me concerning? Disconcerting? God, it feels so good to use my native language again—anytime I want. It's amazing." I pause and follow up, "Concerning, disconcerting, or something else?"

"Both. And other things I can't put into words."

"Tsk, tsk. Lack of words could be a major problem for a writer,"

I tease.

"Yeah, well, I have a case of writers' block right now," he teases back. But his tone is more serious when he says, "I find this intriguing. Can we leave it at that?"

"For now." I wink.

"Thank God."

"Good talk." I stand. "Be right back. I need to use the restroom and grab a refill."

He meets me in the kitchen, watching me mix my half and half. "Isn't that a little strong for this time of day?" he asks.

"Are you the whiskey police today?"

"No."

"Good. It's probably a little much for this time of day, but it is five o'clock somewhere," I jest and look at the clock on the range. "In fact it's a little after five o'clock in Bielefeld right now, and I might still have jetlag so I'm actually right on schedule for whiskey. But," I turn to him, "you should probably cut me off—and feed me—after this. Or you can take me home to fight with my mom in person. I don't think I should get behind the wheel for a while."

"How often did you drink over there? Was it a regular thing?"

"I guess. My friends drank 'round the clock. Lars and I, well, that was how we first bonded, so that's what we did together late at night." I read what I believe to be accusation or a heavy dose of worry on his face. "You told me to let loose." I shrug a shoulder. "I did. And as I told you last Christmas, you were right—turns out any moron can lift a glass to her mouth."

"Lars is the host brother, right?" He's leaning back against the kitchen island, still watching me. Maybe he's trying to read between my lines of bullshit.

"Yup."

"You guys get close?"

"Not in any way that you might be thinking. We became friends, but it was slow moving because he's German, and Germans don't exactly pass out warm and fuzzy feelings like Tic Tacs, you know. You probably don't know." I continue to sip my coffee. "How could you know? You weren't forced to endure it."

"How about we talk about it over breakfast?"

* * *

The Pine Ridge Café on the main highway makes a killer *American* breakfast and has huge red plastic cups for Diet Pepsi and shit-tons of ice with free refills. I ask Braden to drive Cherry because I've had three Irish coffees and his gift is in the extended cab. I want to share it with him over breakfast. We're on opposite sides of the cushy vinyl booth. We've placed our orders. I have my Diet Pepsi, he has Dr. Pepper, and all is right with the world.

"So..." I reach for the plastic bag on the seat next to me. "I'd like to present you with a memento from my most momentous experience during the last year of my life. Sadly, it is not my cherry."

"I'm sure I'll still love it. Probably not as much as your cherry, but..."

"First—or is it firstly? I really need to find that out... I'm sure Mom knows. Anyway..." I pull out the heavy and awkwardly wrapped—because of the shape—gift. It's about the size of an AP Biology text book. I slide it over and explain, "This is a very important piece of *history*."

He unwraps, inspects carefully, and asks me with a hopeful look in his eyes, "Is this a piece of the Wall?"

"Yes." I'm thrilled to see a huge smile spread across his face.

"No shit?"

"Not shit. It's the Wall, Braden. And I liberated this piece with my very own hands. Okay, Marcus helped and he had to use a crowbar. I went to Berlin, obviously, in April, and by then the Wall was pretty well decimated. I mean, there were still sections intact, but the Wall itself was nothing like how I first saw it in September—imposing and enormous and divisive. By April we could clearly see from the West to the East. We could cross the border anywhere we wanted, just run back and forth, and we did." I laugh at the memory even though stupid Curt was there with us. "Marcus was like a kid on a playground. We managed to get this huge chunk free, and my host father helped me make smaller pieces out of it when I got back to Bielefeld. My piece is a match to yours. If we ever put them together, the edges and everything will line up and form an even bigger piece of history."

"What an amazing gift. Thank you."

"You obviously understand that we have pieces of history that fit together. And I think it is a perfect metaphor—a symbol—of our friendship. Even though we're going off to separate places again soon, when we come back together, I hope that we will always fit."

He reaches for my hand across the table, squeezes it, and then uses both of his hands to cradle mine and play with my fingers. "Thank you for the gift and the sentiment. So sweet."

"Right?" And, really, it shouldn't matter to him that Jenny was equally touched when I gave her the formerly conjoined piece of the Wall and used the exact same metaphor. And it shouldn't matter that I hope Tanner is equally touched when I give him his section when I see him in Tucson in a few weeks. I always want to fit back together with each of them, and no single bond makes another any less meaningful.

"This is so special—so, so special—and I will treasure it."

"Good. I'm glad you're so, so moved by it." I smile at him.

It is during this tender moment that we are rudely interrupted. French toast would not be a rude interruption. Becky, however... "Well, hello there." Her eyes note our hand play. "I didn't expect you back in town so soon, Braden."

"I told you I was coming back a little early to spend time with Mandy before school."

"Right." She cocks her head to one side. "I guess time is just flying by this summer. Are Nick and Bonnie home as well?" Her use of Coach and Mrs. McLaughlin's first names is meant as a subtle reminder that she is practically *family*.

"No. They'll be home in about two weeks."

"I had such a great time at the lake house this summer. Nice to have some quality time with you." I thought Braden said that Becky is more humble. I see no signs of said humbled nature anywhere. Her tone is overly sweet and antagonistic at the same time.

"I'm glad you guys could make it up," he replies. He's polite, friendly even, but why shouldn't he be that way with Becky. She's his friend, after all.

Without invitation, she slides into the booth next to Braden, of course. He's forced to scoot over and make room, and in the process of the scooting, I lose his hands on mine. “I can only stay a few minutes,” she says regretfully. “I’m here with Trina. You remember Trina, right?”

She’s addressing Braden but I answer, “Of course we remember Trina. Who could forget Trina after just one year? Not me—I didn’t forget Trina. Braden, did you forget Trina?”

“No.” He smiles at me, and, thankfully, reaches for my hand again. I’m wrought with tension, sitting bolt upright on the edge of my seat, and I’m fighting the urge to roll my eyes or say anything unpleasant. “I did not forget Trina. If we head out before you, we’ll stop by and say hello.”

“Long time, no see, Mandy.” Her smile is like syrup, and her usage of Braden’s nickname for me doesn’t go over my head.

“Hi, Becky. It’s nice to see you.” That is totally a lie, and not a very creative one at that. When my urge to be nasty is somewhat under control, I follow up with “And, please, don’t call me Mandy.”

Her face turns just a smidge pink, but she’s not deterred. That Becky, she’s a smart one. She turns her attention to Braden’s piece of the Wall. “What’s this?” she asks, picking it up for closer inspection. I want to rip it from her hands.

“It’s a piece of the Berlin Wall,” he explains. “Mandy and Brianna’s boyfriend set this piece free with—what was that you said—with your own hands and a crowbar?”

“That is indeed what I said, and that is indeed how it happened.” I grin at him and squeeze his hand.

“That’s a nice piece of history to have. I’d just love to hear about Germany, Amanda. Maybe we can do lunch—or breakfast—before I head back to New Haven.”

"Sure. You know where to find me. Just give me a call." My voice is calm and cool. I hope she doesn't call.

"Oh, it looks like Braden also brought you a present. Nice t-shirt." She gives a nod to Iowa.

"Oh, this? I just grabbed it from Braden's suitcase this morning so I'd have something clean to wear." And, hell yes, I want her to read *everything* into that. I smile at Braden. "It's mine now, by the way. And you really should unpack—you know, scorpions and all. You don't want them making babies in your suitcase."

He can't contain a burst of laughter. He knows that I'm toying with Becky. "Sure, Mandy. The sweatshirt I sent to you will be too warm for Tucson most of the year anyway."

"Well, it kept me cozy in Germany, so thank you." I hold his eyes and smile, and I can tell from the way his eyes dance with mine that, yes, he likes this game.

"I can't wait to hear about your year, but I better get back to Trina. Oh, Amanda, Trina decided to transfer from NAU, so she'll be at Arizona, too. With you and *Tanner*." Bitch.

"That's great to hear. Thanks for the heads up. I'll be sure to look for her."

Thank God for Trina and the waitress who arrives with our breakfast and offers to refill our red plastic cups. Mine is empty except for a shit-ton of ice.

On our way out we stop by to say hi to Trina, and—joy and happiness—she's about to live one floor above me. We promise to connect on campus in a few weeks if we don't see each other around town sooner. While I certainly hadn't forgotten Trina since I've known her since kindergarten, our friendly exchange reminds me how much I liked her way more than Becky.

NINETEEN

BACK AT BRADEN'S HOUSE, WE take to his bed, fully clothed, and curl up to talk some more. I have to go home and deal with my parents at some point, but I'd rather stay in these easy moments forever. Although, right now it's not exactly easy because Braden is in the mood to psychoanalyze everything that comes out of my mouth. He keeps asking me questions about my *feelings* over the Curt *situation*.

"Really, Braden, it's just over. I'll never see the guy again, so what's the point of digging deep on this topic? And maybe *you* should consider changing *your* major to Psychology," I joke. "Because all these questions are exhausting."

"It could be that you were right about something a few years ago."

"Do tell. I love it when I'm right."

"I think we should set some ground rules—for old time's sake."

My tone is dry. "Shall I fetch paper and pen?"

He laughs. "Only if it gets complicated."

"We just have to keep things in proper perspective, and you're pretty good at that already."

"Meaning?"

"My feelings for you are the same. I want this time together with you. It's like recharging the batteries in my heart. And so we have to look at our *situation* the same way that we did before, right?"

"So Option C is still off the table?"

He's laughing, but I'm not. I'm completely serious when I say, "Let's not be hasty. Option C is a very viable option."

He groans and rolls away from me onto his back. "I can't believe I'm going to say this, but I disagree with you. My dick says hell yes, but my conscience says no fucking way. That guy crushed you, and you fell apart on me last night. I get that. We both have feelings for each other that haven't gone away with time apart, but we're saying goodbye again in three weeks."

"Stupid Iowa."

"Yeah... stupid Wildcats."

"At least domestic phone calls are cheap, and we can see each other on vacations."

"Sure, but is that enough for you? Because it's not enough for me. I can't take you with me. I could transfer to Arizona, but I feel like I'd be chasing after you and it's too soon to make a decision like that. It's like prom. I don't want you to miss out on anything because of me."

"Yeah, prom worked out really great for you," I remind him

unnecessarily.

"You're going to be with Rawlings. It's inevitable."

I'm caught completely off guard by this declaration. "What are you talking about?"

"He's in love with you, Mandy. He does a good job trying to cover it up with you, but he's loved you for years."

"Um... I think he proved otherwise when he moved in with my best friend."

"He's not living with your best friend anymore. He's living in the same dorm as you, and your parents think he shits sunshine. You downplay it for me, but you have feelings for the guy, too."

"As a brother—"

"That's bullshit. You proved that on prom night, and *it didn't suck*, remember?"

"God, you remember *everything*. Are we going to waste time arguing about this?"

"I'm not arguing. I'm telling you what's going to happen. It might be a fling, it might be way more, but something is going to happen because he's going to make a move on you. And I don't expect you're going to sit in your dorm room and pine away for me when you have other options."

"You have *the pig farmer's daughter*," I'm getting fired up.

He shrugs. "I have options, too. We're young, Mandy." He rolls back to face me again. "We have three weeks, another *until we meet again*, and a whole lot of time in between. You just said that I'm good at keeping things in perspective so listen to me. After our time is up, I'm going to hand you over to Rawlings—again—and he's going to make his play. You're free to do what you want, and if you want to do Rawlings—*fuck, that was a poor choice of words*—if you want to explore what's there, at least I know he'll be good to you."

"You're insane."

"I'm not. It's the truth."

"You don't know that."

"I do because I heard the words right from his mouth. He told me that he was waiting for you to come home. He was sharing a bed with Jenny at the time, but said that his future is with you. I wanted to punch the guy." I see that because he's clenching his fists.

"Um..."

"Tell me, and be honest with yourself, Mandy, why did you pick Arizona over *fucking* Stanford? Who does that unless there's someone tying you to Arizona?"

"Yeah, I'm tied to Arizona. I didn't want to come back to something completely foreign after, you know, being somewhere completely foreign. I wanted to be close to home."

"You want to be close to that guy, like you have been since the day we met. Tight. Tied to each other. I can't compete with a guy who's in the perfect position to make his move on you."

I take a moment to consider what he's saying. I have to believe there was truth to Tanner's feelings when he saw Braden, but we haven't even seen each other yet. I have no idea how Tanner feels now. "You could if we were on the same campus."

He shakes his head. "No. I can't. If I gave up what I want to do for you, and I lost you to him anyway... Well, that just makes me a fucking idiot."

"But I choose you. I've always chosen you."

"I always want you to choose me. But it's not fair to ask that of you. Don't you understand?"

"Yes. You think I'm going to fall in love with Tanner and give birth to his six children." My tone is already bitter but I roll my eyes for effect.

"Maybe you will. Maybe you won't. This semester, I got into a lot of courses I want to take. I like Iowa. The only thing I don't like is that we're not together."

"You didn't seem to care about that when you fucked *the pig farmer's daughter*."

"This has nothing to do with *Jessica*. If it did, I wouldn't be in my bed with you right now."

"You'd be busy dumping slop into pig troughs..."

His eyes flash with anger. "I'd be committed to someone else, and we wouldn't be having the same fucking conversation we had to have a year ago."

"Fine." I wave the white flag and soften my voice. "What do you suggest we do over the next three weeks to avoid complications and hurt feelings and me slinging insults about the girl you fucked? If we can't be in the present moment together, Braden, and put all the other stuff aside, we have nothing right now. We'll point fingers and argue." I shudder. "And I *refuse* to do that with you. I can't. It would break my heart, but I'd rather walk away right now. I'd rather have only good memories to hold onto than use our time together to destroy them."

"That's why we need ground rules, Mandy. And one of those is no sex."

"*What*?"

"That's how much I love you."

"You *love* me?"

"Of course *I love you*. I *adore* you. I *respect* you. I might lose you in the end, and, for my sake and yours, I can't—this sucks—I won't go all in. That's my ground rule."

"Wait... After all this time, *this* is how you tell me that you love me? You just slide it right in there between ground rules?"

"Saying it out loud is scary, Mandy. It makes it real."

"Gee, Braden, I feel like we should kiss or something right now... At least make it special."

He smiles and leans in for a kiss. "I love you, Mandy," he whispers.

I whisper, "I love you back, Braden." I've waited a long time to hear those words from him... I never imagined I would hear them quite like this, but better than Braden telling me how he feels is finally being able to release my sweetest truth to him. I want so much more than a kiss. I take what I want. I take his mouth and wrap myself around him. We lose ourselves in each other, and we lose most of our clothing in the process.

In typical Amanda and Braden fashion, we get all the way down to our freaking underwear with Braden on top of me. I want him so much. I want to be with someone who loves me.

"Braden, please," I grind my hips up into him.

He throws the fucking flag, or rather, the *no fucking* flag. "No, Mandy. No." He rolls off of me to his back.

I'm wrecked. "Why? God, I want you, Braden." I want him so

much that stupid tears fill my eyes. "I want to be with you."

His hands cover his face and he releases a frustrated groan. "Ground rules. I'm serious. I can't get this tied to you." He drops his hands and looks up at me. "It wouldn't be just a fuck. It would be making promises that we're not in a position to keep."

"I can't believe this," I hiss. "You sound like such a girl right now."

"I don't fucking care. I'm protecting myself—and you."

"So this is binding?"

"One hundred percent."

"I don't understand."

"Tell me something... How do you feel knowing that asshole took your virginity and treated you like shit? Did having sex with that fucking piece of shit make you feel better or worse about the relationship?"

"Worse," I grumble. "But this isn't the same thing."

"No, it's not the same. It means a hell of a lot more. If we go all in and this ends—how's that going to make us feel? I won't be another guy who takes advantage, and I know that you haven't dealt with everything inside of your head. I know you, and all that shit with Curt is still fresh and wrapped up tight."

I release a heavy sigh and reach for a throw blanket to cover myself. "But you still want to fool around?"

"Hell, yes," he smiles. "All the fucking time. We can finish right now if you want."

"Wait..."

He mocks, "You breaking out some sub-bullets, Mandy?"

"How are we going to stop?"

"It's my ground rule. I'll stop."

"I'm going to be so sexually frustrated, I'll turn into a raging lunatic. Like right now, I ache for you. Seriously, I hurt down there. It must be like the female version of blue balls."

He breaks out into laughter and moves his body back to mine. He kisses me, tosses the blanket to the side, and slides his hand into my underwear. "I'll take care of you, love. There are shit-tons of ways to take care of you that we haven't even tried yet."

He called me *love*. My legs part, making room for his fingers to move inside of me while his mouth starts to roam my body. Pushing aside all thoughts of how he learned these new ways to take care of me, I concentrate on Braden. He called me *love* because he loves me.

* * *

My father is, thankfully, already home sitting in the front sun room with a sleeping cat in his lap and a drink on the side table. The cat is a new addition. His name is Sylvester, and he's fat, lazy, and demanding. I can hear Mom puttering around in the loft, likely working on another prayer quilt for her church to donate to someone in distress.

"Hi, Dad," I say charmingly, maturely as I enter the sun room.

"The prodigal daughter returns."

I shake my head and tease, "Daddy, everyone knows it was a prodigal son, but don't worry, I'm sure Tanner will stop by and visit you again one day." I stop and take a seat next to his crossed ankles that are resting on the matching ottoman of his winged back chair.

"What's new?" I ask and reach for his glass. I take a sip off the top and he narrows his eyes. "What?" I shrug. "It was totally allowable with my other family."

He smirks, "Not cute."

"Your expression tells me otherwise."

"What can I say, I have a weakness for brown-eyed girls."

"Poor Brianna."

"Indeed," he responds. "I never had to deal with this crap from Brianna."

"That's because she stopped coming home and then used her Ivy League degree to get herself knocked up. But not this girl—nope, I'm your favorite."

He whispers, "You are, but don't tell your sister." I'm sure he tells her the same thing from time to time, but I know where his loyalties lie. When they're old and living out their final days, I will be the dutiful daughter living on the same continent who caters to their every need. Or I'll hire someone to do that. We'll see how this conversation goes first.

I spend time in my room with my journal, but when I hear noises of dinner preparation, I head into the kitchen to make myself useful. Steaks and sliced rosemary red potatoes on the grill. Mom says the potatoes need a head start so I help slice them and place them on a doubled layer of foil. Per her instructions, I'm heavy handed with the olive oil and rosemary, light with the salt and pepper, and then I pass my fine work over to Dad to put on the grill. Mom and I work together chopping and dicing vegetables for her signature salad while we ignore this morning's confrontation in favor of chattering about things that I might still need for my dorm. Pine Ridge isn't known for fine shopping, and I'm unsure about the size and layout of my room, much less what my mysterious roommate will already have, and I decide to wait to purchase most accoutrements once I'm down there.

"I do need a computer of some kind, Mom—like for papers and stuff. Do you think we can make a trip down to Phoenix with Dad?"

"Sure," she replies. "Your father took a computer course while you were gone."

"Oh?"

"He says that this World Wide Web is going to change everything, including his entire business model."

I don't know much about the World Wide Web, yet. I'm familiar with the concept, but I haven't seen any of it firsthand. There was a sheet in my residence hall paperwork that mentioned the option to pay for two phone lines to support internet accessibility from dorm rooms with more than one roommate and also free access to computers and the World Wide Web in the library. But who wants to spend all that time in the library? My dorm is situated on the far northwest corner of campus, and the library looks to be a bit of a hike based on the map I have. It's a hike that I don't want to make in scorching temperatures if I don't have to.

"Apparently, he thinks that buyers will use the World Wide Web to look at listings."

"Huh, like instead of looking in the paper or those flyers?"

"You'll have to ask him about that. I don't understand the details, but he's really excited about it and eventually wants his agents to start taking similar classes. You know your dad, always trying to anticipate the future, keep up with the times."

"Well, he wouldn't want to accidently fork right when he should have forked left." I laugh good-naturedly.

She joins me, "God forbid, because there's no going back."

Over a delicious meal, my parents put me out of my misery. With few words and stipulations, they give me my Free Will. There is no curfew or restrictions except for those that are illegal, of course. And as long as I check in so they know I'm safe and I make an effort to join them for dinner most evenings, I have free reign.

As we talk, I marvel at this civilized discussion. I was ready to put up a fight, but now we're sitting here around the family table chatting away while eating a delicious meal. I feel conflicted because while I intend to take full advantage of my Free Will, I wonder if I owe them more than a little peace of mind and family dinners.

After dinner, I'm on kitchen detail with Dad. As we load the dishwasher and wash and dry the larger pieces of tableware, I tell him, "I'm going back to Braden's house tonight. I'll be back sometime tomorrow during the day."

He quirks an eyebrow and asks, "How does Coach feel about sleepovers?"

"Coach isn't home. They're still in Michigan."

Dad sucks in a deep breath, his brown eyes storm, and his palm lands with a thump on the counter. "It's just the two of you in that house?"

"Free Will," I remind gently. My voice is even softer when I tell him, "I don't want to lie to you."

He nods, but he's so far from resigned. His eyes are dark

and narrowed, his huge hand still stuck to the counter where he slammed it down.

"I also don't feel like all of this is necessarily your business... anymore... or at all," I draw in my own deep breath and meet his eyes. "So what do we do here?"

My father is silent and clearly struggling to find an answer to my question. Perhaps, he has no idea either. I suggest, "Maybe that question doesn't require an answer. I just don't want to lie to you and Mom. That's not how we do things. So maybe it's better if you don't ask me so many questions—especially if you think that you're not going to like the answer."

"Okay. I won't ask why you're wearing Braden's t-shirt. I'm not going to like the answer."

* * *

Braden smiles as I walk through the slider with a small duffle bag over my shoulder. "How was dinner?"

"Fine."

"What's in the bag?"

"Girl stuff. Change of clothes, a pink razor, conditioner that smells like sugar cookies, and *maybeeeeeee...*" I draw this word out for dramatic effect, "a gigantic box of extra-large condoms."

He turns a little red but bursts out in laughter as he crosses the room, gives me a quick squeeze, a sweet kiss. "Are you going to test my resolve for the next three weeks?"

"Have we met? It's like you don't know me at all. Of course I'm going to test your resolve," I tease. "But, no, Braden. There are no condoms in this bag because your no means no. However, you are more than welcome to amend that ground rule at any time."

"Dinner," he repeats, "was just *fine*?"

"Steak, red potatoes, salad. It was actually more than fine." I drop my bag on the floor and move to flop down on the couch. "You should've been there. It was quite delicious. Some other time."

"Am I welcome for dinner?"

"The jury is probably still out on that one, but I'll let you know when I have a verdict."

"Great," he mutters. "Your dad is big enough to actually kill me with his bare hands. I'm going to steer clear until you're confident that won't happen." This is a wise decision. "Food aside." He makes himself comfortable next to me. "I'm not asking about the food. How are things with you and your parents after that scene with your mom this morning?"

"Was that just today? It feels like a lifetime ago." I smile. "Fine. Free Will prevailed." I wave one hand in a mock cheer, "Yay, Free Will. I didn't even have to fight for it. They surrendered of their own Free Will."

"That's awesome. Maybe I can use some of my Free Will on you?" He wants to play.

"Does it involve your mouth and hands?" I jump from my seat to straddle his lap, wrapping my arms around his neck, tipping my face down so my lips can capture his. When I pull away, I state, "Because I really love it when your mouth and hands are involved, but it's your Free Will, so I guess you get to exercise it as you see fit."

He flips me onto my back and covers my body with his delicious hard one. He abundantly deploys his mouth and hands until we're breathing hard and covered in sweat but not much else. It escalated fast, and Braden's brought me to a luscious orgasm with his hand in my panties. I wonder if I'm going to leave stain on the leather because I'm soaking wet.

"Let's talk about what we're doing tonight," he says.

"Well, I just came all over your parents' couch, and I'm going to have to take a shower and put on clean underwear because these are soaked." I know what I'm doing. I don't want to be serious right now. I want this to be fun, playful, and my banter works. "Not that I'm complaining because that felt awesome."

He kisses my smart mouth and rolls us so I'm on my side with my back against the sofa and he's facing me. Our limbs snake around each other and we're quiet for several beats before he speaks. "I have a question for you."

"Why do we have to talk so much, Braden?"

"I was going to ask if you want to go to Blockbuster and rent a couple of movies. Nothing by John Hughes, though."

"That's a relief because I'm all talked out about my *stupid feelings*. Movies sound great, but let's take a shower first."

We do and it's warm and comforting, and I love the feeling of slick, soapy skin on skin. I never want to shower without him. But he steps out before I do so I can finish rinsing the conditioner from my hair. I call out to him from behind the curtain, "Are you sure you don't want to watch *Sixteen Candles* again?"

TWENTY

THIS IS HOW WE ARE for the next two weeks. We're together in our cocoon on his hill—talking, laughing, snuggling, messing around—and growing closer, but not too close. In bed, on the couch, in the shower, on the outdoor lounger, we do everything but go all the way. We improve our stylistic technique, and our enthusiasm never diminishes. It's sweet and beautiful and physically satisfying. Okay, sometimes it's a little rough and tumble, but it's most definitely satisfying and it's ours alone. We fall asleep together, we wake up together, he starts the coffee while I start the shower, and we fall into a magnificent albeit temporary routine. Each day, I return home in the early afternoon. I help prepare dinner and stay until my parents are ready for bed. Then I go back to Braden.

When his parents return from Michigan, we change up our routine and I start to wean myself. I still go to him each night, but I wake up early and take my coffee, but not my shower, at home. His parents know I'm there. Coach is an early riser and a jogger. He sees my truck in the driveway, but he doesn't say a word to me about what's going on. We still have the same easy conversations about the weather and school coming up.

Sometimes I show up during the day to hang out with Braden and chat with his folks, and other times I don't. He has things to do with his family or I do. I write in my journal, and I make and return phone calls—Tanner's and even Becky's—but I decline to meet her for lunch. I do meet Trina for lunch, though. We have an easy time talking, and we solidify plans for me to knock on her door and head off to lunch next Tuesday. I go for walks with my mom at the park, and I weed through my wardrobe and start to pare things down for dorm life. I make piles and start packing things up, stacking boxes in the corner of my room.

Wednesday before Move-in

I leave for Tucson on Sunday. Today my parents take me to Phoenix and we buy a computer and printer for my dorm room. Jenny meets us for lunch and my parents head back to Pine Ridge without me so I can spend the night at her apartment. Braden is coming down to pick me up tomorrow. He offered and said he has *some shit to do* in the Valley anyway, so he'll just do it on Thursday and drive me home.

Jenny lives in a dingy, old apartment complex in Central Phoenix. There's a pawn shop and bail bond business located conveniently on the other side of 19th Avenue, and the occasional gang shooting pretty much anywhere up or down 19th Avenue, but the rent on their two-bedroom unit is affordable when split three ways. I like her roommates well enough; we didn't exactly hang out together in high school. Heather and Janie loved a good bonfire party back in the day along with half of the defensive line, but now that I've had year of debauchery under my belt, the four of us have more in common. Besides, Jenny is like rubber cement—she can bond any group of people together with her easy-going nature. We lie out by the pool for a while, jumping into the 90-degree water to cool off—which sounds impossible, but it works. We chat animatedly, switching topics often, and laughter comes readily.

Heather and Janie head inside the apartment to refresh beverages and I ask for a shit-ton of ice, which sends Jenny off into a fit of giggles. As soon as they're out of earshot, she pounces. "Have you talked to Tanner lately?"

"I have," I say. "He's helping me move in to the dorm on Sunday."

"Did he say anything about me?"

"Not this time, hun. I think he might be all talked out with me on that subject."

She sighs, her expression pensive. "I loved him, you know."

"I know, Jenny." I feel my skin crawl a little bit. I want to support her, and, if he were any other guy, this conversation would be easy. "I hope that you guys can get past this and move on with your lives."

Her chuckle is laden with sarcasm. "Oh, that won't be a problem for Tanner. He has his *books* and the *gym* and his *stupid schedule* to keep him warm at night. I'm sure I don't even cross his mind anymore."

"I'm sure you do, Jenny." I try to keep my voice even and my tone supportive. "You'll always be the first girl he loved."

She snorts and replies, "Fuck you, Amanda."

I turn my head in surprise. "Excuse me?"

"He loved you first. He probably still loves you and can't wait to show you how much this weekend."

I'm shocked by her words. They are full of venom, but her expression is not. She has a tiny smile playing on her lips, and her brown eyes show signs of humor. I shake my head. "I don't think so, Jenny. I mean, yes, we love each other, but it's not anything like what you and he shared."

"Thank God because that love was *totally* fucked up."

"See, you guys can still agree on something," I try to joke.

"Ugh." She flops back on her lounger and adjusts her top. "He's changed, you know."

"People change."

"No—you should just know that he acts like he joined the Army. He has a stick shoved up his ass, and everything has to be done at a certain time, in a certain way, all on his terms. Including fucking—especially the fucking. Like getting fucked by a robot."

"Jenny," I interrupt. "I'd rather not talk about the fucking, all right?"

She gives me a sideway glance. "You want him."

My sigh is heavy and my response is thought out. "I want Braden, and I have to let him go in a few days—again. And there's still been no fucking with us, so... This is kind of a sore subject for me."

"Got it." She closes her eyes and relaxes under the sun. After a few beats, eyes still closed she says, "You'd be less of a bitch if you just mounted him and made it happen." I snap a towel at her as we both start laughing.

When Heather and Janie return, they bring huge plastic cups

filled with strawberry margarita mix—and tequila. Shit-tons of tequila. We stay out in the sun and the pool, and I go through several drinks before we decide to head inside and order Chinese take-out.

I'm wasted. I have to grab onto chairs and handrails to steady myself, words fall from my lips without a filter, and the rest of the evening brings more of the same until Jenny and I collapse the futon in the living room into a bed and lie down.

It's the first night I've slept without Braden next to me in over two weeks. I'm seriously drunk, and I miss him like someone cut off my right arm. I consider asking Jenny to spoon me and crack up inside my fuzzy head at the image. "Jen?" I say into the darkness.

"Hmmm?"

"I miss Braden."

"You'll see him tomorrow," she mumbles into the pillow.

"I miss him when we're not together."

"You'll be together tomorrow." Poor girl is ready to pass out, but I need a little psychoanalysis.

"I love him."

"Love sucks."

"Would it be crazy if I looked into Iowa?"

"Yes." Still with the mumbling.

"Why?"

"You look better with a tan. You belong here."

"What if I belong with him?" I ask.

"Then he should come to you. Trust me," she mumbles. "Never change up your plans to follow some guy." Her muffled chuckle is bitter. "See how that worked out for me?"

"What if Braden never comes for me?"

Jenny howls with laughter. "I thought you've already crossed that bridge... Ouch! Ah... oh... Laughing hurts. I need sleep."

"What if this is it, Jen? What if he doesn't ever want more?"

"Then there will be another guy. There is always another guy. Let one come to you, and if he looks good, fuck him stupid."

With that sage advice, I'm left spinning in my drunken head while Jenny drifts off to sleep.

I wake to a dry mouth and a major headache. My stomach is churning, and while I consider inducing vomit to purge the tequila, before I can even sit up in bed, Janie pops out into the kitchen/living area and suggests frozen waffles and eggs—she'll cook. The smell of coffee and food helps settle my stomach. I shelter in place and tell the tequila to fuck off.

"Hey, girl," Janie chirps. "Brought you a present." She places four burgundy coated pills in my hand and holds out a cup of flat water. In order to take it, I need to sit up, and I debate the merits of that decision.

"What are these?"

"Ibuprofen. Swallow those down and drink all the water. Go wash up. You have some, um, crusty drool on your face. And then we'll eat." I stare at her with one eye, still unwilling to commit to sitting up. "Trust me, Amanda. I'm a professional."

She's got me there, so I follow her lead.

Over breakfast, Janie serves up tequila sunrises—OJ, tequila, and grenadine syrup, I think. "What the hell?" I ask.

"Hair of the dog," Heather pipes up.

"What's hair of the dog?" The three of them laugh at me, all of them, in unison. "What?" I shrug. "I didn't start drinking until ten months ago, and if the Germans explained hair of the dog to me, it was in a language I couldn't understand. So what the hell is it?"

"It's a hangover remedy, genius," Jenny says. "A little more alcohol will help settle your stomach. I think there's actual science behind it. Whatever." She shrugs. "It helps, so drink up."

After breakfast, I'm nowhere near 100%. I take a shower, and we all take it easy watching TV and talking until there's a knock at the door in the early afternoon.

"Braden," Janie squeals when she opens the door. "Long time, no see. You look good enough to eat," she laughs.

I might have to kill her, but it occurs to me that she's right. Braden is a lot of things, and yummy, handsome, gorgeous—well, he is all of those things, too. I'm not the only girl in the world who sees that and wants him. *The pig farmer's daughter HAD him.* This agitates my hangover symptoms.

"Hi, you." He accepts her hug, and I realize that he didn't greet her by name so he probably has no idea if she's Janie or Heather—the interchangeable best friends and good time girls. *Take that, Janie. He doesn't even know your name.*

"Braden." Heather moves in for a quick hug. "Looking buff, sweetheart."

Ugh, these girls.

He laughs. "This apartment is good for my ego."

"Come by anytime you need a boost," Janie offers.

Another laugh before he asks, "You have Mandy somewhere in there?"

"Sure you aren't here for me?" Janie quips.

No, because he doesn't even know your name.

"Enough, ladies." Jenny hops off the futon to prevent further molestation. She steps in for a quick hug. "I have your girl right here." She leads him over to the futon. "I might have gotten her a little trashed last night." She uses her fingers to demonstrate the Drunk Scale. She downplays it.

Braden's eyes show worry. "You all right?"

I sit up, stretch, and feel like jumping for joy when his eyes move from my face to check out my boobs as I arch my back. "Yeah. Just, you know, learning my limits," I joke. "I still have a lot to learn, apparently."

He smiles and kisses me on the forehead. "Whiskey?

"I wish. Tequila. Stupid tequila."

"Can we get moving or are you too sick?"

"I'm fine." Since he's sitting in my way, I rise to my knees and climb off the futon around him. "My stuff is mostly packed." I move around the room gathering my things and thanking the girls for getting me wasted. Janie continues to screw Braden's brains out with her eyes. She's dead to me now.

Jenny gives me a huge hug. "Come up from Tucson anytime. We can have girls' night and, God knows, I'm not hitting that town any time soon—if ever—so you need to come to me."

I hug her back. "I will—promise. I'll get settled and we'll make that happen as often as we can."

"Yay!" She releases me and smiles sweetly. "Tell Tanner that I said he should go fuck himself."

Braden doesn't bother to stifle laughter as I respond, "I think I'll skip that, Jen. I'm sure you understand why."

"Some friend you are," she grumbles. "Braden," she gives him another quick squeeze, "maybe I'll see you when you're home for Christmas."

"Sounds good, Jenny. I'd like that."

"If you can tear yourself away from Amanda, that is," she continues, and I'm not sure where she's going. "You've been *very* selfish with her time since you got home, and you and me, we're going to have to learn to *share* her if you want me to be nice to you." She pinches his cheek while he grins and shakes his head at her. "All right, kids, off you go."

Braden grabs my duffle bag, and we head out into the sweltering summer day. He left his car in Iowa, so he's driving his dad's black Ford F-150 extended cab. The McLaughlins are not a Chevy family. He's lucky it didn't get jacked during the fifteen minutes he left it parked in this crappy neighborhood. He loads my stuff in the extended cab and we climb in. I'm grateful for the air conditioning.

"Are you in condition to make a few stops before we head up the hill?"

"Sure. I have all day."

We head to Price Club where he buys some bulk items for his mom—paper plates, paper towels, toilet paper, and laundry detergent. He has me check each item off the list so we don't forget anything. We grab a light lunch from the concession area, load up the truck, and hit the road. "I need to stop by my old 'hood—it's nearby. Visit an old buddy. Cool?"

He points out his former old high school and the house they used to live in. It's a beautiful sprawling ranch on a huge city lot in the Arcadia section of Phoenix. He parks a few houses down the street in front of another impressive ranch.

"Who lives here?" I ask.

"Luke. He's kind of like my Jenny, only not as hot."

His depiction of their friendship appears to be quite accurate, however. The door swings open, and a mom figure throws her arms around Braden. She steps back to look him over and comments on his height, how he's filled out, and how handsome he is. We're in agreement on those finer points. He takes it good naturedly. As we enter the home and shut out the hot air, Luke, I presume, joins us in the entry way. They exchange a warm dude hug and a few insults.

"You must be Mandy from Pine Ridge." Luke turns his attention to me, and I'm surprised he's heard of me since I'd never heard Luke's name until one minute ago. We assess each other. Luke is a burly jock dude with tousled light brown hair and dark eyes—handsome and knows it.

"I am Mandy from Pine Ridge." I smile and shake his extended hand. "It's nice to meet you."

"Good to finally meet you, too."

We move into the family room, and Luke's mom asks us what we'd like to drink. Braden responds for both us. "Water—cold and flat, please." He winks at me.

Luke engages me in some get-to-know-you questions, and I discover that he's about to start his second year at Arizona. I ask if he's familiar with my dorm, Manzanita/Mohave. He knows the hall well because—he doesn't mind sharing—he got some hot pussy in good old Manzi/Mo.

Luke is helpful, though, and he draws out a quick schematic of a double room floorplan for me. "Good that she turned the lights on so you were able to see the floorplan," I droll while making a mental note to bring fewer clothes because, if his map is anywhere close to scale, the closets are small. We discuss classes, Greek versus non-Greek parties. Luke is Sigma Chi, whatever that means. He gives his number to me in case I 'need anything.' I don't know what I might need from Luke, but I tuck the slip of paper into my wallet anyway. Braden narrows his eyes and gives him a dirty look, but he has no claim to stake.

As the guys continue catching up and exchanging stories that all seem to start with "remember that one time," I sink into my recliner, pop up the footrest, and nurse my hangover while I consider the fact that Braden rarely speaks to me about his life and friends before Pine Ridge. Meeting Luke and listening to the guys interact with such comfort and familiarity, it unnerves me. Luke's a reminder of how much I don't know about Braden's life—especially when it isn't directly linked to mine. No matter how well I think I know him, there are significant parts of him and chunks of his life that have absolutely nothing to do with me.

These thoughts inevitably lead me down the dark road to the pig farmer's daughter. *Is she looking forward to school starting back up? I bet she can't wait to see Braden, and they'll celebrate their reunion with a hard and satisfying fuck because he had a long dry spell this summer. Maybe he pins her to the bed with one hand by her wrists, a move he loves to use on me to have unhindered access to my body with his free hand. Only with Jessica, he pins her to the bed with his hand and his dick. I hate her.*

"Hey." I'm startled when Braden shakes the footrest because I'm lost in these disturbing images.

"What?" I come back to the world and blink.

"I asked if you're ready to head up north."

"Sure."

Goodbyes are exchanged. Luke's mom gloms onto Braden for another hug and a motherly pat on his rear. Luke tells me to call him even if I don't need anything. "We'll get to know each other and swap stories about this sick fuck." He gestures to Braden.

"Sounds like a lengthy conversation," I return fire.

Luke finds this hilarious. Braden, not so much. *Whatever. Let him stand there glaring and shaking his head at me. Maybe he will go back to Iowa and picture his friend Luke pinning his friend Mandy to the bed.*

Shit... I'm losing myself to the pain of another *until we meet again*. Braden wrecked me without even trying. I can't handle this. *I feel too much, and nothing he shares with me, gives to me, says to me is enough. It will never be enough because I will always have to send him back to the pig farmer's daughter—back to a life that we can't share*. For all my big talk a few weeks ago about keeping things in perspective, I love him and I can't bear to let him go again. If I have to hear "We've Got Tonight" again, I might slit my own wrists. And fuck, I'd kill for a dark room, whiskey on ice, and a conversation with Lars—who had a proper, healthy, and not at all confusing place in my life.

TWENTY-ONE

We're both quiet as Braden navigates rush hour city traffic. As we pass through Fountain Hills, he asks if I need to stop before we turn onto the highway to Pine Ridge. "Food? Bathroom break?" There are no facilities except cacti and brush for the next 70 miles until we hit Pine Ridge.

I decline and he drives on through the last signs of civilization, pulling into the left lane to turn onto the highway.

"You're really quiet, Mandy." He breaks the silence several miles into the twists and turns of the road.

"Tired," I reply.

"Still hungover?" he asks.

"I don't think so, but Jenny and I stayed up really late last night in addition to all the tequila, so..."

"You're welcome to conk out on me. I won't be offended."

"I might take you up on that." I turn to rest my head against the window of his dad's truck. *Maybe his car is parked in the pig farmer's barn right now.* It's early evening, and the sun is starting to go down. The scenery may be breathtaking, but this can be a dangerous, even deadly, stretch of highway, especially as the sun keeps switching sides and obscuring the driver's vision from different angles. You have to make sure that you spend less time fighting with the sun visor and more time accepting the sun's glare in order to focus on the road.

I study the jagged red rocks studded with cacti of all shapes and sizes. I especially love the giant saguaros with their huge arms. They remind me of people of all shapes and sizes. Maybe they have weird conversations in the dark of night. But right now they're in quiet repose with enormous shadows drawn out by the setting sun. Braden turns on the stereo and fills the cab with my favorite lake music—the Eagles' Hotel California album.

It's before our generation and the closest thing to country Braden will entertain listening to. I relax into the window until the fourth track, *Wasted Time.* Fuck, if Glenn Frey and Don Henley didn't pen this song for me, I don't know who it's for. And as I stare out at the darkening desert landscape, I feel every single word burn down to the bottom of my heart. I let the lyrics eat through my heart until the contents bleed into my gut and turn my stomach sour filling my throat with a vile burn.

I know every twist and turn of this road. We're approaching a pull-out for trucks to test their brakes before the road makes a sharp descent into a canyon only to face a quick ascent a few miles later. "Pull over," I demand.

"What?"

"Pull over right now." My voice is loud with urgency. He glances over to see my hand clasped over my mouth. I fight to hang on as he slows quickly and navigates the truck off the pavement and onto the gravel. Before the truck comes to a complete stop, I'm already gagging on my vomit, clawing at the door, searching for the handle and panicking.

Braden jumps out and runs around the hood to throw open my door. I stumble out of the truck and land on my knees. Gravel meeting bare skin is not a good combination. After my initial vomit launch, Braden moves to my side and pulls my puke covered hair off my face. Vomit meeting gravel—also not a good combination. When it hits the ground, it bounces and splatters, and I know we're both getting hit with it. Still, he holds my hair and rubs my back while cars zoom by and I spill my guts on the desert floor until there's nothing left but a few dry heaves.

"Hey... you get it all out, Mandy?"

"Water," I choke out and look up at him. He helps me to my feet and leads me to the tailgate, which he drops so I can sit down. He grasps me by the shoulders and leans in to look at my puke coated face. Ugh, the smell... He needs to step back. "Water," I repeat.

He leaves me momentarily and I can hear the reprise of *Wasted Time* change over to *Victim of Love*. Stupid Eagles—because I'm that, too. He returns with a bottle of water. Handing it to me he gently warns, "It's flat but not cold and I'm fresh out of shit-tons of ice." Funny. I take the bottle and start to chug, but he pulls it back almost immediately. "Slow down or you'll get sick again. Slow sips," he softly but firmly orders. As if he doesn't trust me or feels the needs to demonstrate, he doesn't relinquish his hold on the water bottle until he dispenses several small sips to me.

He places the back of his hand on my forehead and cheeks. It's still blazing hot even with the waning sun and throwing up is a taxing exercise, so of course my skin is hot and I'm perspiring like I just ran a marathon. "Is this because of the drinking last night or something else?"

I shrug, but I'm certain it's combination of hangover, stress, and despair served with a chaser of *Wasted Time*. "I threw up all over you," I say followed by more tears.

"It's not that bad. But you're bleeding. Hold on." He disappears again. This time he cuts the engine and the music stops. *Thank God*. He returns with a gallon jug of water and a roll of paper towels from Price Club. A wise Arizonan always carries extra water when traveling in the desert heat. It doesn't matter if it sits in the car and boils in the sun, when you need it, water is water.

He dampens paper towels, and while I wipe my face and attempt to extract chunks of puke from my hair, he washes my bloody knees before cleaning up his own vomit-splattered lower extremities.

"God, I stink... My shirt..." I'm a complete train wreck as tears roll down my face. I know Tanner wasn't a Boy Scout, but maybe Braden was because he disappears again and comes back with a t-shirt from my overnight bag. I slept in his light blue lion tee last night.

"Good to see this is getting some use," he teases as I attempt a smile. He positions himself between me and the highway and says, "We're going to change this real quick and not get you arrested for indecent exposure. Quick, Mandy." He helps me pull off my disgusting shirt and quips while helping me into the lion shirt, "See, I'm not even slowing down to stare at those gorgeous tits."

Once clothed, I gift him with a dead in the eyes smile and say, "Thank you."

"Have a little more water, okay?" I do while he retrieves a few plastic grocery sacks from the extended cab. He wraps my tee in one and ties it tight, then he does the same with puke, blood, and water soaked paper towels. He hands me a piece of gum, looks me over again, and asks, "Do you think we can make it up the rest of the hill? I need to get you home."

I nod. He helps me slide off the tailgate onto shaky limbs. I'm drained. "You steady?" Another nod. He leads me around to the passenger side and jokes, "Don't look down. I won't let you step in anything." Once seated, he buckles me in and closes the door. I feel the thump of the tailgate lock back into place, before he climbs into the cab on the other side. The start of the engine brings the sweet relief of AC to my overheated skin.

It also fills the cab with the sound of the Eagles. "No music," I say.

"Sure." He quickly turns it off. "You okay if I get us back on the road?"

"I think so."

"Good. Oh wait..." He reaches behind him a digs out another grocery bag. He hands it to me. "In case we're not in a spot where I can pull over." That earns him another weak smile. He turns on the blinker and looks over his shoulder for traffic before easing the truck back onto the pavement. "I'll keep my speed down—make the turns less traumatic."

We drive on in silence until I break it by asking, "Braden, were you ever a Boy Scout?"

***

I open my eyes and see lights from the town and oncoming traffic. We are home. I shift and stretch in my seat. "How are you feeling, Mandy?"

My mouth is dry, my head is pounding, and my eyes burn. "Other than a headache and suffering from humiliation, I'll live—I think."

"Five minutes, you'll be home." He turns off the highway and down Main Street toward my house. He hasn't been there since he left me sitting on Cherry's tailgate over a year ago. He pulls up in front of the house, parks, and sets the emergency brake on the slope. "Stay put," he orders. He hops out, collects my things, and comes around to the passenger side to open my door. He makes me test my legs before he walks me up to the front door.

We can see my parents through the glass moving toward the door. Braden opens it and helps me inside. Dad takes in my disheveled appearance and bloody knees. His eyes thunder and land on Braden who is holding my stuff in one arm and has the other wrapped around my waist.

Braden slides my stuff to the floor but doesn't release his hold on me. "Mr. Harrington, Mrs. Harrington, very nice to see you again." Fun fact, Braden was indeed a Boy Scout during his formative years. This explains why he's very level-headed during a time of crisis and also incredibly polite to all adults.

"Hi, Braden. It's wonderful to see you again, too," my mom offers graciously while Dad glares.

"Mandy got sick on the way up. We had to pull over and do a

little clean up." He looks to Mom, who is not glaring at him. "We actually had to do a lot of cleaning up. She needs some ointment on her knees and her shirt is in the plastic bag."

"Braden did all the cleanup," I offer quietly. "I did all the messing up."

"Sweetie..." Mom moves to me and again I have another hand placed to my forehead. I read somewhere that a hand test for a fever isn't even remotely accurate, but it's something every parent and concerned second party does anyway. Perhaps it's more a gesture of comfort than a gauge of temperature. "You threw up?" I nod. "Are you still sick to your stomach?"

"Not anymore... there's nothing left, so..." I shrug.

"She's a little sticky," Braden shares. "Her hair was loose and I couldn't get to it fast enough."

"Honey, can you handle a shower?" Mom asks.

"Yes. A shower sounds great."

"All right, baby, let's get you cleaned up." She takes over for Braden by putting her arm around me and pulling me toward her. And then she declares, unnecessarily, "Whew, you do not smell like a rose right now."

As we walk from the room, Braden clears his throat and announces, "Mandy, I'll stick around until after you shower, if that's all right with Mr. Harrington." I stop and turn around to look at the two most important men in my life. Dad doesn't say a word.

"You don't have to wait around here." *My dad might kill you while I'm in the shower.* "Thank you for taking care of me, Braden."

"I'd rather wait, Mandy." *Do you have a death wish, Braden*? "I need to see for myself that you're okay before I head home."

Dad continues the silent treatment so Mom steps in. "Of course. You make yourself at home, Braden, and we'll be back in a few minutes." Mom turns her eyes on Dad and says, "Michael, you offer this young man a beverage and see if he's hungry while I take care of Amanda."

"Daddy, he could probably use a washcloth and some soap. He caught shrapnel while holding my hair back."

Dad doesn't even look at Mom or me; he's too busy giving Braden the stink eye. Finally he speaks without taking his eyes off Braden, "Sure thing, girls." *What the fuck, Dad?*

Mom sits on the closed toilet seat while I take a shower. She insists—worried I might get dizzy and fall down. I wrap myself up in a plush towel before I step out. She picks up my dirty clothes and takes them to the laundry room off the kitchen and meets me back in my room while I put on fresh PJs and run a wide-tooth comb through my wet hair.

"Did you check on Braden?"

"He's in the living room with your father."

"Still breathing?" I qualify.

She laughs. "Yes, honey. He's breathing, drinking, and talking."

"Dad is talking to him now?"

"Of course."

"Will you send him in?"

"In a minute." She looks around my room with boxes and piles of clutter that are perfectly organized in my mind. I have a system. "I need to ask..." she hesitates.

"Yes?" I prompt.

"Is there a chance you're pregnant?"

"What?"

She sighs. "You haven't been around much this summer, and morning sickness doesn't just happen in the morning. I have to ask—are you in trouble?"

"No, Mom."

"Are you absolutely certain?"

"Mom, I'm pretty sure a woman still has to have actual sex in order to get pregnant."

She closes her eyes and doesn't attempt to restrain her relief. "Oh, thank you, God. I've been so worried this summer, and then tonight... Well, my mind went to some pretty scary places."

"Tell your mind to rest easy, Mom. Braden and me, we haven't—you know, ever—so it's not even possible."

She leans in for a hug and kisses my cheek. "I'll get you some ibuprofen and water and send Braden in."

* * *

Braden is spooning me from behind in my double bed. I asked him to shut my door, which probably caused Dad's blood pressure to sky rocket. Hopefully Mom is sharing the fact that Braden and I aren't lovers so he'll relax and give us a few minutes alone under his roof.

Braden plays with my hair and caresses my skin as we talk. "If your dad sees us like this, he's going to kill me. I should probably keep my distance."

"No," I whine. "Just stay here a few minutes. They'll knock first—I think." I sigh and settle back into him for closer contact. Almost immediately his arousal pokes into my backside. "Seriously?"

I peek over my shoulder at him. "After what you witnessed today?"

He laughs. "What can I say? You smell like fucking sugar cookies now, and I want some dessert."

I adore his filthy talk, but I elbow him and feign insult before I respond, "I'd love to be your dessert. Speaking of which, are you hungry? No, really, are you hungry because we didn't grab dinner before heading up the hill?"

"Yeah, but I'll take off in a few and eat at home—no dessert there, though."

"Dad didn't offer you anything to eat?"

"No. He was too busy asking me if I knocked you up."

For the second time tonight I'm incredulous. "Jesus," I sigh. "I'm really sorry, Braden."

"Actually, your dad did bring Jesus into our conversation, Mandy. But I did not."

"I don't even know what to say..."

"It's fine. I'm grateful I could tell him there's not a chance without having to worry about that myself."

"Yeah, how fortunate for you that you kept your paws off of me."

"Oh, I've had my paws all over you," he says, and he demonstrates his level of proficiency with his paws by delivering a thorough grope while sucking on the back of my neck. As usual, this play escalates quickly when I react—because, how can I not? With his thumb flicking my nipple through my sleep shirt, he switches topics. "I want to help you get settled in the dorm on Sunday. I can stay with Fiona a few nights."

"You do?"

"Yeah. I can take any overflow down in Dad's truck, help you move stuff in, and, if you want, we can buy ourselves a few extra nights at Fiona's. She's fine with that. So is your dad—well, the helping you move stuff in part. I made no mention of taking you off campus and assaulting you." He says all of this casually while continuing to fondle me. Braden and boobs—he can't keep his hands off of mine.

I giggle. "I think it's only assault when it's unwanted."

He kicks a knee between my legs to part them from behind and his hand slips into my sleep shorts and panties. I'm already wet from the groping and neck sucking, so his access is easy. His fingers slide over and into me. He adjusts our bodies so I'm brought further onto my back and he gives me some of his weight, along with his mouth and more of his fingers which are skillfully massaging my now pulsating clit. He whispers into my mouth, "We're going to have to do this fast, and you're going to have to be quiet." While our mouths meld together, I focus on his instructions and complete the task at hand with flying colors. After he leaves, I have to change into dry panties and new sleep shorts, but I'm just fine with that.

Tell the Team to Bear Down

At Tanner's suggestion, we load everything I have into Coach's truck so I can park Cherry in a nearby garage with my parking pass, and we'll have all hands on deck to unload one vehicle and get it out of the way. It's blistering hot. Hundreds of parents and students are competing for unloading space, and inside I'm sure they're competing for elevator space, hallway space, and soon to be closet space... Utter chaos under the blazing sun.

As Braden starts to unload my things onto the veranda in front of the dorm, I run inside and call up to Tanner's room. "Yo," he answers.

"Downstairs."

"Be right there." And he is. We exchange a huge sweaty hug—well, I'm sweaty. Tanner is not, but Tanner doesn't care. He has a huge smile on his face when he releases his hold on me. "I am so fucking happy to see you. You look great, babe—more grown up." He looks over my shoulder to Braden. "Oh...Hey, dude."

Braden glares but accepts Tanner's outstretched hand. We work together to unload the rest of my things while Tanner teases me relentlessly about how much crap I have. Once unloading is complete, Tanner gives Braden directions on where to park his truck, and I give Braden my room number before he drives off. Another loaded-down car immediately moves into the abandoned spot.

I'm a little winded and a lot sweaty when I squint up at Tanner and thank him for helping me. "Of course. Let's get going—make quick work of it." He commandeers a hand cart from an exhausted looking parent and searches for another. "We can get everything up in one shot," he determines.

I've been on campus several times in my lifetime, but I'm not familiar with the finer details. Manzi/Mo is enormous—nine stories, two huge wings off the center elevators. One wing is called Manzanita and other is Mohave. Tanner is three floors below me, and we're both on the Mo side. Squeezing in to the elevator, he pushes six.

We walk a ways down a long hallway, dodging boxes and other sweaty, confused-looking people until we locate my room. My name, along with another, is written on a dry erase board underneath the room number placard affixed to the wall. The door is wide open, and I'm the first to arrive which is perfect—I get to pick my side. I choose the side that overlooks the campus while seated at my desk. We unload the carts, and Tanner runs them back downstairs while I try to figure out what to do with all my baggage. When he returns a few minutes later, Tanner flops down on the spare bed and watches me make a half-assed attempt to start organizing my closet.

"Sweet," he says eyeing my computer boxes. "I'll help you set that up later. It's gonna save me a lot of time."

"Who said you can use it?" I tease and look up to see Braden standing in the doorway. "Climb over some boxes and have a seat," I offer. He eyes me warily and then finds a place for himself on my cluttered bed—opposite Tanner.

"Panda..." Tanner gives me the puppy dog eyes, "Come on. You're gonna share your toys with me, right?"

I grin in return. "We'll see." As Tanner and I fall into our typical pattern of giving each other good-natured shit, Braden remains fairly quiet. Is he worried? Jealous? Sad?

"Where are you?" Braden finally asks Tanner a question. "Where's your room?"

"I'm three flights down. Same side but all the way at the end where the singles are."

"You have a single?" I ask, suddenly wishing I'd made a different decision. I don't know who this Charlotta Begay chick is. What if she's a nightmare?

"I don't need to deal with someone else's bullshit, Panda. I have eighteen credits this semester and zero time for roommate or crazy chick drama."

"So you're just going to hole up in your room when you aren't in class?"

"Yeah, when I'm not running up the stairs to use your computer and web access. You're getting that right?"

"Yeah, but you could take the elevator."

"*Naw*... Just enough distance to give us a little exercise, but not enough to get *winded*." I watch his eyes dance with humor. I know that look. He's going to throw down in front of Braden. He hops off the bed, drops his voice, and delivers the line, "Although if you wanna get *winded*, Amanda—"

"Tanner," I warn.

He holds up both hands in mock surrender and laughs, as always, because some things never change, right in my face. "Babe, I was gonna say, you wanna get *winded*, I'll take you over to the Rec Center with me. I try to hit it at least four days a week. Hopefully, more now that I'm living on campus." I breathe out a sigh of relief as he laughs again and steps into my personal space but doesn't touch me. He looks down right into my eyes and asks provocatively, "What'd you think I was gonna suggest?"

"Tanner," I admonish, but he's pleased with himself. Braden—not so much. He stands, involves Jesus and the words *fucking asshole* in the conversation, and stalks from the room. "What did you do that for?" I hiss at Tanner, who gives me a grin and a shrug.

Braden's breathing fire outside in the hallway but slows when I wrap my arm around his bicep and apologize for Tanner's behavior. "He's just messing with your head. Not cool. I'm sorry."

He's pissed, and it's my responsibility to diffuse the *situation* and assuage his feelings. Parents and fellow Wildcats be damned, I tilt my head and step in with my lips; I lock him in with my arms around his neck and pull his hard body against mine. "Come on, let's finish up in there and head over to Fiona's," I suggest.

"You sure you don't want to stick around here—get *winded* with Tanner?"

Back in the room, Tanner offers an insincere 'my bad, just fucking with you dude' apology. He offers us a tour of his room, but I decline for both of us. "We're going to do a little unpacking. Maybe my roomie will show and we can compare notes and color preferences before I pick out some bedding and accessories."

"Cool," Tanner replies and takes the hint. "When do you want me to hook up the computer?"

My first official class is on Wednesday. Braden is heading back to Pine Ridge on Tuesday morning, *and leaving to reunite with the pig farmer's daughter* next weekend. "Tuesday?" I suggest. "I'm meeting Trina for lunch. You can join us and then set up the computer. Crap, and at some point, I'm going to need these things called books. Maybe we can do the bookstore before lunch on Tuesday?" I suggest.

"Deal. I know my way around the bookstore. I'll meet you here around ten, yeah? Just make sure you bring your course list and Michael's credit card." He grins at me and turns to Braden. "Am I gonna see you again?"

Braden's lips form a smirk—or maybe it's more of a sneer. "Not if I see you first."

Tanner laughs in his face. "Right, dude. Well, if I don't see you, have fun in Iowa and we'll hang again over Christmas break, yeah?"

"Sounds good."

Tanner offers his hand for another dude shake and, *oh my god*, he says, "Thank you for helping *us* get Panda's things moved in today." Damn it, Tanner. I roll my eyes at him and glare because, really, he's seriously working to get a rise out of Braden. "Later, babe." He smiles at me and takes his leave.

"That guy..." Braden starts in and he's, of course, pissed again—fire in his eyes, fists clenching, and veins visible on his neck. "I told you, Mandy... *Fuck*."

"No, no." I shake my head and latch myself on to him. "Look, I'm so glad you're here with me today. So, so glad." I attempt to elicit good feelings with my facial expression and utilization of double so's. For added measure, I press my forehead to his and speak against his lips, "I love that you get to see where I'm living so when we talk on the phone, you'll be able to picture exactly where I'm sitting. Although," I look around and come back to him, "I want you to see it with cool bedding and some of my favorite things on the walls—makes for a nicer picture, right? And I want you to picture me being nice." I nip at his neck. "So, so nice."

I feel his frame relax. I watch his eyes warm with my words and touch. I hold his hand loosely and walk to the door so I can swing it shut and block out some of the noise. I step back into him, and of course it escalates until I'm backed up against the edge of the large desk that divides the room. We're deep into making out and his hand is inside my unzipped shorts and panties, right between my legs. I'm about to rock into his hand for beautiful finale, and right then—yes, right at that moment—my door flies open.

Braden and I jump apart. He immediately stands between me and the door as I quickly put myself back together, silently lamenting the fact that I did not get to finish. Once I'm decent but still quite embarrassed, I step around Braden and face my stunned roommate. What's the best strategy in this *situation*? Apologize? Pretend it didn't happen?

She's a tiny thing who doesn't look a day over fourteen-years-old, and her black eyes are *huge*—most likely from the shock of discovering that her roommate has loose morals. Her parents don't look pleased either.

"Your hands are full." I smile and move to relieve her from a box. "Braden, help them unload, please." We both spring into action. I'm going to pretend it didn't happen unless I'm forced to call another play. So I start to chatter. "Hi. I'm Amanda—Amanda Harrington. First year, went to Pine Ridge High School. You're Charlotta?"

"Charlie," she says.

"Great!" I'm overly enthusiastic because I'm beyond uncomfortable. "I love nicknames!" I laugh while Charlie and her parents just stare at me. "Where are you from?" I prompt.

"San Juan," she replies.

I wrack my brain. She's Native American, for sure. I think San Juan is up near the four corners, where I think, but I'm not entirely sure, there are two large sovereign Indian Nations. "Hopi?" I venture a somewhat educated guess.

"Navajo." Her eyes narrow and hostility replaces wariness.

Great. Now I'm a whore and a dumbass.

I do my best to salvage what I can from my first meet the

roommate and her parents experience. Braden offers to help them make another trip up with the rest of Charlie's things, but they decline and pull her by the arm out of our room.

"Oh my god," I breathe out, my face turning bright red as I relive the moment in my head. "Should we leave before they come back? Or maybe you could just kill me now?"

Braden, who doesn't actually have to attend this school much less *live* with this girl, finds this hilarious because he responds to me with full body laughter that bring tears to his eyes.

Braden goes off to wash his hands—for obvious reasons—and we wait for them to make one more return trip. I help them unload the dolly, and Charlie and I stiffly discuss my side of the room choice—*fine,* signing up for World Wide Web access—*whatever.* I haven't bought any bedding yet, but I adore hers and will get something that compliments it—*fine*. I leave my stuff mostly still pushed to the side of the room in boxes, fish out what I need for two nights, and make sure I have our room key secured to my key chain.

Since Charlie's parents are either mute or they hate me—likely the latter—I tell Charlie that I'm going off campus for the night, and I'll be back at some point to unpack. She nods, Braden grabs my bag, and we leave without making eye contact with Charlie's parents. *Bear down, Arizona.*

TWENTY-TWO

WITH MY SHOPPING COMPLETE AT a nearby Target and my embarrassment somewhat under control, Braden and I are now ensconced in the tiny living room of Fiona's quirky historic off-campus bungalow near 4th Avenue. And Fiona, well, she is laughing her ass off as Braden recaps the meet the roommate *situation*. I hardly know Fiona, and normally this level of shared detail would not be okay, but there's something about her that makes me feel at ease. Quite frankly, she reminds me of Brianna—not in looks, but in smugness, intelligence, and sense of humor.

As Fiona laughs her ass off at my expense, I sip from the semi-dry glass of white wine that she offered earlier, and I join in. Braden and I are on her small loveseat. My legs are tucked underneath me and we're leaning on one another, my glass of wine resting on his thigh, his arm wrapped around my shoulders.

"You two," she chortles and wipes tears from the corners of his eyes as story time comes to an end. "I like the two of you *together*. This *pairing* is so sweet." She provides her big sister blessing. Glad to know she approves, since her little brother just told her that he didn't have the chance to *finish me off* before the door flew open so he *owes me one*.

But the words *together* and *pairing*—aren't those misleading? As brother and sister continue to chitchat about different topics, I polish off my wine and ask to use her shower. It feels amazing to wash the sweat and grime and the shame of the day down the drain.

After my shower, I change into a simple knit sundress that hits right above the knee. Fiona refills my wine glass and we decide to grill salmon and throw together a salad.

Fiona is in graduate school now—something about feminist linguistics... I don't quite understand it. Braden excuses himself to take a shower as Fiona and I chatter while we prepare dinner. I bring her up to date on Brianna's life, and then she nails me with a question. "Are you and Braden just fucking around, or is this serious?" There's no malice in her voice; it's just a question, albeit a very direct question.

I drain my wine glass before responding with sincerity and humor, "I love your brother, but we're not, um, fucking. There is zero fucking going on."

She laughs and slides the wine bottle toward me, "Well, that's too bad, Mandy." Fiona may call me Mandy—that's how we were first introduced. "If you love a man, you should be able to enjoy fucking him."

Can she read my mind? Did she drive by KFC last time she was in Pine Ridge? *Braden won't fuck Amanda*. I sigh, refill my glass, and return to chopping vegetables. "I don't know how to describe my relationship with Braden, except that I've loved him since I was fifteen years old. He's going back to Iowa next week and I'm staying here."

She nods sagely. "Iowa has such a good creative writing program. One of the best, and—"

I interrupt, "I would *never* ask him to give up his interests or dreams for me, but this whole topic sets me on edge and doesn't bode well for a future with Braden. Maybe we can talk about something else?"

She grins, reminding me of her brother. "Say no more. Let's eat, drink, and be merry, and tonight Braden can finish taking off your edge."

Tuesday

We had two nights together at Fiona's house. We tried to keep it light, but I had a few tearful moments and he had a few angry ones when he talked about Tanner. He pulled up in front of Manzi/Mo and helped me unload my shopping bags.

"Do you want me to help you take that upstairs?" he offers.

"No, I got it." I put the bags on the ground. "If I take you upstairs, I'll want to keep you with me always."

He gives me a long hug in the blistering heat. "I wish I could stay with you."

"It's not too late. You can tell Iowa to fuck off."

He laughs and kisses my neck. "I might think about that when the weather turns to shit and I can't get you off my mind. I love you,

Mandy."

"I love you back."

He sighs and pulls me closer, "Listen, if you and Tanner—"

I pull back to look at him. "Please don't."

"If you do, I want to know. I mean, I don't want it to happen, but I need you to tell me. Promise me."

"I will, but if you and the *pig farmer's daughter*... I don't want to know because it will break my heart."

"I'll call you next week. We'll talk and write, and I'll see you over Christmas break."

"Are you sure you don't want to make any other promises?" I offer. "It's not too late."

He shakes his head. "I promise that when we're ready to make promises, I won't break them."

"God," I sigh and settle back in to him, my nose brushing his neck for a final hit of *Essence of Braden*. "I wish..." I trail off.

"Me, too," he whispers in my ear before tipping my chin up so he can brand me once more with another *until we meet again* kiss. Our lips part and he says, "I love you, and I love those freckles—so freaking adorable."

"I love you back, Braden. So, so much." With one final kiss and a shared smile, I watch him get back into the truck and drive away. *I love that beautiful boy.*

Charlie jumps when I walk into the room. At least she was just reading a book. It's not like I interrupted *her* orgasm. Still, after she startles, she glowers and resumes her reading.

As I find places for my books and clothes and whatnots, I

try—and fail—to make headway getting to know her. I ask all the questions and she provides one or two word responses in a dull flat voice. She asks me nothing—not even, *hey, where's the guy who had his hands down your pants on move-in day*? It's a disaster—both my side of the room and the potential for a decent relationship with Charlie. I'm itching to get both organized. Her side is all fixed up. She favors black, purple, and heavy metal bands.

The tension in the room is so thick that I call down to Tanner's room and meet him earlier than planned. After the bookstore, we meet Trina for lunch and walk back to the dorm together. Tanner, who's helping me carry my book bags, follows me up to my room. I have a shit-ton of reading in my immediate future.

I swing open the door to my room and walk in. Charlie glowers momentarily then her eyes fall behind me to take in all that is Tanner. Yeah, he's cute, and her expression softens slightly. I leave the door wide open because the thought of enclosing all of us into this shoebox-sized room with Charlie is suffocating.

"Tanner, this is my roommate Charlie." I'd already told Tanner and Trina everything that I knew about Charlie over lunch, which wasn't much. I even gave them a very toned-down version of our first meeting. Tanner is convinced he can win her over with his charm and charisma.

"Hi, Charlie," Tanner greets and attempts to dazzle her with an award-winning smile. She stares at him, but her eyes don't narrow. This is hopeful.

"Charlie, this is my very good friend Tanner. We grew up together in Pine Ridge. He lives on 3-Mo. You'll see him frequently, and I apologize in advance for anything we may say or do, more him than me, to offend you. Tanner's a sophomore this year—pre-med. You might have some classes together."

"Are you pre-med?" Tanner asks.

I prepare to answer on her behalf, but she surprises me. "I'm here for the Veterinary Sciences program."

"Cool," Tanner replies and shoots her a grin. "All forms of life start out as cells, so I'm sure I'll see you in some of the basics before we spin off into separate species. And I plan to hog Panda's computer, so you'll see more of me than you probably want." He turns to me. "Speaking of which, are you ready for me to set it up? And, by the way, I love what you've done to your place." He eyes my mess. "It's really inspiring."

"Yes, now's a good time." I tilt my head toward the computer boxes. "And thanks. I've been busy." I glare while he laughs in my face, which is so Tanner and still annoying.

Leave it to Tanner to set up a computer and turn it into an endless string of sexual innuendos—every part, connector, plug in, etc. You get the idea. I spend a lot of time clearing my throat and scowling at him. He spends a lot of time laughing in my face. Charlie spends a lot of time pretending that she's not amused by his antics, but I see her crack a few smiles. I make excellent progress with my room while he gets all the hardware set up and operational.

"We need another telephone cord," he states. "Then we'll be able to connect to the web and take over the world."

"No sexual innuendo, Tanner? Really? You're just making a simple, straightforward statement about a cord?"

"Awe, Panda, are you disappointed?" He grins. "I'm gonna snake a long one around your backside and plug your hole with it."

Even Charlie can't contain her laughter.

* * *

My adjustment to academic life is far easier than my adjustment to exchange student life, except for one thing—one majorly disappointing thing. I can't get anywhere near the football team. While Arizona has a sports medicine program and student trainers on the field, it will take years to earn one of those spots. In the meantime, the closest I can get to working with the team is volunteering as an usher. I pass on that, but do I purchase home game season tickets for me and a friend of my choosing—likely, Tanner or Trina.

I'm not exactly branching out very far from the homestead in the friendship department. My classes are huge, my attention span short, and I'm still fundamentally shy around strangers. I have Trina, and we've meet a few girls in the dorm on Melrose Place night in one of the lounges, but we're only able to talk during commercials or after it's over. I nod and smile at people on my floor, and we have conversations at odd times of the day or night. This dorm is full of life 24/7. It's loud and active, and I'm settling in. I strike up conversations with a girl named Katie in my German lit class. She's from Scottsdale, blonde with a beautiful face and engaging blue eyes. She also spent last year in Germany and had way more fun than I did.

Braden and I have talked on the phone a few times since he got back to Iowa. He's really excited about his classes. He doesn't mention *the pig farmer's daughter*, but he does ask about me and Tanner. I share most of it because there's nothing scandalous to tell.

Tanner and I are tight—together, but not together-together. During these conversations with Braden, I force myself to hold back and keep things on the surface level. Our first conversation was full of deep and heavy sentiments, and I cried buckets after we hung up. Because Charlie was in the room, I went down the stairs and threw myself in Tanner's arms. Some things never change.

Tanner and I have picked through the last year of our lives. After I gave him his piece of the Wall, I admitted that Germany was a less than stellar experience because I was pathologically shy, and I told him about Curt. I also shared that Braden wouldn't put out. That made him laugh hard, followed by his opinion of, "Dumb fucker. If I had you willing and underneath me, I'd make you forget that Curt ever existed. That's a standing offer, by the way." I punched him in the arm.

During the first month of school, Tanner and I form a set routine. We eat breakfast, hit the gym, go our separate ways for the day, and in the evenings, depending on his work schedule and his need for my computer, we meet in my room or his to study. His studies require way more effort than mine, and his focus is admirable while mine is all over the place. Even with AP credits, I have prerequisites in English and Math, my advanced German Lit class, Sociology 101, and Intro to Women's Studies. Tanner finds this hilarious. He says I'm going to wind up weaving baskets underwater like my sister. I remind him that Brianna got knocked up and is raising a baby. "Same thing," he replies.

I don't tell Braden that our study time usually involves physical contact. Tanner is still affectionate. He likes his hugs and cuddles, and when we're sitting on one bed or the other, we're usually touching—shoulder to shoulder, our legs resting against each or draped over one another.

I don't tell Braden that Tanner is a control freak at the gym, and he insists on proper form when using a machine or free weights. His correction of my improper form involves the placement of his hands somewhere on my body to complete the motions with me. His hands, yes, they linger. His mouth, yes, it's a smart one, and he's free with compliments and fluid in innuendo.

I wouldn't classify any of these behaviors as a sexual advance, so there's no reason to tell Braden. He's Tanner, my dear friend who injects my daily life with humor and wit. I disagree with Jenny about how different he is now. Of course, I knew him better and I'm not the one who had a torrid love affair with him, but Tanner seems pretty much the same to me.

Mid-October 1990

Tanner and I are studying in his room, which is exactly like mine except cut in half. *Come to think of it, a wall down the middle of the room is almost like living with Charlie.*

He's sitting sideways on the foot of his bed, his back to the wall with a textbook sprawled across his bent legs. I'm in my favorite reading position, curled up at the head of his bed, my head propped on his pillow with my feet tucked between his back and the wall. The book I'm reading is crap, and the paper I'll be forced to write will be crap about crap.

At first glance, I thought my English TA was hot. Then he started talking. *On the Road* by Jack Kerouac is the third book on a ten-book list of male authors with angst and underlying mommy issues. I decide to write my paper about his beloved Sal Paradise from that angle. This drivel is in juxtaposition to what my Intro to Women's Studies instructor is trying to drill into my head. I'm torn...

I break the silence with a groan. "Ugh..."

Tanner looks up from his textbook, "What's up?"

"Nothing. Sorry, the groan just slipped out; I didn't mean to disturb you."

He snaps his book shut and slides it to the floor at the foot of the bed. "I need a break—I think I just read the last sentence five times."

"Not six?"

"*Sex*? Great idea. Glad you offered." He grins, eyes alight with mischief. "Let's make out," he suggests and hops off the bed. He dips a knee into the bed next to me and peers down. "Come on. Let's roll around together."

"Uh... *NO*."

He climbs over me and spoons into me from behind. "Then let me hold you."

"It appears that you already are. Thanks for asking first, though." I mark my place in the novel from hell, put it aside and settle back into his warmth.

He slides my hair out of his way and asks against my ear, "You ever think about prom night?"

"Junior or Senior?"

That earns me a tickle, followed by a poke in my rib cage. "Do you?"

"Ouch!"

"Do you?"

"Seems like a lifetime ago."

"One year, six months. Not a lifetime, Panda bear."

"Did you mark the days off on a calendar?"

"Yup. Missed you."

"Same," I reply.

"Look at me. Flip over," he demands. I turn over but make sure to grumble and sigh while I do it. We don't meld together like magnets after I assume my new position, but it's cozy nonetheless.

"What do you want?"

"Great question, Panda. Because I wanna talk about where I want you." His eyes tell me right where this is going. He's not teasing.

"Tanner—"

"We're getting along really well, right?"

"Of course," I answer as his hand begins to travel up and down my back.

His next play is huge. "I'm so glad you're back—that you're here with me. Just gonna say it like it is. I want more with you."

There it is. Braden called it, and now I have to decide what to do with it. I close my eyes like I can make him disappear so I don't have to deal with this *situation*.

He keeps talking. "Last year you made your mistakes, I made mine. You had your little summer fling with Braden, and it's time to stop fucking around. Actually, it's time to start fucking around," he corrects himself. As if his point isn't already crystal clear, he leans in and punctuates the statement with a touch of his lips to mine.

When I don't throw the flag, he gives me more, and, as it was before, it doesn't suck.

The kissing escalates to wandering hands before I pull back and finally throw the flag. "Wait. Stop."

He grins at me. "Am I gonna have to talk you into this again?"

"I still love Braden."

"Who is still not here."

"Right." I roll my eyes but take that topic no further. "You want more. What does that mean, besides," I gesture to our entwined bodies, "this?"

"It could mean everything. I don't wanna *fuck* you, Panda. I mean, I totally do, but I wanna be with you in every way that matters. Feels like I've waited around for years trying to get you to see what we could have."

"We have our friendship..."

"That's my favorite thing about us."

"We could ruin it."

He shakes his head. "Impossible. This," he kisses me midsentence, "doesn't suck. It's right. I know it. Don't you get it? I love you, and I love you in a way that I'd kill for you AND die for you."

"Holy shit," I breathe out.

He laughs in my face. "This can't be a shocker. Told you I wanted to revisit this when we were back in the same place. Sick of waiting around for you to figure out what I already know."

"But I... Braden..."

"I'm willing to bet that if we start something serious, those feelings will die off because I can offer you today and tomorrow, next week, next year—forever, if this works out the way I know it can. I need to know, do you see that?"

"I need to think."

He sighs and his chocolate eyes are serious. "You think too much. How do you *feel* when you're with me?"

"Secure." My response is immediate.

"That's good." He smiles and touches his lips to mine. "How else do you *feel*?"

"Is this like that word association game? You say *Tanner*, and I say whatever comes to mind?"

"That might move this conversation along a little faster." He laughs and his next kiss is deeper, hotter. "I say *I love you, Amanda*, and you *feel*... Use all your words—ready, go..." I laugh in his face. "Come on, play this out with me. It's cute, but I'm being serious. I want to know how you *feel* when you're with me."

I take a deep breath and dive in with the first words that come to mind, "Safe, content, amused, happy, comfortable, warm..."

"Those are all good things. And when I kiss you, touch you—how do you *feel*?"

"Well, it doesn't suck," I answer with a small grin.

"Ha! Right?" He proves his point by taking my mouth and kissing me just shy of tipsy while pinning me to the bed with his body and hands which roam everywhere north of my waistline.

When we break apart, I'm *winded* and his knee is wedged between my legs. I'm aroused and wet; I'm flushed and *I want more*. "I know you love me, Panda. You've said it a million times, but do you—can you—love me as more?"

"This is not a fair question, Tanner. I can barely breathe right now, much less think straight." Because I want Tanner, but do I love Tanner as more than a friend?

Of course I do… I love his sense of humor, ambition, and decisiveness. I love his chocolate eyes, the feeling of his mouth on mine, his hands on my skin. I love his friendship, honesty, and certain parts of his bossy side. I love that he admires my father and is part of my family. I love that I don't have to explain myself to him. I love our history. I love that he's so sure about us. I love that he's completely part of my world and we don't have to make any decisions based on *maybe someday*.

"Yes," I whisper.

"Yes, what?"

"Yes. I can love you as more."

With no delay on the game clock, we're frenzied and feverish as we kiss and grope and become frantic to reach bare skin. Grace and form don't matter at all as we reach our common goal. We laugh when our teeth scrape together, our heads bump, and my elbow catches him in the face when he pulls off my shirt.

This isn't planned. I haven't shaved my legs in three days, and there's no setting of a certain mood. The lights in his room are shining bright, with no music to drown out the noises of student life outside the dorm room door. *We want more*, and that's all that matters.

He sits back on his knees and runs his palms down the inside of my legs spreading them apart. He slides his fingers over me – flicking and massaging. "Oh, fuck, you're wet," he growls. "Drenched for me. *Fuck…*"

He slips his fingers inside of me, and my back arches off the bed when he hits the best spot *ever* with precise accuracy. "*Oh my god*," I cry out. "*What is that*?"

He smiles huge and reads my reactions as he *works* me with his fingers. His comforter is clenched in my fists while I writhe beneath him. He's clearly proud of his supernatural ability to pleasure me in no time flat. I feel the burn turn to an inferno, and I'm *this* close when he drops over me to cheer me on. "That's it, babe. Yeah... Fuck, let go for me."

I do with a guttural groan, a conversation with Jesus, and trail off with whimpers. "*Oh my god*," I smile up at him. "That was..."

"That was beautiful," he praises and congratulates me with a kiss. "So beautiful."

I release my death grip on his comforter and wrap my arms around his neck. I savor both the taste of his mouth and the sensations still rolling through me.

"You've been missing out," he grins.

"I totally have," I whisper my agreement into his mouth, but this is not one-sided because he's also been missing out and I want my turn to use some of my newly acquired life skills on him. I try to help him with his shorts, but he's happy to remove them himself, tossing them across the room. I reach down to touch him for the first time, and while Jenny sometimes has a tendency to exaggerate, in this *situation*, she absolutely did not. I blurt, "*You are huge*."

He grins. "Just told you, you've been missing out."

"*God, Tanner*." He has my full attention. "That thing of yours is... um, *giant*. Flip over. On your back," I order.

With laughter, we change our positions on the field. I kiss my way down his body, and I take as much of him as I can in my mouth, but I need assistance from my hand at the base of him. He's long and thick, and tastes utterly phenomenal as pre-come drips from his tip. I control the *situation* until Tanner is the one writhing and moaning beneath me. When he can't take it anymore, he pushes me off by my shoulders and orders me to my back.

"Don't wanna come in your mouth. I wanna come in you." He moves to open the drawer of his side table. I watch him sit back on his heels between my legs and rip open the foil. As he rolls the condom on, I question the next play.

"Tanner, wait—are we really going to do this?"

"Yes."

"Tanner—"

"You wanna stop, say it now, Amanda."

"Tanner—"

"Say no or this is happening. You say no, it's still gonna happen—tomorrow, next week, next month. It's happening."

I'm in danger of being called for delay of game. I decide he's right. "It's happening now," I call the play.

He laughs in my face, and hooks me under both legs, lifting my lower body off the mattress with the crook of his elbows connecting to the bend in my knees. He strokes his magnificent cock (because that's the only word that seems appropriate for it) a few times, positions and rubs himself over my clit like he has all the time in the world to make me wait, which, I guess, is close to the truth. He has all night.

"Mmmm..." My body is mush, my brain more so. I groan, "Tanner, please, I want you inside me." I anticipate a slow entrance and the phenomenon of him filling me. Not Tanner—no way. He *slams* into me. No glide, no tease, no chance to adjust to him. He buries himself balls deep, and I protest his play on my field with an astonished, "Ouch!"

"You okay?" All signs of *cocky* arrogance are immediately replaced by furrowed brows of concern.

"You really should be more careful with that thing," I grumble, but it's not a complaint. "Give me a second, Tanner."

"Relax, baby." He runs one hand down my skin, over my breast. "Spread your legs. Wider. That's it. Relax for me. So beautiful." He locks his eyes on mine, "This is not gonna suck."

I break into giddy laughter for the first time while I'm having sex, because this man—I trust him with my soul because I know that he loves me. He seeks my permissions to continue with a nod and a "Yeah?"

"Yes," I breathe. He slides out slowly, all the way, and obliges with a full and forceful thrust all the way back inside. This time I offer no words of protest, because it feels so fucking amazing—it totally does not suck. As he sets our rhythm, I think that I might lose my mind. I have him adjust our position after a few minutes, so our bodies and mouths are as close as humanly possible while he makes love to me.

This is making love. This is the difference, and it's so beautiful that he gives me another first during sex. I feel it build and burn, and the orgasm tears through me all the way down to my toes. "God, Tanner," I cry out, grasping desperately at his face so I can taste his mouth.

"You came so hard for me, babe." He smiles down and gives me a moment to recover. He controls the rest of this play thrusting deep and hard inside of me until he follows my lead and he rasps, "You're so beautiful. We were made for each other. I love you, Panda."

He quiets and as I hold him, tears of happiness fill my eyes. I'm filled with warmth, laughter, and love. I whisper, "God, Tanner, what have you done to me?"

He kisses me before responding, "I made you mine, and now I'm yours."

He withdraws carefully holding on to the base of the condom. I watch him slide it off, tie it and toss it off the foot of the bed. He lies down next to me, wraps me in his arms, and presses his forehead and lips to mine. I have zero feelings of sadness or regret. It's just Tanner and me—sweaty, sticky, satisfied, and temporarily rendered speechless.

TWENTY-THREE

November

No single bond makes another any less meaningful. Remember that little nugget of wisdom from this summer? That is not true. It's complete and utter bullshit. When Braden calls about a week after Tanner and I changed the status of our relationship, I offer up the information without being asked. There's a part of me that wants to keep it to myself, but he specifically asked me to tell him and our lives are linked through friends and friends of friends. I want so much to keep Braden as a friend, so he has to hear this from me. I still love him. That might sound wrong, but it's true.

It doesn't matter how I feel about Braden because he does not take my news well. He explodes in anger and yells at me. There's a whole lot of *I fucking knew it* and *I fucking told you so,* and *I fucking can't believe it*, even though he both fucking knew it and fucking told me so. He's so enraged that he eventually suggests that *we go fuck ourselves*. Evidently that is all the guidance he's willing to offer, because he hangs up on me.

I leave five messages over the next few weeks. I send a letter pouring out declarations of how important he is to me and how much I want to remain friends. He doesn't respond. Tanner is not concerned whatsoever with Braden's adverse reaction to our coupling, but Tanner is perfectly happy to take Braden's suggestion to go fuck ourselves and run with it.

Chemistry is not on my schedule this semester, but I'm totally taking the class. Sex is a part of our daily routine—like hitting the books or hitting the gym. For weeks, we experiment and conduct research. But there's no hypothesis to test. We love each other, the physical part of relationship is incredible, and our friendship is better than it ever was.

I float between Tanner and classes and campus life with a stupid smile on my face. Half the time I'm thinking about our exploits when I should be focused on school, but, whatever. Tanner is incredibly organized and compartmentalized; I have plenty of time for everything. We fit without discussion or effort, consternation or explanation. We strike an immediate balance, it doesn't suck, and we keep on going.

I carry a slow burn in my gut whenever Braden crosses my mind—which is often because that beautiful, framed photo of the four of us from graduation day has a position of honor in my room. I often stare at those four faces—younger, happier, and innocent. We hadn't yet inflicted any deeps wounds that left scars in the aftermath.

It's not lost on me that I stand between these two boys—now young men—and I have feelings for Braden and Tanner that exclusively belong to each of them individually. Despite the way our arms wrap around each other in the photo, my feelings are not intertwined. It is also not lost on me that I've betrayed Jenny in a way I haven't yet reconciled. I stare at her beautiful smile as she stands on Tanner's other side, tucked under his arm. She has no idea that I've inflicted a wound—one I'm certain will leave a scar.

I should tuck the photo away in a drawer, but instead I use it to draft a list in my journal—turning it into a flow chart of sorts. It's a wasted exercise to organize my thoughts, sort through the complexities, study the dynamics, and, perhaps, make some decisions about what it is I owe these people whom I dearly love—each of them, uniquely.

The Holidays

We drive home together to Pine Ridge over Thanksgiving along with our huge piles of dirty laundry. Not our figurative dirty laundry—our actual dirty laundry. There are never enough available washers and dryers in the dorm, and doing laundry is an arduous chore. To spare us both the pain, I took on that chore for both of us but slacked off in anticipation of Mom's clean, quarters not required, laundry room.

We opted beforehand to keep our *situation* off the record with my parents. With Tanner's family life in such a screwed up state, he's afraid of disrupting the dynamics with my family. I successfully avoid Jenny over Thanksgiving since she doesn't want to see Tanner. She finds nothing odd about him staying with my family. Why would she? My family is his.

***

I return to Pine Ridge for Christmas break several days ahead of Tanner. With his first priority being his studies, his time and effort far exceeds mine, and he's going to use the quiet time to get ahead in anticipation of another 18-credit spring semester.

I place a nervous call to Braden's house. I know he's home. Mom ran into Mrs. McLaughlin at Safeway a few days ago and discussed his return and their excitement to spend Christmas with the kids. As the phone rings on the other end, my heart pounds in my throat. On the fourth ring, Coach answers with a friendly, "Hello?"

"Hi, Coach. It's Amanda Harrington."

"How's my favorite Wildcat?"

I laugh. "I said this is Amanda—not Fiona."

"How's my favorite, Wildcat?" he booms in response.

"Great, Coach."

"Excellent. You making any headway with that sorry-assed football team?"

"We earned that Territorial Cup fair and square *again* this year," I say, referring to the annual grudge match between Arizona and Arizona State.

"We'll get you next year."

"Yeah, maybe the *tenth* time will be a charm."

This elicits a huge laugh since Arizona has taken the Cup nine years running. "Maybe so. Every devil has its day. Speaking of the devil... you learning anything down there? Hit me, Harrington."

I love it when Coach says that to me. "I am, but... my interests are taking a turn. Like, I'm considering other options than a life tending to the needs of athletes."

"Really?"

"It's an instant gratification thing, Coach. It's going to take years before I can start to fight for a spot on the sidelines. I'm impatient and the appeal is declining at a faster rate than the slow passage of time."

Like his son used to do, he responds to my repartee with another bark of healthy laughter. "Keep me posted there, Harrington. Whatever you decide to do, you'll do it well."

"Thanks, Coach."

"Are we going to see you up at the house soon? Don't wear any of that red and blue crap over here, though. I won't let you in the door."

"Um... I'm not sure. I'd love to see you."

"Did Braden tell you that we're having our annual New Year's party? You and your folks are more than welcome. But you can darken our doorstep anytime between now and then."

"Thanks, Coach."

"I suppose you didn't call to talk to this old fart, though, did you? Let me track down Braden."

"Aww... you know you're one of my favorite old farts, Coach. I could talk to you for hours."

He laughs. "Come by then—we'll do just that. Hold on, Harrington."

I do hold on—and on and on and on. I think I hold on for at least five minutes until I hear Braden's flat and cold greeting. "Yeah?"

"Hi." I attempt playfulness, "It's nice to hear your voice. I thought maybe you got lost in a cornfield never to be found." *Nothing*. "Braden?"

I hear him sigh and it's a big, broody one. "What?"

"Are we... are you..." and the stammering is back because I'm not sure what I want to ask him, much less how to ask him. I take a deep breath and express a coherent thought. "Can we get together and talk?"

"No."

No? How can he possibly say no to me? Don't I matter to him? "I understand that you're upset, but, you know, we talked about all of this over the summer, and I thought our friendship would survive. I thought that's what you wanted."

"Not anymore."

"So that's it?" I ask. *Nothing*. "We're not going to be friends anymore?" The silence is deafening and it's breaking my heart. "Braden..." I search again—for words, for hope, for an end to this excruciating one-sided conversation. "After everything we shared over the years, you have *nothing* to say to me?"

After another prolonged period of more awkward silence, he finally speaks, "Yeah. I have something to say."

"Thank God. I'm listening."

He goes in for the kill. "I should've just gone ahead and *fucked* you when you spread your legs for me." The line goes dead.

I try to stand, but my legs give out. I tumble to the unforgiving wood floor, curl into a ball, and sob. I could try to describe my feelings, but they pretty much just suck. Once the sobs subside to whimpers, I sneak into the kitchen and listen for the sounds of my parents watching TV in the next room. As quietly as possible, I locate the largest plastic cup I can find. Afraid the clinking of ice will draw attention to me, I pass and move straight to the liquor cabinet. I grab a bottle of whiskey and tip toe back to my room. I drink until the pain recedes, but that's only because I pass out. When I wake in the morning, I throw up until I dry heave. I rest and then dry heave until they finally subside.

Mom thinks that I have a stomach virus and coddles me for the next few days. I accept. When Tanner arrives on Christmas Eve Day, I rally, uplifted by his charm and laughter. Normalcy is restored, and I push my inner turmoil aside in exchange for my family, Tanner, and all the wine with dinner that Mom allows me to drink. We celebrate the New Year together with a quiet evening at the house. With my parents asleep well before midnight, Tanner and I try to time our orgasm for midnight. I have several, but he's off by a few minutes because he prides himself on longevity. We head back to Tucson a few days later, and I manage to avoid seeing Jenny.

Spring Semester Freshman Year 1991

Like many young women searching for the meaning of life, I gravitate to the social sciences—sociology, women's studies, psychology, and I explore my flair for the creative— German and English literature, creative writing. I have no clue what I want to be when I grow up. Tanner remain steadfast to his goals and routine. While my future is undecided, this structure provides the framework for my academic achievements.

Halfway through spring semester, Charlie basically has a single. Tanner and I relocate my computer and transfer the second phone line for web access to his room. My room is a staging area.

It's where I change my clothes, and I prefer to shower and groom on my floor. It's where I journal and stare at that damn picture. It's where I go when I'm not out and about campus or with Tanner. But Tanner's room is where my parents usually wind up reaching me most evenings. I'm under the impression they've started calling his room first. They don't ask. We don't self-incriminate.

No matter what day of the week, it almost always starts with him—breakfast followed by the Rec Center—and it ends with us falling asleep together in his bed. We are both in excellent shape from all the working out, treks across campus, and our healthy sex life. He's always been in great shape, just more so now with defined arms, a broad chest, six pack abs, and thicker leg muscles. I worship his body. As for me, I'm still curvy in all the usual places, but I've trimmed down and gained lean muscle tone and stamina. I alternate between swimming laps in the pool one day and working the machines or free weights with Tanner on the others.

I've made some new friends—mostly women from my floor and courses, but I'm still not outgoing by any stretch of the imagination. I prefer to listen and observe, mull my thoughts over in my head, and pour them into an assignment. I rarely engage or debate my beliefs in the classroom. Perhaps it's because those beliefs don't seem as passionate or thought-provoking or controversial as others.

The women's studies classes and the very strong opinions of many of my classmates cause me to reflect deeply, introspectively on my relationship with Tanner. I wouldn't share this level of self-examination with him because he would laugh in my face. He already rolls his eyes when he takes a brief interest in a book I'm reading or thumbs through a paper I've written. That's really the extent of his curiosity about my classes.

My relationship status, according to my women's studies cronies, would be defined as traditional, and therefore potentially subjects me to inequalities and assuming a subservient status in relation to men. I don't *feel* unequal or subservient. He loves me, encourages and supports me, and I do the same for him. We don't argue—we laugh, tease, banter, and push buttons. Nothing we say or do with one another is mean-spirited. Our roles are assumed, often little to no discussion, and we serve them well.

I *feel* that our partnership works for both us. *Except,* I've ditched my best friend—or maybe we just grew apart. *Except*, I haven't sewn a single wild oat. I don't party, we don't go out much, and sometimes I wonder what I'm missing. *Except,* my parents have no idea. *Except,* I don't take up the counterargument in class and profess the merits of traditional roles. *Except,* I don't know what I want to be when I grow up. *Except,* I know that Tanner wants marriage and family sometime during med school, which means he is moving fast. *Except,* I can't stop wondering what Braden is doing right this very second and who he's doing it with. Other than these exceptions, everything is just peachy.

I glide through freshman year, and towards the end, we discuss changing residence halls because Manzi/Mo is one step down from a frat house—I think, I've never actually been to one. I research other dorms in search of a quieter environment and a larger single for him. One with a private shower and bathroom would be ideal, but those don't seem to exist within budget. I fill out paperwork for both of us requesting Yuma or Gila Hall, and impress upon the housing powers that be, often and annoyingly, that we can't be separated. We end up with two singles in Yuma Hall, which is more centrally located on campus. He'll be one floor above me and several doors down. Perfect.

Age Nineteen
Summer Break 1991

Tanner changes residence halls on campus for summer school. I leave him the computer and two-thirds of my possessions, and I return home and work part-time doing office work for Dad. I become part of a small tribe of college cast-offs stuck on Pine Ridge Island. I hang out with Trina and enjoy reconnecting with Kyle who—FYI—loves Stanford and causes me to second guess myself. Unfortunately, this tribe includes Becky, who returns from Yale and a week in Michigan and piles on her tales of Braden and his family.

When she knowingly and snidely asks me if Braden's coming back to Pine Ridge to spend time with me this summer, I bite my tongue, I ask *Wisdom* to join me, and I manage not to react in front of her. *God help me, I miss him.* Even after he ripped me to shreds, I still sent him several innocuous postcards and letters since last Christmas break, but to no avail.

Trina, bless her heart, tries to help me out but only succeeds in informing the tribe that Tanner and I are very much involved, thus increasing the likelihood of word getting back to Jenny. Braden's words from the day after senior prom haunt me: *You know, Pine Ridge is such a small town. Everyone knows everything. They like to get in other people's business, tell stories out of school. Do you know what I mean, Mandy?*

It blows up in my face the following weekend. For all the time I spent avoiding the Jenny *situation*, I should've at least used some of that time to prepare what I'd say during the eventuality of this confrontation. She knocks lightly on the front door and enters before anyone gets up to respond. She looks beautiful—tanned, fit, coiffed. She also looks pissed but holds it together to chat up my parents. I keep a wary eye on her. I *know* that she *knows*. I *know* that she's going to use fuck as a noun, verb, adjective, and adverb.

"And so..." she trails off with a laugh, "everything is going really well. Thanks for asking." With that, she turns to me, fire in her brown eyes, and says, "We need to talk."

I convince her that we should go grab a bite to eat. She won't scream at me in a public place. That is my hope at least. We take Cherry to Denny's in silence. We're off hours, so the restaurant is mostly empty. We grab a corner booth, order diet sodas, and prepare to face off.

"What the fuck, Amanda?" Jenny doesn't mince words.

"I couldn't figure out how to tell you. It was a shit move on my part, and I'm sorry."

"Which move was the shit one? Fucking my ex or not telling me that you're fucking my ex?"

"Not telling you. I'm sorry," I meet her eyes because my apology is absolutely sincere.

She thinks this over, her lips pursing and expressing different shapes of surly. The waitress drops off our diets and asks to take our order, but Jenny waves her off dismissively. "How long?"

I sigh and look down to study the front of the sticky menu and buy myself a little time. "Since October—and we're not *fucking*, Jenny. It's a serious relationship."

She rolls her eyes and cackles. "No. No. This is a sick joke."

"Look at me." She glances at my face and her eyes dart away. "Look at me, Jenny."

"I can tell you're spending so much time with him—he always demands the eye contact. Especially in bed."

"Please?" I wait until I have her eyes on me. I swallow a sip of diet and wish I had a whiskey chaser. "I am so, so sorry that this hurts you. I hate that—for you, for me. But you guys didn't work out, right? It was pretty awful."

"It was beyond awful... It was the worst experience of my life," she snaps.

"Okay. It was a horrible relationship that *ended* with a crash and burn. And as your friend—as a friend to both of you—I'm sad that you guys went through that."

She responds with a scoff.

"But Tanner and I have something that does work. It works beautifully, Jenny. And it would mean the world to me if—"

"No. Not gonna happen."

"When I found out you two were together, when I got that third letter from you, I got physically sick from the shock and... grief. The thought of you and him..." Tears fill my eyes while hers narrow in disgust. "I felt like I'd lost him to you. I felt like you took him from me."

"He was never yours."

I shrug. "You're right. So I had to push that aside and try to be happy for you. And if things had worked out, I'd be supporting your relationship. But things didn't work out, and—"

"You just moved right in before Tanner's cock got cold?"

"I hate the word cock." I do, even though it's the best word to describe all that is Tanner.

"Tanner *loves* it. '*Look at my big cock, suck off my hard cock, gonna fuck you with my hard—*'"

"Stop it!" The vehemence of my tone and the anger in my eyes shuts her up. "I love you, Jenny. Always have, always will. You are *finished* with Tanner. You guys damn near destroyed each other with your fucked up head games. You didn't fit together. And don't make some smart-ass disgusting sex comment because that is so beneath you." I stop and stare her down. "I love Tanner. He loves me. We have something beyond special. It works. We fit."

"And Braden?"

"He's not in my life... I think he hates me." I roll my eyes to the ceiling to gain composure, but it's impossible so I let the tears fall. I give in to the sniffles and sob into my napkin.

Jenny places her hand on mine, and I startle. When I look at her, she's gentle. She's my Jenny, and I open my heart to her. "I regret hurting him and I still love him, but he's the wrong guy—wrong place, wrong time. My heart fucking hurts. I was honest with him, and I lost every piece of him. And if I have to lose you, too, I... I can't bear it, Jenny. Please don't hate me, too. Please. I'm begging you... I will do *anything* to make this right again."

"Will you stop seeing Tanner?"

I'm shocked that she would ask me to choose. But as I study her face and see compassion, I realize that's not really what she's asking. I shake my head slowly. "No. I'm keeping Tanner."

She nods. "Okay."

"Okay?" I hold my breath and ask her with my eyes for more.

"Are you hungry? I could go for a grilled cheese—fries for sure."

I exhale. "Jenny?"

"Keep him. But don't come crying to me when he drives you insane. And don't break his cock either, because it's still the biggest one I've ever seen."

I'm so relieved that I laugh right through the rest of my tears.

TWENTY-FOUR

Fall Semester 1991 – Sophomore Year

YUMA HALL IS MUCH SMALLER in terms of the number of students, and the building is beautiful and historic. It's quiet and has a convenient location to the College of Social Sciences. My room is the size of a postage stamp, but I don't care. It has a sink, and it's all mine. Well, mine and Tanner's since we fall into exactly the same routine this semester, except he's busier than ever because his classes are becoming increasingly more difficult. As he explains, my eyes sometimes glaze over.

I branch out, though. I have friends on and off campus now, and one of them, Katie from my German classes, encourages me to live a little. I go to my first college party in a house off campus. Yes, I'm still painfully shy, but I hit the keg several times—both to kill the taste of the beer and to loosen up. At the end of the night, I'm anxious to get home to Tanner. But it didn't suck, so I go out with her several more times.

Eventually, I introduce Katie to Trina, and it's a hit. Trina and I are totally tight. I adore her roommates, Violet and Michele. She's funny and quirky, and she also knows how to live a little but on a scale that I much prefer. We usually gather in smaller groups at her house where we have heady discussions and deep debates about the meaning of life. I have some pretty strong opinions, after all, and in these smaller settings I find my courage and use my voice.

Tanner doesn't like the beer on my breath or, God forbid, the smell or taste of cigarettes which I'm known to light up when I've had a few too many. He's so buried in his books and routine that he can't imagine taking time out to act like a college kid.

My world is forever rocked over Thanksgiving weekend. After a nine year winning streak from Arizona, Arizona State wins back the Territorial Cup and they do it huge—37-14. We sit in my parents' living room with stunned expressions as the clock runs out. Even though we saw it coming the entire game, it feels like a shock. Losing sucks.

Spring Semester 1992 – Sophomore Year

I love most of my classes. I'm into feminist theory, women in religion, and more sociology. I'm also taking a Biology class, so at least I have one thing in common with Tanner. My class is child's play in comparison to his, though.

Socially for me, it's more of the same—small groups, talking, drinking, and strengthening friendships while Tanner works his ass off. It's during one of these Saturday nights in February that Trina shocks the shit out of me. I know that her roommates and some of the guys sneak outside for weed. I know because I'll join them for a cigarette. I always wave my hand when I'm offered weed—it's not my thing. Then again, I've never tried it, so maybe it is.

We're sitting on the back porch on a crisp desert night. I light up a smoke while the bong is passed. Nicholas from a few of my Sociology classes passes it right to Trina. I expect to see her pass it on over to Connor, but... She takes a hit. A huge hit. Smoke billows out of her mouth and she doesn't even cough. I say nothing as she passes the bong to Connor. He does his thing then the bong is in my hands. Normally I'd pass it on, but... Trina just took a monster hit.

"Um..." I look at Trina, "I've never done this before. What does it feel like?"

She grins. "It's relaxing... Mellow. Different than being buzzed. Wouldn't you say?" She poses the question to the group.

"I like it more than drinking," Michele tells me in her wicked New Jersey accent. "I don't have to worry about throwing up if I have too much."

"Just eating too much," Katie chimes in with a laugh.

I swing my head in Katie's direction. "I've never seen you smoke pot."

She shrugs, "I do it all the time—usually at my apartment because I don't want to drive high. Plus, it kind of kills my ambition."

Knowingly, the group cracks up. But I don't know because... I look at Connor, "How do I do this?"

He explains the mechanics. "Your lips go inside the tube. There's a small hole right here on the back. Keep your thumb over it until you're ready to inhale the smoke. When you're ready, pull out the bowl, take your thumb off, and suck it in. But start small... Better too little than too much."

My grin is wicked. "What happens if I suck too hard?"

Nicholas laughs. "Normally there's no such thing, Amanda. But in this case, you'll inhale bong water and that's some nasty shit."

It takes me a few tries, but, what do you know? It *is* my thing. After a couple of tiny hits with Connor's coaching, I pass the bong on. The next time it comes around, I take a bigger hit. Several turns later, my body feels heavy, my mouth is dry, and I have a case of the freaking giggles. I'm dying over here, but, then again, so is everyone else.

Trying pot for the first time did not suck. I'm definitely going to do it again.

March 1992

"I'm going out tonight with Katie and Trina," I inform Tanner, who stopped by my room after his shift at work in the bookstore. He moved out of food service this semester and smells much better after work.

"Cool. Where you going?"

"Well, Katie told me that I'm way too young to be this boring, and she's insisting that I experience a real honest-to-god frat party in case I get hit by a bus..."

"You're not boring."

"You have to say that, Tanner. If your girlfriend is boring, that would be a direct reflection on how boring you are."

"You think I'm boring?"

"I think you're amazing." I go for broke, "Handsome, smart, dedicated, loyal, and incredibly talented in bed."

He laughs in my face. "You don't have to lay it on so thick, Panda. I don't care if you go out. Besides, I have a hot date with Pathogenic Immunology, and if you stick around here there's a good chance I'm gonna get distracted."

"I don't even know who that is, but should I be jealous?" I tease, moving into his personal space to kiss his neck. "Am I going to have to kick her ass?" Within three seconds, I find myself flat on my back on the bed looking up at him. "How do you do that?"

"Talented in bed, remember?" He grins down at me before calling a play that lasts the next forty-five minutes.

I have a smile on my face, and Tanner goes upstairs to his room while I get ready to go out.

"Oh my god." I take in the sight of the enormous Spanish-style mansion north of the campus. It looks like a scene from *Animal House*, or perhaps *Revenge of the Nerds* which, incidentally, was filmed on Arizona's campus. The lawn is littered with garbage and plastic Solo cups while girls/women stagger around in tiny dresses showing lots of leg and even more cleavage and boys/men shout obscenities to anyone within ear shot.

I try to step back, but I'm flanked by Katie and Trina who each hold me fast by an elbow. "Oh no!" Katie insists. "We're going in!"

"This is a nightmare. This is worse than a nightmare. Good god, please don't make me go in there," I plead, feeling horribly overdressed. And not because my outfit is dressy—it covers too much skin in comparison to others.

"We're going in," Katie confirms. "You have to—"

"Live a little—blah, blah, blah," I smart off. "Look, this isn't my thing. I hate crowds and germs and strangers and half-naked girls. Don't make me go in there."

"We're already here. You put on makeup and everything," Trina chides.

"I thought you'd be on my side," I protest.

"Nope," Trina says with a smile, "you never wear makeup anymore."

"I'm in a serious relationship. I have no need for makeup." I defend my uber-casual look.

"And yet, you're wearing it, we all look good, and we're going inside," Trina shoots back. "You shouldn't waste that look. We don't have to stay all night."

"I'll stay five minutes," I grumble as we approach the door to Animal House being manned by a group of guys wearing Greek letters.

"IDs, Ladies," Kippy the frat boy says.

"No need." Skippy the frat boy steps in after giving Katie, who is half-naked, a full-body scan. Kippy stamps our hands and gestures us inside. The house shakes with the vibration of bass from *Humpin' Around*. Good lord, what's next—*I'm Too Sexy*? I shouldn't have asked, because it makes the play list a short while later.

Katie splits off to find herself a frat boy, and I stick to Trina like a conjoined twin. Every move she makes, I follow. Eventually, our stamped hands get us a beer from one of the kegs because, apparently, it's proof of legal age. Hmmm. One beer turns into four to kill the taste, which turns into Trina flirting like a rock star and eventually abandoning me.

I find a seat in the far corner of the backyard on a concrete planter surrounding a Palo Verde tree. I lean my back against said tree and plot my exit strategy while I take in the unruliness unfolding before my very eyes. This is so not my thing—and a lesson learned. It's everything I can't stand—too crowded, too noisy, too impersonal, too...

"Mandy from Pine Ridge?" I look toward the direction of the voice, half expecting to see Braden standing there. Instead, my buzzed eyes come to rest on a burly jock-looking dude with light brown hair in need of a serious haircut. He looks vaguely familiar, and I try to place him from one of my classes... maybe... the Rec Center? One of Tanner's study partners? No. No. No. He called me *Mandy.* No one calls me that except...

"Luke? Right?" I squint up at him.

"I thought you were going to call me?" he teases. "But it's nice you stopped by instead."

"Turns out I didn't need anything," I remark dryly but with a smile.

He sits down right next to me on the planter. Right next to me. No personal space. "What's it been—two years?"

"About... I don't know. Time flies when you're getting educated."

His brown eyes flash with humor. "What brings you by? I haven't seen you anywhere on campus."

"I was forced to come here to experience college life, but my friends ditched me. Now I'm sitting here alone in a corner pretending this is a sociology observation so that I feel less self-conscious. I'm surprised you recognized me..."

"Took me a minute to place you."

"You must not be as drunk as I am."

He chugs back his beer. "How drunk are you, Mandy?"

"I'm not drunk enough to stick around much longer. I'm going to head back to my—"

"Oh no, you're not." He stands abruptly and swipes the red cup from my hand. "I'm getting us refills and we're going to get reacquainted."

"We were never really acquainted."

"Then it's time. Don't move."

With chaos all around us, we sit and talk and drink and drink and talk until I feel acquainted with him. He's easy to talk to. He's funny and not the least bit reserved or self-conscious. He is also a connection to Braden.

When Luke broaches that subject, in my drunken state I mist over just a little bit and I shake my head and share, "He hasn't talked to me in over a year." I then confess, "He won't return my calls or emails, and so I just stopped trying."

"He has a girl."

Why did he have to tell me that? "Is her name Jessica?"

"I don't remember her name."

Why did I have to ask him that? I'm sure he's with the pig farmer's daughter. Not to be out-relationshipped by Braden, I make sure to tell him, "I have a boyfriend—and it's serious."

"How serious?"

"So serious I should probably get back to our dorm so he knows I'm still alive." I stand up and sway.

"You're wasted."

"I am. And now I have to pee." *Stupid gravity.* "Ugh, really bad." *Stupid beer.*

He laughs. "All right. I'll show you where the bathroom is." When we go back inside, every bathroom has a huge line of people waiting and my *situation* is getting dire. "Come on." He grabs me by the hand and leads me upstairs, navigating past a crush of student bodies drinking, making out, and talking smack up and down a long hallway. He unlocks a door and we step inside a dark room. "My room. I have a half bath in here."

While I'm in the bathroom, it occurs to me that by following Luke up here to his room I've broken every cardinal rule in the *Party Smart College Playbook.* Go to frat party—check. Drink too much—check. Get separated from friends—check. Drink way too much more with a guy I hardly know—check. Go upstairs wasted off my ass into dark bedroom with a guy I hardly know—check. Come out of the bathroom only to find myself in another *situation—check.*

In the dim lighting, I instantly recognize that look on Luke's face as he eyes me up and down from several feet away. I've seen that look many times on Tanner's face, when his brown eyes flash and turn almost black, he crosses over midfield onto my side and goes in for the touchdown. I've already scored once tonight with my boyfriend.

He closes the gap between us. His lips meet mine while his body backs me into a wall and his hands take liberties. My drunken body responds to his. Easy. Way too fucking easy. My dress lands on the floor followed by my bra, and my back lands on his bed. My panties are stripped off, I hear the rip of a condom packet, and Luke is inside me. It's too late to throw the flag. I didn't offer one word of protest, but I don't want this.

I close my eyes and pretend that he's Tanner, but he doesn't sound or feel like Tanner. He doesn't say anything kind or caring. He barely kisses me. He doesn't touch me gently or coax an orgasm out of me. And when it's over, I'm mortified—stunned... so, so ashamed. I just had sex with two different men on the same night, and one of them was not my devoted, faithful boyfriend/best friend. *It makes me a horrible person. I am a horrible, horrible person.*

After Luke disposes of the condom, he comes back to the bed and curls up with me. "Normally, this is the time I'd ask the girl to leave."

Wow. This is a first. I've never been kicked out of bed before. Mortified to be sent off drunk in the dead of night doing the walk of shame, my face burns hot and I try to pull away to sit up.

But he holds on tight. "You're drunk. I'm drunk. I think you should stay."

I actually do want to leave, but on my own terms. And I don't want to walk home drunk in the dark. I sleep fitfully and throw up a few times during the night. Luke sleeps like the dead, never waking once, but his body and warmth gravitate right back to mine each time I return to the bed. In the early morning, as soon as the sun comes up, I get dressed quietly, intending to slip out.

As I gather my things, his voice surprises me. "You want to go again?" he suggests.

My laughter is nervous. "No, thank you."

"You sure?" He looks under the covers—probably to assess the state of his hard on.

"I can't believe what I did last night, and—"

"We don't have to analyze it, Mandy." Damn if it doesn't cut me hard to hear him call me Mandy in this moment, but I don't correct him. "Take my number. You want to get together again, call me. But I don't want—"

"I thought we weren't going to analyze this," I interrupt.

He shrugs. "I was just going to say that I don't want anything serious."

"I don't care. I already have something serious."

"Can't be *that* serious," he remarks dryly but without judgment.

Jesus. What have I done? I don't respond. I finish getting dressed, grab my small purse, and make for the bedroom door. "Maybe I'll see you around," is my goodbye, and I do not ask for his phone number.

And then I do the 'I'm hungover and I fucked a frat boy last night' walk of shame through the Sigma Chi house, out the front door, and back to Yuma Hall, where I spend the next hour in the shower trying to scrub Luke from my skin and wash him out of my mind. I fall into my bed, assume the fetal position, and cry my hungover self to sleep. I'm never more thankful not to have a roommate in my entire life.

The phone eventually rings. I feel like throwing up again, and I listen to Tanner start to leave me a message about breakfast and going to the Rec Center. He's about to hang up when I grab the phone. "Hey. I'm sleeping in—sleeping now, so... I need sleep," I mumble.

"Rough night?" He laughs.

"Um... yeah. I might have gotten a free pass to the keg, and I don't think there's anything left inside to barf up, so... sleep."

"Babe, not good."

"Not good. Very bad. Need sleep."

"All right, Panda. I'll bring you something to eat from the Student Union after I work out."

"Nothing runny or smelly," I groan quietly.

He chuckles. "Okay, babe. I'll look for other hungover people and ask for food recommendations."

TWENTY-FIVE

I CAN'T FALL BACK TO sleep. I use the time figuring out how to handle this *situation*. I try to rationalize my appalling behavior... It was a one-time thing—a huge, drunken mistake—and it's pretty much Luke's fault. He plied me with beer and he knew I was drunk off my ass. Easy pickings for a predatory frat boy. Yes, I participated, so it was consensual—not rape. But if he hadn't kept bringing me beer after beer, I would've gone home. And if I'd gone home, I wouldn't be in this really stupid *situation*.

If I tell Tanner, I'll break his heart and he'll probably dump me. I deserve to be dumped, but I wasn't thinking straight. I made a mistake. *One mistake*. I won't do it again. No one needs to know.

When Tanner shows up with yogurt and granola and coffee, he looks me over with a wry grin and he doesn't say *you fucked some other guy last night*. He says, "You look exhausted. Maybe you should take it easy with the keg stands next time."

I sit up in bed to sip my coffee. My head is throbbing. Tanner uses his indoor voice. "I hope strawberry yogurt is good. I couldn't remember which you like better—strawberry or peach."

"I like them both pretty much equally," I reply.

"Probably why I couldn't remember which one is your favorite." He brushes a chunk of hair off of my face.

"Thank you for taking care of me, Tanner."

"I always will, Panda."

Yes, I betrayed him last night in one of the worst possible ways. He's given me nothing but the best of him. I can't bring myself to tell him the truth. It was a mistake, and the truth will serve no purpose other than to hurt him and destroy our future. He can't find out. He can never know. I'm taking this transgression to the grave.

As the rest of the semester winds down under the guise of our routine, Tanner and I are more than fine. We're normal. We study, we talk and laugh, we hit the Rec Center, and we spend almost every night together—naked and worn out. I've almost convinced myself that night never happened.

Late on a Saturday evening near the end of the school year, I'm sitting in Trina's living room with her two roommates, Katie, and a few friends from miscellaneous classes. We're on the floor in a circle passing the bong around.

Connor suggests, "Let's play *Two Truths and a Lie*."

It sounds like a great idea. Michele jumps up to grab a bottle of Jack and shot glasses. The person whose lie is outed on the first guess or the individual who calls bullshit first when it's actually a truth, has to take a penalty shot.

As we take turns, some of the lies are blatantly obvious and send us off into fits of stoned laughter while the bad liar is forced to drink. Others are so good at this game, it's impossible to discern truth from fabrication. Trina is a perfect example. She says, "Okay, okay... I cheated on an exam this semester. I'm a virgin. I can hold my breath underwater for two minutes."

I turn to her and request, "Please repeat that."

She giggles and repeats, "I cheated on an exam this semester. I'm a virgin. I can hold my breath underwater for two minutes."

My mouth falls open while I try to figure it out, but I'm stumped. "I have no idea, T. I thought I knew you so well." I shake my head and laugh, "It's like I don't know you at all."

Her smile is smug. "Are you going to guess and risk a shot if you're wrong?"

"I wouldn't know where to begin because, remember, I don't know you at all." I giggle.

I'm surprised when she's outed by Connor who says, "You're not a virgin."

Trina offers him a sheepish grin, "I should have excluded you from answering." She accepts her shot. "You had an unfair advantage."

Trina and Connor? I like him. He seems like a good match for her.

When it's my turn, my mind goes blank. I ask the room, "Before I go... here's a question. If you keep a secret from someone important in your life—something awful that would hurt him," I add quickly, "or her—is that the same thing as a lie?"

Trina questions, "Is omission a lie? Hmm... it totally depends on the *situation*. I mean, it's not black or white. But if the omission would cause harm, then I guess it depends on what the other person expects from you."

Katie jumps in. "Right, like it depends on the intention of the person who is keeping the secret. Why keep the secret? You don't want to hurt the other person, or you're afraid of the consequences of telling the truth?"

"Both," I answer.

Connor throws in, "But the definition of a lie is making a false statement. It's something you deliberately say to deceive someone. So omission of information isn't necessarily a lie, because a lie isn't something that you *don't* say. It's what you *do* say."

Michele argues—and I love it when she argues because her New Jersey accent comes out in full force, "You're missing the point, Connor. Katie was on to something about intent. You don't owe just anyone information about your life, but if you're withholding important information from someone who expects you to be truthful and you do it in order to avoid or change a particular outcome, then it's definitely a lie."

Connor questions, "So you're saying that the purpose of telling an actual lie or omitting critical information in order to hide the truth, makes both things a lie?"

Michele nods. "Exactly. If the purpose of both is to hide the truth and there's an expectation of truth with this someone special, then it's a lie. For example, if you're in a committed relationship, and let's say you cheat on your boyfriend but you don't tell him, then you're lying because that person has an expectation of fidelity."

"I agree with the ladies." This comes from Nicholas, who

articulates further. "If what you're omitting is a relevant fact and you have a specific motive for its exclusion, then it's absolutely a lie. Deception is the same thing as giving out false information—even if you deceive by saying nothing at all."

"Okay." Connor nods. "That's a convincing argument. I'll buy it. Let's take it a step further. If you lie by omission when it goes against your personal morals or ethics, then you're lying to that person and yourself."

"Right," I agree quietly on a wince. They're right. I suppose I was hoping someone would convince me otherwise.

"I think," Connor says, "that unless someone is a sociopath, people generally lie or omit information because they're afraid of the consequences of telling the truth."

Michele adds, "In any case, keeping track of lies and omissions gets complicated."

"I heard this expression once... I have no idea who said it but it went something like '*a lie may take care of the present, but it has no future*,'" Trina shares.

Connor grins. "Yeah, here's a good one that my mommy told me. One lie is actually two lies. There's the lie we tell the other person or, in this case the information we omit, and then there's the lie we have to tell ourselves in order to justify it."

"Fuck," I mutter.

Trina giggles. "Come on, Amanda. *The truth will set you free.* Throw your little secret into the game and let's see if we can guess."

I groan and roll my eyes. "You know what? I'm going to pass on my turn."

"Then you have to take a shot," Katie orders.

"Oh, I'll take a shot." I accept her terms willingly, and the whiskey burns going down. I follow it with a long pull from the bong and pass it to Trina.

"Here's another cliché—try this one on, Amanda," Trina says before she takes a hit. "This one is from Buddha and most Buddhisms nail it. *Three things cannot be long hidden: the sun, the moon, and the truth.*"

What am I going to do about Tanner and this stupid *situation* I put myself in?

Summer Camp
Thursday, July 12, 2012
Day Five

As I stare at the Timeline covering the first two decades of my life, I wonder how it will compare to others in my group, especially the three youngest members. They're half my age and already in rehab, and according to my timeline, I haven't even touched on my demise—the first one or the second one.

Amber and Mark are just nineteen, and Melanie is a few months shy of her twenty-fourth birthday. They're all finished with their Timelines. Sure, their lives are significantly shorter than mine, but maybe I'm giving this assignment too much thought. It would be just like me to create a detailed flowchart with bullets and sub-bullets, albeit with markers and crayons, when I should stick to the surface.

Still, Jeff, our therapist, instructed us to dig deep. That's what I'm doing—I mean, what else am I going to do in this place besides wish I had an endless supply of drugs and pills to turn off my *stupid brain*? I have nothing but time on my hands to think about all the forks in the road I should have taken instead.

What have I learned about myself thus far? There's nothing exceptional about me. My Timeline tells a story of a near-idyllic childhood with parents who were loving and supportive. I was privileged—downright spoiled. My parents gave me practically everything I wanted and every opportunity to go out into the world and find my way in life.

Braden, the first boy I loved, protected me in his own misguided way. We were so young—way too young to deal with those feelings and hormones. Braden—*God*, these memories make me miss him all the more. He had such integrity, despite those hormones. Sure, things fell apart when I followed my heart down a different fork in the road, but I've long since forgiven Braden for cutting me out of his life.

When I left home for Germany at the age of seventeen, I discovered that I didn't possess any internal strength or true sense of self. My roots were ripped out from under me, and I didn't know how to replant them somewhere else. Instead, I retreated into my head and stayed sheltered there until I was forced to pull my head out of my ass. It's so cliché that it could be a script for a John Hughes production... except John Hughes sadly died back in 2009 at the age of fifty-nine.

Although, all those drawings I made of beer steins and glass tumblers representing whiskey *are* cute. That year in Germany was when I began drinking alcohol. Who wouldn't drink in the same set of circumstances? Alcohol was accessible and legal, and it helped with my pathological shyness and anxieties. It broke down my shields and made me become a more outgoing person. So, yeah, maybe I used the whiskey and beer to cope with tough times. Okay, maybe I spent the better part of that year buzzed and/or drunk. That year sucked.

Shit—the whole cherry popping *situation* with that asshole Curt... I was buzzed and/or drunk throughout my entire relationship with Curt. I was drunk when he felt me up against the wall in the disco. I was wasted when I had sex for the first and second time. I ignored my inner voice and the warning signs. Was it because I was so lonely and desperate for attention, or because I was anesthetized by copious amounts of alcohol?

Still, I can't believe that I stayed with that asshole until the game clock ran out. He was such a dick. If he could see me now—well, *fat* would certainly be an accurate description now, and *whore*—well, that's probably fitting after my twenties.

What if I'd gone to Stanford instead of Arizona? There's no telling where I'd be right now. Probably not here, but I would've missed out on some incredible times with the second love of my life, Tanner. His name is everywhere on my Timeline, and I illustrate the status of our relationship with hearts of different colors—yellow (friendship), pink (more than friends), red (love), and grey (confusion). I haven't gotten to the black hearts yet. I'm saving those to represent devastation.

A lie by omission is a lie. *Why do I spend so much time lying to myself and other people?*

To be continued...

For a sneak peek at book two in the Now & Then Series, turn the page for the first chapter of A Woman Like You available Fall 2016.

A WOMAN LIKE YOU: NOW & THEN SERIES

Summer Camp
Sunday, July 15, 2012
Day Eight

Why am I an addict? When I started smoking pot, it felt like no big deal and yet it turned so horribly wrong for me when it didn't for most of my friends. It started out as nothing; introduced by someone who is a dear friend to this day, and Trina has her life together. Why were her experiences with the drug so different than mine? Why did I lose my self-control and dignity?

I'm eight days in to this Summer Camp experience, and I would kill for a joint right now. Okay – maybe not kill, but I'd definitely maim someone. I'm not sleeping, not thinking clearly, and I feel sick inside from emotions breaking through my defenses and threatening to explode through my skin.

There is nowhere to hide. We have to leave our cabin by 8 a.m. each morning. Thereafter, the doors are locked until 12:15 p.m. After that, they remain locked again from 12:45 p.m. to 4:30 p.m. I can't even try to sneak in a catnap which is probably their point. I have a daily schedule and some choices to make about which workshop or meeting I want to attend, and twice a day we have Community.

The Sonoran Desert in July is obviously hot, and the sun beats down from every direction. Even grabbing a smoke is inconvenient. The women can only smoke on one part of the property. There's nowhere to sit – just a bunch of gravel and scrub brush, and it's almost too scary to smoke at night. This place is alive with wildlife and assorted creepy crawlies. My least favorite are the gigantic tarantulas that come out after the sun goes down and meander down the walking paths like they own the place. I'm not fond of frogs either. They squawk and cry all night looking for another frog to love. They are also known to jump out from nowhere which might induce a heart attack in my current state of anxiety.

I get to know my fellow Summer Campers during Community and over meals. Community takes place at 11:30 a.m. and 9 p.m. Every Camper is expected to attend because we're all part of this highly dysfunctional Community. We sit in a huge circle and go around the room – first name, malfunction(s), and one word that best describes your Core Feeling at the moment.

What the fuck am I doing here is not a Core Feeling.

In case you can't think of a Core Feeling, there's a handy chart on the wall with round, yellow faces whose expressions match the word next to it: happy, lonely, sad, grateful, proud, fear, loved, hopeful, hurt, peaceful, guilty, shame, relieved, anger. If a Camper is feeling creative, he or she can use a combination of Core Feelings.

The Patient Advocates use the time to update the Campers on Summer Camp News, and there are a lot of reminders about following the rules because there are a lot of Campers breaking the rules. Campers have to volunteer for chores that help the Community, and I'll pick an assignment next week.

Then things get interesting. Campers get to give *constructive feedback* to other Campers with any issues they might have with a fellow Camper, but it has to follow a very specific formula: [NAME], when you [BEHAVIOR], I feel [CORE FEELING(S)].

There is always drama at Summer Camp – especially with the younger ones. I steer clear, but admittedly I enjoy the show because it is the main source of entertainment. Too bad John Hughes is dead; he could produce and direct *The Rehab Club*, which would be way more interesting than *The Breakfast Club*.

While the Campers are varying degrees of fucked up, most fall into distinct categories. We have the Alcoholics – with a division between the Hardcore and the Chardonnistas. Addicts are mostly Hardcore – heroine, meth, crack, cocaine and a bunch of stuff from the list Jacob rattled off to me on my first night here. Pill poppers and/or pot smokers are not Hardcore. It's difficult for the Addicts to take a pot smoking Klonopin-popper seriously. I know this because they laugh at me when they find out why I'm here. It's not mean-spirited laughter – they simply can't understand because to them, even though most of them are practically still children themselves, marijuana is child's play.

Oh, there was a Gambler here, but she went through Family Week and walked around in tears when she was outside of sessions. She went home with her husband today.

Meals are a whole other adventure and exercise in social hierarchies. Our cafeteria is gourmet – it's staffed with professional chefs who prepare delicious organic meals and present them with flourish. By day two, every chef memorized my name. There's no sugar in the place – I'm not kidding. Choking down coffee is a challenge so I switch back to Diet Pepsi.

Meal time is kind of like eating in prison except the food is gourmet and we don't segregate by race. We primarily segregate by age with sub-segregation of Alcoholics versus Addicts. Jacob, that kid I met on my first night, was right – there are not many people here my age. We have a well-represented under twenty-five crowd, one woman in her early thirties, me on the brink of my fortieth birthday, and the over fifty set. Since I'm a wife and a mom and a person with actual life responsibilities, I mostly hang with the over fifty.

Sometimes the Adult Camper tables are full so I have to slide in with the Child Campers. Initially a hush falls over the table when I crash the under twenty-five set. An Adult Camper can kill a Child Camper conversation in less than two seconds flat, but I quickly learn that I can start a conversation by asking a question or introducing a new topic.

I also pick up bits of Child Camper gossip over mealtime – that new guy/girl is totally hot, So and So had sex in the shower when the rooms were open before Group yesterday, Haley got caught smoking crack and now a PA has to follow her around 24/7 for the next two weeks. Yes, *The Breakfast Club* would have nothing on *The Rehab Club*.

I see so much of my younger self in these Child Campers, and it drives me batty. Like me, most of them have had everything handed to them on a silver platter. They took what was handed to them and then used the silver platters to bash their parents over the head. *My parents are stupid. My parents don't get it. My life is so hard.* I fight the eye roll because I'm trying to act like an adult these days and, even though they don't have a clue, they already know everything.

I'm sure most of them have no idea how expensive it is to attend Summer Camp. They probably have no idea that their horrible parents are most likely broken hearted and desperate to get them healthy and on the path to becoming productive members of society. I room with two child Campers – Amber and Melanie from my Group. I'm a Resident Advisor of sorts.

Amber and I are building a decent relationship, although every time I say her name out loud, I remember another *Amber* from the night before I married my husband. I have a hard time not telling her about that whole *situation*. I'd love for her to see me as a cautionary tale, but she isn't there yet.

She comes from a life of privilege; an only child forced here by her parents to help with her head and her pending legal charges for underage consumption and possession of marijuana. Amber says that she's not an Alcoholic or Addict; she's no different than other college students except she was unfortunate to get caught – three times. If she can get out of her legal *situation* without serious repercussions, there's no doubt in my mind that she'll continue on her current path which means she has a good chance of winding up like me one day. She doesn't understand that her behavior can spiral out of control and suck her into a dark vortex.

Also by Kate Ryan

NOW & THEN SERIES

***

A Girl Like You

***

Coming Soon:

A Woman Like You

A Wife Like You

A Family Like Yours

Everything to Me

Playlist for A Girl Like You

Aerosmith – I Don't Want to Miss a Thing
Bad English – When I See You Smile
Billy Vera & the Beaters – At This Moment
Bob Seger – We've Got Tonight
Bon Jovi – Never Say Goodbye
Boston – Amanda
Bryan Adams – Heat of the Night
Chicago – Look Away
Crowded House – Don't Dream It's Over
Cutting Crew – (I Just) Died in Your Arms Tonight
Cyndi Lauper – True Colors
Dan Seals – One Friend
Eagles – Wasted Time
Heart – Alone
INXS – Never Tear Us Apart
John Mellencamp – Small Town
Keith Whitley – When You Say Nothing at All
KISS – Heaven's on Fire
Patrick Swayze – She's Like the Wind
Poison – Every Rose Has Its Thorn
Richard Marx – Right Here Waiting
Scorpions – No One Like You
Simple Minds – Don't You (Forget About Me)
Sinead O'Connor – Nothing Compares 2 U
Whitesnake – Here I Go Again

About the Author

To receive notification of new releases, sign up for the Kate Ryan Newsletter

Bit.ly/KateRyanNewsletter

Twitter: @KateRyanBooks

Facebook: Facebook.com/KateRyanBooks

Made in the USA
San Bernardino, CA
02 August 2018